THE INCREDIBLE EXISTENCE OF YOU

—

A NOVEL

DRUE GRIT

ISBN: 978-1-7374794-5-1

*This novel's story and characters are fictitious. Certain long-standing
institutions, businesses, and monuments are mentioned, but the characters
involved are wholly imaginary. The incredible state of Arizona; the town of
Prescott, known as "everybody's hometown"; and the great Yavapai and fellow
indigenous peoples who once roamed the land are all real parts of our fading,
but beautiful, American West.*

Copy Editing by Jessica McKelden Cave
Front cover image by David Erickson
Book design by Danna Mathias of Dearly Creative
Typesetting & Interior Design by Lorna Reid
Proofreading by Shannon Cave
Editorial Assessment by Lindsay Guzzardo

Printed and bound in the United States of America
First printing September 2021

Published by Grinta & Colibri

www.theincredibleexistenceofyou.com
www.druegrit.com

This book is dedicated to *you*.

PREFACE

WHAT INSPIRED THIS STORY?

My life.

My family, my experiences, my pain. People, places, and things. Beating depression. Fighting suicide. Helping others fight it too.

The spirit of Prescott, Arizona. The love of this town.

The love of my family, who showed us what family really means, just by spending time with them.

My Grandmother, who, even at 87, took her own life. My Grandfather, who loved her 'til he was 92, then died of heartbreak 30 days later.

My Dad, rest his soul, who loved cinema, literature, and rock and roll. Who I helped fight suicidal thoughts. Who fought on and died of other illnesses. Who relentlessly supported me in pursuing my dream to make cinema and stories. This story is part of that dream.

My mother, who taught me love — the greatest gift of my life.

My Kid Sis and my cousins, who continue to teach me love through their spirits, their passion, their existence.

All my friends in the entertainment business and mental health advocacy spaces who fight for recovery, education, and most importantly, love.

Being stuck in Prescott for over three weeks with my cousin, David, my best friend. Our car broke down and our cousins rescued us, including cousin Danielle, who had helped raise me as a boy when she was still just a little girl herself. I was able to see firsthand how loving and inspiring she and her husband Tony are to their kids, and how they are raising three great young men. They showed me a part of family I almost felt like I forgot.

My aunt Terri, who, like my mother, is a powerful, loving, incredibly inspiring woman.

My Stepdad, my second Dad, a true father to me and others, and who also believes in second chances.

The people I know who passed by suicide. The people in pain. My friends, family, and loved ones.

God. Because I believe God is love and love is God.

Love. Because it is the reason for my existence.

Storytelling. Because, like love, it has the power to change the world.

You.

Because I can't do any of this without *you*.

THE FIGHTER

The halls were narrow and dark. A murmuring could be heard—the low hum of voices crowded the other side of a cement wall, anticipating what was yet to come. Dusty fluorescent lights flickered through a hall into a dry, dim boiler room. At the end of a long bench was *The Fighter*. His back was riddled with scars and tattoos, the face of a vicious wolf, printed deeply in black and white ink, spanning from shoulder to shoulder and reaching down to his thick lower back. His upper body was broad and wide as he hunched over the bench, completely still.

Those piercing eyes were fixated again—somewhere, some place, lost in time. It wasn't until the rising murmurs shook the old piping that his eyes returned to the present. The Fighter started to wrap aged cloth around bruised and purpled fists. In the same room, fervent conversations in Spanish could be heard from behind his wolf-printed back, whispering echoes in the musky hall.

They were talking about him, crude, threatening, but The Fighter paid them no mind. His swollen ears were attuned to the vibration of the crowd, a slow rising and subsiding, much like the tide. Much like the ocean that he once remembered. The voices in the room hissed their words. They came from his opponent's coach, speaking to his prized fighter, Ezequiel, a proud and strong Mexican man whose eyes stalked The Fighter from across the room.

"Do it for your family," the coach implored. "For your children, mijo."

Ezequiel soaked in the words, pounding his fists into the palm of each hand, rhythmic, sweating—ready to fight. And still, across the room, The

Fighter hardly moved. His hands were fully wrapped, but he was holding on to something that tore his mind and attention from this place. He held it with a tenderness unnatural of a man of his stature.

It was a Polaroid photo—faded celluloid on glossy three-by-four paper.

A dying relic of his time.

His eyes were locked on the photo. It was as if he could not blink—or, for whatever reason, perhaps he chose not to. As if what he was looking at would cease to exist, that if he turned away for even a second, it would fade into particles of sand and slip away into the past with the rest of him.

"I need at least four good rounds," a burly man barked, bursting into the room.

He was a middle-aged white man named Fletcher. His white tank top was stained yellow from sweat, and his palms soaked a booklet of bets and a wad of American dollars. Ezequiel and his coach were eyeing their opponent. There were only immigrants in this room, and what they were fighting for was more than dollars.

"He's not going home," the coach said, affirming the very thing they hoped to avoid, but Ezequiel ignored them both. He scowled at The Fighter, who still kept his back to him from across the room.

The coach stood, and Ezequiel launched to his feet, his jaw clenched, and his entire anatomy tightened with a single flex. He was ready to fight, or even kill. His life depended on it. The two walked out of the room.

Fletcher turned to The Fighter. "And you?" The head of the wolf tatted on his back was snarling right at him. Still, The Fighter didn't respond. His eyes were buried alive in the Polaroid, gazing, reluctant to look away.

"Three minutes," Fletcher said, shaking his head, then left through the cellar door. With a deep inhale, The Fighter's thumbs grazed the sanded corners of the Polaroid, stuttering on its edges. He exhaled. Everything inside him turned. He was staring into the picture, and to the person inside it.

It was *Her.*

There was only one *Her.*

Even inside a fading photograph, everything about her was aglow. Her smile. Her bright, sincere eyes. Her hair and lips that shimmered. She was in her late twenties, and timeless. Every photo he'd ever seen was like this. Everything about her shined. You could feel it just by the way she smiled.

She was happy.

As was the man in the photo standing next to her.

It was him. The Fighter, once a clean-shaven man in his early thirties with high cheekbones and a helpless smile. They stood on a beach somewhere, his arm around her and hers wrapped around his waist, pulling him in. It was a picture and place he would never forget.

And in The Fighter's gaze, he was returning to it.

It was the end of the sun and moon changing places. They sat on cool, pastel blue sand, illuminated by a symphony of bright stars and the rising blue moon. Its crescent was brilliant, clear, with only a sliver of a shadow hugging its fullness. Their feet had been in the sand for hours as they'd talked through the night. They had only been together for six months, and even in the brevity of their time, The Fighter *knew*—she was his person.

Under that moon and the warm summer air, he knew he had to tell her. He had to say everything he felt. There were things he had never told another person, but with her, everything was different. As the tide stretched to their toes, then trickled away, she smiled and told him a story about growing up in the States. How she'd moved coast to coast and many places in between. He related closely to this, because his entire life had never been in one place.

She was watching the cool blue waves, telling him glimmers of her childhood, but all he could do was watch her. His heart was pounding. His lips were moist from the ocean mist and the yearning to tell her, to kiss her, to show her everything he felt. To tell her that, in the last six months, he could not possibly say all that she was to him, all that she now meant to him. The tide rolled higher, and his heart rose with it. He wanted every thought and feeling to pour out of him and into her. And when the tide released and her voice softened with it, her eyes turned to him, and it felt as if he could touch his own soul.

Then it happened.

The tide, rolling to and fro, began to shimmer.

Cool, bluish light stretched to the shore in gentle waves. Below the glossy ocean surface, luminescent molecules shimmered as the waves calmly churned. It was bioluminescent plankton, a type of rare phytoplankton that would appear only on some lucky summer nights and find their way to shore.

They were living, breathing microorganisms, smaller than the eye could see. But together, they would illuminate in a chemical reaction called chemiluminescence, causing a glimmer and glow that would emit within the tide. The ebb and flow twinkled blue and white, softly gleaming in the ocean. And such was the light inside him, beaming, ready to bare all.

To witness this once-in-a-lifetime occurrence made her glow. Her lips and her eyes smiled. A wonder in the dark waters that was so rare that some searched all over the planet to find it—and it was here, on this beach, and they were sharing it from Earth's front row.

The Fighter was astonished, and yet, he could not stop looking at *Her*. She beamed, telling him how she had always wanted to see this and how truly lucky they were to share it together. She told him that very few people in the world have seen it—but, more so, that very few people in the entire world would ever *feel* it.

And that struck him, thinking how her views about things were so different. She was always like that. A blooming optimist. This wide-eyed, wild woman with her brightly shining soul that poured passion into everything and everyone and into her words and her stories and her smile. It was magic. Everything about her. And in that moment, he could no longer contain himself. He pulled his hands from his pockets and took hers from the sand. Her lips became still, and he held her eyes with his.

And then he told her.

"I love you."

The Fighter blinked.

The boiler room was empty.

He could taste the mold in the musky air. It was the farthest from the ocean and her lips that he could possibly be. Droplets of soiled water leaked through decayed piping as the vibrations of the crowd on the other side of the wall cheered for their spectacle. He was no longer that young man, open to the magic and the wonders of the world he had once seen. He had aged in ways that only pain could say, and yet, it had only been two and a half years since that night. His beard was thick and full, and his eyes stayed narrow, trapping faded blue ovals that now appeared almost gray. He took one last look at *Her* and at the person he once was.

They were both gone now.

The Fighter tucked the Polaroid in his boot, leaned his head back, and closed his eyes. With a deep inhale, his chest rose, and his heart began to thump. It was rising faster and faster. His chest surged up and down, the pressure of curdling remorse clenching his body. His breathing escalated, flooding the veins and muscles in his neck with hot blood. The crowd's noise beyond the wall grew, and his bare chest seethed with sweat and anxiety.

The Fighter stood, towering at six foot five inches. His fists shot out, striking particles of dust in the warehouse light like the desperate jaws of a starved animal. His breathing was fast and sharp, hissing through his teeth with each strike. He inhaled faster, fists flying through the air and...

He thought of *Her*.

The pain that fueled him. The thought of her looking at him, with her smile. Their hands, locked in the sand. Some time, some place, forever gone. Thoughts and memories that once filled his soul, now slowly killed it.

He veered into the halls, his shoulders twitching with each powerful stride. The undertone of the crowd rose with each step as he trudged through darkness. He burst into the warehouse arena with its blacked-out windows. Filthy construction lights obscured the faces of the audience. It was a melting pot of noise and people, saturated by tourists, American businessmen, and college students, who all came to splurge. In the back of the crowd were the desperate locals from nearby towns, and the immigrants. Whether for pleasure or for necessity, all walks of life came to this spectacle for a reason.

Ezequiel was sweating and waiting in the ring. Without even looking up, The Fighter cut through the rambunctious crowd and jumped into the nine-foot-tall caged arena. Ezequiel was jumping and warming his muscles while the packed onlookers hooted and cheered, thirsty for brutality.

The Spanish-speaking announcer flicked his tongue, describing the two men through a thick South American accent: "The Stinger," Ezequiel was declared, for his viper-striking eyes and fists that matched. He hailed from an old, run-down village on the Sea of Cortez.

On the other side of the dilapidated cage stood Fletcher. He studied

The Fighter, who still had his back to his opponent. Fletcher could see—
The Fighter's eyes and mind were elsewhere. The Fighter didn't even move
as the ring announcer described him as "El Lobo Blanco," pointing to the
wide face of the wolf that covered his entire back.

"The White Wolf!" he yelled, translating for the Americans.

The crowd booed, cheered, and murmured. Still, The Fighter did not
move. His back remained to Ezequiel, something that frustrated all of his
opponents, who expected to lock eyes, wanting to threaten and intimidate
their foe. But The Fighter didn't care. He was never intimidated. Nothing
scared him. Nothing made him feel. Not this, not anything. Not anymore.

His eyes were low and inert. The crowd muttered, confused but
intrigued by the towering man's stillness. His breathing was rhythmic and
deep. No one understood but him. He was in another place.

That place with *Her.* He was focusing on what he'd once had, and how
that single thought stabbed at his insides. That very pain pulsed through
him and his arms shot out, stretching the density of muscles that coiled
throughout his entire body.

The warehouse was pungent, humid, and packed. Faces and hands
pressed against the rusty cage where the two opponents stood. Fletcher was
now ringside with a group of enthusiastic gamblers—young men dressed in
suits and loose ties. They were the type who would come to the border to
throw money at spectacles and debauchery. Ezequiel hopped up and down,
pumping adrenaline, keeping his eyes locked on The Fighter.

Still, The Fighter barely moved, but his breathing was constant and
rapid. Beads of sweat slid down the aged ink of the countless tattoos
covering his coppered skin. His eyes wouldn't move. He was remembering.

How they had laughed all night on the beach. How he had felt alone
his entire life. Until *Her.*

The jeering crowd was relentless, but, between breaths, all he could
hear were the silent whispers of her eyes and the dance of lips and dimples
that smiled when she told him things. He'd give his life to feel those things
again. The crowd barked. They wanted it. So did Ezequiel, sneering from
across the ring. The Fighter couldn't hold on, as much as he wanted to, as
much as it hurt. They were fragments of *Her,* glimmers. Because she was
gone.

In every way, she was gone.

And someone needed to be punished.

Fletcher peered at his man, trying to understand his prolonged behavior. The announcer looked to Fletcher, confused, still waiting for the cue. Suddenly, The Fighter turned and looked up. He found Ezequiel's eyes. A bead of sweat rolled down his forehead. The rhythmic control of his breathing was now erratic, ready to implode. Fletcher saw it in one look. He waved to the announcer.

The bell rang and the two men catapulted.

Fists went flying. Knuckles to flesh, spit to sky. They exploded at each other. The Fighter's speed was astonishing. The crowd squealed at his instant dominance. A spearing jab hit Ezequiel's shoulder and threw his entire body back, staggering him into the rusted cage. The Fighter lurched with the advantage, his fists striking Ezequiel's face faster than anyone could see. Ezequiel desperately shot a kick to The Fighter's abdomen, pushing him back. But in the milliseconds of stillness, a gouge over Ezequiel's right eye was revealed, already streaming with blood. And before he realized it, The Fighter swarmed him again with a frenzy of knuckles into his sternum.

Ezequiel fired a right hook, but it was blocked. The Fighter pounded his fists into Ezequiel's stomach now. Ezequiel swung an elbow back—but every desperate measure was blocked. The pounding was so rampant that Ezequiel couldn't even see what was happening to him. Wind and spit geysered from his lungs, and within seconds, he was seeing black. The bell finally struck, and the warehouse shook with an uproar. Ezequiel collapsed, and The Fighter stood above, fuming, emotional…starving for more.

The coach jumped up. Ezequiel crawled to him on hands and knees, desperate to catch his breath. Through the cage, the coach applied jelly to Ezequiel's temple, but the gouge above his eye was already split wide and streaming blood onto the mat. The crowd cheered in satisfaction while The Fighter simply turned, averted his eyes to the ground, then went to Fletcher's corner.

His eyes narrowed and he was gone again. Remembering the way she had been. Her laughter echoing through the memories of a hundred nights they'd been together. The way they'd laughed together. Her brown hair falling to his cheeks, then her lips. Her smile that had made him wonder if anyone had ever smiled at him before. The Fighter stared at the blood-soiled mat, but he was remembering all the things that *were*.

Because they were all the little things that now made him hurt. That made him want the pain.

That made him fight.

The sudden shrill cry of a woman jolted him from his mesmerized gaze. He turned in the direction of the sound. Against the cage, a woman cried manically. Her hair was dark, and her eyes were wide with terror. It was Ezequiel's wife. She pressed her face against the fence with unstoppable tears. A woman next to her held their two children, no older than six, petrified by their mother's hysteria. The woman desperately yanked the children away while Ezequiel's wife lost herself, pushing her fingers through the cage and cutting them just to try and touch him. The crowd laughed and cheered.

"Vete, vete!" Ezequiel gurgled through blood-soaked teeth, telling her to leave.

But the woman wailed with agony. Ezequiel spat blood, telling his coach to get her out.

And the Fighter just stood there, mesmerized by it all.

The bell.

Ezequiel leaped to his feet and charged. The Fighter quickly defended himself, landing hits easily, but The Fighter's velocity had changed. A fist cracked against Ezequiel's split temple, shooting a streak of hot blood into the audience. Then he heard the shriek again, like metal colliding and screaming, cutting into The Fighter's ears and chilling his bones. It was the woman, horrified by every second of this. The Fighter couldn't help it—he fixated on the woman again, and yet, for some reason, he remembered *Her*. He remembered the way she had cried, he remembered her slow nights of insurmountable pain, the pain he had shared in his chest just by looking at her pale skin, her frail face. Holding her hand in the hospital all those days. How, treatment after treatment, she had fought, and nothing worked.

Nothing could help *Her*. Not even him.

Crack! A right hook blindsided him. Ezequiel seized the opening and attacked in retribution. The Fighter took hit after hit to his mid-section. With his guard down, a pummeling of fists shoved him back. A high-flying knee collided with The Fighter's sternum, launching him backwards. Fletcher's eyes widened. It was as if The Fighter wasn't even defending himself.

Another steep right hook caught The Fighter's chin, but he fired back, his fist shooting into Ezequiel's temple and instantly drowning his eye in blood. Ezequiel almost collapsed, tripping over his feet, walking sideways. Then the shrill cry came again, stabbing The Fighter's insides. That woman screaming—putting a knife slowly through his ears. His eyes flickered to her. She buried her face and her screams and her tears into shaking hands.

The Fighter couldn't stop staring at the distraught woman. He felt her every time he struck his opponent. As if he felt every moment of this through her—and it was destroying her. The Fighter's eyes broke away to scan the arena. The unruly crowd hollered and hooted while Ezequiel desperately tried to control the blood running into his eye. He was half blind and defenseless, and The Fighter knew it. His chin lowered to his clamped fists. They were throbbing and discolored. He suddenly unclenched them, slowly releasing the hypertension in his body. Ezequiel's brows furrowed—he saw the opening and desperately jumped up. He charged and launched a high roundhouse kick that swung across The Fighter's face. The Fighter practically toppled. He stumbled, disoriented in his footing, but finally squared up his body to face Ezequiel again.

The Fighter's temple was already beginning to bruise, yet his fists were held far below his jaw, defenseless. Ezequiel threw a sharp right hook and clipped The Fighter's chin. His guard was wide open now, Ezequiel saw it, and with all of his remaining strength, Ezequiel threw a fury of fists, pounding into The Fighter.

The Fighter took it—even allowed it—opening his guard further, lowering his arms, hit after hit.

Fletcher watched in disbelief, baffled by what was happening.

He was letting the man punish him.

The crowd wailed at the turn of the match while Ezequiel's fists pounded harder and harder against The Fighter's body, pushing him to the other side of the cage. The face of the crazed wolf on his back spread across the rusted metal, the cage wires cutting into sweaty flesh, while his opponent packed fist after fist into his body. The wind gushed from his lungs, and he doubled over at his waist. Ezequiel's leg sprung up and drove the hot bone of his knee into The Fighter's temple.

The Fighter dropped.

His face instantly bruised. It swelled with lactic acid and water like a rotting melon. Fletcher stared as Ezequiel mounted The Fighter, pounding down on his face, ricocheting The Fighter's entire skull against the mat. His head bounced off the ground and his swollen face landed on its side.

The Fighter blinked.

Time was gone.

His eyes found only one thing: the woman. Her face full of fear and terror, looking back into his eyes…until a fist packed into it. Then another, and another, hammering his skull into the ground. The woman trembled, looking through her fingers, trying to watch. It wasn't just her husband's face in blood—it was all a horror. The crowd. Their pleasure. The uncanny violent spectacle. These people cheered for every brutal moment of it. They cared nothing about these men or her family or her children who had to endure this. They believed nothing was at stake but their satisfaction and petty cash. It was only her, her husband, and The Fighter who knew.

The Fighter gazed at her. He knew all that she could lose if his opponent did not win. He knew, because he had lost everything when he lost *Her*. In those last moments of light, the crowd faded with the suspension of time, and he saw his last moment with *Her*.

That very last breath before her eyes closed.

How the world around him had disappeared. And, in a single moment between silence, peace, and pain, it all disappeared again. Ezequiel lifted his bloody fist and cracked it against his skull. The Fighter's entire world went black again.

Like the day she died.

SECOND CHANCES

The decrepit warehouse stood tall in the sunset. It rested in the barren desert peripherals outside of Nogales, a town just along the southern Arizona border. It was a place that tourists came in private shuttles from either side of the border to spend money. It was a place that others came to survive. Surrounding the warehouse were various homeless encampments, and vehicles and trailers parked by travelers and immigrants.

The warehouse was engulfed by empty desert that, after every brutal spectacle, would become a village of desperation for those who came to fight. Ezequiel's wife was preparing food amongst their large family of cousins and brothers. They celebrated together, drinking cervezas and awaiting the carne asada that she cooked on a charcoal barbecue. Ezequiel was cleaned up now, as all the winning fighters were allowed access to the boiler room hoses to shower off, but he was still inflated with countless bruises from the fight. Half of his face was covered by a patch and old tape that kept the slit under his eye and his temple at bay. But it made no difference to him, for he was the victor now, and holding his five-year-old daughter.

She was still disturbed by the spectacle and continued to ask her father questions about the fight and why Mother had had to seal his eye shut with tape. Still, it was a good day for their family. They had made it through another day in America, and Ezequiel had provided for all of them, one more time. The taste of chilled cervezas in the desert after a fight was nearly as good as a victory. But what mattered most now was that he was here, standing amongst his family, living for the moment to celebrate. Living for another day that he could provide, and they could survive.

Inside the warehouse's dim halls, Fletcher walked furiously. Deep in the back of the boiler room, he found The Fighter, hunched over the same bench where he'd found him before.

"The hell are you doing?"

But The Fighter was silent. He raised a bottle of warm whiskey to his swollen lips. Fletcher shook his head.

"Two fuckin' rounds and you give? You think I didn't notice?" Fletcher barked, studying him from the end of the hall. He didn't know what to make of it. The Fighter could have torn Ezequiel apart. He had watched The Fighter destroy men for eight months now—this behavior made no sense. "What is it? Huh? The bottle? Too old and beat? Not enough money? What? What do you want?" But The Fighter still didn't move. Fletcher laughed. He realized he was just going to be talking to himself—like always. The Fighter barely talked already, and he sure as hell wasn't going to talk about anything tonight. "You don't even know…"

Fletcher huffed, then turned to the only window in the cellar, matted with dust. The setting sun glistened between the particles and the last remnants of light pushed through the glass. There was a long period of silence. Fletcher thought of what to do and how to recoup his wagers with the young attorneys who had come over the border to celebrate a lofty legal victory. Fletcher's Fighter had built a reputation on both sides of the country lines. "El Lobo Blanco" was fierce, cunning, and cold. There were rumors he was "a killer," but no one knew to what extent or who he was or what he had done in his life. They didn't even know his name or where he had come from. The only true stories that could be found were in his tattoos—words, numbers, and symbols scattered across his body. And yet, no one ever got close enough to see the details or to ask about the symbols, such as the hummingbird on his shoulder. The distance prevented them from seeing anything but the face of the wolf across his back and the wounds scattered across his body. There were always rumors and stories about who he was, and those nefarious speculations helped Fletcher sell fights within the circuit. But right now, to Fletcher, his fighter was a failure.

He was dead weight.

The Fighter stood and peeled his white T-shirt off. It was painfully glued to his frame, soaked in sweat and blood. The stained white cotton slid over his bruises, still hot from the fight.

The Fighter finally spoke. "I'm done." His voice was stoic, deep, and reflected some faded foreign accent.

Fletcher stared a long moment before he laughed obnoxiously. "*Done?* Yeah, and then what? What are you gonna do?"

But he was met with silence again.

"Don't let your pretty eyes fool you," he prodded. "You're a fucking immigrant. How long before cash runs thin? Or they catch you?" Fletcher laughed, keeping the upper hand over his prized cage fighter. "You ain't special cause you're different," he continued.

But The Fighter didn't care. He'd stopped caring a long time ago. He stashed his soiled clothes and wraps in an aged leather duffle, then checked for the Polaroid that was hidden in his boot. Fletcher watched. He realized that this was no bluff.

"You know I'll get you sponsorship," he called out. "You know you get that, and you can do whatever you want." He was being open now, even truthful, attempting to lure him back in. "You can do whatever you want with your life. Give me a few more big fights and you got a second chance."

The Fighter turned. A massive purple bruise covered a swollen eye and ran through his temple and beard.

His words were firm and cold.

"There are no second chances."

And he walked out the door.

A "GOOD FIGHT"

Outside the warehouse, the sun descended quickly, and the encampment was coming to life with its true locals. Old pickup trucks and jobless denizens milled about, chatting, and making trades for the night. The once-raging arena began to vacate, less it be the desperate few that camped outside. It was a place many immigrants were hoping to get a shot at a fight or a winning bet. It was a chance to fight for everything—a stack of cash, a way to move forward, a way to stay in the country. Whatever it was to the individual, it was a crossroads between the land of opportunity and the land of despair, a polarity between those trying to survive and those who had come to feast upon the desperation of others.

The Fighter stepped out of the building wearing a clean white T-shirt, stretched open below the neck, an aged, leather duffle over his shoulder. The dark hairs of his tanned chest sprouted from his powerful neckline. His dark blue denim jacket with wool collaring gripped his broad shoulders and taut, sore arms with every stride. His jeans were black and dusty, his boots the same.

It was April, and the prick of desert winds became enduringly fierce as the sun dropped. The Fighter always walked firm and steady, never allowing anyone outside the arena to believe he was ever injured. As his boots collected sand, he eyed the many new tents that had popped up. This included Ezequiel and his entire family as they celebrated around their small encampment. Ezequiel's wife was the first to see The Fighter as he walked away. His boots thudded into the dusty earth, heading toward a 1977 Ford custom pickup truck. The vintage paint was chipped white, and its steel frame mounted thick tires that lifted it as large as a tank and higher than a horse's back. The Fighter tossed his duffle into the truck's open bed and swiftly unlocked the high driver's door.

"Lobo!" A voice hurtled through the wind.

The Fighter turned. It was Ezequiel and his two cousins heading right toward him. His family and children watched from behind, and his younger cousins stared intensely, staying closely behind Ezequiel and ready if they needed to bum-rush. But The Fighter just stood there, boots planted.

Ezequiel stopped within a few feet, enough to land a high kick to his temple—the same kick that had bruised the entire right side of The Fighter's face. Ezequiel's wife held their five-year-old daughter while the entire family watched their hero plant himself in front of his opponent once again. All the cousins and uncles gazed, ready to follow Ezequiel's lead, whatever it might be. They knew if they had to take him—or take from him—they could. Outside the cage, fighting was different. But not to The Fighter. He stood there, waiting, focused on Ezequiel and the man closest to him.

Ezequiel was calm, looking into The Fighter's bruised eyes through his own sole good eye. He was considering his words. He wanted to say more to the man in front of him than he actually could. Then, humbling himself, he spoke softly with his Mexican accent, saying the only words he could: "Good fight."

Ezequiel put out a bruised hand.

They were words he meant.

The Fighter looked him in his one good eye. The other he had ruined.

"Buena pelea," The Fighter said, then took his hand.

Ezequiel smiled and held his firmly.

They both knew what had really happened in the ring.

GIVING UP

The enormous desert sun dipped below the dusty horizon. The air was still, and the last white clouds traversed a sky that faded in shades of orange, red, and citrus. The white Ford truck was parked next to a small motorhome from the sixties. In the middle of nowhere, the vehicles were two metallic specks, the only sign of humanity in an endless, flat desert.

From wall to wall and covering the windows, the motorhome was plastered in Polaroid pictures. They were stuck to cabinets and cupboards and even the ceiling. They were all pictures of two people. They were pictures of who The Fighter once was. And *Her*.

Trips they had taken, memories, moments: Yosemite trees from tent windows, tall New York ice cream cones, and endless photos of the ocean. What was only a year looked like an entire lifetime of adventures, all in photos, all across the old yellow walls and faded wood cabinets. The Fighter sat in the miniature kitchen, a whiskey neat on the torn linoleum table next to a stack of more memories captured in faded celluloid. His knuckles and his hands were purple and completely bruised, holding on to their Polaroid from the beach. The picture of the night he had told her. And sitting beside it all was a loaded .45 Ruger pistol, lying next to his drink.

He finally let go of the picture, his eyes wincing with exhaustion and alcohol. He had thought about that night for hours. For half a bottle. His eyes traveled the mess of memories splattered across the table, till he chose something else: A handwritten list. He picked it up and scanned it slowly, reading it over and over again, like he had done a thousand times before:

~~NIAGARA FALLS~~
~~CHINATOWN, SAN FRANCISCO~~
~~WALK THE GOLDEN GATE BRIDGE~~
~~SLEEP IN CENTRAL PARK~~
~~MOTORHOME ACROSS THE STATES~~
~~LOS ANGELES~~
~~YOSEMITE~~
MAKE A FAMILY
SEE THE GRAND CANYON
LIVE THE MOST BEAUTIFUL LIFE

With one eye crusted in dried blood and the other sharing a yellow swollen temple, he stared at the last three items, like he had always done on his worst days:

MAKE A FAMILY
SEE THE GRAND CANYON
LIVE THE MOST BEAUTIFUL LIFE

His breath stuttered and his heart pounded against its cage. He read the words again, over and over again in his head. His face was too inflamed for tears to leak, but inside, he was erupting over what he had once had: a best friend. A life. A reason. And now, a life without *Her*. His erratic breathing now shook him in his seat. He lurched from the table and smeared the Polaroids everywhere. He tore down a wall of photos from the cabinets, scattering them throughout the motorhome. It wasn't enough. He snatched up the handle of his .45 and burst through the door into the desert abyss.

What was the point? Why did any of it matter? Nothing would be the same. Nothing would change now. He had been given the love of his life and she'd been ripped away, like all the people he had ever loved, over and over again. Sand and sweat trailed behind as he trudged into the void of twilight desert. He passed his truck, gripping the pistol in his palm. He was an insignificant speck in the horizon, careless, senseless, dying, dead, or soon to be all of it and nothing at all. His boots pounded into the earth, plowing further and further into the nothing of desert until he could no longer stand feeling any more. No more torturous feels, no more torturing thoughts. It had to go. The Fighter stopped and rammed the barrel under his chin.

He winced—seething, hating himself, hating this sky. His neck tightened in veins, looking up at the cold blue yonder and the collage of memories and feelings and words that forever haunted him. He saw the twilight moon, the old dreams, photographs, smiles, and stars. It didn't matter what he did or what they had once had. It was all gone, and he had nothing. He had given her all that he was and all that was left of him. And now he was nothing—truly nothing, standing alone in the desert like a speck of nothing, a piece of nothing, ramming the gun to his chin. He flicked the safety off, inhaling. His finger found the trigger, exhaling.

He could be with her now.

Right now.

His eyes fixated on the endless blue above and whiskey sweat dripped from his bruises. His temples squeezed, the last pain he would ever feel. The light slowly faded as his eyes slowly closed.

And then it happened.

A shooting star.

High above. In the blink of an eye. It soared.

But he saw it. He knew he did, because it was the only thing that could possibly take his mind from the pain or the trigger. A shooting star. They were *Hers*. Her favorite things in the world, ever since she was a little girl. The corner of his eye twitched and his breath stuttered in, then out, a locked finger grazing the trigger. He had to do something. Anything.

They were her signs, she'd say. Her secret reminders. The things that told her she was never alone.

His eyes tightened, as tight as his teeth could clench. He rescinded what tears dammed in his eyes and were desperate to pour. He held them, tightly. Until everything became slow again. His breath followed. Then his jaw, releasing. His chin descended from the sky.

"Okay…*okay*…"

And he lowered the pistol.

He had seen a shooting star.

Why?

What were the chances?

They weren't his signs—they were *Hers*. Deep in his chest, something churned everything that was inside. Something agonizing him and invigorating him all at once. Some deep truth, hidden, waiting to be discovered. He was perturbed, his whole body was full of pain...but he'd seen a shooting star.

If he hadn't believed anything in his life before that very moment, he could have ended it—but he believed in one thing:

He had seen a shooting star.

And it was *Hers*.

The Fighter stood there, his trailer behind him, the stars above. He was there again. Some place between the past, the present, the pain, and the middle of nowhere.

THE BREAK OF DAWN

T he break of dawn cascaded across the desert. Light moved like shards of glass, spiking across endless sand, then holding itself there, for only a brief moment before shooting across the horizon. In the city of Nogales, outside the warehouse refuge, many tents, trucks, and campers were silently still. Only the animals of the land were up at this hour. In the back of a pickup truck's camper bed, Ezequiel slept next to his wife and their two small children. Outside, the motor of a large vehicle pulled up beside theirs. Ezequiel's eyes popped open. He worried it might be a bust—federal officers coming to break up the place, or identify its inhabitants. But it could also be someone or something else. He peeked through a corner of the newspaper clippings that covered all his windows, but he couldn't tell who was parked next to them now. If it were federal agents, he would have already known. Ezequiel carefully reached over his children's sleeping heads, nestled into his wife, and grabbed his hidden knife. Without a sound, he lifted himself out of the back of the packed camper.

Parked right beside his small truck was a vintage sixties motorhome. Ezequiel eyed it up and down. He had never seen this camper before and didn't like that it was now next to him. The perimeter was clear—no one was awake this early, or moving. With his knife concealed, he walked along the side of the truck. On the door of the camper, a set of keys hung next to a piece of paper. Ezequiel's eyes carefully read what it said:

Buena pelea.

He took it, then scanned the motorhome up and down in disbelief. His eyes held back tears. He didn't understand why, but he knew—The

Fighter had given him more than just the fight.

Across the desert cactuses and the infinite particles of dust and dirt, The Fighter walked alone. A cowhide bag was slung across his shoulder, and his head was low, deep in thought. He walked for three hours that morning, in the middle of nowhere, until he reached his white Ford truck. Without a moment to waste, he launched the leather bag into the bed next to his duffle bags, then hopped up into the truck, which easily stood four feet off the ground. His bruised hand opened the glove compartment. Inside it was a map and his Ruger pistol. He unfolded the map and trailed his hand from the southern Arizona border to the north. His finger slid across the heart of the state toward a big body of land illustrated above it that read: "The Grand Canyon."

He took a long, deep breath.

"Okay."

The truck's engine roared awake. He yanked the gear, hit the pedal, and took off into the open land.

OF MEMORIES AND FIRE

The massive white Ford thundered down an empty two-lane road. The gurgling sound of exhaust and horsepower was roaring strong and steady. It was how The Fighter always drove, the pedal firm under his boot, with all the windows down, the air whipping through his coarse beard and dark hair. It was midday now, and the sun shared the horizon as he flew up the highway. He was trying not to think. The idea of *Her* was always there, with him, within him, but the constant horizon and the rushing winds helped keep him from falling into *Her* memories again. He didn't want to. Not now. The open road was one of the last few things that brought him peace—that expression of movement and sound and the comfort of its consistency. It was an opera he had known his entire life—the open road, the constant driving, traveling, changing, always moving on, and always moving forward. He felt as if he never had a choice in the matter, and this part of his life was no different. And so, he kept going, keeping his eyes on the road and his mind at bay.

The winds were powerful at his first pit stop. They whipped sand and dust and gusty currents to his ear. The Fighter perched his swollen lips around the old metal of a faded canteen. He stood outside an old Native American trading post with three yellow teepees that served as road markers for travelers to see. Above them was an old tribal flag that waved wildly in the air. Two children, no older than six, ran about the grounds, just outside of a log cabin-like building that served as the trading post. The children were of a new generation. Young Native Americans of this land, and now the youngest. It was a special landmark that seemed almost out of place now, and perhaps soon it would pass with the sands of time, like all things did. The owners would, perhaps, choose to move on in their stories, traveling further east, or west, or perhaps, even cease to exist. And yet, the children's grandmother, a woman who looked as old as the land, shared the love of the sight with timeless, glowing eyes. Eyes that had seen much change from the delicate past to the ever-present, and even the prospect of the future. They were eyes that knew that life was never a matter of time, but always a matter of choice, what one chose to do with the time they had. The grandmother watched, just a few yards away from The Fighter. She gave him her proud, trusting, endearing eyes for only a moment, then, together, they watched the children chase one another, wind flowing freely through their hair as they beamed and shouted with joy. The Fighter smiled.

Something he had not done in a long time.

Rock and roll blared through the heavy speaker system of the white Ford truck. He was riding alongside a sherbet sunset now and was nearly in the heart of the state. With one more half day, he could reach the Grand Canyon. But as he rode into the fading light, his mind finally started to drift with it. What would he do when he got there? What *could* he do? Was this going to be his way of honoring her final wishes?

Or was it his way of saying goodbye?

The Fighter didn't know. But one notion stayed in the back of his mind. Something that loomed inside. Something he planned to do there. He had no words to explain his feelings or thoughts, but they were there, fighting him, fighting what was left in his heart. He was going to make a choice. It was already remorseful to think of what that choice was, because he had already made it. As the Ford truck roared down the single-lane road, he tried to distract his mind. He didn't want his conscience to know.

He didn't want *Her* to know.

He was going to the Grand Canyon.

And he wasn't coming back.

The Fighter set up a small tent and fire before the last shades of twilight turned to darkness. The sky was a dark blue now, and the desert became shockingly cold as it would after sunset in these months. He leaned against a small cooler, sitting on the dusty earth, as the flames danced above his knees. His denim jacket and wool collar complemented the warmth, as did the bottle of rye that he had started back in the trailer. The slow burn of oak and wood spiced his throat, and after a day of fighting and travel and memories, his mind and his heart were finding new places of stillness. But it was more of a numbness that he felt now, or wanted to feel. And like so many nights before, he couldn't help where his thoughts would lead his heart. The Fighter dug into the large duffle containing the last of his belongings. In it was a small rucksack that he pulled out and carefully unzipped. Inside were countless Polaroids he had taken. They were all of *Her*.

He didn't want to stare, quickly flipping through the many trips and moments they had shared during their time. It was all of memories and fire. He knew this vicious circle—this morose way of living—would never end, as it had never stopped since the moment she left, one year ago. All he ever wanted was just to see her face again. The way it had been when she was next to him. How she would turn, and her eyes would smile when she wanted to tell him something. He wanted it to be like so many nights before, when she would be right by his side, somewhere, anywhere, and he could ask her how she wanted spend their night or their next day. He would ask where she wanted to go next, or what she wanted to see. And it never mattered to him what or where, as long she was with him. It was a deep, indescribable love. It was the deepest thing The Fighter had ever felt.

He had changed in that year with her. Never would he have imagined that he would depend on someone like that, because throughout his life, he never could, so he never did. But with *Her*, it was as if he had found refuge. She had become his best friend—a true friend—and, in so many ways, so many things from his past made sense now. So many pains and losses and people who had come and gone—it all came to pass in his heart, just because he met *Her*. It was as if none of his past mattered anymore, because she had come. And sometimes, that was just how simple it could all be when you met your person. When you met the one that was ready for you, and when you're ready for all of them.

The Fighter was holding a heap of pictures and Polaroids. He knew every single one of them better than he knew his own hands. His memories would never fade—but he would. His hands were mangled with bruises and split knuckles that held dried blood and purpled flesh. And with his ruined hands, he held these photos—seeing them, feeling them, all at once, one last time.

Then he tossed them into the fire.

With one deep breath, his head tilted back, and he grimaced, hearing them burn. He stared at the stars, holding back what tears would come. But they didn't. So, he hoped that another sign would come instead. To show him something he couldn't see. For if he could never escape what he felt, if this vicious circle could not be broken, then perhaps he could at least understand it. The bed of black sky receded to the shimmering freckles of white and silvery stars that glistened. And as the pictures burned and singed into nothing, he waited for a sign… something, anything, but all there was was the openness and endlessness of the night above. And he was there, in that place again—somewhere between the past, the present, and the middle of nowhere.

THE COYOTES

The night was dark. The campfire burned low, and the ashy logs were charged a fiery red. The Fighter was warm as he lay on the cold Arizona dirt. An echo of a voice came to him in his sleep. It was some sort of cry, then a sharp whine. It intensified with another. The rustling of the earth could be heard as the voice turned into the call of a pack. It was the cry of coyotes, and they were close. Their echoes traveled the plains, and their paws came closer and closer, crackling brush and bushes. Their howls were so close now, that even in his sleep, The Fighter knew he was in danger.

His eyes jolted awake, and he ripped his Ruger pistol from his sleeping bag, swinging the steel barrel over his shoulder and pointing it behind himself. His head snapped upward, looking upside down, only to find a dog, covered in blood.

The fire danced flames in its dark eyes as it stood there, mangled, panting. There were dollops of blood and dirt on its shoulders. The Fighter stared, upside down, with his pistol trained on him. Just a few feet from his head, the dog collapsed. The coyotes howled again, this time, even closer, circling the bushes outside the camp. The Fighter quickly pulled himself out of his sleeping bag and got to his feet. The dog laid there, just within a kiss of the fire. The flames exposed the countless bite marks and flesh torn under its light brown fur. The Fighter palmed his pistol tightly and scanned the area, but it was so dark that even the moon could not expose what was lurking beyond the dying fire. But The Fighter knew—the coyotes were all around them.

He lifted his .45 to the dark sky and snapped off two rounds. They thundered with an echo, and the squeal of the canine pack followed as they skittishly bolted away. He could see the larger ones racing from the bushes and around the tires of the white Ford. The pack was afraid, but they must have been starving, because they were far too close for their safety.

The dying campfire had just enough embers to show the dog's gashes. The Fighter examined him, standing above. If this dog had been traveling or running from the pack, he had barely made it.

Suddenly, the dog's eyes opened. They gazed up at him, pain and fear expanding them. The Fighter towered above, pistol in his hand. He exhaled, knowing what he had to do. He swung the barrel over and pointed it down at the dog's head.

But the dog just stared at him, panting, his tongue dry from fear and exhaustion. The Fighter looked down into his eyes. Within the shadows and the last embers of burning wood, he saw his own reflection in the animal. He saw his own bruised face. And in a split second, he felt all that the dog had gone through. The hurt, the pain, the abandonment. His finger slid delicately down the arch of his trigger. He held the pistol trained to its head. The dog's eyes struggled to watch, quivering on each side of the metal crosshair.

And then he holstered it. A breath released from The Fighter's swollen lips, then he slowly squatted next to him. The dog, too scared and too exhausted to fight, or to even whimper, only stared. The Fighter took the bottle of whiskey in his sleeping bag and doused his wounded neck. The dog finally whined from the cool burning, but The Fighter held him down with his strong hands.

"I know, mate, I know…" he said tenderly.

The dog kicked, but it couldn't fight any longer, its eyes wincing at The Fighter as the burning rushed through his wounds, fighting blood and infection. With paws quivering, the dog started to shake. The pain and fear was so sharp that the animal suddenly passed out. The Fighter took his sleeping bag and ever so gently wrapped the dog in it. When the dog awoke moments later, his breathing intensified, but he was too weak to even yelp now. The Fighter picked him up, cradling him to his wide chest, and headed for the truck.

"Okay," he whispered. "Let's go."

He placed him in the passenger seat and put his pistol in the glove compartment. The Fighter took the map inside and quickly scanned it. His finger trailed the mountain highway road and stopped at the first town up: Prescott.

The Fighter took one last glance at the dog, then fired up the engine. "Hang in there."

And the Ford thundered into the night, heading north.

PRESCOTT

T he glow of dawn permeated the mountain mist. As the sun crested miles of range, light beamed through the peaks and valleys and trees, then pierced the windshield of the truck. The Fighter's sore hand carefully held the dog's neck through the sleeping bag, keeping a firm hold on the animal's wounds that were now crusted into the fabric. The dog was no longer bleeding and had been asleep for hours. They drove all night like this, and although The Fighter's hand was bruised and ached like the rest of his exhausted body, his piercing eyes were still sharp and focused. It was the same way he would operate in any fight, channeling his energy and concentration on his breathing and the task at hand. His hand was numb, but he knew he had to get this creature to help. He had already made it through the night, and the nearest town was coming up quick.

He was still heading northbound toward the Grand Canyon, and he thought that this overnight detour actually sped up the time he would have taken driving upstate. More importantly, whatever might happen with this dog now, he knew *She* would be happy. Because he knew he'd done the right thing. He was giving the dog a second chance.

That same morning, light struck the tall spring pines that shared the northern town of Prescott. The trees lined the mountain range and enclosed the town in its surrounding hills, summits, and valleys. A flat mountaintop just outside of town overlooked every direction of the land. The Yavapai Indians, known as the "people of the sun," had once called this fixture the "Mountain Lion Lying Down." To the white settlers, it had been known as "The Sphinx," but to the locals of modern day, it was the shape of a thumb, and hence the beloved landmark was called "Thumb Butte." It was the first and largest monument in the town's history. The second was at the heart of downtown: an old stone courthouse. The columns were tall and bare, like the trees lining the courtyard, awaiting the blooms of spring. From the saloons to the brick buildings, it was an old western town, someplace between the forgotten past and the history of this country. Just south of the courthouse were neighborhoods that had stood since the era some called the Wild West. There were rows of Victorian-style homes, some with paint that had been pressed by settlers over a hundred years ago. On this particular row of historic homes, the sun pierced the pine and cut across a modern road, which irrigated a neighborhood rich with 160 years of history. Some homes were renovated and looked as if they'd been built just yesterday, while others, withering but proud, had somehow withstood the tides of change.

The cast of morning light extended down the historic block, kissing the windows of a rustic Victorian and entering its bedroom to glaze the blankets of a warm bed. A woman in her early thirties slept there. Her hair was dark, and her overworked but honest eyes slowly opened. Her name was McKenzie. Sleeping next to her was a boy, Aiden, eleven years old with short, sandy-blond hair. It was just past six in the morning, and she started to rise with the sun. But, as she sat up from the bed, Aiden's arm flopped onto her, halting her. She let out a small smile, realizing he was still fast asleep. Somehow, the kid was always ready to stop her from leaving, and he always slept better knowing she was there. She gently tucked his arm back into the warm quilts, then turned from the bed once more. Aiden's arm flopped over onto her lap, holding her again. McKenzie smiled, shaking her head. With no choice, she wiggled her way out of the covers as his arm scrambled to hold her to stay just a little longer.

The coffee pot gurgled hot and rich. The kitchen was an old renovated '60's design, its second life since the original Victorian build. It was dated, but charming and well-kept. McKenzie was still in her pajamas and a warm blue flannel shirt, overlooking a spread of books on the kitchen counter: *Marine Biology*, *A Survey of English Literature Pre-1930*, *College Algebra*. She was focused, and the cold ambiance of spring's early mist cast bluish morning light outside her window. The town was always quiet at this time, and to McKenzie, the moments before sunrise until eight a.m. were paradise. If she could, she would spend this time on her porch just listening to the world wake, while enjoying hot coffee. Those moments before sunrise were sacred, her solace, and they always echoed what she hoped for at the end of the day: a sunset and a clear mind that was finally calm. But seldom was this the case, and this time in her life was no different.

Her gaze was intense, with her head deep into the next book on her list. It wasn't even seven a.m., and McKenzie had already reviewed three study guides of the five subjects she had to prepare for. She was on a roll. There was a true satisfaction she felt in these early mornings or in the latest parts of night. It felt like the whole world was asleep, except for her. No one would bother her, no one would call or send a message. The soft discourse of nature's movements at her window were always soothing. She was never bothered by the morning birds or the crisp air or the warm splashes of sun that reached through the pines. But, of course, in the way things seemed to do in life or in our minds—always challenging or disrupting our pinnacle moments of peace—McKenzie heard the porch door creak open. A set of keys jingled, then scratched metal, trying to unlock the bolt. McKenzie stared, surprised, watching as the door opened.

It was Jason, her oldest. He was sixteen, handsome, fair skinned with high cheekbones. He looked as if he had already entered adulthood, as he was tall, and his face had already thinned out and trimmed the fat of his adolescence. On the outside, it looked like he had already morphed into a man that had discovered himself. But he was not there yet, despite the deeply hidden gem of his old soul. Jason was a kid who could talk to anyone—make friends with anyone from anywhere and at any age. He was a talker and a listener, but only when he wanted to, because he was still a kid—frustrated, confused, and emotional. Jason had a better sense of morals and integrity than most kids his age, yet much of that greatness was suppressed by anger and confusion during this stage in his life. And when Jason walked through the door, he stopped right in his tracks, seeing McKenzie glaring from the kitchen counter. His flannel was torn at the shoulder, and his eyes were sunk from a lack of sleep.

"You're just getting home…" she said, realizing it as she spoke.

He stared. His eyes couldn't hide his tiredness, or his intoxication.

He was still drunk, and she knew it.

"Are you kidding me?" she snapped.

"What do you care?" he bit back.

"Hmm, where do I begin? Uh, maybe you're gonna get arrested one day?"

Jason let the porch door slam behind him, stepping in and shaking his head at her. It became a stare down, but McKenzie wasn't going to let up.

"I don't even know what to say to you anymore, Jason. You wanna tell your dad you're riding around drinking?"

"I wasn't riding."

"But you *were* drinking."

He stared.

"Why don't you call him and wake him up right now?" She pushed.

"I already fucking talked to him. And we aren't staying with him this weekend—*again*," Jason lashed out, then charged for the bedrooms. She was shocked. He had no shame storming off and slamming the door. He didn't realize he was so much like her. He didn't realize he was on a path that so many people McKenzie knew had gotten on, and she knew, wherever it was going, it wouldn't get better. She knew people who'd drunk their lives and their dreams away. People who had become too angry to overcome what life had dealt them. She knew those people all too well, because, for most of her life, she had been one of those people. Jason, whether he knew it or not, was just like her. But deep down, he also had her same strength. He was sensitive, but he always knew what was really right, and what was really wrong. And maybe that was why they could never talk anymore—because he was frustrated, deeply frustrated, like McKenzie had also been throughout her life. But to McKenzie, Jason was still her second chance. And to her, his life was just beginning. She just didn't want him to follow any of the roads she'd seen growing up. There weren't many, and they weren't good. He'd been reckless and angry like this for a year, and he wasn't getting better. She knew she had to do something. And it was the last thing she wanted to do. She had to try and speak to his father.

The sun sat low in the pines during midmorning. McKenzie was furious, pacing across the long wooden deck of her home. She had her phone between her ear and her shoulder, arguing with someone on the other line while picking up moldy food containers and garbage scattered down the deck.

"We went over this three times—it's finals week, Turner. You promised them and you promised me..."

"I messed up the dates...I might get a rider's spot in Tucson."

McKenzie dropped down from the wooden porch and scurried to pick up a large tuna can and soiled lasagna tray with her free hands. The front walkway of the house was a mess. The local pig-like rodents, known as javelinas, had swarmed the neighborhood the night before, tearing up and devouring everything—rubbish, plants, flowers, and anything pungent their snouts could find.

"You *might*!?" she snapped. "Turner, this is my one chance to study. I've got work all weekend— Stupid javelinas!" she interrupted, kicking over a pair of chili and pineapple cans scattered from a knocked-over recycle bin. "Do you know how much I gotta study this week?" she pushed while bagging the rest of the trash in the bins, then heading back up to the mailbox.

"What do you want me to say, Mac?" he asked. "This is my shot right now."

McKenzie stopped. All she could do was bite her tongue and shake her head. This man would never understand what he was doing to her and to their kids.

"What about your *sons*, Turner? Do you even know what Jason's been doing? Or how he feels when you flake? He's tired of it—we all are."

"I'll fucking handle him, Mac. But work is work. What do you expect? It comes when it comes, you know that."

McKenzie pulled a wad of envelopes and junk mail from the mailbox, then stopped. She had to take a deep breath before clarifying her words. "I expect you to keep your word when you give it, Turner."

She held the silence. The words stung him for the simple fact that Turner knew he had done wrong and that he was lying to her. He always lied if it meant he got his way. It didn't matter if it was McKenzie, or work, or anyone. Turner did care about her. He did think of himself as a man and as a father. But in this moment, he didn't know what else to say. He wasn't going to help her through this—he had other things on his mind and McKenzie knew it. His silence spoke for him. And he would never understand the damage he had done to her children, let alone to her.

"Thanks for letting us down, like always," she said, then hung up.

McKenzie stepped back up onto her wooden porch, trying to think through everything. She had to study as much as possible now, and in between everything, if she was going to do well on her exams. She sat on the end of the wooden rail overlooking the neighborhood. The boys were going to be devastated. The energy was going to be toxic for everyone. She shook her head. She had been enrolled in community college for years now, scraping by on a class or two every year, and this was her chance to actually finish two years of college level education that had taken her eight. She had no more time to lose and no more time to waste. She headed for the door and quickly flipped through the barrage of mail. A large letter from Arizona Public Services stood out. It was the electric bill. In bright red ink, an excessively large stamp read: *Past Due*. McKenzie stopped halfway through the door.

"Shit..."

It was the second notice. And it wasn't the only unpaid bill waiting to greet her.

GOING TO GRAM'S

McKenzie was doing her best to study. It was midmorning now, and the fact that she'd have to tell Aiden and Jason that Dad wasn't coming to get them again, was just going to stifle her from doing her best work. She didn't know what to say to them. She couldn't make excuses anymore and Turner would never give them the time or day. It always fell on her. At this point in her life, she was completely fed up with Turner. But she was also truly worried about Jason. She could feel him growing up and changing faster than ever before, and in ways she couldn't even speak with him about. They just didn't talk anymore. His childhood was fading into rebellious teens, a time in life she knew all too well. He needed a dad, now more than ever. But his father was always going to be like this—picking and choosing to see his children when it was most convenient for him, and not when it was best for his boys. They were always afterthoughts—second, third, or even fourth to his career and lifestyle as a rodeo man.

It was this same fantasy that had drawn McKenzie to Turner to begin with. He was ambitious, talented, and had become a town hero as one of the youngest and best bull riders in local history. And while he wasn't always self-centered, McKenzie knew now—for better or for worse, Turner was never going to change. It was something that had taken McKenzie a long time to understand, let alone come to terms with. They had met in high school when Turner was a senior, and she, a junior. With talent, and ego to boot, everyone knew he was going to be a rodeo star, even McKenzie. It had been impossible not to be swept up in the glitz and glamour that dating a town hero had come with. Her hometown held the country's oldest rodeo. It was a beloved tradition that the entire community would share all week amongst friends and family. The town of Prescott would throw a fair, parades, car shows, cowboy shows, concerts, and a bustling street market. The businesses, the schools, the elderly, and the young all loved Rodeo Week. It was a way of life. It was their own slice of history, preserved in a communal country soul that all the people cherished, but that only few in this country still really knew. The west was fading, but her hometown had prevailed. It was a rich town—rich in the strength of character, community, and kindness. Prescott was even the state's first capital, and anyone who had ever been to, or been raised there, or had just heard about it, knew that it was called "everybody's hometown" for a reason.

Yet who Turner was now was not the person McKenzie had grown up with, and he certainly was not the person she thought she'd spend her life with. Her life and Turner were far from what she had ever imagined. But all that really mattered now was how she would break the news to Aiden that Dad wasn't going to take them for another weekend. It was the weekend she'd needed it most, and now the fourth weekend in a row that she'd had to say, "Your dad's not coming around."

She shook her head, pulling away from her marine biology book. She tried to dissipate her anger through long, deep breaths. But just as she took a moment's break from studying, her eyes crossed the electricity bill again. McKenzie exhaled so deep that it made her feel more out of breath. This weekend was her last chance to study before finals week. She had already spent eight years taking night and morning classes anytime she could afford it, or whenever she could schedule it while working doubles at the bar, and now she was finally in the last semester of her life at Yavapai College. It had taken eight years just to scrape through general education, giving up weekend days for classes, and studying before working all night at the bar. And now this was it—her final exams, to end her final term. McKenzie didn't know what she could or would do after. She didn't even know why she'd committed to going back to school. McKenzie just wanted to be something—anything—if it could get her and her boys a better life. It was always like this. Just trying to get by. She didn't even know what a better life would look like. She was just trying to survive.

If it wasn't her children's father, it was the bills, or the neighbors, or work, or school, or her mother, who had been disappearing in and out of rehab programs since McKenzie was in high school.

McKenzie, in every way, was on her own and always had been.

There was only one person she could ever depend on, one person who she actually looked up to, and she was racing to pack clothes, toiletries, and food to take the boys to where that person lived. It was the only person who was ever there for her.

"Aiden, you up and ready or what?" she yelled from the kitchen.

"I'm packing for Dad's right now!"

She stopped and became still again. Even from the other room, she could feel his excitement. The pit in her stomach went sour. She had to think about what to say to him this time. Turner would always over-promise and over-sell them "guy time," and he was just as quick to let them know he had something else really important to do. For Turner, it was always the prospect of work or touring rodeos. McKenzie never understood why he was so selfish. There were countless times he could have taken them to the rodeo or even on his tours with him. It took McKenzie almost ten years to realize that the real issue with her relationship called back to something she'd had to learn earlier in her late twenties: some people just love you when they *want* you. But real love was to *need* someone because you love them. It wasn't that you couldn't live without them; it was that you *chose* to live with them, because you love them. That was that mature, lush, truth of love that only grew from vulnerability, and ironically, she had learned it from Turner the hard way. She had learned it not through his love, but through his absence. It had been all too familiar, like everyone in her story—coming and going. But now, in this chapter of her life, trying to make a better life as she entered her thirties, she recalled something that her grandmother always said: "Everything happens for a reason."

McKenzie was halfway through packing up school supplies and bags for the boys when she heard someone step up to the porch door. "Morning, Kenz."

She stopped, surprised. It was Kyle, a neighborhood friend since elementary. She took one look at him before returning to packing the bags. "Hi."

"Are you mad at me?"

"No, Kyle. What do you want?" she asked, already annoyed.

Kyle opened the screen door and carefully stepped in. They were the same age and had known each other since the first grade. And while Kyle had always been a good friend, in her mind, his world and hers were too different. He'd grown up in a stable, strong, middle-class family and had left town to go study finance at the University of Arizona. It had been a good experience for him, then he'd immediately come back to Prescott and started in real estate. Kyle was a good ol' local boy in every sense of it. He was smart, ambitious, and because of his love of home, his pride of country, and his large family, he'd always known he wanted to come back to Prescott. He wanted to help his family members in their businesses while starting his own life and making his own name in town. McKenzie had known him since he was a good boy, and now he was a good man. Kyle was soft in ways that McKenzie was not. But today, she couldn't even look at him.

He was a handsome guy with short, clean-cut light brown hair gelled to the side. She looked up for a second to see that he was still there, smiling at her. But with one glimpse of his University of Arizona polo shirt, she immediately ignored him and went back to packing. Ever since she was a little girl, the University of Arizona had been her dream. The idea of going felt like an escape. An opportunity. A path to a new life. So many of her friends had gone or left town, but McKenzie had had no choice but to stay. Going to the U of A was something she'd had to give up a long time ago. It was a pipe dream, and she hated his shirt and any little reminder that wouldn't let her forget that dream.

"Well?"

"Oh, I was wondering, I know it's just you here…" he began, referencing the fact that she'd been the boss of the household since Gram had left.

She stopped packing to actually listen now. McKenzie knew enough men to know the sounds they made when they wanted something from her.

"And you know this here is a historic home…"

"And?" She held her ground.

"You in the market to sell?"

She stared. "You walked all the way down here to ask me that?"

He thought about his answer. "I mean…I was gonna see how that went first, then ask you to dinner."

She immediately averted her eyes to her books. "I start finals on Monday. I need to focus." Without making eye contact, McKenzie began to quickly organize and pack food from the cabinet. She knew, with bringing the boys to Gram's on such short notice, that she may not have much to feed them.

"Aiden, Jason, come on!" she yelled down the hall. Kyle was still standing in her front doorway.

"All right, well can I just say something then?" he finally implored.

"Hurry up, I gotta take my boys somewhere."

Kyle took a breath. His heart and his ambition were finally coming out. "I know you got a lot going on…but you know me. You know my family. And I know Turner puts you through a lot. I get it." He stopped to take another breath. McKenzie pretended to repack Aiden's backpack, listening to everything he was telling her, but keeping her back to him so he couldn't see that she felt vulnerable. "I'm not him, Kenzie. You've known me since the first grade. I just think we're getting older and…I want to help you."

She turned to finally face him. "What do you want, Kyle? You want to date me or sell my Gram's house?"

"I want both."

He stood there, firm, clear, looking right in her eyes. McKenzie heard him—she believed him, and it scared her. Right then, Aiden walked in, interrupting the moment.

"Mom! The javelinas are back!"

"Yeah, I know." She continued packing.

"Hey, bud," Kyle said cheerily, but Aiden didn't even look. He hated the nicknames Kyle used. They varied from "bud" and "buddy" to "chief" and "little guy," all of which annoyed him and Jason. The boys had just never liked him—not because Kyle was a bad person or because of the nicknames, but because Kyle's sisters and brothers had sons and daughters all around Aiden's age, and to him, they were all brats and certainly had more than they did. The whole family was better off. This didn't bother

McKenzie, but their clan-like mentality did. Kyle's family was big—he was the oldest of six siblings and they were a known and respected family in town. Kyle was a good guy, but the idea of assimilating into their clan just never felt right to McKenzie. She was never going to be someone's prize or accessory. She was already that with Turner. Plus, according to Aiden, an eleven-year-old, Kyle was a "complete dork."

Aiden quickly charged the window, seeing the javelinas and pointing. "No, they're here right now! We gotta scare them!"

McKenzie was making sandwiches now, swiftly multitasking like she always did when doing her motherly duties.

"No, Aiden. Get your stuff," she said.

Kyle chimed in, "Javelinas are dangerous, bud. Best to just leave 'em be." Aiden rolled his eyes. Kyle quickly returned to his previous subject. "Kenzie, what if you sold the house and made a good profit? Imagine what you could do right after you finish school."

Aiden interjected, "Mom, they're right outside! Can I spray 'em with the hose?"

"No, you can't, Aiden! Get ready, please. We're going to Gram's!"

"What!?" he yelled back. "What about Dad's!?"

It had just come out. She hadn't meant it to. McKenzie finished packing sandwiches into a bag then admitted, "He canceled. I don't know what to say…"

She could see it on his face. He was crushed. Again.

"That's bullshit!" Aiden yelled, then stormed back to his room.

Kyle, uncomfortable with the new tension, tried to keep the conversation moving forward. "I was just saying…I think we could sell the house and make a profit. I could be your agent."

"Dude." She turned to look him in the eye. "I don't have time for any of this."

Right then, a dirt bike's high-pitched motor squealed through the neighborhood. It gunned up the driveway, then the motor screamed from being throttled in neutral. On the brink of a blowup, McKenzie headed for the door. "Jason! It's not even nine a.m.!"

Kyle followed her outside to find Jason in the driveway, straddling his dirt bike, while a wave of javelinas squealed and flooded down the street.

They were large, coarse-haired animals that resembled pigs, but were the size of medium dogs, and some had sharp tusks. They scurried like ants all over the neighborhood as Jason revved up his bike, screaming the engine with a high pitch.

"Cut it out!" McKenzie yelled from the patio.

Jason shouted back over his screaming motor, "I'm scaring 'em off!"

"I don't care! Turn it off! We're going to Gram's!"

"I'm not going to Gram's!"

"You're going where Aiden goes, and where I say you go, Jason!"

But Jason was already furious from the news, and with a shake of his head, he dumped the clutch, kicked the gear, and blasted out of there, the engine screaming the entire way.

"Jason!" she shouted as she watched him fly down the street without a helmet. "Jason!"

But he drowned out her voice by gunning the throttle and skidding his tires out of the neighborhood. Like so many times in her life, she stood there, stuck again. No matter how bad they fought, Jason always worried her more than he angered her. In so many ways, he reminded her of herself and her own mother: rebellious, independent, and always angry at someone or something. She couldn't blame him because she understood him. He was just a smaller version of her, frustrated with life's constant shuffling of poor cards. But Jason never thought that way. He just thought about how his parents played games with each other, and how his father would sell his love for them so hard, only to let them down over and over again.

It was silent on the porch now. McKenzie just stood there, trapped in her head.

Kyle watched. He pitied her. He knew there was always so much on her mind and on her plate. He wasn't naive to her family's story or their struggle. "Do you want me to take Aiden?"

She took a breath. "I want you to leave, Kyle. Thank you."

But Kyle shook his head and stood there until she acknowledged him. When their eyes finally met, he told her something she always needed to hear and that very few ever said: "You need to trust some people, Kenzie."

"Yeah? Like you?" she fired back.

"Yeah—like me." He stood firmly, only a few steps below her on the old wooden porch. "And you know why?"

She waited.

"Because you know me, McKenzie. And I know you. And you know what? I actually care about you."

Kyle walked off, leaving her on the porch. He had had enough, and he wasn't going to fight with her, even though he knew she needed help. She always needed more than she would ever admit.

She stayed quiet, watching him head back up the street to his mother's house. She took a deep breath, trying to curb her feelings.

She had to keep it together.

Aiden and McKenzie cruised across town in her old, green 1987 Jeep Cherokee. Aiden was face-first into her cell phone, his thumbs wildly jamming to a video game. McKenzie was sorting it all out in her head—how many hours of studying could she actually do after getting off work tonight? She thought about how she might entertain or keep the kids occupied while she focused. How would she handle Jason if he came home? Then she thought about how she had to pace herself and her coffee intake today if she was going to have enough time and hours to study. But what stressed her most now was whether Jason was going to be out drinking and being reckless again. It killed her how hurt Jason would get. So much of his frustration with her mirrored what she had felt about her own mother, someone who had voluntarily stepped out of her role as mother, and stepped into a vicious cycle of partying, addiction, recovery, and relapse. But McKenzie was strong enough, and smart enough, to no longer blame her mother for anything in her life. She just didn't want to deal with her in her life anymore. She had her own kids to raise now. And that commitment took precedent over everyone and everything, including herself. Aiden's game zipped and zapped as he mashed the phone's screen with his thumbs.

"Aiden, don't drain the whole battery. Jason might call," she said. Her voice was somber.

"Okay," he said, putting it down. "Mom?"

"Yeah?"

"Can we get a dog?"

"Nope."

"Why not?"

"Because."

"Because why?"

"Because I got two animals already, and there's a hundred other things we need first."

"Like what?" he prodded back.

"Like your own bed?"

He nodded, finally piping down. She looked over at him twice, inspecting him, seeing how he was actually feeling. She could always read her kids just with one word, one look. She reached over and rubbed his neck. "Does your back hurt today?"

"It's okay…" he said timidly.

She knew what that meant: his back was sore, and he hadn't slept well. He was a charming little man, and for whatever reason, he had chronic joint pain to go with it. McKenzie sighed. There was nothing worse for a mother than to know her child was in pain. She'd happily give up her life if she could take away just a fraction of life's challenges that would come his way.

"Mom?" He looked over. "Are you freaking out?"

She nodded. "A little."

He reached over and rubbed the back of her neck. "You're gonna do good, okay? You're a good studier. You're way gooder than me."

She smiled finally. His playful words always softened her. She didn't know what to say. She was just grateful for him—just for being him, exactly the way he was.

"Thanks for staying at Gram's," she said, softly. "I'm sorry about your dad…"

He tried to hide his disappointment. "It's okay."

She knew, just like his back pain, he was trying to hide how he felt. She put her arm around him and tugged him in like he was stuck with her forever.

And he was.

Aiden smiled. He loved it when she roughhoused him. It was the type of play and love he craved from his father and his brother. Aiden gave it another minute before trying to be clever again. "Can we get a dog now?"

"Nope!

A SURPRISE

It always felt like a long a ride to Gram's new apartment. Probably because she was no longer living at the house with them, which was the one stable thing McKenzie had ever known. These last two years, watching Gram "get old" had been hard. She could feel Gram slowing down, just watching her think and listening to her talk, and now that she was living across town on her own, everything going on had become especially harder for McKenzie.

Gram was now thirty-five minutes out of town in a small housing complex, one of the most affordable places to rent in town outside of the halfway homes that McKenzie's mother had been in and out of. This apartment was to be Gram's last home, as it was only a few miles from the hospital, which now helped with the in-home care she required daily.

Gram was everything to McKenzie. In all ways, she was her savior. She was a mother, a father, and a protector. Watching her get old and lose her edge was something that made McKenzie ache. Gram was the one who was always there for people. Everybody in the family, and really, anybody in town. From lending money, to opening up her home to neighbors who lost theirs in the fires. Every Tuesday, she had the ritual of visiting the oldest living resident on the block, buying him groceries, then cooking him a meal. Gram didn't shy away from anyone who needed help. She stepped in and stepped up for anyone in need, without question, and she had been like that her entire life.

To McKenzie, she had the strength and intelligence of a great woman *and* a great man. As a little girl, McKenzie never saw Gram get out of line with anyone. Instead, she carried a powerful, but quiet, demeanor with the people who had done wrong. She was firm with her feet and her eyes, and seldom did she ever need to raise her voice because of it. She showed how a person could be strong and kind enough to forgive, and even show compassion and forgiveness for a person who had done her wrong. And yet, she was just as strong and wise to let someone go, or to move on. All her life, McKenzie saw Gram take someone in, or take someone back. And this included her mother, throughout her addiction.

Gram was older now and outgrowing the image McKenzie had always had of her. Her later years had caught up with her real quick. She refused to stay in the family's longstanding home with McKenzie any longer, even though she had spent her entire life in it, raising her little sisters and brothers there, her daughter, and even McKenzie. When her unreliable legs and fading memory came, Gram had felt like a burden—although she never was, not even now. It was just how she felt. And while McKenzie had had to grow up with the excuses and heartbreaks from her mother, Gram had never broken her word. She had spent her entire life helping others in the family get on their feet, and then helped them get on with their lives. And this was no different than for her daughter, who she'd had to raise on her own when her husband died.

"Kenzie, you best understand—if you don't help those that are weak, then you are the weak. But if you can care about someone who can't even care for themselves, that there is what makes someone strong."

They were words that had often come when Gram took her mother back in, time and time again. McKenzie could never forgive or accept her mother, but with Gram, she always tried.

Gram was one of those rare souls who could see people for who they were, but also who they could be. She could see the truth in people, and she believed in helping people to see and understand those truths. More than anything, Gram understood that people just wanted to be felt and understood. And maybe that's why it was easy for her to forgive. McKenzie took more after her mother—she forgave no one once they did her wrong.

Gram never expected her same degree of kindness or attention from anyone; she never wanted that same attention, especially now with in-home service coming twice a day to help with chores, cooking, bathing, and the restroom. It made Gram sad to not be the caretaker of others, to do the daily chores of life, because she had always done them. To have a stranger do these things for her was beyond foreign, and still, she knew the time had come that she could no longer fully take care of herself, and she didn't want McKenzie to inherit that as well. When Gram's daughter entered rehab for the third time, and McKenzie was just about to attend her junior prom, she had seen how confused and sad McKenzie became. She knew she had to step in. And, as a result, she became more of a mother to McKenzie than her own mother could or ever would be.

Throughout her youth, McKenzie had been terrified of losing Gram, because she was the one person who was there. She was the one person she could trust. Besides her boys, Gram was the only person she had ever really had on her side. But Gram was more than her saint. She was the most loving and selfless person McKenzie had ever known. And that type of living and loving is a way that can change anyone for the better.

McKenzie compared everyone she met to Gram. She had realized, at this point in her life, that if someone didn't reflect the kindness and integrity that her grandmother did, every day, just by being themselves, then they weren't her type of people. And while she'd had to learn the hard way through her twenties, McKenzie understood now that there wasn't time to waste with anyone who wasn't even the smallest sliver of greatness like Gram. McKenzie gave Gram credit for everything, especially for the wisdom and confidence that made her strong and independent. And she had to be. McKenzie was the last of her family's line. She was now the matriarch of the house.

When they arrived, Aiden instantly hopped out of the Jeep and grabbed his backpack and weekend bag.

"Hey, tell Gram I'm late and I'll call her later."

"Okay!" Aiden said, hauling up the hill to the apartments.

"Hey, punk!" she got out of the Jeep and crossed her arms across her chest. "Gimme a kiss."

Aiden shook his head then ran back down. He planted a loud one on her cheek.

"Love you." She smiled.

"Love you back! Hope ya crush it!" Aiden raced uphill once more. McKenzie watched as he bolted through the front door. The door was always unlocked for anyone and everyone—that's just who Gram was. Echoing down the street, a dirt bike flew around the corner. McKenzie turned, shocked—it was Jason. He pulled his bike right up to the Jeep and killed the engine.

They were both quiet. She hadn't expected him to show up. This was how it was. Always fighting and frustrated with each other. But, deep down, McKenzie knew who Jason was: he was her—scared to trust someone. They both idled, thinking about what to say. Their feelings and healings were always found in what they *didn't* say to each other. Sometimes, it would just take one single look to understand again, and let go.

"Thanks," she opened up, "for watching over your brother..." Jason nodded. She walked up and gave him a few bills from her pocket. "Get some takeout this weekend. I can drop stuff off late tonight if Gram needs anything."

Jason took the cash, but he was preoccupied. "What did Kyle want?"

She thought about it. "He wants to sell the house."

Jason's brows furrowed. He was trying to understand what that would mean. "But...where would we go?"

"I don't know..." McKenzie said, honestly.

He huffed, then looked away from her. Between his father's flippant changes and McKenzie's uncertainty, Jason was fed up. "Do you guys even care about what *we* want?" He stormed up to the apartment.

"Jason..." she called gently, hoping not to end it this way. But he was already around the back, disappearing again. She looked down. They had been through so much already, just in his teens. Turner coming and going. Trying to work. Trying to get through school. Fighting to make sure the boys also got through school. Once Gram moved into assisted living, McKenzie had inherited more than she could handle. It was all up to her now, and between the bills and Mom's rehab, nothing she did was ever enough. Was she ever going to get through to him? It was only in those quiet moments where neither said much that their understandings felt real. But they were few and far between now, and she felt so much of their separation came from just one single truth: Jason *wanted* his father—his dad, the rodeo star. But it was deeper than that. He *needed* a father. And McKenzie, what she needed—what she wanted now more than ever—was her own courage and answers.

GOLDIE

The white Ford was parked outside a small, run-down office just south of the courthouse. The Fighter leaned against the large metal frame, his hands tucked into his denim jacket. He had been waiting since sunrise. After an hour, a rattly old Ford Bronco II pulled up and parked next to him. An old man in his seventies stepped out. He had kind, gentle eyes, resilient silver-blonde hair, and a small smile that seemed welcoming to all walks of life.

"You Goldie, the vet?"

"Depends." The old man eyed him up and down. "You the IRS?" Then he smiled.

The nearly empty office had a wooden desk at the entrance, a plant or two, and the backroom where all of his tools and instruments rested. It was minimal, and it had to be—the old man ran the practice by himself. This was his twentieth year serving the town as veterinarian, and he'd decided that simplicity was the best approach for even the most complicated matters in life.

The dog lay bare and sedated on a steel examination table in the back room. The Fighter unfolded his blood-soaked sleeping bag, while taking soiled T-shirts from it. He had used them to absorb and stop the dog's blood as best he could. Goldie carefully examined the dog's wounds, wearing large bifocals and using a pen flashlight. His finger traced the multitude of teeth marks scattered and buried in the dog's soft hazelnut hair. He was a strong, mid-sized dog, his hair as fine as a puppy's, but now it was all matted with dust, sand, dried blood, and saliva. The Fighter watched from a distance. He could feel the cold, polished steel on which the dog lay. The smell of sterilizing chemicals and the sharp, cold, filtered air entered the room in silence and made his skin prick with chills. He swallowed back. He knew places like this too well, and he knew deep wounds when he saw them.

"You did a fine job…a fine job," Goldie said.

The Fighter took a small breath through his nostrils, not wanting to taste or smell this place, but forced to breathe.

Goldie stroked the dog's tightened eye—he was dreaming now, possibly running or defending himself from his attackers.

"Strong pup," Goldie insisted. "He fought back…fought hard." The dog's leg suddenly kicked in his sleep. Goldie nodded. "Yup. Still fighting."

"He gonna make it?"

"He might. He needs more blood, that's for sure."

The Fighter was trying to control his thoughts, staring at the dog sprawled across the operating table. He had been there before. In more ways than he'd like to remember.

He finally conceded, breathing in deep from his partially open lips. He had detoured to help this dog, knowing that he may not make it. Whether he actually helped him now or not, he felt like he'd done the right thing. And in an odd way, he thought that *She* would have expected this of him. All it took was looking into this animal's eyes, to see his trepidation—he had felt it, and it had been enough to awaken something in him. The dog was here now, with this kind old man, and The Fighter knew then that he had done the best he could.

Goldie double checked the intravenous therapy needle plugged into the dog, then washed his hands.

"Nature sure is powerful, ain't it? It can be the most beautiful thing, and at the same time, the most harsh and unfair."

Goldie wiped himself up, then turned to face The Fighter from the operating table. The Fighter was in the doorway, as if he were seconds away from walking out. Goldie saw this. "One thing's for sure," he said. "It's a miracle he's alive. Thanks to you."

The Fighter disregarded the thought. He didn't want any 'sap story' or medal of honor—he had just followed his gut, and that was the end of it. Whether it was for *Her* or for himself, he didn't want to think about it anymore. This place—this operating table—it was all too much and all too familiar. He looked up at the clock then tucked his hands back inside his denim jacket. "How far is the Grand Canyon?"

"Grand Canyon? Couple hours. That's where you're headed?"

"How long will this take?"

"I'd say by midday. If he makes it."

From across the room, Goldie now examined The Fighter. He could see he was trying to work something out, though he didn't quite understand what this young man was wrestling with. He just knew it was more than what he had brought in.

"You outta see our town," he offered sweetly. "Lots of history worth seeing, if you're passing by."

The Fighter considered. He was trying to make a decision right then and there: to stay or to go. He had come this far with the dog, but he didn't want to live with any more guilt. Even if he wasn't going to be around long enough to feel it.

The old man's eyes were big and patient, waiting for the young man to respond.

"All right," he gave in, and opened the front door.

Surprised, Goldie called out, "Hey… what's his name?"

The Fighter turned. "Don't know. He ain't mine." And he walked out.

Goldie gave it a ponder. The young man wasn't one for much talk, but he certainly was a thinker. He reminded Goldie of an old part of himself. An older version of who he had been in his own youth. Right then, something dawned on him—he didn't even know the young man's name. "Well, what's yours!?"

But The Fighter was already gone.

THE BELL

The Fighter flipped up his wool collar then tucked his hands back into his denim. The days of April were dramatically cooler in Northern Arizona. It was a place unlike any other, The Fighter thought. He looked at the old courthouse and its sand-colored stone. Trees symmetrically lined the courtyard, though their leaves were bare and their stems frigid like the air. It was crisp and still, something very different than his previous residence in the desert, or the many places he had seen in his time.

His boots and their wooden heels clacked against the pavement as he walked the downtown sidewalks. It was a quiet Thursday morning, and only a few denizens perused the corner shops. A sign next to a brick building identified it as *The Beginning of Whiskey Row*. The Fighter stopped and thought about it, observing a line of bars down the block.

At any other point in his story, it wouldn't even be a thought, but he was tired of drinking, and he was tired of thinking as well. It had been a year since *She* had left, and the pattern of replaying all the things they had had and all the things they had lost was torturous and never-ending. Over and over again, it all played in his head like it was yesterday, today, every day. It was a distinguished pain, a loss far more than any other in his life, and he had known many. The Fighter had already gone through a lifetime alone. Meeting *Her* changed everything.

As he walked down the boulevard of the old western town, he couldn't help but be drawn back to the things he had seen and believed in her. How she was boundless, in possibilities and ideas. How everyday was an adventure, where she loved him. It felt nothing short of infinite, but complete. It didn't take effort, it didn't take thoughts—it was just how it was and how it felt to be around her. She had loved him in a way that he had never understood, or had ever felt, until she came. And he had loved *Her.* He had loved her in ways that even made him learn to love himself.

Things were forever perplexing to The Fighter. To have felt so much with one person, to feel an entire lifetime of missed emotions found, and to think of all the adventures and memories still yet to be made. But they were only thoughts and feelings now, that had come and gone in the blink of an eye. The story was over. She was gone. And all he had left was this Polaroid photo that he clutched inside his denim jacket every time he hid his bruised hands.

Whether the dog would live or not, he knew he had done the right thing. But he had to ask himself, *what was left to do?* He stopped at the corner's intersection. Whiskey Row was behind him, an empty road ahead. He looked back again and considered the Row once more. He stood there, staring, until the powerful toll of a church's bell shook the town and rattled his ribs.

He turned, feeling the reverberation inside his chest. Up the road, a handful of people were congregating. The church was old but stood tall and triangular with lush red brick. The Fighter thought about it, then looked back at Whiskey Row once more. Until the bell tolled again.

REPENTANCE

The old church was quiet and one of the very few places still shared by the very young and the very old. There was a light musk from its aged walls. The faded scent of dusty wood and bricks filled the air. The church was nearly empty. The very few inside all faced the pastor, a man of kind smiles, who stood at a chipped wood podium. He was calm with his sermon, thinking it through as he spoke. In many ways, he was speaking as it came to him. The Fighter walked the entry aisle cautiously, already uncomfortable with the choice he made.

Behind the pastor was the large hanging body of Christ, pinned to the cross, looking down into the church. The pastor, standing just below it, spoke calmly. "Peter came and said to him, 'Lord, how often will my brother sin against me? And I forgive him? As many as seven times?'"

The few occupants listened carefully. The Fighter took a seat by himself, his hands stuffed into his denim and his right hand clutching tightly to the picture of *Her*.

"Jesus said to him, 'I do not say to you seven times…but seventy times seven!'" The pastor laughed, as did a few of the elders who already understood. It was a small group, held mostly by the elderly who had been coming there their entire lives.

"Funny thing, this forgiveness," he digressed, thinking the matter through. "The whole of life becomes a matter of forgiveness. People…places…things. Us. Because through forgiveness, we find ourselves opening up to life. Opening up to God. Peter tells us 'that the Lord is not slow to fulfill his promise, as some count slowness.'"

The pastor smiled, looking to the tall windows. The stained-glass pattern diffused the late-morning light that projected lines into the church. "But the Lord is patient toward us, not wishing that any of us perish, but that all of us reach repentance. And in that is the gift. The gift of life. The gift of another moment. The gift of love. The gift of God."

The Fighter's eyes dropped. They were words he felt more than he could understand. It had been a long, long time since he had last sat in a church, and he had seen many in his time.

"Let us share in this prayer," the pastor said, looking to the people. "To forgive ourselves, so that the gift of the Holy Spirit may enter us and show us His miracles. Please pray with me."

The few locals closed their eyes and folded their hands. Yet, The Fighter did not. He was the only person in the room with his eyes open. He stared up at the body of Christ, trying to control his breath. The sounds of the church started to subside and all that could be heard was the aura of silence that filled the brick walls and the windows' stained glass.

In that brief moment, The Fighter's chest relaxed. His eyes finally closed.

But then he heard something. Without moving his body, his eyes drifted. It was the sound of tears. He knew it was, because he could hear it in their breath. Very carefully, The Fighter turned his head over his shoulder and saw a woman. She was young, maybe in her late twenties, but even through her tears, she was beautiful.

Everyone inside the church had their eyes closed. No one saw her but The Fighter. And for a moment, he wondered if she was real. It was hard to understand, as she stood out in this place. But before her scattered breaths and tears could disturb any further, she stood up and walked out. The Fighter turned away as the large church doors closed and the old steel lock rattled behind her. When he turned back, he looked up, and the eyes of Christ were facing him.

Before the service was finished, The Fighter slipped out. His hands were in his pockets, and he looked up to see the placement of the sun. It must have been midafternoon already. The Fighter did not carry a watch or phone. He had no one to call and time didn't matter anymore. His routine at the arena in Nogales was the only structure he'd had, and the only clock that had served him had been the one on his coffee pot in the motorhome. He'd stopped carrying a watch a long time ago, and often forgot what day it was. It had been a year like this, where every day was the same.

He walked through downtown, debating if he should just get on the road now or stop to see if the dog had lived. He thought that if he could just kill a little more time, he could finish what he'd started, and he could see if the dog had made it or not. *She* would have wanted that. He took a deep breath, and when he looked up, he found himself looking at the long row of bars again.

He had to make another choice.

SEEING HER

T he Fighter stepped through the door into a dim and empty bar. He
sat in the closest seat to the entrance, in front of an old '60's jukebox.
"Be right with ya," a voice said from the back.

He finally took his bruised hands from his pockets and held them on
the bar. He had spent more time praying in bars than he ever had in church.
It was all a thing of the past now anyway, and seeing any more of the town
didn't matter much now. He just wanted to ease his mind, which was still
drained from the night of driving. He wondered if sleeping in the truck
tonight would be easier than trying to haul through the night again. The
bruises on his face were healing or hiding in his thick beard, but his head
was clouded and aching with the rest of his body. All he wanted was just
one more moment of peace.

A napkin floated to his hands.

"What'll it be, early bird?"

The Fighter looked up. His brows flickered.

It was her.

The woman from the church. Her white and gray flannel's top buttons
were now undone, showing her busty shape, but The Fighter was locked
onto her face, still surprised.

"Hey, beard-o, you awake?"

They held eyes. He stared until she was the first to flinch. And for a
moment, she wondered if she had met him before.

"Why were you crying?" he asked.

"What?"

"The church… I saw you. You were crying."

She recomposed herself. "Yeah—I was in church, feeling the feels, so what? What kind of question is that?"

The Fighter shook his head. He was befuddled. So was she.

"I don't mean nothin' by it. I'm just wondering why."

She studied him like she could study anyone to get to the truth. And for whatever the reason, he was being honest. She could feel it. "It's been a long time since… So, I was praying… and then I was crying."

They held eyes again. Neither of them was backing down now. It was perfect honesty shared between two strangers.

"I understand," he finally said, relaxing his eyes from hers and drifting down to his swollen hands. His thumb rubbed his knuckles, and she saw that they were bruised and torn, with dried blood holding them together. She studied him a moment. "Where's the accent from?"

"California."

She blew hot air. "Right. You on vacation or something?"

He thought about it. "Just passing through… Trying to keep a promise."

"Yeah? You always keep your promises?" Her tone mocked him.

He took a long, deep breath. It was something that actually hurt him to say. "I used to…"

And his eyes lowered as if he were looking for something—something he could no longer understand or explain.

Whatever that meant to him, she knew he meant it. She didn't understand, but she watched his eyes as he thought. She believed him. And for whatever reason, something compelled her inside to say more.

"I'm Kenzie."

The Fighter looked up.

"Nolan," he said.

TUPELO HONEY

The old jukebox spun "Tupelo Honey" by Van Morrison. The late-afternoon sun shared the height of the pines, and the bar was now filled with locals. McKenzie was chatting with a handful of regulars at the end of the long bar top that stretched to the other side of the shotgun-style room. It was busy now—the same type of crowd you'd find at any bar at any time in the history of this country: the lonely, the hurt, and those desperate to be heard.

At the end of the bar was a tall cup of cold, black coffee. It sat there for an hour, untouched. And beside it was Nolan, his back to them all, and his eyes staring between the illuminated blinds at the entrance's window. The light was hazy and poured into the bar. It was mesmerizing for him. Or perhaps because *Her* photo was clutched in his hand and the song on the juke was taking him to their places. He held the photo tightly, remembering moments in their story like so many times before. He was always like this—stuck in his head, replaying old memories, choices, and thoughts. But it was torture. He knew that it was all just a vicious circle that he put himself in, perpetually sinking into the reflection of thoughts and feelings that he could never escape, and perhaps, that he never wanted to.

McKenzie was listening to one of the Local 500 boys when her eyes darted to the other side of the room. Nolan stood out, no matter what he was doing. He was a presence. His back had the wingspan of an eagle, moments before flight. His left elbow rested on the bar, and his blue denim jacket stretched up his back to meet his sharp posture. He was calm, almost meditative, looking into the light that glowed between the blinds and diffused throughout the room.

Nolan finally turned back to the bar and sipped his cold coffee. He didn't even know how long it had been sitting there, nor had he realized that there were a handful of people in the bar now. He looked up and scanned the room, finding the many old faces of the town. Then he saw McKenzie, serving people, smiling…giving them her attention. Her real attention. It was plain to see that the people she talked to cared about her. She listened to people, not just with her ears, but with her eyes. That stood out to Nolan, as it was something that a fighter must do to understand their opponent. The eyes either dissuaded you, or they told you everything.

She looked over. They caught eyes. He was first to look away. There were many elements dancing in his mind—the song, the light, the Polaroid. He quickly tucked it back into his pocket and cupped his coffee mug. He thought about the times riding in his truck with *Her*. They had never listened to this song when they were together, but he wondered if she'd known it. He thought that she would've actually loved it, and that it'd be something they'd both smile over, driving somewhere, anywhere—it wouldn't matter where. So many nights were spent just like that—finding themselves somewhere, some place. They would forge dinner from provisions at any store or gas station they could find, then take their dinner and sit under a new night sky, or find the best place in town for a sunset. It didn't matter where they went or what they did. As long as they were together, it was an adventure. A discovery. And this song, blaring through the jukebox, reminded him with a melancholic sense of gratitude. The gratitude for what she'd brought into his life. He had never known true friendship or love until he met *Her*. And he missed her. He missed all of her. He even missed the way she would intentionally annoy him, just to get a reaction. Or how he would use every trick in the book to scare her, hiding around corners or tickling her ear with the tip of a napkin. They had been playful and sweet, fearlessly loving, like the way children were before they became too grown. And this song took him there, to those places he'd once felt.

Crack! The record stuttered, then scratched up the rhythm. It was being shook by the hand of Clayton, a local rodeo man, and Turner, who stood right next to him. Turner wore a flannel tucked into some old Levi's jeans, a gold and silver rodeo buckle, and long pointy snakeskin cowboy boots. He was handsome and tall with thick, strong legs—and completely arrogant. He was a town hero for his stardom at the rodeo and for being a superb football player at the local high school. If he wasn't regarded for one achievement, it was for the other—something that had kept McKenzie on her toes for years, because they were both confident and strong, albeit for different reasons.

"Fuckin' welcoming parade if I ever had one. Mack, can you at least do us a round? Damn!" Turner barked, standing in front of McKenzie at the bar. Clayton walked over to join them as the vinyl record recalibrated in the juke. Turner—and his buddy—had surprised her at work, something McKenzie always hated. Everything was always a competition or a power play with Turner. He never could be seconded by anyone, especially McKenzie, who made demands with their kids. And she was not ready to play his game.

"Listen, shithead," McKenzie fired off. "If you wanna throw a fit about it, do it when I'm not working."

Turner gawked. "I don't got all goddamn day to work around your new schedule, McKenzie. Are they staying with me this weekend or what?" he barked back.

"Are you kidding me? I already took them to Gram's!"

"For how long? What about Easter?"

"Turner, you'll know the rest when I figure it out for myself."

Turner smacked the jukebox. The needle scratched the record, distorting the vocals. The sounds of Van Morrison skipped loudly, trying to catch up to speed. "Well, we can just sit here until you figure your shit out, so I can figure out mine," Turner said, as Clayton rattled the jukebox again.

"Stop messing around, dickheads!" McKenzie sneered from behind the bar.

"Great service! Rodeo Week will be a hoot hanging here!" The two laughed while Clayton slammed the juke, throwing the record off completely. The music skidded to a stop as everyone in the bar watched uncomfortably.

"Oi…" The foreign voice came from across the room.

Turner and Clayton looked over. Nolan was staring from the far end of the bar, his hands in his pockets and his eyes locked on them.

"You're pissing her off, mate," he said calmly. "And you're pissing me off."

Turner and Clayton looked at each other, almost shocked, but completely amused.

"Do I fuckin' know you, *mate*?" Turner mocked, leaning against the bar.

But Nolan didn't look away, he kept his eyes right on Turner. McKenzie didn't know what to say. The other patrons, some much older than all of them, could only watch. Turner took his time approaching Nolan, slowly, letting his boot heels make all the noise. Clayton trailed behind with a little smirk. Nolan simply watched, his hands shoved in his pockets, but he wasn't holding the Polaroid—he was holding fists. Turner stopped closer than an arm's reach. He wanted to show his alpha prowess by getting close to Nolan, demonstrating how confident and intimidating he could be. But Nolan didn't flinch for even a second. Clayton stepped closer and hung over Turner's shoulder as the three locked stares. Patrons watched, unsettled, but not making a sound.

Turner looked him up and down. "No, I don't. So, mind your business or I'll bash your head in."

"Enough, Turner…" McKenzie said from across the bar.

With his knuckles tightened and hidden in his denim, Nolan carefully stood up. He kept his eyes on Turner's, and stood face to face with him. "You will?" Nolan asked, sarcasm in his accent.

Turner took a step closer. There was no space between them now. Turner grinned. Neither was backing down. He pursed his lips, then blew hot air into Nolan's face—

Crack! Nolan's whole body sprang forward, plunging his skull into Turner's nose. Turner toppled backwards to the floor, taking a barstool with him.

Clayton immediately stepped forward to swing, but Nolan sunk his entire boot into his abdomen, throwing Clayton across the room and crashing him back into the jukebox. The machine shook and jittered, skidding "Tupelo Honey" back on through the speakers. Clayton's arms flailed, then he dropped to the ground, completely winded.

Both men rolled on the floor, Turner's nose gushing blood and Clayton coughing uncontrollably. McKenzie just stood there, watching with the patrons, speechless. Nolan slowly released his fists and took his hands from his pockets. He took his cold black coffee and chugged it slowly to the last drop. He wiped his mouth with the back of his fist, then dropped a twenty on the bar.

He looked her in the eyes once more. "Take care." And he walked out.

Turner groaned, trying to stop the nosebleed, while getting back to his feet. McKenzie still had no words.

Moments later, Turner and Clayton burst out of the bar.

"Where is that son of a bitch?!"

They looked in either direction, until the rumble of Nolan's truck came shaking down Whiskey Row. With his window down, Nolan casually lifted a hand and waved. Turner held his nose, and Clayton held his abdomen, disbelieving as they watched Nolan drive away. They had never been humiliated like that in their entire lives.

CHANGE

G oldie's office door swung open, and Nolan casually stepped through. He found the old man in his veterinarian coat, packing up for the day.

"Well, hello there. Get in any trouble?" he asked playfully.

"Not much," Nolan replied nonchalantly. "How's the guy?"

Goldie smiled. "Come see for yourself."

In the back room, the dog was bandaged from his lower neck down to his chest. The IV system was monitoring his vitals as he slept. Nolan noticed the dog was still twitching, maybe dreaming. Goldie observed a small monitor for a few beats.

"He's taking blood and his vitals are steady. He's definitely a fighter, this boy."

Nolan leaned in. He could hear the dog breathing, every once in a while stuttering, trying to get through it. Nolan's hand was still sore, but he carefully ran it up the dog's snout, then to the back of his head and ears, thumbing behind them. Nolan knew all dogs loved it, and he was just hoping that the dog could feel something, if anything.

Goldie watched. He could see that Nolan was the type to conceal his feelings, but things like this were evident for an old man like Goldie. He could see that Nolan cared for the dog.

"Where'd you find'im?" Goldie asked.

Nolan gently stroked the dog's long nose, watching his weak eyes squirm in his sleep. "He found me."

Goldie examined Nolan as he pet the dog carefully, looking at his various lacerations and bandages, avoiding where he might hurt him. He gave the dog one last pat, then headed for the door. "Thanks for your help, Doc."

"Hey—where you going?" Goldie asked, surprised.

Nolan stopped and looked back. "The Grand Canyon."

"Oh, son. You head there now, and you won't even have the light to see it."

Nolan considered. Through the window, he could see that the late-afternoon sun was already falling fast.

"He's still critical. He's gotta make it through the rest of the night."

Nolan ran a bruised hand through his beard and peered out the window.

Did it matter if it was at night or during the day?

Did it matter anymore when he did it?

That simple, secret notion that he was hiding made him remember the pain. The old man could see—he was thwarted by something much more than he could say.

"Tell ya what," Goldie urged. "You come stay at my ranch tonight. I got a guest room and all that."

What would *She* have done?

Nolan's eyes fell to the floor. He didn't know what he was doing anymore.

"When we get back to town, we'll check on the pup, and you can be on your way, first thing," the old man said, standing beside the dog. Nolan, unsure, looked back. Goldie's smile was faint, but it was honest and true. He knew there was something deeper happening within Nolan—he had felt it the moment he met him. He wasn't a man of words, but there was something in his energy and poise that reminded Goldie of an older version of himself. Those days that he was most afraid or frustrated. Those days that he felt truly alone. But he knew, whatever was going on with this young man—if he could just spend a little bit of time with him, then maybe he could have an impact on him. If he could have been there for his younger self, he wondered how his life may have been different.

Sunset cascaded over downtown Prescott. The light was changing quickly, and the town's warm old street lamps, some over a hundred years old, were beginning to ignite. Nolan followed Goldie out to his white Ford parked beside Goldie's rusted red Bronco II truck. It had been nearly thirty-five hours since Nolan had last slept, and he was completely drained. He looked back to the office once more.

"He'll be okay…alone?"

"Oh sure. He's just gotta get through this moon. Then we'll see if he starts to heal."

Goldie unlocked his Bronco and got in while Nolan gave it another thought. "I'll follow you out," he said.

"Ride with me," the old man insisted. "I'll save you the gas."

Nolan looked back at his truck, unsure.

"They'll both be here when we get back," Goldie assured him. "Come on, gets dark quick out there."

Nolan finally agreed. "All right, hold on…"

He went into his Ford and took his Ruger pistol from the glove compartment, then dropped the metal clip, checking that all ten rounds were still there. Making sure the old man didn't see, he tucked it into his waistband, then took the road map. But something stopped him. He patted his pockets and knew right away…something was missing.

The Polaroid. His hand quickly dove into his denim's left pocket where it always rested, but the thin celluloid wasn't there. He rechecked the glove compartment, then the folds of the map—but nothing. Nolan quickly dug into every pocket in his jeans and his denim again, then his boot, the place he hid it during a fight so that, if he had died in the ring, at least he would have been found with her. But it was gone—it wasn't in any place it would have possibly been if it wasn't inside his denim or clutched in his hand. He froze. He was completely baffled. It was their very last photo. The impulse of worry sent him peering under his seats, then fishing his pockets once more to know for certain.

"Well?" Goldie said from inside the Bronco, his windows down, waiting, smiling.

Nolan hesitantly looked over. He had to let it go for now. He had no choice. But it wasn't just the change of habit that made him uneasy, it was the fact that he never lost things. He didn't have much already, and he certainly didn't carry much, so the Polaroid was always with him, touching him, being held by him in his denim. Nolan's thoughts raced. When he looked over, the old man was still staring, but smiling. Nolan let out a deep exhale. He snatched up his duffle from the back, then jumped into the passenger seat next to Goldie, and the two rode out.

POEM

T he sun was low as they rode out of town. With his bruised hand
holding up a swollen chin and his exhausted head, Nolan gazed out
the window, observing the homes and trees and all the nuanced textures of
the rustic country town. He had been all over the United States in his life
and was no stranger to the countryside, but this place was *different*. The
aura, the energy. It was if this place had not changed in a hundred years.
Whatever it was, there was something distinct and timeless about the town.
The winds were forgiving and gentle, and the air was cool, crisp, yet somehow
familiar. It was nothing like the desert. Prior to this voyage, he'd thought the
entire state was covered in sand or desert, as, for the past year, it had been the
only landscape he had ever really seen of the state. When he'd first come here
from the north, leaving the last of his life behind, he hadn't made it far. He'd
thought he would go to Mexico, and maybe, he wouldn't return. He'd been
senseless and empty, departing only days after *She* had passed. The pain was
despairing, isolating—but worst of all, it was eternal. Nolan had found out
quickly that running or traveling, near or far, would never be a remedy. It
was always there. Always with him. Always haunting. The desert's vastness,
its void, its perpetual emptiness—that was the only thing he could
understand. And it was the only thing he could relate to now.

And yet, this old town was far from the desert or his past. The hills
rolled into mountains like flowing tides, and the old red-brick and faded-
stone buildings reflected a panorama of the town's preservation. In some
ways, it felt as if the entire country's soul fit into this small patch of land—
all the history and agriculture and landmarks that one would see in an old

western painting or in historical pictures were forever preserved and real in this land.

Only, for Nolan, it was all just a stop at the crossroads of his life. He knew where the road headed. And he knew where it now ended.

They were driving a small single-lane road far out of town. It gradually expanded and turned into a straightaway stretch into Williamson Valley. Here, they ventured down the middle of open farmlands and plains, which expanded in every direction and ran to the mountains in the deep distance. The valley's grass was faded green, subsided and thirsty for spring, and the light was falling fast just beyond the highest points of the valley. They had been silently sharing the empty valley road for twenty-five minutes when Goldie began to fidget. He abruptly steered the Bronco to the side of the road.

"Ah shit…" he said.

"What?" Nolan looked over.

But Goldie was already halfway out the door. "Hurry!"

Nolan, unsure, hopped out.

Goldie left his door wide open and walked up the side of the road. His suede boots skidded across the gravel, breaking the silent, still air. He was completely engrossed in what lay ahead, and Nolan, keeping his guard up, followed at a distance from behind, watching the old man's energy and the way he moved, as any fighter would. He was trying to assess what was happening or anticipate what the old man's moves or motives might be.

But then Goldie stopped, and without a witness, he took a deep, satisfying breath, then smiled to himself. Nolan came to a swift halt, keeping his space, but watching the man closely. The air was still and the land silent. He observed the old man's firm, unmoving stance, but then, his eyes looked beyond him to see what lay ahead.

He was stunned. Far beyond the low, rolling hills and the sprinkling of trees—a gargantuan sunset. Powerful. Orange, blue, red—it was a kaleidoscope of colors that stretched down the road for miles and kissed the entire horizon of mountains. Nolan stood there, blindsided. He had been so transfixed on his thoughts and the old man's behavior that, even in his peripherals, he hadn't realized the enormous sun and strokes of color that were just before them.

They stood there, silent, standing in the center of the empty two-lane road, each man looking ahead as wondrous light cast upon the land and a tremendous sun descended before them.

"It's even better at the ranch," Goldie said with a faint smile.

Nolan couldn't help but stare into the array of color in the sky. At first, the intensity and the grandness of it all angered him, but, as quick and as strange as that feeling was, the very same thing calmed him, even cooled him. It brought him to a place of peace. It was rare that he felt this place. It was rare that he could feel it, once again.

After a few minutes, Goldie finally spoke. "It makes you feel, huh?"

But Nolan couldn't say a word, sharing the silence, just looking on.

"Hmm…" Goldie smiled and nodded. It was a pleasant notion, he thought.

The sky was a vista of color, an orchestration shared between the melody of their thoughts, their feelings, and the colors of their souls. It was all a spectacle, laid before them, as it was, waiting within them. Looking into the waves of watery color, Nolan could feel a montage of sunsets that he had once shared with *Her*. It was as if they were all connected and always had been. He could see them and feel them all at once, the many they had experienced and cherished together. The many moments between their eyes and the sky, between light and quiet tenderness.

Now he was here, he thought, grateful to see one more, in one of his last days. And in that single sentiment, Nolan couldn't remember a single sunset before *Her*, or during his life, when he had shared a sunset with anyone else. Now that she was gone, he could barely recall anything before *Her*. And he never imagined anything after *Her*.

The old man bit his dry lower lip. His faint smile returned, and his eyes drifted to the gravel on the road. He was remembering something himself. Remembering his own *someone*. And after a moment of long, wandering eyes, he remembered some words. They were words that meant more to him and to *someone* than he could ever express. And he finally spoke:

"How I see you in me.
How you see me in you.

Fire, brimstone, sunset, rain.
All my dreams, all my history
All my life, all my pain.
You unlock
everything
As you say I do for you.
It inspires me
It terrifies me
and it
opens me.
To everything.
Everything I should be.
Everything that is me.
Everything that is you.
The Incredible Existence of Me
is found
in The Incredible Existence of You."

Nolan's eyes were full, but he held it all down. The words were painful and true, like the fading colors and the hues of countless memories fading with them. They were all beautiful and pressing. They were words he could never express himself, but they felt like they were his. They were words that felt like *Hers.*

Goldie let out a slow, releasing breath. "Wrote it for my wife," he said, still looking ahead.

Nolan didn't move, wrestling inside, holding what deep tears fought to rise. Because those words meant more to him than he could possibly say.

"You know what her name was?" Goldie smiled. It was his favorite story and his favorite word to say. "*Poem.* Her name was *Poem.*" Goldie finally laughed. "Fuckin' hell, was she hard to live up to." His laugh subsided and, after a moment, he turned back to Nolan. "But worth every effort."

It became quiet again as the sun finally set beyond the valley.

Goldie grinned. "And there she goes..."

And in the blink of an eye—another day was gone.

Goldie headed to the Bronco, renewed in his step. He patted Nolan on the shoulder as he passed. But Nolan just stood there, without words, watching as the last of the light continued to change before him.

NORTH STAR RANCH

I t was nearing dark, and the sky was twilight blue. The Bronco rumbled
and swayed on a long, winding dirt road. They passed farms and ranches
that had been operated by families for decades. There were cabins standing
from logs cut in the pioneer days, still steaming with stone chimneys. In
the fading light, he could even see the newly built ranch homes with long,
paved driveways and their own fencing of land. There were properties
scattered amongst the plains, where you could see the outlines of crops,
stables, and fields freshly plowed—the ways of the past where the fruits of
the land were how one made a living, contrasting with a new world, where
people sought out to build the ranch and life of their dreams. It was all
separate from the constantly moving industrialized world. The earth was
changing, but the land was still fertile, and the air still tasted green. It was
drastically different from Nolan's past home in the desert. The notion that
there were still families and people who lived on this beautiful, open land
triggered something melancholic inside him. It made him remember *Her*.
It made him remember *Her* dreams and the things she would muse about
under the night sky with him. And when they saw their first shooting star
together, up high in the mountains of Yosemite, he, too, had thought that
anything was possible. That was what she gave him. That undying gift of
believing.

They rode for a mile on that dark, dirt road before turning onto
another narrow road that bore no sign. The road became rougher and
dusty, and there were no streetlights to distinguish where they were now,
only the Bronco's old orange headlights as they swayed down an unmarked

path. They had said nothing since sunset.

Nolan was looking through his window. He could see the sky holding those last moments of deep blue before true darkness would silence the horizon. It seemed as though the old man lived miles out from the valley's main road, far from everyone. But, with little light, and no markers in the land, he had no true perspective. Goldie finally slowed the Bronco as they came toward the mass of a tremendous, dark hill, silhouetted to the night sky. They turned around the bend of the hill, and from Nolan's view, the unknown mass looming above seemed like a mountain. When they cleared the bend, Nolan finally saw an old, wooden sign carved by hand: *North Star Road*.

Goldie let out a little smile when he saw it. They turned onto the lane, and, after a quarter mile stretch of dirt, gravel, and rock, they reached another stretch of land that was lined with old, chipped, white wooden fencing. Some pieces were strong and standing, while others dilapidated and completely broken apart.

"Here we are."

The old fence spanned a few hundred feet of dirt road before it turned inward and led them up to a large property at the base of another tall hill. The night was true dark now, but the stars gleamed bright enough that Nolan could finally see the silhouette of the ranch. There was a modern steel barn, a gated corral with more decayed wooden fences, and at the end of the road, a large three-story modern ranch home. It was all highlighted by the cast of a white and blue full moon that stood high above the ranch and rested atop a mountainous hill overlooking the property.

Goldie pointed to it. "See there, up on the hill?"

Nolan lowered his head to see up high enough through his window. At the top of the hill, the moon was illuminating some sort of rocky structure, half pronounced and in disrepair, but still standing at the highest point of the hill.

"Indian ruins," Goldie explained.

Nolan stayed silent, looking up to the ruins and the moon behind it. The Bronco had finally pulled up to the ranch.

It was a large, cozy ranch home with taupe and cherry brown walls. Artifacts and art from all over the world covered every square inch and filled every corner. From a stone Celtic cross with chiseled etchings, to various African tribal masks and European paintings. The entire house was full of photos, tapestries, Persian rugs, craft sculptures of animals, the busts and statuettes of natives from different lands, and much more. It was clear that the old man had seen many things in his time. Nolan's eyes wandered the intimate museum as he perused the living room.

Meanwhile, he could hear the noise of dishes clinking in the other room. Goldie was cooking loudly and proudly. In an attempt to relax, Nolan had removed his jacket and was wearing just his flannel now, something Goldie had insisted on, as he busied himself in the kitchen. Nolan stepped to a set of large, sliding glass doors that led to a wide patio overlooking the ranch. All of Williamson Valley could be seen here— bushes and trees were scattered throughout the immense plains just beyond the barn and were cast in unobstructed moonlight. The air was so pure, and the visibility so clear, that Nolan could actually see miles beyond the ranch now. In the furthest distance, staggering silhouettes of mountain range covered where the sun had set. From this second-story view, the land was a panorama, wide, open, independent. To Nolan, it felt like they were the only two souls out on the land. And maybe they were. He didn't know much about the old man or why he was here, or why he was alone, but there was a sense of comfort in knowing he was a well-traveled man. Nolan had seen a few things himself in his own time.

The melodies of soft and pleasant French music emitted from the kitchen, accompanied by the playful whistling of Goldie. He was in one of his favorite moods, in one of his favorite places, joyously preparing a few dishes in his large, warmly lit kitchen. It was a treat for him to finally cook for another person.

"Hope you don't mind French oldies!" he called from the other room. "Not that you got a choice!"

Nolan smiled, hearing the ruckus of music, whistling, pots, and pans. He turned from the view of the valley and spoke loudly so the old man could hear. "I'm allergic—to both," Nolan said sarcastically.

"Oh, shut up!" Goldie hollered back.

With his flannel sleeves rolled up, Goldie basted a small batch of chicken drumsticks on the kitchen's large center island. His hands ran through herbs and spices that he freckled the drumsticks with, then he was quick to wash his hands before slicing fresh potato scallops and thick stalks of organic broccoli. Goldie's favorite part of cooking, as it had been for years, was to season his food with his very own blend of hand-ground spices that had come from the garden and fields of his ranch.

Nolan was in the large family room, observing the various African art and French paintings. He found an old cabinet with glass windows that had not been dusted in quite some time. Inside were a set of old, silver picture frames, lined up side by side. They were photos of what seemed to be a younger, vibrantly smiling Goldie—and a woman. The photos must have been from thirty years ago, progressing from black and white film to faded Kodak color stock. In every photo, they were full of life, both young Goldie and the woman, smiling through decades and growing older in each picture Nolan found. Nolan smiled to himself, looking at young Goldie's smile, then to the woman.

He knew it was Poem.

When he looked below the series of photos, he found another shelf inside the cabinet. This one held a collage of an entire lifetime—photos of them together in different countries, beaches, homes, with various animals, and smiles. They were always closely together, arms locked, or with Goldie's arm proudly around her. Nolan's smile subsided. It was all too familiar.

He turned away, trying to change his thoughts.

"So…how long you been out here?" Nolan called.

"Twenty years," Goldie hollered back. "By way of the Colorado River. And you? Down under?"

Nolan turned to the kitchen, surprised. "How'd you know that?"

"Ah, mon ami. L'habit ne fait pas le moine." His words poured with a beautifully dancing French tongue.

"What does that mean?" Nolan immediately asked.

"It means 'The vestment does not make the monk.'"

Nolan's brows furrowed. "And what the hell does that mean?"

Goldie shouted, "It means don't judge an old fart by his cover!"

Nolan smiled again. He took a last glance at the expansive moonlit valley and barn. He could feel the sense of repose that came with its complete stillness. It was all beautiful, and it felt like something he would always remember.

"Now we're cooking!" Goldie shouted excitedly as Nolan entered the kitchen. Goldie was dressing the scalloped potatoes with his fresh herbs and spiced oil that he had bottled.

Nolan watched from the doorway as the happy old man whistled through the final touches.

"Big place. Could use a dog."

Goldie laughed. "I've had plenty of pups in my time. Peace is what I seek now. Although...the love of an animal really is the love of God. Even when they shit on the carpet."

Nolan squinted. "I can tell you're wise, old man," he sarcastically added.

"That's right. Now pour us some Scotch from that cupboard and let's eat!"

The dining room was lit only by a few candles and a faint moon that brushed the valley blue. They ate at a large dining room table that was much too large for the two of them. The food was delicious, and the music was warm and soft to their ears. To Nolan's left was another set of wide porch doors facing the valley. He kept turning to it. Beyond the glass, he could hear the chimes of various insects singing to the moon, faint and rhythmic. A thought came to Nolan—it was special to him, this place. There was something about it. It was all truly peaceful. He wondered if the old man had raised his family here on the ranch.

"This dish is one of my favorites. Southern French comfort, I'd say." Goldie smiled happily, finishing a piece of creamed lemon chicken. "You been to Paris?" He asked.

"No..." Nolan spoke quietly. "Didn't get the chance."

"Ah, you're young. You got the rest of your life. 'Qui vivra verra'—he who lives, shall see."

Nolan lowered his eyes and took a bite of food. He kept his gaze low and took a sip of his Scotch neat.

Goldie was smiling to his own thoughts. He was remembering Paris and his wife. Sometimes he wondered if he was lucky, spoiled, or actually unlucky, depending on the day and how he remembered things. After a moment, he looked up and could see that Nolan was in that familiar looking place again—his eyes out to the valley and his mind pondering. Goldie watched him a moment. He could feel that he was a truthful man, but that he was deeply hurt by something. Whatever it was, and whatever he was feeling, it was honest and pure, and not something Nolan hid well, at least from a man like Goldie. Nolan looked up, catching the old man's eyes. Goldie smiled.

Nolan searched for something to avert this attention. "How do you know so much French stuff?"

"Easy—my wife. She loved it, so I loved it. But she was an Italian, believe it or not." His eyes then hopped up to the ceiling, remembering how she would correct him. "Well, a Roman, to be exact."

Nolan looked to the valley again. It was as if there something out there, tugging at him. Goldie studied him now, trying to understand his mannerisms. "And the Grand Canyon?"

Nolan turned back.

"A place you always wanted to go?" Goldie asked, chewing.

Nolan thought about it. "It's just a place I said I'd go. With someone."

"Someone you love?"

Nolan took that in.

She was more than someone he loved. The thought was grabbing him now, clenching his insides and squeezing the center of his throat. He turned back to the valley—he didn't want to be caught looking vulnerable. Or perhaps, he thought his own words could not say or mean what he actually felt. She was more than someone he loved.

She was his entire world.

"Yeah…" he finally spoke.

It was all he could say. And yet, in that single moment, Goldie finally saw Nolan. All of him. As if he knew all of Nolan's heart right then, reflecting some time and place of Goldie's own. It wasn't something he would yet understand, but it was something, there at this table, that he could feel. Goldie saw something in Nolan. Something that reminded him of his worst days. Some with Poem, some alone, some long before her and many days after her. Whatever had happened to this young man, Goldie believed he could do some good for him. He believed he could help him.

"Good. We can celebrate with more French music!" He turned the old record up, allowing the sweet, joyous melodies to fill the room to its vaulted ceilings. Nolan snapped out of his daze and turned to the old man. His smile was truthful, but above all, it was happy.

He was a good man, Nolan thought. If anything, he knew that Goldie was lonely, too, and just happy to have his company. The old man was relentless with positivity, and in its own way, it was comforting. Nolan finally smiled back.

Later that night, Nolan had his flannel's sleeves rolled up and his sore hands plunged into the sink, washing all their dishes.

Goldie ambled in with his Scotch glass and rosy cheeks. "Well, young man, the downstairs den is all yours. This old timer can only fit two glasses of Scotch."

"That's a lot of glasses," Nolan replied.

"You shoulda seen my heyday," Goldie retorted with a grin, then splashed a little more into his glass. "Train leaves an hour after sunrise."

Nolan nodded, drying their dinner plates and putting them away. "Sounds good, old man."

Goldie turned to walk out of the kitchen and took a strong sip of his Scotch. But then he stopped. Something came to him. "Ah, I forgot to tell ya…"

Nolan looked over his shoulder. The old man was standing there, his head down, really thinking through his words.

"That Grand Canyon…" His eyes wandered. "Everything about it…it's poetry." His eyes were low, reflecting. He finished the thought with an affirming nod to himself and, when he looked up, he could see that Nolan was observing him closely. The old man smiled. "Help yourself to anything but the '82 in there. We'll save that for a special occasion."

Then he left to his bedroom on the third floor.

Nolan was still, thinking to himself. The faucet ran warm country water over his bruised hands, softening them and his scabs. He wondered what Goldie had meant. It was as if the old man was remembering his own memory or story there. Whatever it was, Nolan knew that Goldie had meant what he said.

The Grand Canyon must be a beautiful place, he thought.

Midnight came quick. The blue moon was peaking in size and shape. Nolan held the remainder of his Scotch, looking up to the black sky and its endless stars. There was a softness to them in the way that they shined. Nolan often wondered what she thought of now, or if she was thinking of him. He wondered how she felt and if he disappointed her. He wondered if she was frustrated, like him. He wasn't looking for signs or shooting stars anymore. He just wanted relief. He wanted to quiet his thoughts.

After a long, hot shower, Nolan unpacked his things in a small but cozy country bedroom. The Scotch glass sat empty on a dresser next to his steel Ruger pistol. He dug through his duffle and his denim, searching for the Polaroid again. It was still nowhere to be found, and it was infuriating. He looked through all of his clothes and possessions twice—he had to—including his socks, and even under the interior sole of his boots, but it was nowhere.

Finally, he exhaled and sat on the small country bed facing soft, translucent white curtains. The blue moon was beaming on the barn. Nolan inhaled, trying to regulate each breath so that it would deepen and slow his heart rate. He knew the Polaroid was gone. He must have dropped it in town somewhere. He ran his hands through his thick, dark hair and his palms skidded across his bruised temple. He winced, feeling his sandy palms graze his temple. He had completely forgotten about the injury and that part of his eye was still swollen with a bruise that reached down into his beard and jaw. He had been injured so many times now, and in so many ways, that he always seemed to forget that side of pain. That pain was always there. But the physical was just a lesser extension of what truly hurt him. He was exhausted, frustrated, and uncertain of his choices, coming here to the ranch. But all he could do now was be at peace with it and for where he was tonight. He knew there was nothing else he could do.

His feet swung up onto the small bed and dangled over, then he turned his sore head to the window. At least he had that—the view. Everything was calmer in the country. And much like in the desert, sometimes the sound of silence felt overwhelmingly loud. A sort of humming drone that one could hear if they listened closely or could sense in the late night or early morning. But not tonight. He took a deep breath. He was here now. There wasn't any use in being angry. And with one last chest-expanding inhale, Nolan filled his lungs to the brim and exhaled with the last of his frustration.

He was thankful for a long day's end.

THE WHITE BEAST

All was quiet throughout the ranch. The morning sun peeked above the Indian ruins, dispersing light across the valley and open plains shared with the mountains afar. The sun was moments from cresting over the peaks, and the ambient presence of silence was peaceful and still. Until the deep, echoing shrill of an animal broke it.

The creature screamed long and sharp, crying in pain. Inside the lower den, Nolan shot awake. His head turned toward the glass patio window— the shrill had shaken it. Was it something of a dream, he wondered? It wasn't likely—he never dreamed anymore. If anything, they were nightmares. They were always about losing *Her*.

The scream came again.

Nolan knew now it was an animal and it was real.

He haphazardly threw on a navy and black flannel and dark denim jeans, pulled on his boots, then headed down to the barn. He held his Ruger pistol with the barrel pointed to the earth and his finger perched alongside the trigger. Everything became still again, and the valley was eerily quiet, as if the pained cries of the animal had silenced the land. He looked back at the ranch house. The sun was just above the Indian ruins and its morning rays cut into the icy air with a needed warmth. As he approached, another shrieking whinny shook the entire barn and its thin metal doors. Nolan eased slowly toward the barn, not wanting to spook anything. He wondered if the animal had been hurt or attacked.

He slid sideways into the barn with one step and without touching the parted doors. Steaming nostrils and heavy hooves throttled the stall at the end. Nolan inched forward, wary of startling the beast any further. He came closer, reaching the metal window of the very last stall, then made a clicking sound with his tongue against the roof of his mouth. The hooves immediately stamped and planted with an attentive snarl; his presence had become known. Nolan eased around the metal windows, and he finally saw it:

An enormous white stallion.

His hair was long, silvery white, and his eyes were bold obsidian. The stallion instantly spotted Nolan and confronted him with another shrill whinny. The sound was so violently piercing that it shook all the metal in the barn again and lingered a moment after, rattling their ears and the entire structure's frame. The beast was strung with distress. Nolan stood there at its gate, cautious, letting the beast hear his tongue click again. He took a slow step forward and tucked his pistol between his jeans and the small of his back, then calmly opened the stall's metal window. The stallion's nostrils fumed and flared with steaming air, locking its eyes on Nolan. His head was high, and his daunting size dominated the entire stall, even with the back door open. But Nolan was not timorous. He knew the animal had been spooked or was in some sort of pain.

"All right…it's all right," Nolan said, calmly. He made the soft clicking sound again, drawing the stallion's tall, pointed ears toward him. Right then, another whinny came from just outside the pen—it was an older, brindle horse, who had come to watch from outside the stall. He was keeping his distance from the alpha, who had no hesitation in its snarls. Nolan stepped fully up to the pen now and extended palm.

The stallion approached pensively, its massive hooves smashing the dirt below. Its long cranium lowered, then inhaled the scent of his skin, but kicked his head up, seeing that there was nothing in Nolan's hand.

"Okay…okay…" Nolan said, ever so gently, as he reached up and stroked his face. But the stallion jerked its head, boiling. Something was wrong with the beast. It was more than something Nolan saw—it was something he could feel.

"You hungry, mate?"

He moved gradually and reached for a bale of hay behind him, then plucked a handful to offer. The stallion, unsure, lowered his head and pulled the aged golden hay quickly from Nolan's hand. Then, having tasted the offering, he was compelled to eat, taking gigantic bites from Nolan until he had to reach back and offer him some more. The stallion pulled and tugged, eating and breathing quickly, though Nolan could sense that he was calmer now. He was no longer huffing. Nolan kept this up as he wondered what troubled him. Maybe it was the sunrise or another animal he had seen in the pasture? Or perhaps the horse just needed the right attention.

Goldie quietly stepped into the barn. He was dressed in a camel-colored suede jacket, an old red flannel, blue jeans, and weatherproof boots. He was ready for a day's work. But he stood there, silent, watching as Nolan hand fed the stallion. Nolan's mannerisms were deliberate and calm, which the stallion now reflected in his own movements. His temperament and behavior had finally reduced to just the simple act of eating from Nolan's hand. Nolan turned to Goldie, keeping his voice low. "What's wrong with him?"

Goldie thought about it. There was more to say than he would. But it was a simple reason. "My wife used to feed him," he said mildly. "He was hers."

Nolan turned back to the white stallion, who was now casually taking from his palm. Nolan knew a beast of this type was always leaning on the ledge of fury or force, and in the flicker of an eye, it could be spooked and swing its massive skull into Nolan or the metal gates. Its dark nostrils flared as he continued to chew from Nolan's hand.

Goldie could only watch. He was quiet, his heart heavy. He was remembering Poem. He was remembering how she'd loved that horse and how deeply it had loved her. To see his wife have a sacred relationship with such a raw, pure, powerful creature had been a true gift in his life, as it had been for her. He thought of the way she had looked at the creature and how she had tended to him. The way he would follow her on the dirt road, towering high above her, but moving gracefully right by her side. It had been magic to him, her control and tenderness with the stallion—it was all effortless. And it was all completely the color of Poem's character. She had been somehow magnetic, kind, and gentle with everything and with everyone. They were things that had radiated from her. Everyone had seen it. Everyone had felt it. And over the years, as if she were a great teacher, those qualities had begun to reflect brighter in Goldie's own being. They had become a part of who Goldie was. Because Poem was a part of who he was.

Standing there, watching Nolan, Goldie saw that familiar tenderness again. It struck him, like a train of a million memories and journeys shared all at once. At this stage in his life, thinking of Poem did not make him hurt or sad. It made him feel grateful. And yet, watching her horse with Nolan and seeing that sacred bond live again, it was a force that his heart was not prepared to take.

Goldie turned and quickly trekked back up to the house. Nolan noticed him just as he slipped out of the barn doors. Something got to the old man, he thought, then he turned back to the stallion, who immediately peered directly into his eyes. They were large and glassy, like flawlessly polished obsidian, reflecting back at him, showing his own face within them. Nolan looked into them. He knew that the horse's wavering emotions could surface at any moment, whether at the whim of his beastly nature or the spark of his temperament's choosing. But Nolan still wasn't afraid. He had shown him that he was not a threat and continued to offer feed. What would come within the beast, would come and pass like all emotions. Anything could happen, Nolan knew, but he still chose to feed him. He wanted to feed him, and so he stood his ground.

To Nolan, it was just easier understanding animals. Their rage, their fears, their need for touch and for nourishment. It was something he had always understood, since he was a boy and on his own. And it was something he would always relate to. From his time ranching, to hunting wild fish, to even spending a night or two with a stray dog. There was a truth to the behavior of animals that made more sense to him than most things or people in this world. And as the white stallion finally relaxed and its belly grew full, Nolan thought of the dog. He hoped that he had made it through the night, like Goldie had said. The thought weighed heavily. The dog had come this far in his own journey, whatever it was. But he was alone now and injured. Maybe even hurting.

Nolan knew that, no matter what happened, today he had to set forth on his own path. But he had to keep his promise. It was one he could keep.

And it was a promise made in the same way he had with the stallion, just by looking into its eyes. There were words spoken between creatures that only eyes could say. Of destiny, fate, and love. And those special moments in life were always something you could feel. Nolan looked into the reflection of the stallion's wide eyes and saw himself there, standing. Right then, he decided that he had to make sure the dog was okay.

She would have wanted that.

TO WALK AWAY

Nolan and Goldie entered the office together. Nolan had his large duffle bag slung over his shoulder, with the last of his belongings ready to go, no matter what they might find. Goldie flipped the office lights on and led them to the back room, but he stopped in the doorway, surprised by what he saw.

The dog was standing, awake in his cage, and happy as hell to see them.

"Well look at you! Better than I expected!" Goldie said through a big grin, inspecting the dog through his cage. Nolan couldn't help but smile, seeing that the dog was well, but more so, that he was wagging his tail inside the cage as fast as he could. Goldie started to unlock it, but before he could open the gate even halfway, the animal busted through and charged Nolan. The dog was wobbly and completely elated to see Nolan, sniffing him up and down and pressing his body happily against him. Nolan dropped down to his knee and nuzzled the dog, who panted and flicked his tongue wildly with joy.

"Hi there…Hi…" Nolan said, pensive, but smiling.

The dog was weak, and his whimpers were suppressed, but he pushed hard through his swollen throat so that his cries could be felt. Then he licked Nolan's bruised hands and kept his sore and bandaged body leaning against him. Nolan smiled, pulling him in and wrapping his large palm across the dog's snout. He pushed the tips of his strong fingers over his face, then into his wavy auburn hair.

They were both bruised, sore, and smiling, just happy to see each other again. And Goldie grinned, witnessing it all. He was thinking then that Nolan was like him in many ways. Better yet—that, in some special, restrained way, Nolan was like Poem. Keeping her deepest emotions tight and protected in her chest.

Goldie headed to the cabinet to get his tools so he could check the dog's vitals. The room became quiet again as Nolan and the dog shared smiles. All the dog wanted to do was look at Nolan—it was the one familiar face that hadn't abandoned him. And it was still happy to see him. Goldie cleaned up the dog's cage, then prepared his IV machine and needle.

"A damn shame about animals—how pure they are," he reflected. "Most people don't even deserve them. And the ones who do…are often too scared. No different than children, really."

Nolan disregarded this. They were all things he already thought about with *Her*. And they were things he did not want to face. The dog was finally relaxed, staring up at Nolan as if he expected Nolan to give him some command that he knew—all dogs lived to serve and to give to their family, and they are helpless and anxious if they cannot. It was an innate part of their beings to give everything they could to their pack. And now, without even knowing it, Nolan was *his*.

But Nolan just kept petting, running his hands under the dog's eyes and down his spine, avoiding the bandages that held his neck's flesh that was stitched and jellied. He kept eyes with the dog, who he could tell just so deeply wanted to be seen by him. The dog hadn't been loved by a familiar face in a long, long time. It was a thought that even Nolan couldn't hide from.

Nolan looked up at Goldie, who finished preparing a dose of medication in a tube. "He gonna be all right?"

"We'll keep him on some meds, but he's on the right path."

Nolan's mind trailed, looking away from the dog. He was hesitant before he asked. "You'll find him a home?"

Goldie half laughed. "A home? He's yours, son."

"Hey…" Nolan said, firming up. "I told you. I found him."

"I thought you said he found *you*?"

Nolan blinked and looked away. He adjusted his duffle and stood there, thinking of what to tell Goldie—some excuse or reasoning as to why he couldn't take the dog. He knew the old man was smart and that he cared. But he also thought that he couldn't tell him what he planned to do. He wouldn't understand. No one would. And it wasn't his choice, anyway.

"Listen," Nolan said, looking for the right way to explain. "Where I'm going…I can't take him, all right?"

Goldie looked right through him. "You can't? Or you *won't?*"

He gave it one last thought. He had the answer, but he wasn't going to say it. Nolan stood up and straightened his long, bruised body. The dog stopped panting and watched him closely.

"Thanks for everything, old man…"

Nolan adjusted his duffle bag and headed for the door. But the dog, too weak to chase, stood there with his mouth closed, his eyes wide, watching. It was if he were still waiting for that command—some sort of sign or clarity about what Nolan wanted him to do. Goldie looked at the dog, then to Nolan as he walked to the door. Goldie was shocked—and in many ways, deeply disappointed.

And Nolan felt it. He knew the old man could see right through him. Nolan turned back, looked to Goldie and to the dog, but tried not to show his eyes too long. He let up a small nod to the old man, who respectfully nodded back. And though Goldie had hoped for otherwise, he knew that was it.

There was nothing else to say. Goldie's smile was his goodbye.

Outside the office, Nolan approached the white Ford. He threw his duffle in the large steel bed next to his cowhide satchel, unlocked the high door, and hopped up. He gripped the worn leather steering wheel with one hand and sat there a moment. It was one of the last few satisfying things in his world, every time he was back in this saddle. It was the only thing customary. To travel and to roam was in his blood, and now that she was gone, it was the only thing Nolan thought that he had left.

He could come and go as he pleased. He could set sail at any moment in time. It was the one constant current in his life. And yet, deep inside, he'd wanted the very opposite when he met *Her.* Even in loving her, and being loved by her, there had been some sort of freedom that had come with *Her*…and through *Her.* And while Nolan knew deep down what it was, it, too, was gone. And what was left was what he always had. The road of nothing.

With one hand he gripped the steering wheel, put the key in the ignition, and turned. But the roar didn't come. The truck stuttered, then wrenched with a terrible grinding noise. His brows furrowed. He knew every possible sound his truck could make—this was none of them. He turned the key again, but this time, it was dead.

"You gotta be kidding…"

He jumped out and tossed up the wide metal hood to see what was wrong.

It was completely thrashed. Wires were cut, the battery caved in, and the alternator was bashed into its frame. Someone had beat the hell out of it.

And he knew who.

The tow truck pulled out, leaving a trail of dust and Nolan behind it, standing at the open garage of Adams Specialty Automotive Repair. He turned and stepped into the bright and airy garage. A couple of mechanics worked on a vintage '66 navy Mustang that was up high on a rack, next to his own Ford, just below it. The mechanic, a kind and happy middle-aged man with a greased shirt, took a final scan under the truck to see if there was any structural damage.

"First guess is the alternator—

Nolan didn't hesitate to interrupt. "It's the serpentine belt, the battery, and the alternator. I want them replaced."

The mechanic stared for a moment, making sure he understood Nolan's Australian accent.

"You work on cars before?" The mechanic asked, not sure what to make of him.

"Yeah," Nolan said, with no time to waste. "How long's it gonna take you? I'm trying to get somewhere."

The mechanic hesitated. Nolan's firmness and knowledge was clear. The mechanic knew he had to shoot straight. "I gotta get an alternator from outta town, won't be till tomorrow…at the earliest."

Nolan looked him up and down, then to his truck. He knew the mechanic's word was true, but he was frustrated because he knew that leaving his truck in town the other night had been a bad idea. And now his plans were being delayed once again.

Nolan shook his head. "Make it happen," he said, then took off for the road.

90

HARROWING OF THE SOUL

N olan walked, his head low and his hands stuffed into his denim pockets. His thoughts were always a siege. His mind was a never-ending pendulum that fought with what he felt, and what he thought he should do. Both sides teetered and were muddled by sorrow. He could never explain himself inside. He simply just hurt. It was a pain beyond his scars or the soreness in his temple or the countless markings on his back. It was a pain much deeper that clenched tightly around his entire soul. There were times after a fight that he didn't even know he was injured, because all Nolan ever thought of now was one single, torturous thought: that no matter what moments of relief he could find in a day, she was no longer with him. He was going to be without her, until the end of time.

Unless…in some version of life after death, he could be with her again.

This was what he held on to. It was always that same repeating thought that came back to him, over and over again. He had to get back to *Her*. He wanted to feel her presence, her touch, her everlasting smile that had made him feel alive for the first time and for the last time in his life. It was a burden he could not bear nor bury—the pain was simply not going to pass. And it was all he ever thought about.

Nolan crossed in front of the Elks Theatre, an ornate, old auditorium in the town. It was empty, like most of the town at this hour. The flyers showcased a new play about family, coming this spring. Nolan wondered if *She* liked theater. It was something he wasn't sure about. They had talked of music and movies and travel, shared some themselves, but never had theater come up in their time. He wanted to know. He wanted to know everything about her. And that became an innate feeling and lesson that he had learned from her:

To love someone is to seek to know all of them. To see all of them. Through anything and everything. To want them to truly grow to their greatest potential. Although these were words never shared between *Her* and Nolan, it was something he felt. Something eternal, unspoken, and true. Because they were things he had learned through *Her*. So much of what they'd had had been effortless, a constant sharing and learning about one another. And the other part, the greatest part, was experiencing things together. As long as one of them had been excited about something, they both were. That seemed to be one of the universal truths about the great loves of our lives—they always share true and common passions with us. They always share spoken and unspoken understandings. They always share who they are and who they desire to be. But most of all, our great loves help us share each other. They help us share who we are.

Nolan made it to the end of the block and stopped at a corner intersection. His head had been hanging low in thought since the mechanic's. He didn't know where he was or where he was headed. Not in any sense of it. But he knew he wasn't going back to Goldie or the dog. His heart was already too heavy. He had to commit to the choice he'd made. Nolan lifted his chin and realized that he was actually standing back in town. He had been walking and thinking like this for three miles. Without even knowing it, he had walked through the neighborhoods twice, almost in a full circle, until he found himself back in a place he had already been. Straight ahead was downtown and Whiskey Row. Behind him was the community square and the mountain range afar. Beyond Whiskey Row and in the distance was Thumb Butte, the flat rocky mountain overlooking the town's horizon. He licked his lips and the cool air quickly glazed them. This would normally be the time of day he'd finish fighting, and his guilt was telling him to have a drink. But deep down, he was sick and tired of that too. All he ever really wanted was to stop the pain inside. The years of punishment his body had taken through fighting, traveling, and hunger was unparalleled to the pain that dwelled within his heart. Nolan finally looked up and scanned to the east, then west of the intersection where he saw the church. It was still and quiet. He looked ahead to the long row of bars again. His eyes sank, wanting another drink, just one last time.

The stained-glass windows glowed and flooded the empty aisles with warm light. Nolan was there, sitting alone, in the left aisles of the church. Hours must have passed. He felt the colors of the sun shift in the stained-glass light. Ahead of him, towering above the church altar, was the body of Christ. It hung from a tall wooden cross and under its thorn crown, narrowed eyes gazed upon Nolan. He looked at them carefully while his mind churned. But he was only thinking of one thing.

He remembered the way she had smiled when his jokes hadn't worked. Or her laugh when they had. He remembered laying with her, swallowed in soft linen sheets during summer nights. He remembered how sometimes they would just stare at each other under the covers, their eyes traveling each freckle, wrinkle, and scar, then asking the other to tell the story behind it. They didn't judge each other for their pasts, and they each believed in the prospects of the future. They had deeply admired and respected each other. Everything about each other. He was a man who had lived many lives in many travels. He was independent, strong, and held his morals close to his heart. But to him, *She* was something else. Something beyond.

She was the first person to truly love him for what he was, and what he wasn't. She believed in the goodness of people and the importance of hope. She believed in the power of true forgiveness and kindness to strangers. She believed that everyone has their own purpose and their own special journey. And she believed that sometimes, those journeys cross in life, and are meant to be shared with another. She was the most hopeful person he had ever known, with the innate ability to glow in everything she did, an undying optimism for life that defeated the cynicism of his past and his pain, and stirred him in a way that he could touch his own soul.

She was everything.

He remembered how she would lean against him on their couch and run her fingers through his hair, and he, with his large, strong hands, would carefully hold the side of her face, so he could see every detail in her eyes. And every time he did, she would smile and want to do the same. Nolan would never forget that, or her touch. How she would place her hand against the line of his jaw, and he would lean into it, sending her palm up and down his face. It was amazing how much love could be expressed by the simplest of eyes, words, or actions. And how easily it could be felt, by the littlest of any of them at all.

He had no sense of time, sitting there alone, just remembering *Her*. The way she was. The way they'd been.

He looked up, holding tears beneath his eyes.

"What do you want me to do?"

But he wasn't asking Christ. He was asking *Her*. Could he go through with it? Would she hate him for it? Would he actually see her again? Or were these all just the freckles of memories and scars, like her eyes and the details he would soon forget? Images and stories becoming pigments of sand in the wind—glimmering, glowing, then gone.

"I miss you...I..."

But his whispers stopped. He didn't even know what he wanted to say.

"I just miss you..."

He was confused, defeated, and more alone now than ever in his life. He looked up to the body of Christ and stared at the stakes embedded in the palms. He would rather have that pain. He would rather have any, than his own. And he wished that, if God had a role in any of this, that he could have traded his own life, if he knew she could have kept hers. She was stronger than him in every way, and in Nolan's mind, she was more important to the world than him. She *was* the entire world to him.

"Hello there," a soft voice said over his shoulder.

Nolan turned.

It was McKenzie.

She smiled.

Nolan quickly turned, hiding the tears sitting just beneath his eyes.

"Did I miss anything?" she asked sarcastically, looking around the empty church.

He held his head low, quickly trying to clear his mind. He didn't want anyone to see his vulnerability, let alone her, who caught him completely off guard.

McKenzie shrugged and slid into the pew next to him, side by side.

She was confident and nonchalant, and as the church became silent again, Nolan kept his eyes averted. He didn't move, and he tried his best not to think. But after a long period of silence and trying to clear his head, he wasn't even sure if she was still next to him.

He turned.

She was still there.

Her eyes were closed, and she was gently inhaling, in and out. She was praying, and at the same time, melodically controlling her breathing. McKenzie felt her prayers most through the quiet spaces between breaths. Sometimes her prayers were clear, as if she had written them down in her mind, and others…were silent. They were things she simply felt. Things she didn't have words for yet. But this all distracted Nolan. She was uncomfortably close in the pew with him. Her shoulder wasn't touching his, but how close she was felt like it. Yet, in some way, the way she was breathing, reminded him of his own method when coming down from a fight. He turned away and began regulating his own breath.

Then his eyes closed.

McKenzie was praying for her family. She was praying for her Gram and especially for Jason. She thought about her family's home. How it had been passed down generation to generation, and now it was all in her name. She felt the weight and the responsibility of being the last of her Grandmother's name. With her two boys, an ailing grandmother, and a mother in rehab, she was the last in charge, and a part of the last line of Americans that had settled in Prescott long ago. Whatever was going to come next, was going to come through her boys. McKenzie took a deep and final breath, taking this all in with her prayers. Then, to Nolan's surprise, she began to whisper her thoughts aloud.

"The hardest thing about being here…is that it always reminds me what I have to do. Deep down…I know it."

Her words were calm and clear, and though he kept his eyes shut, he was listening.

"And I guess that scares me because, I always feel it here… I always know it," she said, her eyes still closed. She was open and honest, as if it were a confession, or perhaps a moment of clarity.

"But I know…I have to be open…" she continued. "Because…that's the only way things can change."

Nolan opened his eyes and turned to her. She was still there, eyes closed, thinking. He stared. He didn't understand why she chose to share her thoughts. And yet, he could sense this was all something truthful to her. The way of her words and the care and freedom of her thoughts—it made him consider his own. McKenzie slowly opened her eyes then turned.

"Why'd you come back?" she whispered.

He was caught, unguarded. He quickly turned away. His mind was imploding with what he felt, and he didn't even know what he could actually say to her. Then, a memory came to him, something inherently painful but true. He inhaled, thinking of the last lines on *their* list:

Make a Family
The Grand Canyon
Live the most beautiful life

Nolan's face was low and held away from hers. Tears wanted to engulf his eyes, but he was still holding back. He inhaled, then whispered. "Because I'm trying to keep a promise…and I don't know what else to do."

He was hiding, but she knew his honesty and frustration was truthful. There was some unspoken dilemma inside, rising and receding, warring with itself. She wanted to understand, but she could feel just by looking at him, this was not something to push. Whatever it was, it was painful. Deeply painful. She remembered seeing that in his eyes back at the bar. And maybe that's why she'd chosen to tell him her name.

McKenzie always had the gift to see how people felt inside, whether they hid or deflected things from themselves or others. She had a sort of third eye that could always find things that were deeper below. It was an ability that had grown from her time trying to take care of her mother, during the lies and the endless battles with her addiction, relapse, and recovery. It was an ability that had grown from the many different encounters she'd had with people at her bar, day in and day out. But really, it was a gift that she had inherited from her Gram. McKenzie, like her grandmother, always wanted to find people's true feelings. And even greater, she wanted to understand and feel them too.

She sat in silence with Nolan, but she was listening with her eyes, trying to comprehend him and what he wanted to say. She knew from her mother and her past, that all people try to hide, in one way or another. But to McKenzie, most people couldn't hide behind their words or their eyes, at least not from her. If anything, she found that people want to share their truest thoughts and feelings. They were just afraid to be judged, misunderstood, or even worse, to feel more alone. But McKenzie didn't think this way. She found good in all people. People, after all, were just people.

In all her years dealing with family and the ups and downs of people throughout her life, she had learned one thing that was universally true in all of her encounters. It was something she'd learned from her Gram and something she tried to do every day herself. It was something about McKenzie that made people care about her and something that McKenzie deeply cared about within herself: everyone in this world just needed a little bit more kindness.

"What do you *want* to do?" she asked, referring to his last words.

But he couldn't say. He couldn't say anything at all. He felt stuck, suspended in time and thought. It was that same vicious circle rotating his past and his pain, recurring over and over again. After a long moment of silence, she turned back to the cross, then stood up.

Nolan's eyes drifted, but he didn't turn until she spoke again.

"You dropped this at the bar…"

She was holding his Polaroid. The picture of Nolan and *Her*.

He was in awe, and as if it could disappear right in front of him again, he carefully took it.

"Take care, okay?" She said it with a whisper and a gentle smile, then she walked out.

Nolan didn't move. He gripped the Polaroid, gazing into it. It was entirely overwhelming. He didn't know what to think, say, or do. When he heard the church doors slam, he woke from this daze. Nolan jumped up and moved swiftly to the doors.

When Nolan came out of the heavy church doors, she was already walking down the street.

"Hey!" he called.

She stopped. He stood there, holding the Polaroid.

"Thanks...for this."

McKenzie smiled. "Thanks for headbutting Turner. It was the highlight of my day."

Nolan nodded. He almost smiled. It became silent again until another impulse hit him. "You going to work?"

She nodded.

"Can I...walk with you?" he asked, unsure.

"If you get angry, will you headbutt me?" She grinned.

"Not if you don't piss me off." He walked up, restraining his smile.

"So you do smile," she teased.

"Well...you're funny..." he replied, shoving his hands in his denim, tucking the Polaroid inside.

"I'll take that as a compliment."

"Good. Most women can't."

"Wow. That's a bold statement."

He looked at her. He didn't think it was. "Well, you're not like most women."

She thought about it until it made her laugh. "No...I don't think I am."

She thought about it some more. She had never met anyone else that was like her. Even though she looked up to her grandmother and aspired to be as wise and as strong as her, she always felt like *she was something else.* People saw it, too, but not in the way McKenzie felt it. McKenzie had always known she was different. She was different than the guys and the girls her age and who she'd grown up with. And in her own way, that gave her pride.

They strolled to the center of downtown where the open park and the courthouse awaited. They were sharing the quiet early evening now, each of their boots gliding along the pavement, clacking heels side by side. He looked over to her, intrigued, but now he wasn't sure what to say. She looked back, thinking he was going to say something. Instead, he clenched his fists inside his denim and kept his chin low. McKenzie looked over again.

"So…fish out of water. How's that working out for you?"

"What?" he asked.

"What are you doing here?"

"Oh, just…passing through."

"Yeah, but to where?"

He thought about what to tell her and what not to. "The Grand Canyon."

She looked over, keeping a slow comfortable stride. "By yourself?"

"Yeah."

She paused. "Why?"

Nolan thought about it for a long time. She was studying him now. She could see he was trying to work it all out in his mind again. He finally shook his head.

"I don't know anymore."

He slowed to a stop and looked over his shoulder. He was gazing at the old stone courthouse. She stopped. "You seen that?"

"Yeah. I like it," he said, his elbows jutting out from his sides while his fists held tightly in his denim.

"What do you like about it?"

"I don't know…I like the whole town." He shrugged. "I've seen a few places."

He turned away and kept walking through the courtyard. She was expecting him to say more, but he didn't. McKenzie almost laughed to herself. This guy had more conversations in his head than he ever did with people.

"Annnnd?" she finally asked. "Is that all you're gonna say?"

Nolan thought about it. About what he really wanted to say.

"It just feels like the whole world's always changing. But this place…I don't know if it does."

"Trust me, it don't."

"You're from here?"

"Since I was born. Prescott hasn't changed much. I guess that's what people like."

"But not you?" he asked, finally looking at her.

She wondered about it. Like it had in church, her mind wandered again. "I wanna see things. Yeah, I'm a country girl, but I haven't seen anything yet. I want to go travel…explore, hear new things, see new places… I don't know. I just want to *feel.*"

He looked down as they walked. There was something about her openness. There was a sense of hope and faith she had. It was something he could see, just in the way she spoke about things. It was familiar.

Nolan looked over. "If you could do anything…what would you do?"

She turned and let out a little smile. "Anything?"

"Yeah," he said, the inflection in his Australian accent heightening with curiosity.

She stopped at the end of the sidewalk, just before the crosswalk between the courtyard and Whiskey Row. She gave it another thought, then inhaled with a smile. She looked around, then turned to him. "I would feel *everything.*"

Nolan's brows furrowed.

He didn't know what she meant or what to make of it. But he did understand one thing now:

She was special.

"Cross here," she said, stepping into the street.

They both ambled up Whiskey Row. The city lights were up and the murmur of a Friday night's crowd permeated the town. There were more cars and more people than earlier in the day. The town was coming alive again with a new energy that had emerged with the evening. People, tourists, and locals were all heading out to drink and to dine.

They strolled through an alley in the back of the Row's old brick building. They walked alongside a structure that had been there for over 160 years, as far back as the days that some would still call the Wild West.

"You worked here long?"

"Too long. I'm just hustling 'til I finish school."

"How much longer you got?"

"I got finals this week…then the next chapter begins."

"And what's that?"

She stopped by a fire escape, then smiled sweetly, musing. "I don't know. Leave town? Trade school? College? I always wanted to go, I just never thought I could. I just know I'm open now…more than I've ever been before." Her confidence and hope was palpable. It was as if she had been waiting to say it like that. It scared her and thrilled her all the same.

Nolan could see it. He took a hand out of his jacket and grabbed the fire escape. He was listening to her. Truly listening. Just in the way she thought about things and talked about them…it made him wonder too. McKenzie wasn't afraid of what could—or what would—happen. She was open to it. She was excited about it. She was different than him.

"Look…" She pointed to the ground.

Nolan did, and found the Polaroid on the concrete between their boots. He was stupefied. How could he have dropped it twice now? But before he could grab it, McKenzie swiped it up and held it out to him, teasingly.

"You got a real problem with that, don'tcha?"

She looked at it once more, then handed it to him. Nolan took it delicately. He didn't know what was wrong with him. How could he possibly be so careless to have lost it twice now?

"You both got nice smiles," she said, the words waking him up.

He inhaled and watched himself carefully place it back in his pocket, to be certain he had done it correctly. Then he tightened his index and thumb at the corner of the fading photo paper, making sure it was secure. He had never been this reckless. Not with anything, even when drinking. But when he looked back up, he found that she was still looking up at him, smiling, honestly, patiently, as a friend would. As someone truly kind would. He didn't know what to say now. He was overwhelmed by all of this. What was he even doing anymore?

McKenzie could see something difficult ticking, and with a softening in her eyes and her words, she sweetly and simply asked: "Are you okay?"

Nolan finally looked into her eyes. He held them there while she looked up and into his, patiently waiting for him. And for a moment, they both felt something else—and it was the same thing.

"*Hey!*" a voice hurtled down the alley. It was Turner, Clayton, and their two stocky rodeo buddies.

Turner laughed bemusedly and took a long drag off his cigarette. "Fancy seeing ya'll here." The bridge of Turner's nose was split from the day before and had been taped shut. He was in a leather jacket and cowboy boots like his buddies. They had clearly been waiting and hoping to catch McKenzie or Nolan coming to her bar. Turner had harassed everyone inside until he'd found out what time she worked.

McKenzie wasted no time in giving him a piece of her mind. "Hey, *jackass!*" she yelled. "Stop coming here! You did enough already, everyone saw!"

The four men cruised up to them. Nolan kept his eyes on Turner. His back was to the brick wall, but he wasn't going to run.

"Saw what? Your fuckin' boy here's what started it." Turner flicked his cigarette at Nolan, sparking his denim jacket with embers. But Nolan didn't even flinch. "How's the truck, mate? It really is a beaut'," Turner pushed with a grin. He was happy that Nolan knew.

McKenzie stepped right up to him. "You know what, Turner? You can all fuck off!" And with both hands, she shoved him as hard as she could.

Turner snatched her wrist, yanking it over her head and bending it to control her. But as soon as Turner made the move, Nolan's palm harpooned forward, upper cutting his bandaged nose. He wailed in pain as dried scabs instantly cracked and blood came rushing down again. Clayton swung first, but Nolan immediately parried it with his forearm, then hammered his entire forehead down onto Clayton's nose. Clayton dropped like an anvil. The two rodeo men charged Nolan, quick-jabbing his mid-section, trying to knock the wind out of him, but Nolan's whole body tightened defensively. The men pushed together, driving his back into the fire escape, then put up their fists, ready to fight.

With flames in her eyes, McKenzie hurdled through them to get to Turner. "*Asshole!*" She yelled, left-hooking Turner's temple, smearing his blood across his face with her knuckles.

"Ergh!" Turner groaned, then pushed her face back, sending her violently against the wall. The back of her head smacked the brick wall, and she collapsed to the ground. Nolan stepped in front of her. His fists came up, then clenched. Now all four men stood on their feet, facing Nolan. Turner's nose ran open with blood, while the other three sweated, irate, and ready to punish him. Nolan prepared, his chin lowering, eyes narrowing, his fists gripped tight and high. He took one deep inhale, then exhaled, and watched as they charged. Turner threw a heavy left hook that swung over Nolan's head, then quickly pivoted on the toe of his boot and threw another right punch. Nolan blocked it effortlessly and shot another painful jab into Turner's nose.

"*Ahh!*" he yelled, stumbling backwards just as another goon launched toward Nolan. The goon swung big, hitting only air. Nolan shuffled around him as the man swung wildly, striking out again and again until his face was met by Nolan's pummeling elbow. His head toppled over and rolled his entire body to the ground. The next man approached Nolan with the swiftness and form of a boxer. Nolan saw it coming and kept up his own sharp footwork. Before the man could even throw a punch, Nolan quick-jabbed, then crushed his eye with a devastating right hook. Each man scurried to stand, racing to Nolan's left and right trying to get an advantage, but they couldn't land a single hit, or keep up with any of this.

Nolan shuffled through them like musical chairs, striking each man efficiently and dropping them one by one. Each stumbled and jumped up in a puzzled frenzy, embarrassed and charging again, but before they could make even move, they were torn apart, fist for fist. Nolan was moving three hundred and sixty degrees, defending himself and attacking from all directions. Each one was struck over and over, tripping off their feet by Nolan's crushing hooks. They outnumbered him four to one, and they were dropping like flies, hit after hit. Nolan's speed and power was faster than any of them could process or even see. And the more they tried to stand up, the more Nolan ridiculed them with his fists or the toe of his boots. With dirt and blood all over them and their clothes, they were the ones being punished now.

McKenzie finally pulled herself together and charged Turner with a roar—she wanted her own blood. McKenzie punched Turner sharply in the side of the neck.

"*Agh!* Fucking bitch!" he screamed back, shocked by her blow. He swung the back of his hand down and smacked her square across the jaw, spinning her entire body the opposite direction. Nolan's eyes exploded. He dove at Turner, grappling him and driving him face-first into the brick wall. With his palm pinned on the back of Turner's skull, Nolan drilled Turner's blood-gushing nose into the bricks.

"*Ahhh!*" Turner cried with a flailing hand. But Nolan then caught it, bending it mercilessly behind Turner's back. Turner wailed in agony, his face smearing against the coarse wall. Nolan leaned into his armlock on Turner, pushing it further and further, clenching his teeth—he was going to break the arm that had hit McKenzie, slowly.

A sudden sting shocked him. His grip on Turner quickly eased. Nolan looked down. There was a knife handle sticking out of his side. Clayton pushed the knife further.

Nolan grunted and released his grip. Turner staggered back, holding his face. Clayton pushed on the back of Nolan's neck, holding the knife in and slamming Nolan face-first into the brick. McKenzie screamed with shock.

"*Ergh!*" Nolan bellowed, the delayed reaction to pain now striking his nervous system.

"What are you doing?!" McKenzie cried in horror.

Turner got to his feet and stood beside his disheveled buddies. Nolan spung around, bringing an elbow across Clayton's face. The force blew Clayton to the side, simultaneously pulling the knife out. Nolan groaned, facing them again. But before he could ready himself to fight, Turner smacked a tight fist against Nolan's bruised temple. Nolan staggered back and crashed into the brick, then collapsed to the ground. The men all stood and gathered themselves. Blood oozed from Nolan's side, already covering his flannel, his jeans, and Clayton's blade.

"You fucking bastards!" McKenzie screamed, dropping to her knees to staunch the blood coming out.

They could all see it—the stab was deep.

"Let's go," Clayton said, still holding the blood-soaked knife. The men rushed out of the alley.

"Are you okay!?" McKenzie asked, trying to see Nolan's face. But he was already crawling up on his hands and knees and trying to get back up. She gripped his large arm and helped him. Her eyes widened—blood was already seeping through his flannel. But Nolan was just annoyed. "Who is that fuckhead?"

She held her palm tightly at his side, holding the blood in. "My ex-husband," she said quickly. "We gotta get you to the hospital."

Nolan shook his head, surprised. He was now feeling all the pain in his body. His swollen hand touched his temple, now re-bruised and puffed purple.

"What? No, we can't do that."

"Are you kidding me!? Come on!" McKenzie pulled at him.

He hunched over, then stood straight again, trying to loosen his wide upper back and the muscles around his stab wound. "I can't go to a hospital."

"Dude, you're bleeding!"

Nolan stretched his upper body, trying to shake it off, but McKenzie just she kept her hand tightly on his side.

"We have to go now!"

"Listen to me! I can't go there!" He waited a moment before admitting, "I don't have papers."

She shook her head. Her palm was soaked in his blood. But for some reason, she understood what he meant: Nolan was not an American. He was here illegally.

"All right, come on. I have an idea," she said, helping him stand.

McKenzie drove quickly out of downtown, her eyes darting between Nolan and the road. Nolan held his stab wound with a navy blue bandana and used his other sore hand to hold up his head. He was spotted with bruises and wounds everywhere now, old and new. But he wasn't hurting or worried by the blood—he was frustrated.

"Stay with me, okay?" she said, her eyes constantly jumping to his.

He nodded, then saw the blood on the arm rest and the car seat. "Sorry about the mess."

McKenzie gawked. "Well just don't die and everything will be all right!"

Nolan shook his head and spoke somberly, "It's fine. Been through worse." And he had. This was nothing new or threatening to him, and, at the moment, it was the last thing he cared about.

"We're almost to the house," she said, keeping her foot on the gas, flying through her dimly lit neighborhood.

Something was bothering Nolan, but it wasn't his wounds. He was puzzled by something about McKenzie that he just couldn't understand.

"Serious question," he said.

She looked over, nervous about what he might ask.

"Why would you ever marry a fuckwit like that?" he asked with his head still low.

She nodded, thinking of her past life and who she used to be. "That's a really good question."

Nolan shook his head. He was more frustrated with that than with his own blood in his hands. He lifted his chin to look out the window, still thinking about it. "You're just a better person," he added.

McKenzie looked over. She knew he meant it. And it struck something. She had wasted so much time on Turner. She had always known it. But for some reason, Nolan's words spoke so much more to her. They were about how he saw her, not how he saw Turner. McKenzie's hands tightened on the steering wheel. She cleared her throat. "Because I was fifteen and got pregnant."

Nolan looked over. She was quiet now. There wasn't much more for her to say. In Nolan's mind, the gash in his side was gone. For the rest of the ride, all he thought about was all the things she must have gone through being that young, and how hard it must have been for her.

Nolan was dazed, sitting on McKenzie's kitchen countertop in a white tank top soaked with blood. He was holding the fabric tightly against his side, waiting as McKenzie dug through her medicine cabinet in the other room.

"I don't know if I can patch you up with what I got!" she yelled.

Nolan snapped out of his daze and checked his denim jacket's pocket. The Polaroid was still there, but with a smudge of blood on it. He wiped it and put it away. On the fridge, he saw pictures of McKenzie and her sons. He thought about her—how young she had been when she'd first had them. He couldn't fathom what it must have been like for a girl that young to have a child. He couldn't imagine how she must have felt, or how people must have treated her. Nolan assumed she was only a few years younger than him, and, in that thought, it brought him back to his own childhood.

He realized then—they had been almost the same age when very strenuous and unfair things happened to them.

"All right, let's see it. Here..." She came into the room with some alcohol and an old wooden box full of sewing materials. She set it on the counter next to him, then helped him peel off his tank top. It was matted to his strong upper body, slowly revealing the countless tattoos, bruises, and now blood. She glanced him all over, seeing both the artistry and the punishment found everywhere on him. He was looking off and a bit dazed, maybe thinking to himself. She carefully pushed his knee to the side so she could get closer to his wound. His chin turned a bit to her. He was surprised by her control and confidence, standing between his dense thighs. McKenzie was focused, knowing what she had to do and that using this sewing kit was going to be a long shot. She soaked a cloth with alcohol, then looked up. "It's gonna burn. You want whiskey?"

"No, thanks."

She pressed the cold cloth against him. He inhaled slow and deep, then closed his eyes. She watched his every move, anxious and surprised that he wasn't showing much of a reaction. In fact, he didn't show anything at all. She didn't know how he felt or what he was thinking.

But she wanted to.

"Are you okay?"

He nodded, keeping his eyes closed. It became quiet again. Her hands were slow, tenderly dabbing his torn flesh, soaking the old and fresh blood, revealing the deepest part of the stab wound. If the knife had been thrust up or down any further, he might not even be alive. The cold air whispered from an open kitchen window, while crickets echoed through the old neighborhood. McKenzie carefully pressed the wound once more, then dried it with clean cotton gauze. She put pressure on the open gash, then looked up. Her eyes crossed his. Nolan looked away. So did she. She held the wound shut with her fingers, trying to slow the flow of blood for a bit before threading. She snuck another glance at his tanned arms and shoulders and all the faded tattoos that covered both. She was curious, but she didn't even know where to begin with him.

"Were you a soldier or something?" she finally asked.

It was a long moment before he responded. "I was a fighter," he said, looking out the window.

She waited for him to say something else, but knew he wasn't going to.

"Okay... Is that it?"

"I was a lot of things," he added.

McKenzie pricked him with the needle, then pushed it through the severed flesh. He inhaled strongly, feeling the thread sift through him, finally remembering the pain. McKenzie inhaled. She was becoming anxious about stitching him up now—not that it was hard for her to do, but because his stoic face and silence were making her nervous. He was still dazed and still bleeding, and she thought he might just pass out or fall over at any second. Even if this wasn't hard for him, it was for her.

"All right, dude, you gotta start using your words and start talking. Where ya from? Where were you raised? Give me something…"

Nolan closed his eyes, feeling the needle thread through him faster, then he slowly reopened them. He knew he had to make effort. Not for himself. For her.

"I was born in Australia, but I been all over. Worked fishing boats off Alaska. A ranch hand in Missouri. Montana. Colorado. Up and down Canada."

"Why'd you travel so much?"

"Never had a home," he was quick to reply.

"What do you mean? What about your parents?"

"They, uh, they left when I was young."

"They left you?"

He nodded.

"How old were you?"

"Fifteen."

She stopped threading. McKenzie stepped back from his thighs so she could look him in both eyes. She was close—closer than either had been with another person in a long time. She was looking at him with a sense of surprise. Her thoughts raced with more questions. She felt anger, confusion, but mostly, she felt sorry for him.

"No child deserves that. I'm sorry."

Nolan looked at her, holding his eyes to hers. She didn't turn. They were looking inside each other, not yet knowing what to think or to feel. But something turned in each of them, and it was suspended in time, right in that moment. McKenzie finally broke their gaze. She turned her eyes to focus on his wound. Nolan was still looking.

It became quiet again. And then she realized it: he had been the same age as her when his parents had left him. And it scared her, because she didn't know what her life would have been like if she hadn't had Gram. It was silent until McKenzie found herself in her space again, reflecting like she did in church.

"I'm just lucky I got my Gram. She's been there for everyone, even before herself. Never lost it on us, never gave up on no one. She's helped three generations of family live in this house."

As she reflected, her own words reminded her of what was to come. It was all up to her now. Gram had given her this house to do with as she pleased. She didn't want to let her down, but she also didn't want to let her kids down and lose the roof over their heads. And, at the same time, she desperately wanted to go to college. She wanted to go learn and study and experience new things. Really, she just wanted a new road in life, something that could be hers and her choice. McKenzie recalled the day Gram had told her that the house was all hers.

"She even left it in my name. Told me to do what I had to do."

It was a heavy thought for her, but she didn't look at it as a burden, she looked at it as a reminder that she was different, with her own path and her own story. Nolan simply watched her eyes. He didn't even feel the needle going in and out of his skin anymore. McKenzie, too, was lost in the process, as well her thoughts. Anytime she thought of her Gram, her heart would show. She smiled. "She's the one I'd go to church with, when she still could."

"Where's the rest of them?" Nolan asked.

"Mom's in rehab. Dad, I never knew. And Gram, she's across town. Assisted living."

"And them?"

She stopped and looked up at him. He lifted his chin. McKenzie looked over her shoulder to see what he meant. It was the picture of her and the boys on the fridge. She was hesitant, unsure if he was judging her. She had always felt it by men. She was a single, young, attractive mother. She had curves. She had attitude. She had strength. And she always felt like men wanted something from her, or would insist that she needed something from them. Whether it be Turner or Kyle or anyone throughout her life, they were all the same in that they all tried to make her believe that she needed them. It wasn't 'til thirty did she realize she didn't need anyone. Trusting men was the last thing she believed in now.

But Nolan… In some strange way, it seemed like he had too much pain to not be trusted. As hard as it was to even understand that, it was something she felt. He was a fish out of water. He was different from anyone she had ever met. McKenzie didn't want anything from anyone, and she didn't believe he wanted anything from her. At least, not yet. She looked up and saw that he was looking in her eyes, waiting for an answer.

"They're with Gram for the weekend."

He nodded. "They're handsome."

"They're my boys," she said sentimentally with a pleased smile.

McKenzie's breathing was rhythmic, concentrating on the needle going in and out of his flesh, but she was also becoming distracted by the different things rummaging through her mind. "I gotta do right by them. I was so young when they were born. I just feel like…I gotta be my best *me.* Because what am I to them if I'm not? I don't want them to see me like how I see Mom."

Nolan studied her as she spoke. How she thought through things as she said them aloud. She was fearless and open. Different than him. He never shared or said what he thought or felt. And yet, she was confident enough to do both. For minutes now, Nolan had forgotten what she was doing or if he was still bleeding, even though he was.

"I don't blame her. I don't even hate her." McKenzie shook her head. "She did the best she could, but she can't even take care of herself. Like Gram. I just…" She paused, her eyes were searching. "I just want my boys to be good men."

She meant it with everything she had, and Nolan saw it. He felt it. "I think they will," he finally said.

She looked up. They held eyes again. She believed him.

But he was still bleeding.

"Shit. All right, this isn't gonna work. We gotta go to the hospital or find a way to patch you up, man."

He looked down to his bruised side and to the wound. It was pulsing and gradually seeping blood through the stitches.

"I know where we can go," he said.

A Second Chance

They drove through the long, dark night. There were no cars to be seen out on Williamson Valley Road. The only light was the Jeep's headlights and the countless stars that shared a pale crescent moon. All was silent except for the old Jeep's humming engine. McKenzie was driving fast and they both had their thoughts. She wondered more about his life and his experiences. He was like some sort of wanderer, lost in his head and the world. And yet, she could see that, beneath all of that confusion and hurt, there was a sense of thoughtfulness. It was clear to her that Nolan was emotionally intelligent. She had known it from the moment she met him at the bar, and had been reminded again in their walk through downtown. She wondered what he was thinking and what he may be feeling through all of this. Her eyes darted over to check in on him. His head rested against the cold window glass, and his palm was holding his wound, packed with a stack of gauze. She could see the white and gray in his eyes, even in the dark. His head was low, but he had to be thinking something.

"You okay?" she asked softly.

Nolan looked over. He was calm. "Yeah. You?"

She looked at him twice before laughing. "You're the one bleeding!"

"Yeah," he said quietly, seeing the humor in it.

It was silent again.

"You should see the other guys," he added.

She smiled, then couldn't help but laugh. When she looked over to Nolan, he finally smiled back.

It was still early evening. The ranch was still except for the chirping of insects and the river of soft wind that sifted into the valley from over the Indian ruins. Goldie saw the Jeep from his bedroom window, hauling down the dirt road.

When he opened the door, he found McKenzie and Nolan with his arm around her shoulder and her hand keeping pressure on his side as he weakly stood. His shirt and gauze were drenched, and her stitching was leaking blood. Nolan was already feeling faint, just from walking up to the door.

"Howdy," McKenzie said.

Goldie gave them a surprised look. "Will you look who it is…"

"Sorry to wake you, old man," Nolan said.

"Sorry? Sorry for what?" The men stared at each other. "You brought a beautiful woman with ya. Come on in now, I ain't stopping ya."

She helped Nolan carefully through the doorway. "Hi, I'm Kenzie. We need your help." She pulled her hand and gauze from Nolan's wound.

"I see that," Goldie said wide-eyed, ushering them in. "Christ, young man, what'd you say to her?" he joked.

"I didn't do that," she quickly replied. "My ex-husband did."

"Well, I'm looking forward to this story," Goldie said.

Nolan sat atop the kitchen counter with his shirt off while Goldie worked on him from a barstool. With his glasses on, he stitched him up with the same thin metal wire he used at the office. McKenzie helped keep the wound dry and passed Goldie tools and wire as needed.

"You young'uns sure know how to have a good time. Oh, speaking of—darlin', can you get that old '82 in the cupboard there?" Goldie gestured to the cabinets above his coffeemaker.

"The what?" she asked.

"Scotch," Nolan aided.

She found what he was referring to.

"Oh, you like the good ol' stuff, huh, Goldie?" She went around the kitchen island where Nolan was sitting on and opened up a cabinet.

"Of course! I'm old—the old stuff is the good stuff." He grinned. Then a thought struck him. "Ah, almost forgot. I got a surprise for you, young man." Goldie stopped threading and wiped his hands in the sink.

Nolan turned with an uncomfortable squint in his eyes. "Is it a horse tranquilizer?"

"Oh, mon ami, much better than that. Go ahead and pour us some there." He looked to McKenzie, then hurried out of the room. "Just a second."

McKenzie poured three glasses of Scotch in short, wide glasses, then brought one over to Nolan. Keeping his eyes low, he looked at her a moment, then took it.

"How ya doing, fighter?"

He bobbed his head, woozy, but no longer faint. "Sore. Tired."

"I hear that," she said, then sipped her Scotch like it was water.

Nolan held his glass a moment, then looked at her. "Thanks for riding this out."

Her smile came softly. She knew he meant more than he could say. "It's the least I can do. You did beat up my ex-husband and his dumbass friends." She smiled. "Lord knows, I tried."

"You had a couple good hooks. I saw 'em."

Her smile grew and she sipped the honey-colored Scotch without even a flinch. "I shoulda punched Clayton first," she said.

Nolan finally smiled. He looked down and took in his own Scotch. When he glanced back up, he found her looking at him. This time, he looked back.

Something was happening.

Right then, an animal's panting and paws came padding around the corner.

It was *the dog*.

He nuzzled his body between Nolan's dangling legs at first sight. Nolan's entire face lit up, and Goldie walked in right after, just as excited.

"Oi!! What's he doing here?" Nolan asked, reaching to pet him. The dog pushed his body against Nolan's shins on the counter and whipped his tongue about.

"I thought he'd like a warm bed for a night or two," Goldie replied.

McKenzie's voice heightened as soon as she saw the happy dog, "Hi, ya big puppy! Who are you!?"

Goldie pointed. "That's his dog," he said, referring to Nolan.

"Old man—"

But before Nolan could protest, McKenzie happily interrupted, "This is your dog!?"

"No," he replied. But he was still smiling and running his hands through the dog's ears. His tongue flailed left and right while looking up to Nolan.

Goldie interjected. "Sure, he is. Now I got two sick pups on my hands."

"He's not mine," Nolan insisted. "It's a long story."

Goldie laughed. "No, it ain't." He grabbed his Scotch glass and lifted it up. "But look here, before we get back to patching up our guy, let's take a moment."

They all lifted their glasses now. They could see that Goldie was glowing in their company. He relished in it.

"Every moment in life is a celebration," he said, looking back and forth between Nolan and McKenzie's eyes. "It is. Because life is a celebration of moments. Even when we've been wronged, or done wrong, or done ourselves wrong, we always have another moment, a moment to do right, a moment to celebrate again. So…" He smiled. "Shall we cheers to this moment?"

"Cheers!" McKenzie rejoiced.

"Cheers," Nolan added.

And the three joined their glasses together.

They were words each of them felt. But to Nolan, they were still just words. And yet he wondered—were they true? Were they true to him?

Nolan sat on the balcony in his jeans, with his shirt off and his torso wrapped in gauze. His bare feet were up, and the glass of Scotch sat in his hand. He was overlooking the barn and the valley from the wide second-story view. The voices of McKenzie and Goldie could be heard behind him in the living room—joking, laughing, looking at old albums of Goldie's youth.

Nolan was quiet. He was listening to the sky and the stars and the happy moments of conversation in between. Goldie talked about his love for Arizona and his wife. How he had built this ranch twenty years ago with her, after a life full of travel and adventures around the world. Nolan felt drained and tired. He was still present, but he tried not to listen to their conversation. It was stirring too much inside, because he had felt like he was just beginning his own life and adventure with *Her*.

He had been around the world alone and had seen and experienced many things, but *Her*—she was an entirely new adventure. And she had been taken away. Now more than ever, Nolan didn't understand why things happened the way they did in life. Why some people come into our lives and just as easily leave. It angered him. But he didn't want that to reflect on McKenzie and the old man. He heard the joy in their voices, laughing and celebrating stories about life together. He had to block out what he felt, as it would just take away from the good things they were feeling.

There was a soft whimper. Nolan looked down from the stars to what lay beside his chair—the dog was there, staring up at him. But the dog did not just gaze, his eyes searched. He searched within Nolan as Nolan had once into him, standing above him with a pistol in his hand. They were both wrapped in gauze and bandages, and they were both here, in this moment, looking into one another once again. Nolan wondered if the dog knew something he did not.

McKenzie and Goldie stepped out to the balcony with an old photo album cradled in her hands. "Look—young Goldie," she said, leaning into Nolan's chair and holding up the album.

Goldie reached over and pointed to a woman. "And there she is…"

Nolan scanned the picture. It was of a happy young man and woman. "*Poem,*" Nolan said softly.

Goldie nodded, then smiled. It was a photo from the early seventies. Her hair, her clothes, and her makeup were simple, but her smile was bright and true. Just like Goldie's.

"She's a babe," McKenzie added, smiling.

Goldie grinned, completely pleased. "You know, young man, I'm very glad you gave it to that ex-husband of hers." Goldie laughed. "If you hadn't, I would have never of met such a lovely woman."

McKenzie smiled. "Good point."

Goldie stood upright and stretched his back, the remainder of his old '82 in hand.

"And now, lady, gentleman, and dog…" Goldie patted the dog beneath them. "Make yourself at home. And thank you for such a lovely moment to celebrate. I think you'll love the Grand Canyon together."

McKenzie's brows furrowed, confused by this. Nolan too.

"Night, Goldie," she said.

"Bonne nuit!" He headed off toward the master bedroom. "Oh, and young man, get a damn name for that dog! We can't keep calling him *Dog*!" Goldie laughed to himself, disappearing into the hall.

Nolan's eyes wandered the valley, trying to understand Goldie's comment. McKenzie quietly sat next to him, wearing one of Goldie's old green flannels over a low white tank top. She clutched her glass of Scotch in both hands and faced Nolan with her knees up on an old wooden rocking chair, the same kind he was slumped in. He was quiet at first, not sure what to say.

"I, uh…I told him I was going to the Grand Canyon with someone," he said. "I didn't tell him who."

"The girl in the picture?"

But Nolan didn't reply.

"She's beautiful… Who is she?"

Nolan thought about it.

What could he say?

He was already holding back what he could.

"She was my fiancée."

"What happened?" She was curious, but attentive and gentle about it.

Nolan sipped his Scotch, keeping his gaze toward the valley and its moon. He thought about his words. And before they left his lips, he realized then that he had never once said them aloud. "She uh…she died."

Nolan tried his best not to move, not to remember it. Not to remember how he'd lost *Her*. How he'd fought alongside *Her* and for *Her*. How she had always been the positive one and how he had done his best to be everything for *Her*. He was trying not to remember that, because he had given everything, what was left of him—and she was still gone.

McKenzie watched as he kept silent, with his eyes low, almost lifeless.

She had never met someone who could radiate such suffering without showing anything at all. She knew from the bar that he was different. She knew that he hid something, some guilt or pain. And she felt it. Now more than ever.

"I'm so sorry," she finally spoke.

"Don't be," he said after a long pause, then finished his Scotch. He remained as still as he could, trying to write off his pain. "Just another sad story with sickness."

It was silent. And yet, without even looking over, Nolan could feel she was somehow moved or hurting by this. He could hear it in her breathing, but he did not want to look.

There were tears in McKenzie's eyes. She carefully reached over and rested her hand atop Nolan's purple knuckles. Her touch jolted him from inside. He turned to see her.

"Or a beautiful story," she said, her eyes looking firmly into his and not turning away. "Where you loved her, and she loved you."

In that moment, he wanted to show her everything.

His tears.

His heart.

His soul.

In that moment, Nolan saw her for who she was. He saw all of her.

Because she was able to see him.

He inhaled deep, looking into her eyes, accented by the bluish moon and the depth of her compassion that looked right back at him. Her hand was holding his, and he was terrified by it. He was terrified by the idea of having to answer anything else she might ask—because he would. He would have to say it.

Until…

His stomach let out a beastly growl.

McKenzie lit up. "Oh my lord! You're hungry!" She laughed, wide-eyed, hearing how painfully loud his stomach grumbled. "Why didn't you say anything?"

Nolan exhaled, then shrugged. "I was bleeding."

She laughed at his unrealized humor, then took her hand from his. "Well, I'm hungry too. I'll find something to make."

She looked into his eyes again. She smiled. He did too. It was a moment of instant relief, even comfort.

McKenzie stood up and took a few steps. They both turned away from one another—'til something came to her. "Hey…"

Nolan turned back.

"It's okay to feel what you feel. It's part of what makes you…*you.*" She said it with confidence, accompanied by a gentle smile, and she walked into the kitchen.

Nolan turned back to the valley.

He thought about this.

He thought about everything.

He looked back up to the stars and inhaled. A sort of calmness came with the cool night air that filled his chest.

For the first time, in the longest time, he felt true peace. Not like before. It was as if he had no worries in his heart or his soul. No pain. No thoughts. Nothing.

Present.

At peace.

And his eyes closed.

INDIAN RUINS

The sun was already high over the Indian ruins. Rays beamed down into the valley, the ranch, and the barn below. Stretches of light streaked across the land while a flock of afternoon clouds floated overhead.

A powerful neigh hurtled down the valley and dispersed, echoing into the sky. It was the stallion. This woke Nolan, who was still slouched in the same chair on the outdoor balcony, but with a stack of blankets across him. He hadn't moved the entire night and must have passed out. He was surprised to have slept into the early afternoon. His body must have needed it, he thought. The stallion's cry woke the dog, too, who stood up below Nolan's chair, looking to the barn. Nolan rubbed his face and looked down to the dog. He hadn't left his side.

Nolan stroked the dog and their eyes connected. He finally felt the soreness in his side and found a small splash of blood dried in the tape and cotton gauze. The white stallion whinnied again, and it railed through the valley. It was a powerful cry, much louder and deeper than most horses. Nolan stood and slowly pulled on his navy and black flannel and denim jacket that rested on the empty deck chair next to him, then he descended the balcony's stone steps to the ranch soil. The dog followed right by his side. His boots crunched the gravel and sand down the long ranch road, but then he slowed in his step. He saw that the barn doors were partly open.

Nolan and the dog entered the barn together and found McKenzie. She was feeding the two horses with apples and carrots in her hands. She turned and smiled.

"You stayed?" He was surprised.

"Thought it'd be easier to check up on ya. Plus, it was late, and we were drinking that old '82."

He was still puzzled, but deep down, he was just happy to see her. McKenzie ran her empty hands through the stallion's long white hair. The brindle horse, who took no measure in being second to his alpha, stood carefully to the side. McKenzie patted the tawny-furred horse and watched happily as he stepped out of the stable and back onto the pasture. Nolan's wound and soreness were catching up now as he slowly walked up to her. The dog was on high alert, seeing the horses, but kept silent and slow as he followed Nolan closely, sniffing the dirt but keeping his eyes on the stallion. The stallion's massive head poked from the stall between Nolan and McKenzie now. They were close again. They took a quick glance at each other's eyes before averting to the stallion, who calmly took carrots from her hand.

Nolan put his fist to the stallion's nose, thinking to himself, almost smiling.

McKenzie palmed some carrots to the stallion, unsure what to say. "How you feeling?" she finally asked, looking up to him.

"Good. You?"

"Good. You heading out today?"

He hadn't thought about it since the church. He nodded, then moved closer to pat the stallion's back. "I gotta get my truck."

"Yeah. I gotta study before my boys get home."

It became quiet again. They both just kept their eyes on the stallion. He was calm, and his hulking upper body blocked them from facing each other, while his head bobbed up and down as he chewed. The stallion was feeding and content, periodically huffing, breaking their silence. They each stroked him from their side, while they both thought about what to say. Neither knew what they were doing here. Nolan was recounting the entire night in his head. McKenzie had thought of it all morning. Inside each of them, there was a small, subdued part that felt the same way—they didn't want to say goodbye yet.

Nolan reached up and rubbed the back of the horse's skull and in between its ears. His hand slid down its thick neck, accidentally grazing McKenzie's soft hand.

She froze, then moved her hand away, up to the neck of the horse. He glanced at her, but she looked away. She reached up carefully and rubbed behind the stallion's ears, keeping closer to her side and far from Nolan's large hand. But each of them felt it. Nolan tried not to over think, and yet…he couldn't help but remember last night when she'd put her hand on his.

He hadn't been touched in a long time. Not like that.

His heart was beating fast. Hers too. And with one accidental glimpse of the other's eyes, they both knew it. Nolan held his eyes to hers. "You wanna ride?"

She didn't look away. "With them?"

"Yeah. You know how?"

"Do I look like some city girl?"

But Nolan didn't stop looking. "You look like *you.*"

And she didn't stop looking back. "I'll take that as a compliment."

"You should," he said, holding his gaze.

"You should rest," she retorted, holding hers.

"I don't want to."

She was looking up into him. He was looking down into her. Neither were petting the horse now and neither were backing down.

"Saddle up," she said.

The air was crisp and the country quiet. The soft hums of insects were the only things to be heard in the plains and its patches of green shrub. It was nothing like the desert here. The hills rolled and perched to small mountains. They stood outside the barn in the corral and McKenzie buttoned up her flannel, then tied her hair back. The brindle horse was already saddled by her, and the dog's focus drifted between her and Nolan, who had carefully placed his saddle on the stallion. The beast huffed and jolted his hooves, but Nolan held the top of his neck then used the back of his other hand to rub him.

"Easy. Easy now."

McKenzie smiled. She didn't waste any time. She jumped right up onto the brindle horse like she had done a thousand times before in her youth. She snatched the reins and straightened them with a commanding tug. The brindle horse kicked its head up, ready to obey. Nolan shot a look discreetly, then continued to buckle the stallion. The beast was hesitant, hearing the stretches of leather against its belly. A sudden whinny rang through the valley, and the dog immediately barked back as if to warn the horse and Nolan.

McKenzie smirked, watching the three of them. "Doing all right over there?"

Nolan shot her another look. The stallion was antsy on its feet, but Nolan was swift to restrain and lock him into the saddle. McKenzie watched closely—she could tell he had also done this many times before—and she wondered where he'd learned. Nolan tightened the last strap and looked the stallion in its wide, dark eye.

His hand slid down the stallion's mouth and pressed his knuckles gently against its nostrils. The stallion snorted, then huffed, taking in the scent of Nolan's skin and realizing there was no food. The stallion yanked its head away, but Nolan returned his hand to its snout. Then, barely moving, his hidden hand drifted behind the stallion's sight and clutched the leather reins, slowly pulling and putting undetectable pressure to its mouth harness.

McKenzie watched closely. Nolan stood firm, keeping his eyes on the horse's ears and movements. The stallion shifted, then attempted to back up, but Nolan's hand was curled in a tight fist, keeping steady pressure on the reins, while the other hand stayed open and close to its nostrils. McKenzie clutched her reins, waiting, watching, intrigued. Nolan was fully listening now—the stallion's lungs were beginning to slow inside the barrel of his massive body. They were becoming rhythmic and acclimated to taking in Nolan's scent. The anxiety of a saddle strapped on its back, along with the pressure of its mouth harness, was starting to be forgotten, and Nolan, firm in his posture and grip, waited.

In an instant, he released the pressure on the reins, grabbed the pommel, and launched his body up onto the saddle before the stallion realized what was even happening. And with a strong tug on the reins, he whipped the stallion's head westward. Nolan became instantly in control. The stallion's blood boiled, and it instinctively wanted to resist, but before he could make a move, Nolan swung him to the pasture gates and booted his rear with a "*hee-yaw!*"

The stallion rocketed them to the ranch gates. The dog barked and bolted after, down to the road entrance. Nolan whipped his head over his shoulder and pointed with an unyielding "*Stay!*"

Hearing Nolan's stern command for the very first time, the dog immediately plopped to its rear, tongue dangling, and watched as he rode off into the pasture.

And all the while, McKenzie was smiling, completely surprised, and completely turned on. She whipped the reins, then jolted her horse. "*Yaw!*" They galloped after, flying past the dog, who looked up from the end of the gates and watched as they disappeared into the plains.

The countryside was empty and serene. The riders were two specks of life amidst the endless plain lands, galloping together through the openness. Thundering hooves, slamming onto the dirt of the earth, were steady and melodic. McKenzie grinned, cracking her reins, keeping herself aligned with Nolan. The cool wind ran through their hair and splashed their faces, keeping their brisk pace and challenging them to keep up. The wind was a flowing river, whipping and whispering between them and the drums of hooves. They rode long and hard and didn't say a word. Both were equal in skill, but different in the way they each handled their horse. Neither had ridden in a long time and each recalled those memories in their lives. But here, on this land, it was different. They were different people, far from their pasts. And the song of wind and hooves was all a reminder of that freedom.

Across the plains, the grass and shrub competed with the dust and dirt of the earth. It was cool and fresh in Northern Arizona, but not quite yet the true taste of spring. The hills and plains were a faded sand-like color, like most of the land, but the mountain pines were lush and resilient, awaiting the first drops of monsoon that would disrupt the land in the following months. Nolan and McKenzie crossed a dirt road and veered around the base of the open valley. It peaked at a ridge of mountainous hills that surrounded the ranch and split the land into two territories.

Nolan looked over his shoulder, catching something beam in the sun.

Atop the small summit, which now blocked them from Goldie's ranch, Nolan could see various slabs of thinly laid stone that were stacked atop the mountain in small formations. It was the Indian ruins. As Nolan eased the stallion, he eyed the hillside leading up to them. From this side of the mountain, he could see a steep but plausible path. Nolan gave the stallion a sharp kick and galloped closer to the base of the summit, searching for an easier path to scale.

McKenzie was just behind him and could see he was inspecting something. As her eyes trailed up the small mountain, she found the secular structure that Nolan peered at. They had been moving competitively this entire ride, and without hesitation, each had displayed prowess on horseback. And while Nolan was one to ponder, McKenzie was one to do. As Nolan circled around the base of the summit trying to understand a way to scale, McKenzie kicked, and the brindle horse launched right up the slope of it, heading up steeply toward the ruins.

Nolan's mouth opened. The way she was headed was difficult, if not dangerous. But McKenzie and the horse rapidly and effortlessly scaled the mountain, maneuvering through jagged rocks and slanted crevices of broken stones. She was nearly at the top before Nolan could even think through his next move. He didn't have much of a choice now. He cracked his reins and headed up after her.

Just before the summit's peak, McKenzie unmounted and carefully walked the brindle horse around heavy and jagged rocks that leaped from the ground like a prehistoric temple. It was becoming too dangerous for their hooves. Nolan was just getting up the hill and followed suit. Here, the gusts of wind were intermittent but powerful. They were loud enough to stop any other sound, including their voices. It rushed from the valley's farms below them, just on the other side of the mountain. McKenzie was ahead of Nolan, exploring the various stone slabs of hand-chiseled sheet rock that created the base for the ancient foundation. There were rocks arranged like tiles, stacked on each other, creating parts of an enclosure.

Nolan was looking at the valley behind him, surveying the wide land of farms that laid just on the other side of the mountain and separated Goldie's ranch from the rest of the valley. This place was vastly different than the desert. He had never imagined that such a town or place existed.

Even in the distance, he could see the flush of pines sprouting from the hills and mountains. He had been in Arizona for a year now, and while he had visited most of the south and the border, he never knew the degree of texture, or country, or life that existed beyond his time in the sand.

"What is this place?" McKenzie called down from atop the structure.

"Goldie said Indian ruins," he yelled up through the wind, then watched her turn and disappear around the highest part of the structure, enclosed by four-foot stacks of sheet rock. Nolan hadn't planned to stop or walk here, but he tied the stallion next to his mate and tromped up the rocks. His hands tucked into his jacket's pockets, and he closed his fists. He had left the Polaroid at the ranch this time, concerned he would make the same mistake twice and lose it on the ride.

He scaled the platform and entered the perimeter of the rocky enclosure. He found McKenzie sitting on a flat, elevated boulder at the highest peak, overlooking the entire valley. Her knees were tucked into her chest, breaking the wind, and her eyes were semi-closed toward the wide expanse and the sun falling into midday. Nolan's boots crunched the gravel, trekking the boulders over to her. He scanned across the ruins through the rays of light and tides of wind. He stood in a space that was as large as Goldie's living room, with four-foot walls around the ledges in what remained. The entire structure sat atop the mountain just behind the ranch and was a natural peak that gave window to both sides of the valley, behind him and ahead of him.

Perhaps these slabs of stone had once been taller and stronger. Perhaps this place had been destroyed by man, or was a home never finished, or maybe even abandoned, Nolan thought. All that was left was its elevated perch, overlooking a three-hundred-and-sixty-degree view of open valley and the range of mountains, hazy in the distance. Nolan walked the stones of a low-rimmed wall, the air rushing his face and beard. He now faced North Star Ranch with McKenzie. The gaps in the stones created twenty feet of distance from each other. The valley was longer than Nolan had realized and stretched to a small mountain range to the north. The ranch was minute from this view, a small, boxed structure in what looked like an abundance of country.

He wondered if the dog had chased them down the old dirt roads or stayed put. He was still injured, like Nolan, and he imagined that the dog would either return to the ranch or perhaps run off again, beginning a new journey and a new life. The thought stuck with him: the dog was a wanderer, too, just like him.

He looked over. McKenzie was still, holding her knees in and looking across the sweeping valley. It was a view she had never seen during her life in Prescott. Nolan watched her a moment. He wondered what she was thinking, or feeling.

He walked over with his hands buried in his pockets, still hiding from the gusts of wind that swirled and swept their hair. The wind rushed McKenzie's face, and her ponytail whipped and flickered with it, but she didn't mind. She was staring off into the valley. After a moment, the winds subsided. They could feel that the other person was near.

She didn't turn when she asked, "Why'd you become a fighter?"

He looked at her. He knew the answer. He wasn't scared of his past or sharing it. To Nolan, he had nothing to lose. But he had also never shared what happened with anyone. Whether it was because no one had ever asked, or he had no one to tell—he didn't talk about *Her*. He had kept it all inside, buried within, for a year.

"When she died," he finally spoke, "it was a way to *feel*." He tried to understand his own words as he spoke them. "It became the only way I'd feel."

McKenzie turned. "You can't punish yourself for what happened."

But he didn't look at her.

"It wasn't your fault."

Nolan thought about it as the wind whispered between them.

"Maybe if I never met her," he said, "it would have never happened." He was trying to figure it out aloud, searching between the stones at his feet and the valley ahead. "Maybe she could of had a different life…"

McKenzie winced. "What kind of bullshit is that?" She stood from the rock and faced him. "You were meant to meet her."

Nolan was as still as the slabs of stone that had laid there for hundreds of years.

"You loved her, right? And she loved you?"

He didn't answer. His eyes averted to the rocks, and his knees locked in defense, trying to keep them from buckling.

"Well, you ever look at it the other way? And think about *why?*"

"All I do is think about *why*," he blurted.

"That's not what I'm saying—" McKenzie wasn't finished. "Look—you think I don't wonder why I got two boys, and they got a shit father? They all said I was gonna be prom queen. I dropped out at sixteen." She stared. "I wasted too much time thinking 'Why me? Why am I a screw up?' And not enough time thinking about what I had to learn."

The winds whisked through the rocks. She was there, looking at him, telling him part of her story, and he was listening, trusting, believing what she had to say.

"My boys are my blessing. I was like any girl, I loved Turner. Even when he left. And when he came back—I loved him again. Then Aiden happened…" she exhaled. "And I stuck with him again." Her eyes were direct and her words firm. "I kept giving him chances, but I never gave *me* one. I gave the wrong ideas one."

Nolan's eyes stayed low, but he hung on to her words.

"I loved him enough, but I didn't love *me* enough." She took a breath. "And that's the problem with you. You gotta stop punishing yourself, Nolan."

He didn't move. He couldn't. But her eyes didn't leave his.

"It's not that you don't feel—you're afraid to."

His eyes pulled from the rocks and could only glance into hers. She was strong, and she was confident, and she stood there, looking into him. Only the wind separated them as they stood, facing each other. Nolan inhaled, tasting the truth in her words, both bitter and filling.

She saw him for who he *was*, and not for the ways he thought he *wasn't*.

And when he looked up again, she was still there, looking at him, patiently waiting for him to speak.

"What would you do…if you were me?" His voice was so low that it could have choked. But McKenzie heard him. She inhaled, then looked out to the valley. He waited, unshielded, vulnerable, ready for what she might say.

She turned back. "I'd go and live the best damn life I could."

In every way, shape, and form, he was astonished.

They were words he had heard before. Words someone had once told him.

They were words he had even once promised.

With all his heart and his soul, they were words he had once shared with the love of his life, and now he was hearing them again, in a different way.

And he was speechless.

The horses trailed behind Nolan and McKenzie, walking them by their leads down the dirt road. They passed many farms and grazing cattle before turning back onto North Star Road. At the end of the long dirt road, just before the ranch, plopped on his rear and waiting at the gates right where they had left him, was the dog, watching and happily wagging his tail.

Neither could help but smile.

"Look at him!" McKenzie laughed. "Has he been there the whole time?"

Nolan nodded. "I reckon so."

He smiled, then gave a sharp whistle. The dog shot up then trotted up to them. He happily circled them and the horses, swinging his tail. Nolan's sore cheekbones rose high and delighted, and he watched the dog follow them with a flailing tongue. McKenzie peeked at Nolan. He did have a nice smile. And for a brief moment, he shared it with her.

Back at the stables, they stripped the leather saddles from the horses. They didn't speak, but there was something stirring amongst their silence, as if they each had more to say, or secretly wanted to share more. McKenzie watched Nolan as he lifted the stallion's heavy saddle off its back. He wasn't a cowboy, not like a few of the rough ones she had grown up with—*but he was something else.*

Nolan looked over and caught her eyes. She resumed unstrapping the brindle horse.

"I gotta get my bags and everything," he said.

She nodded. "Yeah. I gotta get back to studying."

She thought about the amount of work she had to do now, given the two and a half days of studying she had given up.

"Could you take me to the mechanic?" he asked.

"Sure."

He nodded, then headed to the barn's storage to put away the saddle. McKenzie pondered, watching him leave.

The sun was low and the road back to town would take the remainder of the day's light. McKenzie leaned against her Jeep just outside the ranch driveway with her cell phone in hand. She sent a message to Jason asking if he was okay. Then she realized that she had sent the same message earlier that morning and still had no response. She called Jason straight away, but there was no connectivity through her phone. McKenzie realized there must be no reception at all on the ranch. She was worried now—what if they had tried to call and couldn't get through? As if the entire experience of the past two days didn't put more pressure or thoughts in her head, she was feeling guilty now.

Nolan marched down the driveway with his duffle across his shoulder. He was sore and moving slow, and the dog followed him closely. When she saw him, a small smile let up and she got into the Jeep. Nolan threw his bags into the trunk, then looked down at the dog. He debated if he should take him back to Goldie's office or leave him on the ranch. Maybe Goldie had planned on keeping him, he thought. The dog stared up at his eyes, calm, monitoring his every move, wondering what his next command might be. Nolan debated if he could just leave him here, although he did want to say goodbye to the old man and thank him. After everything, it was the right thing to do, and he wanted to do the right thing. For him and the dog.

"All right, come on."

He squatted down to pick him up under his belly and lift him into the back seat of the Jeep. McKenzie smiled as she watched. Nolan got in and returned his own small smile, though, deep down, he was hiding again. She turned the engine, and they began to drive out and down the bumpy old road. The dog pointed his snout between the two from the backseat.

Nolan looked out the window, surveying the ranch for the last time.

McKenzie glanced over. She was looking for a way to start talking but was hesitant. "It's a pretty special place, huh?"

"Yeah, it is." He meant it, but he didn't know what to think. And this time, he didn't know what to feel. McKenzie turned and continued driving. Like earlier on the horses, they didn't speak the rest of the ride. But something had changed.

JUST PASSING
THROUGH

The way into town was a long two-lane road that passed the old farms. On one side of the road stood many new homes, and even housing complexes, where folks could own a ranch and share a part of the land. On the other side was the history of the land—farm homes of a hundred years or more. Nolan stared through the glass, his eyes drifting with the plains while the radio played old rock and roll. McKenzie stared ahead, but her eyes and brows were tight. It wasn't that she was angry or upset—it was the opposite. She was processing everything, and her mind wandered in their silence.

She hadn't felt something for a man in a long time.

Not like this.

She didn't think of Nolan like the others. Everything about him was different. From the melody in his accent, to the way he considered things intensely before he spoke. His wide shoulders and his sharply hidden, faded blue eyes. The way he moved and stood tall and upright at all times, even when he was hurt. He didn't play tricks or say anything he didn't mean. He was different, even in the way he smiled. It was always unexpected, but sincere. In such a short time, she had come to know that he thought more, and felt more, than he would ever actually say. Strangely enough, she felt the very same about herself and her own life. While so many men in her life had judged her, taken advantage of her, or deceived her, she saw Nolan differently. Part of her felt like she already knew him. Part of her felt like she knew nothing about him at all. Part of her instantly trusted him, and another part of her was completely terrified by that.

When they got to the mechanic's, Nolan pulled out his bag and helped the dog get out. He immediately sniffed around and explored the cement lot and the old cars scattered about. Nolan didn't pay him any mind—the dog was just as independent as him. He wasn't going to try and control him, not now, even though he felt responsible for him.

McKenzie reached over and rolled down the passenger window.

They had been avoiding this moment the entire ride. She met with Nolan's eyes one last time.

"Well, that's the most time I ever spent with a stranger," she said, half sarcastic, and the other half just not sure what to even say to him.

"Stranger?" he asked. "I feel like I know you."

They shared unexpected smiles, full of respect and quiet admiration. Neither knew what else to say. Until McKenzie accepted what she had to do next.

"Make the best of it. Okay?"

He considered it. His guilt stung. He had other plans. Nolan looked over to the dog who was investigating the mechanic's garage on his own.

"Think your boys want a dog?"

She laughed. "Oh, I know they do. But I don't."

And with that, they looked into each other's eyes, not knowing what the other felt or really wanted to say.

"Bye, Nolan."

It didn't feel right. But he said it anyway. "Goodbye."

He took a step back from the car, slung his bags over his shoulder, and walked away.

McKenzie drove through town. The same roads, the same stops, the same turns she had taken her entire life. In a strange way, she felt reposed. There was a sense of calming. It was slow and cool like the northern spring air. And now that she was alone, she breathed it in with a sort of relief. She knew, no matter what had happened, she had to continue her goal of finishing school. She had to move forward, or otherwise feel stuck to the circumstances and cards that had been given to her. At this stage in her life, she was no longer going to be a victim of circumstance. Not anymore. She refused it. She was going to be the writer of her own story. For herself and her boys.

But then…then there was this other part of her. Something quiet inside, but speaking. Something aching. It wondered and begged for answers. It begged for clarity. The sun lowered through the clear sky as she drove home, but her heart and her mind were shrouded in clouds. She couldn't remember the last time she had felt *this* way. Part of her felt like she had lost her strength—her defenses were down, and she found herself caring about someone again, like she did for Aiden and Jason.

It was as if Nolan had shaken something in her. Something that energized her, and at the same time, made her feel safe with him. Even through his stoic demeanor, she felt a sense of peace with him. He had this unspoken morality and pain that was somehow truthful to her. His vulnerability was not weak to her—it was a reflection of his integrity. And that was something that comforted her.

She could see that he tried to hide himself, but who he actually was, she felt like she could see. He was his pain and his vulnerability. He was strength and silent compassion. It was all part of who he was, glowing with sensitivity and strength in his spirit. She could also see that he wasn't healed from his loss, but, in her own way, she could relate. Not by her long and tumultuous relationship with Turner, but by the truth that she had never met someone she also felt so deeply about, like she knew Nolan had.

Many a time, she had questioned her own worth. She had spent so much of her life like that, wondering why things happened the way they did. But she remembered something her Gram had taught her and told her time and time again: "Everything happens for a reason, child. Everything."

McKenzie knew in her heart that her time was coming. Inside was this newfound glimmer of hope. It was as bright as the sun in the morning, or the falling sun behind the stupendous pine that had shared her family's home for generations. This glimmer was breathing inside her.

And it would all bring clarity.

It would all bring focus, soon enough.

The white truck sat on the mechanic's lot with the sun's gargantuan eye beaming down on it. It looked strong and proud, and Nolan, who chatted with the mechanic, felt the same way.

"Thanks for gettin' on it, mate," he said.

The mechanic nodded. "You saved me time knowing every issue. You local? I could use a guy like you."

Nolan was surprised by this, but he didn't want to give it a single thought. He shook his head. "Just passing through."

With the windows down, the Ford rumbled through town. The dog was next to him, looking out his window, happily observing from his high perch. His tongue flailed wildly in the wind, tasting the air and scents and changes as they rode. Nolan looked over at him—the dog was a natural. He sat in his seat like a polite old man, simply watching as the world passed him by.

He was a good dog, Nolan thought.

When he pulled up to Goldie's office, he was wondering what might happen to the dog.

Or to Kenzie.

He liked the sound of her name, especially the way she had said it to him. Though, oddly enough, he was afraid to say it. He disregarded the train of thought. He had somewhere to go now. He couldn't look back. He had to stick to the choice he had made. Nolan hopped out, and the dog stood up and watched his every move, waiting for a command.

"All right, come on," Nolan said, and carefully brought his hands toward the dog again, not to scare him. He lifted him from the truck for the last time and lowered him to the ground. The dog eyed the area quickly and looked back up to Nolan, his snout closed and watched Nolan closely.

Nolan could feel it. The dog knew something was about to change.

Goldie carefully unwrapped the last of the dog's dirty bandages and applied some ointment. His wounds were stitched and healing fine. Nolan watched from the back room's doorway. He was trying to make it easier for himself to leave. The dog was chained to a pole as Goldie examined.

"Boy's healing nicely. Glad ya'll took the horses out," he said, then looked up to Nolan. "I appreciate that."

Nolan nodded, watching him work. But for Goldie, that meant a lot more. He hadn't ridden since Poem passed away. It had already been ten years. He loved those horses. As did Poem. The stallion was a big move for him, and although he had known horses his whole life, the stallion was something else. He was a complicated horse, wild, beautiful, and strong. And that was precisely the reason why Goldie had wanted Poem to have him. They were both one-of-a-kind.

All of a sudden, Goldie erupted into a fit of coughs. The dog stopped panting and looked up. His coughs were hoarse and his forehead perspired with them.

"Hey…you all right?" Nolan asked.

Goldie nodded, then walked over to the sink to wash his hands.

Nolan watched him closely. "You sick or something?"

Goldie laughed. "Just an old dog." He turned to Nolan, putting his tools away. "But you know what? You can always teach an old dog new tricks." Goldie grinned.

The crease at the corner of Nolan's his lips raised. "Yeah? There a French saying for that?"

"No, I don't think there is," Goldie said bemusedly.

They shared a smile.

Nolan walked up, adjusted the dog's chain collar, then pat him. "Thanks for everything, old man." He said, then turned for the door.

"Hey…" Goldie said quickly.

They both paused. He knew Nolan was going to leave. He knew he wrestled with a lot. He had felt it the moment he'd met him. He wanted to help, but he also knew that old unspoken code amongst men—that sometimes, all one could do was just show up and reach out. Especially with a man like Nolan.

But it was a shame, Goldie thought. If only this next generation would know what beauty lay within being vulnerable. What honesty and what truth came from that great openness. It was in his age and experience to know, that this was actually the only way to live, in this age now more than ever. If only this new generation would choose to show it more than to hide it, they would find so much more of life's magic. But he knew Nolan was a man who kept his word, no matter the circumstances.

And he knew that Nolan had come to say goodbye. Nolan stood there, waiting for the old man.

"That girl," Goldie said, reflecting on her as he would have his Poem. "She's special, you know."

He was implying something to Nolan, something evident, but true. McKenzie was amazing, and to the old man, he saw them both as they were. But better yet—as they could be.

Nolan thought about it. The old man was right.

"She is…but she ain't going where I'm going."

They each thought about what that may have meant, but, for Goldie, it only meant one thing. "Well, then I hope you find what you're looking for."

Nolan's eyes tried not to wander. Then he disregarded it as he did everything that might show what lay within him. He nodded finally. "See ya, old man," Nolan said.

"See you, young man."

As soon as Nolan left the back room, the dog lurched up and followed him to the end of his chain. Nolan heard the rattle of his chain and turned, putting his hand up. The dog, stared, surprised, but understood what he meant. He didn't know why he was being commanded in this way, but it was a command that he knew, and because he loved Nolan, he was going to obey it. The dog's head jerked, shaking the chain around his neck, staring at the doorway that Nolan was leaving.

"Hey!" Goldie quickly came around the corner and found Nolan halfway out the front door. "What about his name!?"

Nolan smiled. "Call him Dee-Oh-Gee."

"Dee-Oh-Gee?" the old man asked, confused. "Italian?"

Nolan let up an amused smile. "No. American. It means *dog*." And he walked out the door.

Goldie thought about it for a moment. He smiled.

THE NEW ROAD

Nolan swung open the heavy steel door to his truck. This time, his bags were already in the open metal bed. He hopped up the two-foot stepladder, sat inside, and slid his key into the ignition. But then he held it there. His eyes held on his hand and the key, unmoving. After a few seconds, he relaxed back into his seat, and let go of the key. Up the street toward town, he saw that the light was changing. It already seemed dim. But there was something else—something digging at him. He didn't want to think of feelings, thoughts, or even questions. He didn't want anything else in his head now.

He just wanted to go forward.

Whatever it was that stalled him, he shook it off and opened his glove compartment. Inside was his pistol, the Polaroid, and the map. He eyed the black handle of the gun, then carefully took the map out so as to not also pull the Polaroid with it. But when he opened the map, a weathered piece of paper fell to the floor. He picked it up warily, immediately knowing what it was.

It was *their* list. He hesitated, but Nolan couldn't help but read it again, like he had done a thousand times before:

NIAGARA FALLS
CHINATOWN, SAN FRANCISCO
WALK THE GOLDEN GATE BRIDGE
SLEEP IN CENTRAL PARK
MOTORHOME ACROSS THE STATES

~~LOS ANGELES~~
~~YOSEMITE~~
MAKE A FAMILY
SEE THE GRAND CANYON
LIVE THE MOST BEAUTIFUL LIFE

His eyes were alert, intense, as if looking through a magnifying glass, following each sentence on their list. They had created it together, writing one dream after the other by hand, and marking them off as they went. He loved the way she had written things. They had gone so far in such little time and there was something poised and confident about the list. But there was also something about it that haunted him. Because the last three things were all written by her.

He remembered that time—before they'd known she was sick.

They had been in a tent inside a forest, under the largest trees they had ever seen. Their view had been the rounded mount of El Capitan in Yosemite. They'd spent days looking at it, and the trees above, down by the cool stream, and during never-ending summer nights. This town of Prescott, that he had just so happened to cross during the end of his road, exuded something that soothed with familiarity. Perhaps it was the fresh air or the tall trees. Though they weren't the great sequoia he had once discovered with *Her*, they were still stupendous in their density and height. But what amazed him most was that he had never imagined that pine trees could thrive in what he'd thought to be a place mostly in desert. He would have never known that if he hadn't come to this town, he thought. This place was far from any desert. Far from many things he had once known, and yet, it was all familiar.

Nolan took the list and put it in his denim jacket's pocket. He looked once more to his destination on the map, roughly 125 miles above the city of Prescott: *the Grand Canyon.*

He gripped the key again. This time, he turned the engine without hesitation. The Ford roared with a fire inside.

It was time to go.

Nolan left town in a roundabout but scenic way. The white truck blasted

138

up a long, spiraling road through the mountains, shaded by the endless canopy of Northern Arizona pine. The light was piercing through the thickness of the tree-lined road, and glimmering shards of sun struck the Ford's chipped white hood. The windows were down, and wind was flowing. Nolan rode in a calm, meditative-like state. The place he liked to be. Everything forward, everything moving, nothing behind him, keeping his thoughts and his pondering at bay, focusing solely on the road ahead.

The sharp light gleamed into the truck over and over again. Nolan looked to the open passenger's window, to where the sun repeatedly struck. The flash of a memory crossed his mind, looking at that seat next to him. The light beamed between a blanket of thick trees and kissed the faded cushion seat, again and again.

She used to sit here.

She had always been there.

But he blocked any further thought as best he could and put his eyes back on the road. To the truck's passenger side, and following him along the stretch of forestry uphill road, something beamed at Nolan. It had an unmistakable glow that radiated between the rapidly moving trees outside the window. His eyes narrowed and focused as the light struck him over and over again. The Ford thundered up the road, and Nolan leaned forward, escaping a beam of light, finally getting a better view into the woods. Beyond the shadowy trunks of countless pines, he could see the glassiness of a lake. His brows furrowed—he was surprised that a lake of this size could even be possible in this state. He was far from the desert, his last and final home, and he couldn't remember the last time he had seen a body of water as large as this. Maybe the last time was the ocean, he thought. Maybe the last time was with *Her.*

Just ahead, there was a turn off. "Goldwater Lake," the sign said.

He thought about it. What would one more moment hurt? The truck was riding hard and fast, and the light from the sun reflected and glistened on the lake, striking him over and over again. Right then, Nolan made a split-second decision.

He told himself he had nothing more to lose.

The lake was sparkling and calm. The sun was perched high in a bed of clouds that drifted apart from one another, and the same light that had pierced through the truck, now painted the stillness of the water.

There wasn't a soul in sight, only Nolan, who stood at the end of a long wooden dock that jutted out into the body of water. To his right and to his left, he could see either side of the lake's wide oval shape, and he was there, in the middle of it.

The place was serene, but there was a sort of humming and ringing that emerged between his ears. It was a reverberant energy that one could hear and even feel in a place like this, but was often indescribable. It was an ominous resonance that very few in this day and age would ever understand, let alone ever truly remember.

It was the sound of silence.

If you listened closely, this reverberation would whisper and stir within your ears, your body, your mind, and your entire soul. It was a sound that could be heard in the oldest of churches. In the darkest of nights. It made you aware of who you were, and reminded you of both of your physical presence, as well as your emotional presence, and view of the world—whatever that may be.

Nolan felt it, that ever-evolving quiet awareness. It was an aura surrounding him, touching him, making him feel ever so aware of where he was and what he was thinking. He hunched over the fence at the end of the wooden dock. The only thing to share the vibration of silence was his own breath. A flock of birds soared, high and in the distance, but they, too, were silent. He realized then, inside his denim and clutched in his hand, was the list. He felt the folded corners of the aged paper between his thumb and index finger. The folds made it easier to know that it was there with him. He imagined the words, reading them in his mind. Why would he ever be given such an experience? To meet someone like *Her* and to lose her like this? Was he being punished for something? A mistake in his life he had overlooked?

She had never done anything to deserve this. He had never seen *Her* do wrong—it just hadn't been in her nature. She was the opposite of selfish or self-centered. She had never lied, she had never misled, and she had never hurt anyone. She was full of truth and life and optimism. And in every way, she had helped him feel complete. He was a better person because of *Her*.

So, it had to be him. Losing her had to be punishment.

But why?

Nolan carefully removed the list from his pocket. It was folded, waiting for him to open it again. He stared down at both of his hands, holding each weathered corner. And as he leaned over the dock, he saw below the reflection of a man. The water was as still as a mirror, reflecting back at him and the person he had become.

It angered him. It saddened him. And it frustrated him.

Then he thought of *Her*.

What would *she* want?

What would *she* expect of him now?

He thought about how disappointed she must be, seeing how he'd crumbled after her death. How he still crumbled, at the whim of her memory. The strength of his body was nothing compared to the strength of his weakness. So, what was the point now? What did any of it matter?

He had been given his chance—how could he possibly have another? The love of his life had been gifted to him, and then she had been ripped away.

But even these were just his thoughts.

She had never thought like this, or his way.

He remembered how compassionate and how patient *She* had been. Just by her being *Her*, she had nurtured how he thought, how he felt, how he lived.

It had been her undying hope. It had been her smile. It had been who she was deep down and who she wanted to be, for herself and others. In every sense, she had radiated. What would she want him to do? What would she tell him?

Nolan stopped his thoughts. Below him was that man, staring back at him. The two were still, with the small paper folded in their hands. Shards of light streaked across the glossy surface, the only thing to remind him that he was looking at his own reflection.

He inhaled deep.

In a single moment, suspended between thought and clarity, he felt something inside tell him to make a choice.

He let go.

The list fluttered. It patted the lake's surface with a soft tap, radiating small ripples around it that expanded and reached out. The list's folded corners weighed it down until the last dry crevice was submerged into the body of water. It sunk, long and slowly into darkness while Nolan watched.

Then it all became still again, and all that was left was the reflection of Nolan: standing above himself, reflected below himself—showing what was left of himself.

He had made a choice.

The lights of downtown were bright and lively. The people were ecstatic for Saturday night, and everyone was headed to their favorite restaurant or bar on the Row. It was mostly locals who went out on Saturday night, but through word of mouth, many folks from the bigger cities and from every corner of the country had somehow heard about this small western town, a preserved painting in the history of time.

As people laughed and enjoyed their stroll, McKenzie walked through them, her head low and her hands stuffed into her thin black duster jacket. She wore high-heeled boots that clacked loudly and made her tall and powerful behind the bar. Underneath her duster were more revealing clothes—a low black tank top and tight black skinny jeans that accentuated her curves. She walked alone, thinking to herself about all that she had experienced in the past two days. It was a whirlwind to process, and this brief time alone was her last moment before getting back to her hustle and her school plan.

McKenzie had parked her car up the street from the bar, giving her some time and space to think. She would often park in the neighborhoods away from the bar. This made it easier to avoid locals or customers that she didn't want to deal with after a long night. And she never wanted her customers to know what car she had and where she parked. Especially on a night like tonight. More than anything, she didn't want Turner to know she was working. Her goal was to get in, get the job done, and get back to studying. Tomorrow was Sunday and the last opportunity she had at some sort of peace of mind before her final tests would begin and she would have to get the boys. She needed clarity to get through whatever was to come next. When she came to the crossroads of the courthouse, Whiskey Row, and the path to church, she stopped.

She considered which direction to go.

She decided to stop by the church before work. If she was going to make any prayers for all that was to come, it should be tonight. A few older locals were inside the dimly lit church, praying for themselves and their families as the weekend evening had now begun. McKenzie, as always, took time to pray for her boys. Earlier in the day, she had heard from Aiden, who was terribly bored and feeling stuck at Gram's. He wanted to be out and about or closer to town with his friends like Jason had been the night he'd arrived at Gram's. She was annoyed that Jason was in and out of Gram's, escaping at a whim on his bike. No one could control him. But she couldn't overthink it now—she needed to get through all of this. She thanked Aiden for helping her with this favor—it meant a lot to her, and one day he'd know why.

"If I see a javelina at Gram's, can I shoot it?" he'd asked jokingly.

"Sure, Aiden. Spear it, if you want," she'd joked back.

Aiden was always happy to make his mom laugh—he knew she loved it when he got clever, especially when trying to make her smile. He had done this since he was a boy, with his bright, wide eyes and his big, dimpled smile, every time he got an idea. It always meant the world to her.

Jason had been there while McKenzie was on the phone with Aiden, but, of course, he had refused to speak with her, which she'd expected. She knew that once she finished the rest of her studying this week, she would be prepared for all that the week could bring. And that also meant deciding if she had to sell Gram's house or not. With Mom's rehab bills, she was constantly fighting to make ends meet. And the choice between losing Gram's house or losing Mom's rehab were two things she was fighting not to choose from.

She had to make it work.

Right before she got to church, she'd told Aiden she was going to pray and couldn't talk to Gram. Really, she just knew Gram would hear her troubled voice and figure her out in a second. McKenzie would instantly want to confess and tell her all that had been going on in the past two days. But she was trying to stay focused and clear. The idea of selling her family's home, getting through the week, thinking about Jason, and what she had experienced with Nolan, was a whirlwind of thoughts and feeling that she didn't yet understand.

And in her mind, she had little time to.

Yet, one thing was for sure, whatever was going to happen next, she knew she had to be strong. And still, she felt a sort of sadness about what had happened with Nolan. And it was solely because she felt like so much *had* happened, just in those two days alone. There was excitement, respect, truth. She was challenged, she was intrigued, and still…she was wondering.

It was as if there hadn't been enough time with him. As if she wanted more. Despite what feelings stirred within, things she had not felt in the longest of time, there was a peculiar feeling that even made her sad, because deep down, she felt like she had made a friend in Nolan. A true friend.

Someone she cared about and who cared about her.

Now he was gone. Maybe that was the hardest part. But maybe that was the most important part too.

"Everything happens for a reason."

That's exactly what Gram would say in a time like this. Only time and truth would tell. So, she held fast to her faith and her hope—her unbeatable gift that she always had and would never change.

She was just happy to have met him.

And so she prayed for him too. She wondered how far he was now and what he might be thinking. And in her own way, she wondered if she had helped him with his heart. Or maybe, he was meant to help hers? She barely knew him, but she trusted him. She had barely spent time with him and yet she had felt things that made her feel alive.

McKenzie had always known that people came and went throughout life.

Some people came for a moment. Some people stayed for a minute. Some stayed for a lifetime. Others, we wished we'd never met. But then there were those special ones, the ones who showed us a part of ourselves that we'd never seen, or perhaps, hadn't seen in a long time. They showed us our truth, our hearts, and the best of us, buried deep within our walls and fears.

Those special people show us who we really are.

Whatever it was they'd experienced together, she was grateful for it. She knew she would understand this experience more in the time to come, and that coming back to church tonight had brought her back to a place of peace and acceptance. She had to accept goodbye and let go, like she had done so many times before.

Even though she didn't want to. Even though she didn't choose to.

She had to.

But this time—she felt stronger. She felt ready. And she was just grateful that it had happened.

And so, she ended her prayers on Nolan, praying he would find his peace and clarity too.

Then she stood up, crossed her heart, and walked out the door.

THE STARLET & THE SHERIFF

McKenzie stepped out into the cold night. It was a short walk to the bar through the courthouse plaza, but it was already freezing to her. Under her thin duster, she was underdressed for everything but the bar. She unbuttoned her black flannel and re-tucked it into her jeans that gripped her strong thighs tightly. She was ready to get in there and get the job done.

Her heels clacked, walking down the aisles of glowing streetlamps along the church's brick walls.

But then she stopped.

She saw something that completely surprised her.

She wasn't even sure at first what she was looking at. But when she took a moment to relax her eyes in the cold air, she knew.

It was *Him*.

Against a stone wall, under a glowing streetlamp in front of the church, Nolan was waiting.

His hands were in his pockets and, when he saw her, he pushed himself up from the wall, straightening his sore spine.

She was shocked. Her entire chest and stomach rushed her.

"I saw your Jeep," he said.

They both stood there. She didn't know what to say, and neither did he. But he was here, standing in front of her. Nolan's piercing eyes searched hers, and even with thirty feet between them, he could see the feelings in her eyes. He didn't know what to say—he was just happy, seeing her again.

And he knew, just looking at her, he'd made the right decision.

"You going to work?" he finally asked.

"I...haven't decided," she said, confusedly, already forgetting how she'd planned the rest of her evening.

Nolan held his eyes on her, his hands still in his pockets. She was doing the same.

"I'd like to take a walk with you," he said.

"I'll take that as a compliment," she said.

"You should."

They each stared, trying to hide their smiles.

But they couldn't.

McKenzie finally laughed and walked up to join him by his side. They knew they didn't need to hide anything. Not anymore.

They walked together, Nolan with his hands in his pockets and McKenzie with her arms across her chest. They each smiled, sneaking anticipatory looks at one another. Even though she was dressed for work, putting a little more of herself out there as she did when she worked the bar, she could just as easily be dressed to go out.

"You done any studying?" he teased.

"Are you still bleeding?" she hit back.

They were happy to poke fun at one another and Nolan's smile—his true smile—was starting to come out. At the same time, so were McKenzie's eyes—her true eyes. The ones she'd had when she was a little girl—worry free, wondrous, and curious again.

And all her eyes wanted to do was look at him.

The night sky was black, and a bed of glistening stars hung just above their heads. The old shops in town were beginning to close, as most of them did after sundown. Down the long stretch of sidewalk and storefronts, warm light emanated from within, reminding McKenzie that she was freezing.

"Hey," Nolan said, seeing that she was trying to keep herself warm. "Take this." He took off his denim jacket, but she shook her head and stopped in front of a warmly lit store window. It had an old '60s working-woman's green dress, old brooches, and a typewriter on display. She gave him a quick grin. "I got a better idea." Then she practically ran inside.

Nolan looked up at a big wooden sign that said, *Local Antiques*. He slung his jacket back on and followed her in.

It was a museum of old things, trinkets, and antiquity of the past. Photographs of forgotten people, times, and sentimental abandonments. There were vintage clothes, some ridiculous, some interesting, and could be found everywhere. Nolan stepped in, and an older woman with wild, curly hair looked up to him. "We'll be closing soon."

"All right," he said, walking further. He moved through the aisles and bookshelves stacked ceiling high with various things. He came across a huge glass and oak cabinet with hundreds of old-timey photos. Every racial heritage and every type of family, spanning decades, were on display. He liked the old family portraits. Some of them must have been a hundred years old, pictures and portraits of men, women, and children, some in western garb, others in Victorian dresses. Their postures, poised, and straight. Nolan shifted in his boots, reminded of his posture and the sore gash at his side.

He wondered where their journey in life had taken them and how these photos had even ended up here. There were so many faces behind the glass from many decades and eras. He wondered what life had been like then and how different it must be now. Or maybe it wasn't much different at all, as all of life was still full of intricacy and challenges that men and women faced.

"*Boo!*" McKenzie lurched forward with a chipped '60s Easter Bunny mask on her face. It wasn't cute.

"Ahhh?" he said, not even flinching except for a small smile.

"What? You ain't scared of nothing!?"

"Not that."

She grinned. "I haven't been in here for years," she said happily. "They got all sorts of old costumes and dresses."

She dug through nearby racks, amazed by the different generations of clothing. Nolan watched her as she excitedly combed through the racks. But then she stopped suddenly, her eyes locked onto something. It was wedged between two wooden crates full of clothing.

Nolan peered over.

"What's that?"

She pulled out a faded and worn navy hat with the emblem of an "A" on it.

"It's an old U of A hat," she said, carefully feeling it. "University of Arizona. A lot of my friends went after high school," she said, touching the old stitching and fading fabric. It was like a flash, remembering that old dream. Something she had once believed in, over fifteen years ago before she met Turner. McKenzie had always dreamed more than she reminisced, but every once in a while, she would see something that reminded her of the cards life dealt her. Things that reminded her of all that she had been through. A simple sign like this that would find her and rush up her entire body with longing. McKenzie was hopeful and resilient through and through, down to her soul, but, every once in a while, that deep hurt from the past crept up on her and made her question her own worth.

She was a good person, but was she good enough for the things she'd always wanted?

"You can go too," Nolan said softly. "After your finals."

Her back was to him. She felt insecure, even vulnerable, but he still made her smile. His support meant more to her than either of them realized in that moment.

Nolan watched as she carefully put the hat back.

"Come on," she said, changing the subject. "Let's find me a warm coat and you a pretty dress!" Then she took off, rushing happily through the store.

"Sure…if you can find my size," Nolan joked.

She laughed, already zipping around the corner and into the next room. "Come on!"

Nolan smiled to himself. He admired her charisma. It was full of youth. But her hesitation hadn't gone unnoticed. He'd seen how delicate she'd been with the hat, and he could feel that she was reminiscing. He knew the look. He knew the sounds. It was a color of melancholy he knew all too well. It reminded him of himself.

He thought then that if he could do something to cheer her up, even for a single second, he would do it.

McKenzie was in the other room shuffling through coats. She found old hotshot fire jackets, wool shawls, used denim, and then, a long, soft, purple fur coat.

"Oh lord," she said, snatching it up and throwing it on.

She could pass for a street hustler or an actor from the Golden Age of Hollywood. McKenzie threw the coat over her shoulders like the old movie stars did, hamming it up with a flick of her chin to the ceiling.

"Howdy, ma'am," a terrible Texan-American-Australian accent bellowed from behind.

McKenzie turned.

Nolan was standing in the doorway wearing a gigantic cowboy hat. It barely let him fit through the doorway. It was as wide as his shoulders and his hands were on his hips, with his elbows bowing out.

"My lord. Is that how cowboys sound?" She snickered.

"Ain't it?"

"Not where I'm from!" She laughed.

"Well, ma'am, there's a new sheriff in town." He took a big boot-swinging step. "And I gots ta tell you…you is under arrest."

"Oh, Mr. Sheriff Big Head? Why so?"

She stepped forward, tugging her purple coat theatrically over her shoulder. Her hips swung like a classic performer taking stage, front and center.

Nolan pointed to her scarf.

"Well, I see you done kilt a purple buffalo. Them there be the rarest buffalos in the world," he said, confidently butchering an American cowboy's accent and tilting up the brim of his hat, bowing it out like the wingspan of an eagle.

She sauntered up closer.

"Oh, Sheriff darling, you can't blame me. See, if I had it my way, I woulda killed me a pink buffalo instead."

He grinned. She adjusted the brim of his gigantic hat. Between their small smiles and close distance, their eyes connected.

It was only a moment, then she grabbed his hand and ran.

"You're much too underdressed! Come on!"

Nolan's eyes widened. It was the second time she touched him.

His abdomen squeezed as she yanked and ran him through the store.

Her purple coat bobbed up and down on her shoulders as she raced and laughed.

"Hurry, Sheriff!"

Nolan quickly grabbed the brim of his enormous hat to keep it from falling.

"We're almost closed!" The shopkeeper popped around the corner.

"Thank you, darling! We're almost done!" McKenzie shouted back, then tugged Nolan into what appeared to be "The Cowboy" section. There were round tables and hooks displaying all sorts of spurs, boots, and vests, some of them appearing to be truly vintage, and others looking straight out of a prime 1980s Nashville country concert.

"Now here we are," she said with a sly smile.

To McKenzie's delight, everything she eyed was covered in rhinestones.

"Oh man…" Nolan said, a sudden lump in his throat.

"What? Is you or is you not a cowboy, Mr. Sheriff Big Head?"

"All right. Do your worst," he said with an unconvincing laugh.

"Well, what we need for you is a purple saddle, or—how about this!?"

She whipped out a pair of studded leather chaps.

"Chaps?" he asked.

She turned them around. "Assless," she excitedly corrected.

"Far too cold, ma'am." He smiled.

"I reckon so!" she said and kept digging into the bins.

"But this," Nolan grabbed an old yellow hardhat, "ought to keep you safe on a purple saddle or a pink buffalo."

"Oh, yes, and it matches so well," she said, dripping with sarcasm. "But you, Sheriff, darling, are going to need this!"

She pulled out a tight, yellow, rhinestone-covered vest with a bright gold sheriff's badge pinned on it.

His eyes widened.

She carefully slung it around his arms, laying it on top of his denim jacket.

"Would you look at that!" She turned him to face a tall wooden mirror. The rhinestones shimmered in the overhead lights.

Nolan looked horrified.

"You look so proud," she insisted.

"We look like the Village People," he replied.

She sparkled, laughing, then immediately turned and started digging for more. "Oh! A pink scarf to match!" McKenzie beamed, grabbing a long, pink-feathered scarf and twirling it on. Nolan stood there a moment, watching her, smiling.

Nolan couldn't help but want to compete now. He looked through an assortment of wacky, filthy, and completely ridiculous boots. They were all completely worn out or completely impractical, some with tassels and feathers attached to the leather. It wasn't long before he found the worst yet: a set of large, yellow, rhinestone-covered boots with various moon and star charms on them.

"Oh man," he said, feeling his stomach clench.

"Find something, Sheriff?"

"Nope. Not yet," he said, keeping his back to her so she wouldn't see the boots.

"Well, you best find me a purple saddle or something with more stones on it, Sheriff. I don't want us to be underdressed."

"Of course, ma'am. Right away, ma'am." He shook his head and they kept digging with their backs to each other.

Nolan peeked over to her, then smiled—this was fun.

"These!" she shouted. McKenzie swung around, smiling brightly, and holding a pair of pink, snakeskin cowboy boots.

She dangled them with a sly grin. Nolan smiled, too, until he realized they weren't for her. His proper Australian accent came right out.

"Oh, I'm not wearing those."

"But, Sheriff, this is a formal event."

"They're, uh, they're not even my size!"

"You're concerned about *that*?" she poked.

"You try them on!"

"Darling, they're not purple—it just wouldn't work."

Nolan finally laughed, looking at her bright smile. She swung back around and looked through another bookshelf of more outrageous boots. It became quiet a moment before she heard his voice again.

"Kenzie…"

She stopped.

It was the first time he had said her name. She had told Goldie what her friends and family called her, but to hear him say it, stopped her cold.

When she turned, she saw that his eyes were low.

"Can I ask you a serious question?"

She froze, a rush hitting her and tightening her throat. She remembered the last time he had asked her that. It had been about Turner and how she could get with a guy like him. She timidly adjusted her hard hat, sliding it back on her head. He slowly stepped closer to her, fixing his own hat.

He was debating how to ask her.

"Yeah?" she replied, unknowingly holding her breath.

He gathered his thoughts, then looked her in her eyes.

Nolan slowly pulled out a bright, silvery badge that shined with the words "Junior Sheriff."

"Would you be my deputy?"

Then his smile came.

Her lips curled cheek to cheek, then her movie-actress voice returned.

"Oh, Mr. Sheriff Big Head! Do handcuffs come with it?"

Nolan grinned, looking down to her. She tipped her yellow construction hat, then tilted her head up with a glowing smile.

"Hey! You two!"

They looked over. It was the shopkeeper. "The YMCA is closing!"

McKenzie laughed. "How much for the whole shebang?

"What? For what?" Nolan asked, nervous.

She looked Nolan up and down, then shouted back to the keeper. "For everything, darling!"

The shopkeeper smiled. "Come on down, let's get ya a deal."

"Great!" McKenzie zipped down the hall toward the entrance.

Nolan stood there, alone in the big room. "Shit," he said under his breath. He didn't know what to think, but he knew McKenzie was ballsy enough to want to do this. But then he smiled and looked to the other room. An idea came.

McKenzie was leaning over the counter in her new purple fur coat and pink feathered scarf. She set the construction worker hat to the side as she explained to the shopkeeper. "Sorry for the fashion show. It got so cold, I was hoping to get a coat."

The shopkeeper smiled. "Well, you sure found somethin'. You got cards? I closed the register already."

"Oh, all I got is cash…" McKenzie said, holding some loose bills.

"That's fine! We don't need any of it," Nolan said, emerging from the other room and stepping to the register, trying to scooch his big arm out of the yellow rhinestone vest.

"Um, we need *all* of it," McKenzie interrupted and stopped him.

Nolan gawked. He would never be caught dead wearing any of this.

"Well, I don't have any cards. Just cash," he said, his last chance at escaping.

The shopkeeper tilted her head. "You two headed to a party or something?"

McKenzie smiled. "Why, ya know of any?"

"Tell ya what. Ya'll just go and have a good time."

"Are you kidding!?" McKenzie shouted.

"What? Why?" Nolan almost flinched.

"Oh, darling!" McKenzie counted her small bills and handed them over. "At least take something!"

"No, no—you just go and have a good time and let me get home to my man."

"Deal." McKenzie grinned, then looked to Nolan.

He was dumbfounded, standing there like a rock in a gigantic cowboy hat.

"Oh, come on, Sheriff. You look fabulous."

She straightened out his rhinestone jacket, then strutted her way out the exit.

"Shit," Nolan said again under his breath. He couldn't remember the last time he felt nervous about being embarrassed.

The shopkeeper looked Nolan up and down. She smiled. "Good luck…Mr. Sheriff Big Head."

Nolan looked at her, lightening up a little bit. It was too late. He had to commit. He dropped a $100 on the table and tipped the massive-brimmed hat.

"Ma'am."

McKenzie laughed and pointed as Nolan struggled to fit out the doorway. The brim of the hat curved and lodged between the frame, causing Nolan to stop in his tracks. McKenzie burst with laughter again and pulled him out by his denim's wool collar. He wanted to shake his head, but found that his noggin' would just be sloshing around the loose-fitting crown. She covered her mouth, trying to reel herself in, but her eyes were bright and she was enjoying herself too much. Nolan sighed as they stood there under the doorway together, sharing the cold night air while McKenzie glowed with delight. Nolan couldn't help but smile, although he tried.

"Are you happy?" he finally asked, tilting up the ridiculously large hat.

"I reckon! Ain't you?" She laughed.

He did too. But then a thought came across him. "I got you something."

Her lips curled. "Giving me your badge already, Sheriff?"

He looked her up and down, then from his back jean pocket, he slowly tugged at something. She watched, but her grin started to fade when she saw what it was.

The University of Arizona hat.

"Just in case you go. You got something to wear."

McKenzie froze, before she reached out and took it delicately. Her hands and eyes were slow, looking down at the old emblem "A." Her thumbs skated across the stitching of the letter. The fabric was old…and she adored it.

She lifted it, put it on, and instantly smiled. It was too big for her head, and there was something cute about that, to the both of them.

She looked up and tilted the hat's brim to find his eyes. "Now we both have big hats," she said quietly.

They were close in the doorway. Closer than he'd realized. It felt like the first of many things for him, all at once, and he was becoming pensive.

And yet, Nolan's smile—his true smile—returned. She was just happy, here, with him, and he could feel it.

She finally spoke for the two of them. "Let's get a drink."

His eyes narrowed, and his cheekbones raised again with his small smile. Kenzie noticed something—it was a small thing he did when he was happy or in a good place: his eyes would smile. Whatever his expressions were, they were always small and true—an infinitesimal glimmer or the slightest shift of his eyes would tell her how he felt.

Neither of them knew what they were doing. Neither of them understood their feelings. In that moment, they were just *feeling*—without any other thoughts or complications.

Until Nolan realized something horrible.

She wanted them to wear these ridiculous outfits.

"Right now?" he asked.

"Yeah, right now." And she took off up the street, her black boots and bare legs swinging out of her skirt, wearing her new oversized, pink feathered scarf and large baseball cap.

"Like this? You're kidding!" he said, looking down at the rhinestone jacket sparkling across his chest.

She looked back with a clever grin.

"Do I look like I'm kidding, Sheriff?" She tossed one side of the pink scarf over her shoulder.

Nolan inhaled. He couldn't think of an Aussie curse that would accurately express his concern for the embarrassment he was about to suffer.

She marched back then stood in the middle of the street. "What? Are you shy or something?" But he didn't know what to say now.

McKenzie sauntered back over to him in the doorway and confidently fixed his hat so it was straight and proper as a cowboy's would be, except that it was gigantic, and stood out like a giant sore thumb.

He didn't have to imagine how it looked.

Oh, he knew.

Nolan tried to shake his head, but the massive hat wobbled.

"I shoulda kept the helmet," she said. "I'm worried you'll headbutt me."

Nolan finally laughed. He tried to shake his head again, but the hat wobbled like a loose umbrella top. She reached up and straightened it for him. Her eyes widened, and she tilted her head, mocking him with her little sly grin.

"You need to lighten up, Sheriff!"

Nolan inhaled again, preparing, the way he would before entering a ring to fight.

156

She was right.

And he couldn't remember the last time he had actually felt embarrassed. Or really, the last time he had felt enough about the world to give a damn.

"Well? Whaddya got to lose?" she asked, staring up into his eyes and smiling.

He laughed under his breath, thinking of her question. "Nothin'," he said.

FAR FROM FOLSOM

Whiskey Row was bursting. People flew in and out of bars, some drunk, some happy—some happier and drunker than drunk. It was an easy place to find a good time or a fist fight. During this time of year, the Row shared waves of locals, college students, cowboys, tourists, and families who just wanted a fun night out. It was a melting pot of change, of the past, the present, and every walk of life.

And then there was Nolan and McKenzie, coming down the street, looking like a parade without the parade.

Nolan wore his massive cowboy hat, which could be seen in the crowd from every direction, and his yellow rhinestone jacket, beaming so bright that he competed with the streetlamps. On both sides of the busy block, cars slowed down in confusion. McKenzie grinned cheek to cheek, wearing her pink scarf, purple fur coat, and the large vintage University of Arizona ball cap with its low brim perched above her eyes. At that very moment, they were the two craziest-looking people in town.

People stopped and gawked at Nolan, while McKenzie simply smiled and cracked a joke to egg it on. Anything their audience said about Nolan, McKenzie happily amplified with bright eyes and her own punchlines. And when he tried to ignore the attention or evade eye contact, McKenzie would whip her feather scarf across Nolan's face.

"You enjoying yourself?" Nolan asked, the fake feathers splashing across his beard and bruises, smelling of old perfume.

"Maybe." She grinned.

"Won't we run into somebody you know?" he asked, hesitantly.

"What do you mean?" She looked over. "I know everybody."

"Great." He laughed.

Just ahead and blaring out into the streets from a bar, was live rock and roll. The sign atop the establishment read, *Far From Folsom*.

"Drinks on me, Sheriff."

And she hooked her arm into his and dragged him past a long line of people, who all stared, snickered, or commented as they walked on by. Nolan just kept his mouth shut.

Big Pete, the bouncer, was at the end of the line and saw them coming. He was a large Black man wearing a light brown flannel, denim jeans, superbly polished gray cowboy boots, and the biggest smile you ever did see.

"Mac, what the hell is you wearing!?" he shouted through his grand smile, spanning cheek to cheek. Nearly the entire line turned to look at Nolan.

"What the hell is *he* wearing!?" Big Pete shouted again.

"What, this ol' thing?" McKenzie tilted on her toes to kiss him on his happy cheek, then whipped her scarf across his face.

"What you up to, woman? Ain't you got work?" he asked with his never-ending smile.

"I decided not tonight, Pete. But I also decided we gotta getcha something like this for your own."

"I think you're right, Mac. I'm liking this fit!" He said, looking her up and down.

Nolan tried to shake his head, but was quickly reminded he couldn't, which didn't help his monotone response: "You can have mine, mate."

"Mwah, Pete!" She blew him a kiss, then dragged Nolan into the bar.

They had barely made it through the front door, Nolan's hat was already caught pushing against some lady's head.

"Sorry, uh, ma'am," he said, trying to be a good sport about it. McKenzie laughed, wildly entertained. The two stood there, barely a foot past the doorway.

It looked like a moment in an old desperado film, when the sheriff stepped into the doors of an establishment—and everyone turned to look. But there Nolan was, standing with his hands tucked in his denim, rhinestones beaming, uncomfortable, and nowhere near looking the part.

McKenzie looked back at all the people and scoffed. "Well shit, it's crowded."

"There is no way we're getting to the bar," said Nolan.

McKenzie looked at him, then to the guy behind the bar. "Billy!"

His light brown hair was slicked back, with his sleeves rolled up high, and black suspenders pressed tightly against his white collared shirt. He was spinning a mixer when he caught her.

"Mac!? What the hell?" he yelled out, scanning her getup, then the tree-trunk of a man in an oversized cowboy hat next to her.

"It's me! And I brought the sheriff!"

"Fuckin' hell you did! Everybody *move*! That Sheriff there deserves a drink!"

And just like that, the locals, tourists, cowboys, cowgirls, and patrons all parted, as Nolan, the sheriff, and McKenzie, the starlet, strolled right up to the bar. She pulled Nolan by the arm into a corner where there was just enough room for the two of them and his hat. The place was full of smiles, and the man on stage wailed that good rock and roll. The place couldn't have been louder or happier.

Billy ran up with a whiskey neat already in hand. McKenzie happily lashed him with her scarf.

"Thank you, baby," she said.

"What are you doing, Mac?" He laughed, then threw down an extra coaster for Nolan.

"We thought we'd hit the town, since we got alls dressed up."

"Howdy," Nolan said, tapping his index finger to the roof of the massive brim, which could barely move. That was the only move he could make with this monument on his head.

"Fuckin' hell! He's a dangerous man wearing that! She put you up to this, Sheriff?"

Not knowing what he could say, but knowing he couldn't shake his head, Nolan put his palms up.

"She's hard to resist, huh?"

"I didn't have a choice."

"Ha! But you ain't working, Mac?"

"Wayne's on the schedule. He could use the extra bucks. Plus, the sheriff's taking me out tonight."

"Well, alright then. What can I get you, Sheriff?"

"Same as her."

"Whiskey neat, coming up!" he called, running down the bar.

McKenzie turned. "He used to work next door with me. His kid sis was in rehab. I helped them a bit since Mom's there too. Just tried to show up for them, you know?"

"Do you see your mother?" Nolan asked.

"She doesn't want to see me."

"Why not?" he asked, noticing her shift in the barstool.

"I kicked her out of Gram's. Didn't want the boys having that in their lives."

Nolan nodded. The music was rocking in the next room, but even through all the people and noise, their space felt intimate. In a room full of voices, it felt like only they were talking.

"Every once in a while, I go take a peek at her when I go to pay the bill."

Nolan studied her. "You pay her bills?"

"When she's in rehab, yeah."

Billy slid back. "One whiskey neat, courtesy of your friends, Far From Folsom."

"And Billy the Kid!" McKenzie said, lifting her drink. Billy quickly followed with his own cocktail, and Nolan his. They clinked and sipped. McKenzie's eyes darted to Nolan's, but he was looking into his drink.

"I'll be back!" Billy said and shot down the bar yelling at a regular, "Slow down, you bastards!"

It was just the two of them now.

She looked him up and down, then shook her head with a smile.

"What?" he asked innocently.

Until he realized she was admiring the outrageous hat. He had almost forgotten.

"All right...enough of the safety hazard," he said, taking it off and putting it on the last barstool in the corner behind him. The hat swallowed up the stool, and the oval brim bowed out, making it a difficult perimeter to access. She laughed, then pulled off the ball cap and tossed it effortlessly onto the crown of his. She smiled and they sipped their drinks.

Before, they'd always been side by side, whether in the church, walking together, or out riding the horses. But now, they were right in front of each other. The place was so crowded, and their space so small, that they almost had to face each other. Nolan *did* want to look at her, but he was hesitant being this close.

"Why'd you come back?" she asked.

His stomach tightened and he glanced away. She watched his every move. He didn't know what to say. He was afraid he might say too much, or maybe not say the right thing at all. He made the slightest of shrugs, then looked back into her eyes. He didn't know. That was all he could say now.

"I'm glad you did," she said, and smiled in the way she did. The way he was beginning to understand. It was the same smile she gave to her friends and customers. It was honest, pure, and in some special way, something that made her glow.

"Make a toast," she said.

"What?"

"Make a toast!"

"Me?"

"Yeah, you! Goldie says we gotta make 'em count, right? Well with all I put you through, it's the least I can do. So, make a toast!" She lifted her drink. Nolan followed along, but after a moment, he was hesitant. "Come on," she spoke softly. "Use your words."

But he was anxious.

He wasn't truly sure why he was here or what he was even doing anymore. He didn't want to overthink, and he didn't want to say something he didn't truly feel.

But as he looked into the amber in his glass, then to her matching eyes beaming back at him, something came to him. She was there, waiting patiently, kindly, just happy to be there with him. There was something he felt down inside and in such a way that made him feel truly grateful to be here.

He was truly grateful to have met her.

Nolan raised his glass.

"To *you.*"

And with her smile, she brought her glass to his, their eyes not wavering or leaving the other for even a second.

They talked through the night. She told him how she had learned to ride horses from her grandmother on their neighbor's ranch. She shared how she loved the outdoors and how it made her heart ache that kids these days were spending less and less time outside. She felt fortunate that Jason loved to ride his dirt bike—despite his recklessness—and that Aiden was a natural explorer and adventurer.

But at the same time, she felt deep guilt. She was always working or trying to catch up on bills, and never had enough time with them. All the boys ever had was each other and a father who only offered to play Dad when it was convenient for him.

"Turner wasn't always an idiot," she told him. It was the idea of his own success and fame that had taken precedent over the idea of a family. For so long, McKenzie had put her own dreams and ambitions aside, not just to embrace the family she had been given, but to make her family stronger than what they had been before. She told him that her only role model was her Gram, who would stand up to any man or woman if it meant doing the right thing.

"I've never met anyone else like her," she said. They were words familiar to Nolan. It was the only way he thought of the woman of his past. But he didn't share that. Instead, he told her about his life living on different farms. Moving from the Australian outback to Canada to Montana throughout his teens. How he'd barely made it through any schooling because he was always moving. And when his parents had left him at fifteen, he'd really had no one there to tell him what to do. He felt fortunate that he'd always found someone to mentor him in those early years—first, an old couple in Canada who had a cattle ranch. They'd needed the help and took him in, even in their old age. They were the closest thing he'd had to parents.

Then, when he turned eighteen, and they passed away, a middle-aged farmer who needed ranch hands in Montana had come to town looking for men wanting work. He'd gone down to Montana with a migrating group of Mexicans, all in hopes for a better life. He told her the story that, on that Montana ranch, the men had been trying to tame a wild horse that bucked and kicked and snarled throughout the crops. Nolan, with everything to prove and nothing to lose, had chased the horse down. The only reason he could tame him, he said, was because he had been tall enough and lanky enough to hold on tight, gripping with all he'd had, fighting with all he was—because he had nothing to lose. He'd impressed the ranchers and the farmers that day. He hadn't forced the horse or bullied it, he'd simply snuck his way onto its back and cupped his long arms under its neck, tucking his shoulder into the back of the horse's kicking spine. Even at eighteen, he'd been long enough to accomplish such a feat. Immature and fearless enough, too, he mentioned. The owner of the ranch had seen it all, and that was something he had only seen once in his life. He'd taken him in that day, and that was how he'd learned to ride horses, Nolan explained, by first taming a wild one.

McKenzie didn't speak through any of this. She simply kept her eyes to his, listening, watching, understanding. "And fighting? How did that happen?"

That part was easiest to explain.

"Been fighting my whole life," he said.

Whether in the streets, on jobs, or at the ranches, there had always been a competition, and he had always been challenged. Not everyone had wanted him to get a job before they did, and sometimes, he'd had to fight for it. But where he'd really learned to fight, was an old boxer who'd been drafted to the Vietnam War. The man had survived the war, but had returned to the States heartbroken and alone, and had turned to ranching to re-seek his life's peace. Nolan had learned a lot from this man, and he was the closest thing to a father Nolan had ever had. He'd introduced Nolan to an old war buddy who was a street fighter and had done a brief stint in a small fighting circuit in Montana. Whenever Nolan had been able to get a fight that might pay, he'd partnered with the rancher. The ranchers would bet and fight other ranchers around the state, pitting their best set of hands against the next man's. With the other ranch hands, all of which were much older than him, and many immigrants, too, he'd learned to fish.

On their days off, he would hear stories from these men, teaching him about life through their eyes and experiences and the countries they had come from. This was also how he'd learned Spanish.

And one day, he'd taken the opportunity to learn to deep sea fish, when the rancher's client asked if any of his hands wanted to go to Alaska to experience "the biggest catches" of their life. Not only did Nolan go out to sea for a month and catch the biggest fish in his life, but he also saw humpback whales migrating—the largest animals he had ever seen. And, at night, while everyone slept deeply with exhaustion, in the icy lower deck on stiff cots, Nolan had stayed awake and listened to the whales sing. In one season, he had made twenty-five thousand dollars. But he had never had an address, nor a place to go, so all he did was work, travel, and put money away.

"All of this? Before you were twenty-one?" she asked.

He nodded.

"I don't even know what to say. Or what to ask."

She was utterly amazed. She didn't even know where to begin, and she still wanted to understand the stories behind all his tattoos. They covered everything she could see of his body, which, she realized then, he always kept hidden under his denim. Even in a flannel, he rarely exposed them. Like the hidden face of the wolf spread across his back. They must all be stories, she thought.

They were two neats and two beers deep. Little had they expected to be talking here in the corner of the bar without getting up once.

"I mean, I haven't seen even half of what you have...I never even seen the ocean!" she said, laughing at herself.

"Never?"

"Nope."

He was amazed.

"I mean..." She shook her head. "I've seen pictures and movies, you know. But not with my own eyes." And then her glow came, an aura that emanated from her when she daydreamed of things. "I always thought the ocean was some magical place."

The thought stirred him.

It made him remember that night with *Her*.

How they'd been on the beach and how he'd finally told *Her* how he felt. How they'd experienced the glowing phytoplankton, one of life's great miracles, and at the same time, one of the most pivotal moments in Nolan's life, where he'd told the woman of his dreams that he loved her.

He was afraid to think of it, let alone tell her that part of his story.

"Hey," McKenzie said, grabbing his attention back. "How about this—one day, you take me to the ocean, and one day, I'll take you to the Grand Canyon."

Something twisted inside him.

She was smiling big, but inside, Nolan was afraid. But before she could lose her smile and discover that something bothered him, she caught a glimpse of some friends at the other side of the bar.

McKenzie jumped up. "Hey, there's Mark and Bri! I'll get us another round." And she pushed through the crowd.

Nolan was shaken. Did she realize what she'd said? Did she know about it, or was it her just being friendly? He remembered telling her at Goldie's that he was going to the Grand Canyon, but had he told her why? Had he told her what he was really going to do? What did she know? What did she understand? He couldn't remember now. Had he said something else before passing out in the deck chair? For the past hour, Nolan had only been looking at her. Now his eyes were on the floor, trying to figure out what he might have said, or if he'd said too much. He lifted his chin and finally looked around the bar. It was as packed as ever, even more crowded than when they'd arrived. Something was gnawing at him from within now, and it made him second guess himself.

How much had he actually told her? Had he talked a lot? Had he talked about *Her* or...anything? For the past hour, his guard had been down, and he hadn't even realized it. The licks of a slow harmonica and the man performing on stage finally brought his head back to his seat. He checked behind him and saw that her ball cap and the ridiculous cowboy hat were still there. Nolan inhaled, trying to calm himself amongst the boisterous bar. Then, from across the room, he saw Kenzie.

She smiled bright, hugging and chatting with some friends. The way she looked at them and how she smiled, it was true—reserved only for those who deserved it. She was strong and she was kind. For herself and for others.

And he felt it, even from across the room. But he couldn't help but now think of *Her.*

How she and Kenzie smiled in such different, but beautiful, ways. A thought came to him.

When would he say goodbye to Kenzie now? How would he do it? As the anxious and inevitable question scratched at him, he remembered when he'd had to say goodbye to *Her.* How she'd laid in the hospital with that tumor that was spreading mercilessly. How cold the room had been. How the constant beeping of machines and the noise of the halls haunted him awake. How he'd stood by *Her* all the way through the end. How he'd held *Her* hand when she couldn't even speak.

How he'd held it in the very moment when he'd known she was leaving. The love of his life, whom he'd opened all of himself to. Whom he'd given all of himself to and anything that was left of him. Nolan inhaled.

If he could just slow down all those things—the things that tortured him. The pain, the guilt, the memory. But it was too late. He remembered *Her.* He remembered *that* moment. The way her breathing went slow and shallow, her sunken eyes that could not open. He remembered the tide on the beach. How it had rolled and taken things away. How she had been holding his hand, lying on the hospital bed. How her breaths had slowed, until they stopped. That exact excruciating moment, when her hand could no longer hold his. When she had let go.

Forever.

Nolan launched from the barstool. He shoved his hands into his denim, around the rhinestone vest, and maneuvered through the crowd. His wide shoulder plowed through a man who didn't see him coming. He inhaled deep and quick. He was trying to breathe but couldn't. His lungs were choking, with his soul. He pushed through a group of people dancing and finally made it to the entrance hallway.

McKenzie looked over from the bar, but he was gone. She peered around and weaved her way back to their spot, but she couldn't see him anywhere.

She knew—something was wrong.

She turned and headed for the main room where the music played. She held her feathered scarf and fur tight over her shoulders and pushed past the waves of people.

Then she stopped, entering the room before the front door's exit.

He was standing there with his head low, his left shoulder facing the exit and his right lingering inside. He was locked up, still as a statue. McKenzie slid her way through the people until she could stand right in front of him.

Nolan flinched, seeing her.

It was as if he saw a ghost.

In that split-second reaction, McKenzie could see that he was afraid. She could see that he *did* have fears.

It was something hidden, deep within. Something that even Nolan couldn't fully understand yet.

"Hey…you okay?"

Her voice was sweet and her eyes were wide as she looked right into his, holding him there, patiently waiting.

He was trying. He was trying with all of this. But what was he doing? Why was he even here with her? He was trying, but all he could do now, seeing her right in front of him, was nod.

They stood there, frozen with the crowd all around them.

Until she spoke. "Would you like to wear my feathers?"

She let out a little smile, then swung the pink scarf off her shoulders and wrapped it around his neck. She pulled it snug around his strong neckline and nestled it into him with her open hands. Now he was wearing a bright yellow rhinestone jacket and a coil of faux pink feathers.

McKenzie grinned. She tugged at his denim's wool collar so that it popped out, pushing the feathers up his neck. "Is that better?"

Nolan looked down into her eyes. He couldn't smile like her, but seeing the way she could—how sincere it was, just there, looking up at him—something changed.

"What?" she finally asked, watching him try to work something out in his head.

His eyes were fixated on hers. His words were almost a whisper. "You're a beautiful person."

And for the second time since she'd met him, McKenzie was

speechless. No one had ever told her something like that. She instantly remembered the feeling when Nolan had said something of the sort in her Jeep on the way to Goldie's. She had been told many things, being the sort of woman she was, but this—this hit her gut in a way that shook her and, at the same time, made her happy.

They just stood there, holding each other's eyes.

Vulnerable. True. Even scared.

She reached beneath his layers—underneath his rhinestone vest and his heavy denim jacket. Her hands slid inside, where only his flannel rested on his skin.

She hugged him.

He didn't know what to do. His fists were hidden, locked, with his fingers buried tightly into his palms. Her entire body and face held against his chest, and she didn't move. His hands started to release. They slowly left his pockets, and he unfolded them, letting them breathe. He gently put them around her lower back.

And he held her.

They found themselves back at the bar top in an even smaller corner now— the one where they had left their hats. There were people all around, but they paid them no mind. They spoke casually and contently the rest of the night. McKenzie didn't want him to be uncomfortable again, not even for a second. They were entertained by Billy's one-liners and trash-talking to his drunkest customers. They shared a shot of Tennessee whiskey, to which McKenzie happily toasted, "To *you*, Sheriff Big Head."

She spoke of Goldie and how good of a man he was. Nolan believed it as well. There was much still unknown about Goldie and his story, but he thought the old man must have wondered the very same about him. McKenzie brought up how Goldie was so kind to him, and that she could see that he had so much respect and admiration for Nolan too. Nolan was surprised by this. He wasn't even sure how she'd picked that up from the old man, but then it made Nolan realize that he felt the very same for him.

They left the bar to a standing ovation from Billy and his regulars. Everyone clapped, whistled, and watched as McKenzie and Nolan drunkenly parted the crowds. Nolan wore McKenzie's purple fur now, her delightful request, as well as her University of Arizona hat, which fit him like a glove, and she happily wore his oversized cowboy hat hanging loose on the back of her crown while accompanied by her pink feather scarf. They looked like the town parade as they left the bar to a clapping celebration. They were both drunk, but still in control, still themselves, just finally relaxed. And wholeheartedly smiling.

McKenzie insisted they walk home, which was only a half mile from the center of downtown. Nolan, who had walked alone his whole life, was used to it, and happy she suggested it. And while earlier in the night may have been embarrassing for him, none of that mattered anymore. He didn't think about what anyone thought or said, he didn't even care what he was wearing or anything that he might have said or shared. He was just here, with her, in this moment. Everything about the dimly lit historic Victorian neighborhood was quiet and proper, except for McKenzie, singing "Wanted Dead or Alive" by Bon Jovi at the top of her lungs. She didn't have a care in the world, and along with Nolan's smile, she stole the show. She sang and laughed and danced and trotted next to him throughout the street, stomping and tromping, arm and arm, all the way home. All she wanted was to make him laugh and smile. And he didn't mind one bit of it.

STAY

They rambled through the old neighborhood, loud with laughter and unrestrained smiles. McKenzie was wearing the large cowboy hat on the back of her head, and Nolan was not only impressed that she could wail the lyrics of any Bon Jovi song at the drop of a dime, but by the fact that she so proudly wore a long purple fur coat and the awkwardly huge hat that actually made it harder to walk or see. But with whiskey swimming in their veins, it might have just been easy.

They passed an old elementary school that had boulders jutting from its playground. When they entered the heart of the Victorian neighborhood, they passed countless modest and regal homes with warmly lit porches and stoops. There was something about a home with a porch that Nolan always liked. He'd heard there were many places like this around the country, like New Orleans and throughout the south, places that Nolan had not yet seen.

McKenzie lit up to this. She told him that, even though she'd grown up on a porch and played games on a stoop all her life, there was something about them and old wooden stairs that she still always loved. That little sound of bare feet tapping across the wood. The feel of the elevated breeze coming to kiss you. To her, porches and decks were a warm invitation. It was a nice idea, Nolan thought, as they walked the warmly lit street. A porch was something to be shared. Like sunsets and adventures and long stories about returning home. Between Bon Jovi live, the crickets, and the porches of old houses made of wood, their voices were the only things the neighborhood could hear, as if they were the only two people left in the world.

The night was cooler than ever, as temperatures dropped fast after nightfall in Northern Arizona. But their bellies were still full of warm whiskey and laughter, which kept them pleasantly comfortable through the night stroll. When they reached the house, McKenzie was laughing and teasing Nolan about the idea of him wearing the pink snakeskin boots. It still wasn't enough that he was wearing a yellow rhinestone vest. She beamed, demonstrating his "grumpy face" when he'd first resisted at the antique shop. He looked like a fed-up dog, teased with a treat.

Nolan had to laugh. He could see himself in her impression—a recluse and a grump, though no one had ever told him he was. But now Nolan's face was sorer than ever. It wasn't just the bruise that came from the ring fight, or the re-bruising from Turner and his gang—it was the amount of smiling and laughing he had done for the day. It felt like a beating. Everything in his face was sore now.

And he couldn't be happier for it.

McKenzie's narrow cheeks were beat too. He was a joy to tease, and he was a good sport about it. Nothing really made him angry anymore. Not unless it was himself. McKenzie was mid-laugh when she saw that the living room lights were on in her house. Her eyebrows perked. Maybe she'd left them on, she thought. They stepped up on the stoop and porch, and she opened the door, still laughing with Nolan. It was damn near impossible to get through any door wearing his giant cowboy hat, and she didn't know how Nolan had done it in the first place.

Then she stopped. Jason was in the living room, playing a motocross video game on a small television.

"Jase…"

Jason froze and stared at the both of them. McKenzie stood there in the excessive cowboy hat and her purple fur coat while Nolan stood behind her, wearing her pink scarf and the yellow rhinestone jacket.

"What are you doing?" she asked, honestly surprised.

Jason sized them up. He didn't know what to make of them, or his feelings.

Had his mother lied to them about her final exams?

Was she lying about other things?

Did she just want to go out with some new man, like Dad did with his own incessant flings? With just one more thought Jason would have burst out with anger, but he held it back just to say one good truth instead.

"Aiden was begging to come home," he said. "Gram's couch hurts his back."

McKenzie inhaled and her stomach tightened. She finally sighed and gestured.

"This is Nolan."

She set his massive cowboy hat on the kitchen counter then put her University of Arizona hat on top of its high crown. Straight away, she started picking up the bagels, empty soda cans, and wrappers they had already scavenged and littered throughout the entire house.

"Hi," Nolan said calmly, still barely past the doorway. He didn't want to show the kid that they had been drinking like they had. He knew the situation was already complicated enough for him.

But before Jason could think any further or draw his own conclusions, he stormed to the front door and pushed himself forcefully past Nolan's shoulder. Nolan didn't move much, but he budged just enough to let the angry young man pass.

"Hey, what are you doing?" McKenzie quickly called after him.

"Whatever the fuck I want, just like you," he said sharply."

"Jason…" she followed him out the door, but he wasn't stopping for anyone. "Jason! Are you kidding me right now!?"

Jason stomped down to the garage. She took a deep breath, fixing her hat hair and considering what to do. Nolan watched Jason through the porch until he disappeared into the garage.

"He's my favorite," she said after a sigh, trying to cover her frustration with sarcasm. She went into the kitchen and quickly took off the rest of the antique roadshow.

Nolan shook his head, unbothered by it. "It's all right. He's just a kid."

They shared the silence. But Nolan's own words hit him just then.
He was just a kid.

Nolan realized something. Jason was almost the same age as he had been when his parents had disappeared.

"Beer's in the fridge," McKenzie said, then marched through the living room to go check on Aiden.

A dirt bike engine screamed outside in the quiet neighborhood. Nolan turned to the porch. He stepped out and found Jason straddling the bike without his helmet. Jason looked back to the house and found Nolan standing there, watching him. He gave him a high and long middle finger, revved his bike, then screeched into the night.

And again, Nolan barely moved.

What the kid was feeling was all too familiar.

Nolan took off the rhinestone jacket and scarf, then placed them in the kitchen next to the cowboy hat and McKenzie's purple coat. There wasn't much of anything fresh in the fridge, just packaged sandwich meat, locally bottled milk, cheese, some old vegetables, and a case of beer. Either she hadn't shopped in a long time or they weren't eating too well. He took a bottle of beer, then went into the cherrywood bedroom hallway. Without McKenzie noticing, he watched her tuck Aiden into the small bed. He was already fast asleep in the messy room. There were motocross pictures taped to the walls, dinosaur toys scattered on the floor, a Led Zeppelin poster—among others—and chipped old wooden dressers that must have stayed through a generation or two. Then, against a flaking, beige-painted wall, a smaller kid-sized bed was pushed into a corner where she tucked Aiden in. On the floor next to it was a mattress without sheets and a few old pillows with a stack of mismatching blankets.

"Come on, flip. Flip over, honey. You gotta do it." McKenzie whispered, trying to gently turn Aiden over. She carefully turned his growing eleven-year-old frame to its side, and though he was fast asleep, he was so inherently used to the routine that it didn't take much for his muscle memory to kick in. When she stood up, she found Nolan in the doorway holding a beer. Her eyes were stones, hardening and ready to defend herself against what he might be thinking.

She walked to the master bedroom but avoided his eyes. Nolan watched. He wasn't judging her. He felt for her. There was nothing to judge, and, in his own story, by Aiden's age, he had been through far worse.

When Nolan entered her room, she quickly closed the door partway behind him. Her mind was racing with reality and all the little struggles that chipped away at her. She couldn't hide her frustration now, so she tried to clean up the dark room instead. Aiden had left his entire weekend bag unpacked all over the floor and it was clear he had first fallen asleep in her bed.

Nolan stood in the doorway, calm, just watching her pace and scramble about the room.

"I'm happy they're home. I just can't get any studying done." She turned on an old lamp, making it easier to see Aiden's mess. "Tomorrow was my only day, no thanks to you."

"Me?" he said, the alcohol exaggerating his surprise.

"Yeah, you. I missed two days of work and studying 'cause of you."

"You're blaming me?"

"A little bit, yeah."

Realizing she was getting frustrated and loud, she shut the door completely. Nolan offered her the beer. She looked at it, surprised he didn't have his own. She swiped it, popped the top off on her nightstand, and swigged.

"I guess a little is fair," he said.

McKenzie shoved some laundry and Aiden's mess into her closet, then plopped onto the floor. She rested her head against the old bed with her knees out and the bottle between her legs.

Nolan was still standing just past the doorway, watching. "Why's he gotta sleep on his side?"

"Aiden?" She looked up. "He's got a bad back. I need to get them real beds."

"Jason sleeps on the floor?" he asked, trying to understand.

But with a single glance, he could feel her temper rising. Everything about his words, no matter how he meant them, made her feel self-conscious. Even ashamed.

"Aiden sleeps in here with me and Jason gets the bed and that's how it is right now."

She sipped the beer, looking away.

Nolan took his hands from his denim and slowly sat on the floor across from her. Then he leaned against the closet door and yanked his long legs and his knees up to his chest. He was still feeling the whiskey, but he felt her more. His eyes were calm and they were on her.

"I know. You're thinking I'm the shittiest mom ever."

"I'm not thinking that."

She was trying to keep it together, but with the alcohol she was faster to unravel. "I'm just behind," she said. "With bills, with *them*. With *me*. With everything," she continued, trying to make sense of the constant mess she always felt.

And Nolan just watched.

"Jason *is* a good kid, he's just...growing more into his dad, who wants him when he wants him and doesn't want the responsibilities." She swigged. "But Jason doesn't care. He just wants Dad. I don't know. I don't know how to knock sense into him."

Nolan's eyes didn't leave her once. He wanted to help, in any way, if he could. Then his eyes drifted, finally thinking of something. "Want me to headbutt him?"

McKenzie let out a little laugh, then shook her head, returning to her feelings.

They were both quiet. Nolan could see how deeply these things troubled her. Whether it was her biggest fear or not, Nolan could feel it— her guilt was palpable. She didn't want her kids to go through even a fraction of what she had been through, let alone the tribulations her family had endured over the years thanks to an absent mother and a father that didn't even give it a chance.

But now, above anything and everything, McKenzie was just worried about Jason. He was still a kid, despite his self-reliance and intelligence. And he was too young to be drinking and too sensitive to be caught between his parents' constant push and pull.

Nolan tilted his head back. He was thinking about everything she'd said. McKenzie's eyes were low, sipping the beer. She felt senseless. Lost. Something she hated. Something she felt on those dark days. Nolan's eyes wandered the cracks in the ceiling, and when he began to speak, it came from a place that was both open and absorbed in his own truths.

What he said to her next did not come from a memory or any specific experience, but something deeper. It wasn't a lesson that any person had taught him, not even *Her*. It had come from an accumulation of understanding that reflected all of his relationships.

Even his relationship to himself.

"Sometimes we gotta let people be who they are. We can't control them...or what they do. All we can do is love them. Love who we have."

McKenzie stared.

She knew he thought about things in such ways, but she didn't know he could speak about them in such a way. She didn't know how else to respond but with her defensive sarcasm. "Are you drunk?"

"Do I sound drunk?" he asked sincerely, knowing he was a little tipsy. She smiled, then shook her head.

They held eyes. She brought her knees out and rose up on them. She crawled over, close now, inspecting his face. He was surprised, looking up to her. She was close enough to kiss him. He was close enough to want it.

But he wasn't sure if he felt good or guilty looking at her lips.

McKenzie's hand slowly reached over. She carefully palmed the bruise that stretched from his temple and hid inside his beard.

"What's this from?"

Nolan didn't move, looking at her. He didn't remember which bruise it was or from when. His shoulders lifted in a small shrug. "Fighting."

"You gonna keep it up?"

He didn't know. He was looking in her eyes and didn't know anything he was doing anymore. She saw him thinking and she could tell—he was bothered by the unknown.

She stroked the bruise, her fingers gently running through his beard. Their eyes locked.

"Will you stay? Tonight?"

But before he even thought about it, he nodded.

And now they were both thinking about it.

About each other's lips. About tasting.

They wanted it.

"Um." Her eyes drifted away. "If you're in here, my kids..." It was already too much. She was happy and wanted many things, but something was stopping her.

Nolan nodded. He understood, because he felt the same—they both felt guilty.

"I'll sleep out there," he said.

"Thank you." And she gradually pulled back, sitting and pulling her knees back up to her chest and planting her black boots on the floor. Her face was tired, intoxicated, but finally relaxed. And now that there was space, he felt like he could breathe again. She swigged the beer until it was half empty, then passed it to Nolan.

He downed it in one gulp. Everything became quiet. The night permeated through the cold windows. It was silent and calm again. And they sat there, sharing it together.

Nolan was laying on the couch with his heavy head on a pillow. He wore his navy blue and black flannel, with his boots and jacket on the floor. His arms were folded behind his head, and he was content, stretching his long back and the bandaged wound at his side. McKenzie walked in wearing moccasins, a white low-cut tank, silk shorts, and her own red and black flannel. She barely stepped out of the bedroom hallway before typing rapidly away on her cell phone.

"You okay?" he asked in the same soft way she had asked him before.

Her breaths were low. "He does this and comes back wasted, or runs off for days with friends. He gets so hurt. It kills me…"

He could see how much it bothered her. "Wanna go find him?" he asked.

She sighed, giving it a rest for the night. She had been through this so many times now. "No, but if he comes back, headbutt him."

Nolan smiled. So did she.

"Hey, thank you," she said.

"For what?"

"For staying."

He thought about it. "Why wouldn't I?"

Her brows furrowed as he looked at her. They were each puzzled by the other. She didn't know what to say or to think about him. He was just different.

Beyond that. He was special.

She went to the living room lamp that hung over the couch and turned the light out.

"Goodnight, Nolan."

"Goodnight, Kenzie."

They were words that struck. Because the way they said each other's names, said so much more.

HOWLING FROM
WITHIN

T he morning forest sifted the cold mist that flowed down from the
north. Tall, dense pines jutted into the icy sky while the morning sun
cut through them, painting the valley and the town in layers of warm light.

Throughout the old neighborhood, the sounds of wet, nostril-gagging
snorts echoed through the streets, breaking the Sunday morning peace.
They were obnoxious, sometimes ferocious, and often slimy. They were all
the grunts of rotund pig-like rodents known as javelinas. Nolan could hear
them through his sleep, which, for once, was deep and filling, until their
sharp squeals and dripping snorts crackled in his ear drums. Having been
raised all over the world and sleeping in every imaginable corner and nook,
he had a sensitive threshold to sound when it came to sleeping. He was
always attuned to any disturbance that might threaten him.

Laying on his back, his eyes popped open, only to find Aiden, wide
awake, leaning over the couch, and hovering above his face. He stared at
Nolan, both of their eyes wide open.

"You hear 'em?" Aiden whispered.

Nolan whispered back, not moving. "Yeah."

"Javelinas. They killed my friend's dog," he said in his boyish, matter
of fact way. "I hate 'em."

The snorting and squealing became louder as they crashed into the
trash bins just outside in their front yard. They could hear every detail.
Nolan's eyes moved toward the wood frame of a large Victorian window,

then back to Aiden. "Do you know what javelinas hate?" he said in a low whisper.

Aiden perked up, leaning against the couch, still hovering above Nolan. "What?"

Nolan's eyes narrowed with a sort of mischievous youthfulness.

"Big...bad...wolves."

Aiden grinned from cheek to cheek.

McKenzie slept deeply in her bed, covered in a beige comforter and an old quilt that had been passed down from her Gram. It came from a time when the women of her generation would knit the most intricate, thick blankets and fabric designs. It was unusual for her to sleep beyond sunrise, but, for once, she submitted to sleeping without an early rise or an alarm. Until the sounds of scurrying pigs came screeching from outside. McKenzie was moved for only a second. She hadn't slept much in a week and this deep sleep was being demanded by her body. Then, the offset of a man-like beast howled outside:

"*Awhooooooooo!*"

And another childish beast burst out after it.

"*Ow ow awhoooooooo!*"

McKenzie jolted awake and turned to the windows. She could hear the pigs squealing, plowing trash cans and potted plants and old chili cans that tumbled down the road in a complete frenzy.

"Raahh!"

"*Rah rah* rah!"

It was definitely Nolan and Aiden. With hazy eyes and a heavy head, McKenzie could only think and say one thing "What the fuck?"

She flung the porch door open and stepped into the cold spring morning. She was barefoot and still wearing her low tank top and short boxer shorts. "You gotta be kidding me," she uttered, immediately finding them.

In the middle of the street, Nolan and Aiden howled at the top of their lungs, bare chested, swinging their shirts high in the air at the pack of javelinas. There were twenty of them—fat and muscular with tusks jutting from their mouths. The adults were obnoxious and aggressive, as were the babies. And they were scurrying every which way as the two shirtless humans hollered and hooted like maniacs.

Before McKenzie could even come up with something to say, she watched as Nolan and Aiden went running down the street, swinging their shirts like lassos.

"What the hell are you doing!?" McKenzie finally yelled.

"We're scaring the javelinas away!" Aiden proudly shouted back.

Nolan turned to see her. Her arms were folded across her chest, looking at them incredulously. Nolan grinned broadly, then let out another wolf cry. "*Awhoooooooo!*"

"*Ow ow awhoooo!*" Aiden followed, cupping his hands to his mouth, intensifying his howl.

Her hip was out and her folded arms didn't move. She stared them down like she was about to give them both a lecture. "Yeah, you're scaring me away too," she said with a sly little smile. "And our pancakes."

"*Pancakes!?*" Aiden practically squealed.

McKenzie finally smiled, then… "*Ow ow awhooo!*" she howled.

Nolan grinned brightly, looking at her and her legs. "*Awhoooooooo!*" he called in return.

"*Ow ow awhoooooooooo!*" Aiden cried, bolting up the wooden stoop and flying into the house.

OLD DOG, NEW TRICKS

Old '40s rock and roll blared from the radio in the kitchen. The record was Wynonie Harris's "I Want My Fanny Brown." Aiden was stirring a big bowl of batter while McKenzie flipped golden tan, fresh pancakes. The smell of sweet batter and warm butter filled the house. Nolan was slicing bananas onto a red plate as McKenzie smiled and re-enforced her instructions to Aiden, reminding him that this was batter, not frosting, "so *don't* eat it."

But of course, when she wasn't looking, he'd sneak a lick and dart his eyes to Nolan, who caught him every time. But instead of convicting him, he smiled with him.

The upbeat old rock and roll soul filled the room with the warm aroma. McKenzie had a twist in her step, cooking barefoot while the boys kept busy behind her.

Seeing an opening, Aiden flicked his tongue out to lick the spoon just to rile her, but with the sixth sense of any mother, McKenzie's eyes darted over.

"I'm joking!" Aiden smiled, playing as though it were all a ruse.

"You're not gonna like it, dude, I'm telling you."

But he did like it, and what he liked most was the act of irritating her while simultaneously amusing Nolan.

McKenzie finished another hearty pour of batter onto her 1960s steel griddle, the same griddle Gram used to cook for them with. She gave the big pot of batter and wooden spatula back to Aiden, then made sure to give him her "short temper" eyes so he knew not to mess around.

Aiden peeked over to Nolan, only to discover that Nolan was waiting for him to see what he was about to do. Nolan's eyebrows danced for Aiden, then he flicked a quarter-sized banana in McKenzie's direction. It smacked a teapot next to McKenzie's hand and stuck to the side of the metal. She immediately looked back. Nolan had his back to her, stalling a second before glancing over.

She was waiting there, staring.

"Sorry," he said, in his nonchalant tone.

Aiden giggled. McKenzie gave them both inspective stares before writing off Nolan's seemingly innocent mistake. She held the wide spatula under a blanket of crisping batter, then flipped an "Aiden-sized" flat and thin pancake. Nolan waited a moment, slicing a thinner sliver of banana and shooting a sly grin at Aiden. Aiden's eyes beamed. Nolan was preparing to strike again. Nolan flicked the sliced banana over his hip—this time, the slimy little coin flung onto the back of her arm and slid down to her elbow.

"*Ahhh!*" she gasped.

Aiden burst out with all his belly.

"Ah, sorry," Nolan said calmly, trying to take advantage of his stoic demeanor. But now she saw right through it.

She dropped the spatula onto the griddle, crashing it with a bang. "Do you think you're clever?"

Nolan stopped and turned back to her. His eyes darted between Aiden and McKenzie.

"What?" he asked, pretending to be confused.

But she knew he was messing with her—the longer she spent looking into his eyes, the harder it was for him to hide.

"Hurry up, banana boy. I'm hungry! And you—" She eyed Aiden. "Keep stirring, not licking!" Then she flipped a pancake with a swift hand.

Aiden, of course, was better at playing innocent and simply gave her his best "I don't know what you're talking about" face. He always knew, however. So did she. But he did it anyway.

McKenzie reached up to grab a set of pastel-colored plates and while her back was turned, Nolan saw the wild in Aiden's eyes—he was holding his wooden spoon, loaded with a glob of batter, dripping, and ready to launch.

Nolan gave him a look—they were pushing it now. McKenzie looked over to Aiden. He quickly plunged the spoon into the batter. She stared now.

"All right. Whatever you two are doing, knock it off or you're gonna get it."

The boys waited, then exchanged sly smiles and big eyes, but when it became quiet again, Nolan looked over to see that Aiden had re-loaded his spoon…and with one last bolt of excitement flashing in his eyes, he flung the golden goo right at his mother, splattering it all across her neck and shoulder. But, in half a second, ready for war, McKenzie yanked the dish hose, swung it over, and sprayed them both down from head to toe.

"*Ahhhh!*" Aiden screeched and jumped from the stool, running and screaming through the house. Nolan staggered behind him, his heavy frame thrashing through the kitchen stools while McKenzie drenched him with merciless pride.

"Little shits!"

Water shot like a geyser in the air and all over the kitchen. The boys' hollering quickly turned into a pleased howling.

"*Awhooo!*"

It was still early morning and the air was crisp. Their clothes were all damp, but they still didn't care. They devoured stacks of warm banana pancakes. Nolan took his thick and fluffy, Aiden liked his thin and crisp, and McKenzie made hers somewhere in the middle but drenched in maple syrup. The sweet melody of "Sleep Like a Baby" by Roger Clyne & The Peacemakers kept their spirits awake and alive. They sat at the messy kitchen counter that intimately held them all. Aiden was still in his flannel pajamas, as was McKenzie in her shorts and wool moccasins. Nolan wore his navy blue flannel and a dark gray undershirt, all damp. They were so hungry and happy that they hadn't even bothered cleaning up the water puddled all over the kitchen floor. It was a beautiful breakfast and, in between satisfying thick bites, Kenzie and Nolan snuck looks to one another.

"Oh, I forgot…" McKenzie popped up. She jumped from her stool to look into the fridge, then pulled out a canister. "We got whipped cream."

"Oh! Me me me!" Aiden said, and she carefully pointed the nozzle at his plate. But what she served, was less than a dime's size.

"Hey! What the heck!"

McKenzie nonchalantly looked to Nolan. "And how about you?"

But he could tell she was hiding something behind her slow-growing grin. Nolan stopped chewing, but before he knew it, McKenzie swung the barrel of whipped cream right at him. And with no remorse, her finger jammed the plastic tip, spewing streams of whipped cream all over Nolan's face.

"*Agh*!" he yelled, laughed, and practically fell off his barstool. Whipped cream covered his beard and forehead while Aiden screamed in delight. McKenzie swung the barrel over. Aiden tried to escape, but he was met with a hissing slosh of cream all over his cheeks and curly hair.

"Have some extra!" McKenzie yelled, chasing him out of the kitchen. When she turned around, Nolan was back on his feet, foamed cream and sugar across his face, trapped in his beard, dripping down his neck.

McKenzie laughed wildly, pointing the barrel at him. Nolan stood there with a cream-covered grin, accepting the punishment. McKenzie's stomach ached from delight. She could barely point at him, seeing the foam stuck on his chest hairs like tufts of clouds. Nolan just shook his head. All he could do was surrender. And laugh.

He couldn't remember the last time he had laughed so hard. But then, for a moment, he did. And if it wasn't for Kenzie's pure joy, he probably would have felt that pulse in his gut to reminisce about another time, another place, when all he did was laugh with *someone.*

Instead of falling back into that empty well, he just looked at Kenzie, hunched over, practically crying from satisfaction. And in that laughter, he cast away the pain of the past that always lingered. Instead, he laughed at what was there, glowing, shining, right there in front of him.

It was early afternoon. Aiden and Nolan were on the lawn just outside the porch. Aiden held his fly-fishing rod proudly, high to the sky. He was teaching Nolan how to cast with the proper posture and form. He was just a boy, but his maturity and intelligence shined brilliantly in his demonstration. Like a wise little man, he focused on the details of the task at hand, explaining everything about fly fishing as all a matter of fact, as if he were already a master. Aiden's enthusiasm was contagious, and Nolan listened carefully for an hour, impressed by his confidence as Aiden told him the importance of specialized knots, twists, and flies.

He could see that the boy was not yet disturbed by the great world around him, or the pains and lessons that came with adolescence. There was an innocence and purity in Aiden, and Nolan was enjoying every second, becoming a student once again and learning something new from a child. It was a complex idea to him, because it was hard to even remember the last time he had learned anything new—that was, *truly* learned something. With an old metal box of trinkets, Aiden spared no detail, describing different rods, reels, and proper fly knots.

"Fly knots are tough. You can't get angry 'cause you mess up a lot. It's not like tying shoes or nothing. You gotta make sure it's a good fresh fly and a strong tie. If it's too big, with extra lead, the fish might think it's too big and not bite and that's the whole point. You gotta think like a smart fish, but you gotta be patient and wait a lot because fish are smart, and they can wait all day and not move and not be hungry."

Nolan nodded. All he did was listen to the little master, feeling a sort of youthful joy. Although Nolan had deep sea fished on some dangerous and choppy seas, he never experienced just good old-fashioned sit-by-the-river fishing. His experiences deep sea fishing had been a fight for the entire body and for survival—it was either catch the fish or there was nothing to eat, nothing to can, and no money to put in his pockets. Aiden was teaching it as an art. It was nothing particular he said, Nolan thought, it was simply how Aiden described it and how it made him *feel* about fishing.

Fly fishing was an art of patience, but also perseverance. Nolan listened with his eyes and ears closely, watching the little man's hands navigate the fly rod and reel. Nolan focused, absorbing every movement of Aiden's hands like he would do in any fight or task—a skill he'd developed as a fighter. And in this deep-focus learning, Nolan was already forgetting that constant voice that took shape in his thoughts and memories, always finding ways to interrupt him. In this moment, the things that disturbed him weren't present at all. All he could hear was the young boy who spoke proudly and with poise.

"You gotta cast between ten and two. That's the sweet spot. It ain't like normal fishing—you gotta do it just right. Your cast gotta be good or the fish will know."

Nolan's bruised hand reached for his chin. He eyed the thin and flexible six-foot rod that Aiden held gingerly in his hand, bringing it up high above his head and waving it to and fro like a marsh's cattail with the wind. Nolan was already assessing and re-assessing fly fishing situations like a fight.

"But what if you catch a big fish? Won't it break?" he asked, watching Aiden wisp the rod calmly into the sky. But then he stopped and looked up to Nolan.

"How big we talking?" Aiden asked.

"Swordfish."

Aiden's eyes widened. He had heard about them and had seen old paintings of a swordfish once in a merchants' store, but he'd never thought they were real. Like McKenzie, he too had never seen the ocean.

"A swordfish! Have you ever caught one?"

Nolan nodded, a simple matter of fact in his history of experiences. "Yeah, a big one."

"Where!? How!?"

Nolan smiled. "Gulf of Mexico. But you know what?"

Aiden leaned in, imagining what little he knew of the creature.

"It was hard. He was a really good sword fighter. *Ha!*"

Nolan lunged, jutting out his hand then swinging it like a crazed swordsman. His knees bent and he shuffled forward then twirled erratically, fighting invisible enemies everywhere with his fencing moves.

Aiden's cheeks jumped higher than the rod, laughing.

From the porch door, McKenzie smiled too. She had been watching them the entire time, still in her pajama shorts, bare toes, and a white tank. As the boys played and told stories, she thought about it.

All of it. How Aiden spoke and talked with Nolan. How Nolan always listened more than he spoke. How he talked back, kind and deliberate.

It was effortless. All of it.

And it made her smile.

Back in the kitchen, everything was clean, dry, and put away from their pancake feast and water fight. Even the whipped cream. Since it was Sunday and supposed to be her last day of studying, McKenzie didn't want to spend any more time not doing the work. Through the porch screen door, she could hear the swooshes of wind as the boys practiced casting. McKenzie had just finished rereading a chapter in her marine biology book. She turned the book over, hoping to break from the subject and power through another. As she did, she re-discovered her stack of mail from earlier in the week. An opened white envelope showed the words *Past Due.*

It was the electricity bill. McKenzie took a deep breath. It was one of the many little distractions she was competing with now, and as that surge of fear hit her, she couldn't stop herself from thinking about Jason either. His phone was off, and he still hadn't replied to her messages. Jason only turned his phone off when he was truly angry. It would always upset McKenzie because there was no way to know if he was okay.

He was so much like her and didn't even know it.

He had inherited Kenzie's strength and rebellious anger, but also, in a special way, he had taken on the sensitive, compassionate, and emotionally intelligent side of her too. All of their family saw this and thought this about Jason, including his father, because they always got the best of him, sharing a visit or two each month, or seeing him at a family function. Yet McKenzie, like any single mother, had the challenge of facing him and raising him through his best *and* his worst, all on her own. Jason had never had family around to support him or talk him through his adolescence or early teens. Unlike Aiden, he had always been a troubled kid, even though McKenzie knew, deep down, just like her, he was a good kid. To her, Jason had just never had the same opportunities or parents that she knew others had. He had never had the same consistent presence of two parents or love from a bigger family. And he certainly wasn't used to the presence of a father.

McKenzie's fear and guilt were getting the best of her. She hated thinking like this, and she desperately wanted to know if he was okay and if he was safe, and if, deep down—which she could tell in half a second just by the sound of his voice—he wanted to give it all a rest for now and just come home. She didn't care about studying or grades or anything else, she just wanted to know that Jason was at least okay for one more day. She snatched up her cell phone and dialed again. It rang for half a second before going to a voicemail. "It's Jase. Leave a message."

She wanted to be sweet, but she was too worried. She had already called five times this morning to no avail, but at least she knew his phone was on because it rang sporadically before transferring to his voicemail. Whether he was awake or not, she was tired of waiting.

"Dude, you can't keep this up," she fired off. "Get your ass back here or call me right now. I'm not playing, Jase."

And with that, she exhaled and hung up, just as Nolan walked through the porch door. It took one glance for him to know she was worried. They were beginning to understand each other.

"You okay?"

"I can't get ahold of this little shit. And I can't get my head around this."

She was holding her face, staring down at her next textbook.

He stood there, overlooking her spread of books. He caught a glimpse of the past due notice that was wedged between the pages. When she felt his silence, she looked back up and realized he was looking at the notice. McKenzie quickly tucked it back into the book pages.

She was stuck. She didn't know what to say, what to do, or what to think. She had truly enjoyed her morning with Nolan and Aiden. It had easily been one of the most fun times she had had with Aiden in a long time. They'd both needed it. But now she was sitting in front of a stack of realities, and she was feeling more discouraged by the second.

Nolan finally spoke. "I gotta run an errand. Maybe the little guy can cruise with me," he offered. "Then you won't have any handsome distractions."

Her brows furrowed. She looked up to him. "Did you just compliment yourself?" she asked with a flare.

Nolan smiled, knowing he got her attention. "I was talking about the kid."

Then he went and picked up his denim jacket slung around one of the kitchen stools. But his eye caught something else. McKenzie exhaled, shuffling over the pages in her study guides. Studying for a test while having multiple jobs felt like moving in or moving out of a house alone. It was an uphill battle that she was never winning. McKenzie had scraped by on quite a few grades and quite a few tests over the past eight years at Yavapai College. She had even retaken a couple courses in math and science until she received a passing grade. It wasn't that she wasn't capable of good grades, it was that her life didn't give her the room to do the work needed for good grades. And now she was here, the last semester of her life. She had come this far, and she didn't want to wait any longer. She had been waiting for this opportunity her whole life.

She had to make it.

"Hey," he said, his voice softer. "I never thanked you for my hat."

When she looked up, he was wearing the massive cowboy hat, filling up half the kitchen and blocking the windows.

Kenzie shook her head. She couldn't help but smile now. "Thank you for mine," she finally let out.

He smiled back, then picked up her vintage U of A ball cap. His words were sweet to her, because what he had done meant so much more to her than he knew. Or maybe he did.

"Put it on," she said.

Nolan set the enormous hat down, then slipped on the old baseball cap. The bill was curved and low on him. It fit like a glove. He looked like a ballplayer as he tucked his hands into his jacket, his eyes hidden high up under the brim. Yet, he was still mysterious, even in his unassuming, kind, gentleness. McKenzie looked him up and down. He was taller and stronger than any baseball player she'd ever known, and more handsome. The low hat drew attention to his strong jawline and the bruises hidden in his beard, which she inspected as he stood there. But his eyes were still bright and looked more bluish now than gray, even from under the shadowy brim.

"It looks good on you."

He smiled. He was happy to see her relieved, even for that instant. He took his hand out of his pocket and tapped the top of her hat, the same way he had with the cowboy brim.

"We'll holler if we find him." And he walked out the door.

She took a deep breath.

He wasn't like anyone she'd ever known. No baseball player, no cowboy, no roughneck, no man she had ever known. He was a man with a faded Australian accent, who had been around the world twice before he was twenty-one. A man who said so little, but she knew felt so much. A man that she knew felt just as much as her.

And it scared her.

Because she realized then that he must be feeling about her just as much as she was feeling about him.

True spring was coming closer and closer, and the sun was warm through the clear sky, elevating the day's temperature fast and comfortably. Aiden and Nolan walked briskly through the neighborhoods toward downtown. Aiden hopped and skipped, telling Nolan about his old elementary school they were crossing by. He pointed out that he used to always climb the big boulders in the schoolyard. Nolan smiled, recalling them from his walk home with McKenzie the night before.

Everything must have been real, because even with a bunch of whiskey and beer in him, he remembered those rocks during their loud night walk home. And that meant everything that he remembered feeling that night, and everything they had woken up feeling, was real too.

Aiden and Nolan walked and chatted happily for a mile in the bright afternoon. Nolan didn't speak much—he didn't have to. Aiden was just happy to tell another person—a man—things that he thought were cool or funny. Really, Aiden was just happy to have someone listen to him. To have someone care.

Nolan had never forgotten about the loneliness of his youth. How scary and how isolating it had been, not knowing who to turn to or who was an adult that he could trust. He had been betrayed, deceived, and manipulated more than once. But none of that mattered anymore. More important now, he cared about Aiden.

The truck was across from the courthouse in a local neighborhood. When they got to it, Aiden raved. "This is the biggest truck in town!"

Aiden beamed, which surprised Nolan. He'd seen plenty of large rigs in the state. Nolan double-checked under the hood and saw that everything was still in order. He came around the passenger side and took his hands from his denim to unlock it for Aiden.

"Can ya make it?" he asked, seeing that the truck's step bar was half of Aiden's height. But Aiden didn't even second guess it—he reached up, yanked the truck's door handle, grabbed the doorway's hinge, then pulled himself up.

Nolan was impressed.

He went around the front of the truck and jumped up, effortlessly, like he did when he mounted a horse.

"Ready for the best part?"

He looked over at Aiden and slid the key into the ignition. Aiden waited with a smile. And with a flick of the wrist, the white beast roared to life.

The Ford rumbled through town, every window down, blaring Led Zeppelin. Aiden was riding in the truck bed now, happily bouncing up and down. He popped his head in through the back window, then twisted sideways to look at Nolan.

"Now where!?"

"We're gonna get Dee-Oh-Gee," he said.

"What's that?" Aiden's brows arched.

"You'll see."

Nolan let out a small smile and the truck continued roaring down the boulevard.

Nolan and Aiden stepped into Goldie's office. D.O.G. came flying from around the corner with his tongue flailing.

"Doggie!"

Aiden beamed and ruffled his eyes and ears. D.O.G. was still wearing his bandages, like Nolan, but refused to wear his protective cone, which Goldie had learned the hard way earlier in the week. The dog was stubborn, though surprisingly, he did not pick at his wounds. He was smart enough to leave them be. D.O.G. was healing quickly, as was Nolan, who still had bandages and stitches under his flannel and shirt. Goldie came around the corner in his old white, knee-length veterinarian coat, with his suede boots popping out from his jeans.

His eyes widened.

"You cease to amaze me, young man." Goldie said, his eyes turning into a grand smile. He wasn't even sure what to say or what to ask—he was just thrilled to see him again, as was D.O.G.

"Long time no see," Nolan said to Goldie and the dog, who was ecstatic as ever to be petted by Nolan and the newcomer, Aiden.

"And who's this handsome feller?" Goldie looked down at Aiden.

"I'm Aiden, the javelina hunter. Who are you?"

Goldie's brows raised, not sure how to distinguish himself. "I'm Goldie…the…animal helper."

"Hmm." Aiden nodded, accepting the title, then returned to petting D.O.G.

"You come to get Nolan's dog?" Goldie asked.

"This is *your* dog!?"

Aiden was thrilled by it. Nolan stood upright with his hands in his denim, watching the two excitedly.

"Sorta."

"He don't hunt javelina, this dog, but he does fight coyotes," Goldie followed with his smile. Nolan knew what he meant. But the reunion became stifled by a fit of throat-scratching coughs. Goldie's face flushed red in an instant, and he quickly took to the back office. Nolan watched him move to the other side of the back-office doorway, then half turned, taking out a handful of pills from his desk. Goldie breathed through it, downing a few pills at a time then chugging some water.

Nolan watched closely.

Goldie walked back into the room with a smile, but Nolan had been around that sight plenty to know the look—something was wrong.

"So, what could I possibly ask you first, mon ami?" Goldie sipped more water and smiled while Aiden played tug-of-war with D.O.G.

"I got a question for you, actually."

"Shoot."

"You want help around that ranch?"

Goldie's smile slowly grew.

As did Nolan's.

The white Ford hurtled up the road, windows down and Led Zeppelin blasting. Nolan wore McKenzie's hat, brim low, air rushing over his beard and face. He lifted his eyes to peek in the rearview mirror. Aiden and D.O.G. were riding in the back, waving and barking at people on the streets.

"*Awhooooooo!*" Nolan called.

"*Ow ow awhoooo!*" Aiden immediately called back.

The Ford truck pulled up to some storefronts just around the corner from Whiskey Row. Nolan pulled out what cash remained in his jacket pocket. It wasn't much, not more than a couple days' worth. He hadn't planned on more than that. He hadn't planned on a lot of things that had been happening. He wondered how much cash was left in his duffle bag sitting in the bed with the boys, and how long he could stretch it. Then he thought about the small duffle full of cash he left on the kitchen table in the motorhome, and what Ezequiel must have felt when he or his kids opened it.

With a slow inhale, Nolan reached into his glove compartment. His Ruger pistol was there, waiting. He pulled it out and double-checked the magazine, accounting for every single round, but made sure Aiden didn't see. He tucked it into his black jeans behind his belt. But before he closed the glove compartment, he saw something else.

It was the Polaroid.

It was *them.*

The way they'd been. He shifted in his seat, the .45 pressing tightly at his waist. He held there, staring at the photo. It was the very last of them. And he returned to those same questions that he incessantly wondered— what was he doing? What should he do? What would she think of him now? It was all coming to him, rushing him, a storm on the brink of thunder, like every time just before a fight, waiting for the bell, waiting to unleash. With the gun ready, Nolan knew what he had to do. He tucked the photo into his left side denim pocket, where it always was, and always was supposed to be.

"Where we at?" Aiden asked, popping his head through the window and pulling Nolan out of his own.

"I gotta make a quick stop." He made sure his denim was hiding the pistol. "You two guard the truck in case any douchebags come mess with it."

"What's a douchebag?" Aiden stared.

Nolan shook his head. "Just howl if anything happens. Or if you see your brother."

Nolan jumped out and headed toward one of the storefronts.

The silver Ruger pistol was sitting on a glass counter. Above it, Nolan's eyes were fixated, and in front of him, an old clerk with a thick beard examined the weapon.

Nolan looked up to find the man smiling.

"She's a beaut'. You get 'er from Mike?"

Nolan was puzzled, but the clerk went about counting cash next to a final pawn shop release form, then set it on the counter for Nolan.

"What?" Nolan asked.

"Mike at Ruger."

"I don't follow," Nolan said, looking at the old clerk, who looked back, surprised.

"You know where this piece comes from, right?"

The clerk pointed down at the .45 with his pen. Etched on the side of the gun's narrow squared barrel were the words *Made in Prescott, AZ*.

Nolan read it, then read it again.

He'd had this gun for two years, and even when he'd purchased it somewhere in Colorado, he'd never once realized the fine, meticulous engraving on the side of the barrel.

"I never noticed," Nolan said, still surprised.

"Made right in the heart of town."

The clerk finished the paperwork, then tapped the wad of cash resting on the receipt of sale and final documents. He tapped the place for Nolan to sign.

"God is in the details," he said. "The devil, too, depending how you look at it." The clerk smiled.

Nolan took the pen resting atop the paperwork and tilted the ball cap. He wondered then if he'd ever noticed the name, or simply forgotten it. It wasn't his first handgun, but he had planned it to be his last.

He had planned many things. Things he felt shameful thinking about now. He thought of *Her* and how she'd disliked weapons. But when they'd started traveling the country together, he'd known he had to be prepared for anything. Even if that put his deportation at risk.

Little had he known then that this pistol would one day not be used to defend himself. He had planned for a far worse use of it. And now he was here, in the very home it was made, and he was selling it back for cash to do something right with it. Something on a whim of an impulse, something good that he thought he could actually do for others. And still, Nolan was surprised. Of all the towns and all the weapons made in the world, of all pistols—and he knew his way around all of them—he had never once noticed where his pistol was made. And now he was here.

Nolan read the engraved writing one last time, then collected the cash.

"Don't spend it all in one place, they say." The clerk smiled.

Nolan adjusted the ball cap, tilted it to the man, and walked out.

Early spring's midday light was cooling. Kenzie stood on the porch wearing a pair of warm, tan Ugg boots, tight blue jeans, and a long, loose cashmere sweater that was long enough to cover her hands and dripped below her neckline and shoulders. Her chest filled the sweater out and the fabric hung comfortably past her curved hips. She loved being warm and cozy at home, but right now, her entire body was so heated that she broke a sweat. Kenzie was on her cell phone, arguing with Turner in one hand, and with the other, leaning on the porch's wooden rail, looking at an array of books and study materials. The porch rail was lined with note sheets and books, all side by side, in order of completion and task.

At the end of the line was a stack of finished paperwork, notes, and books that she had plowed through during the day. It was an assembly line, a strategy she had thought of to keep herself focused on what she needed to review and re-review. But right now, her blood was on fire.

"If he's there, then you need to tell me, Turner! He's been gone all night."

"He ain't here, Mac. Fuck. I'm not gonna lie just 'cause you pissed me off."

"Look," she demanded. "I'm sitting here, worrying and trying to study. I told you how important this is. If he shows up, you need to talk to him as his *dad*, not his once-a-month buddy."

Turner breathed heavily through the phone, his voice deepening. "You know I'll talk to him…" He said it in a way that McKenzie knew. He was being cryptic, alluding to what he would do, and he knew that if he said what he really meant, she would throw a fit.

Kenzie stopped pacing to make her point clear. "Turner. Don't lay a hand on him."

It was the one thing she could never forgive him for. Beyond being selfish, he was physical with the boys. Jason, especially. But Jason wasn't your average teenage boy. He naturally took more of Kenzie's independence and guarded sensitivity. Turner thought that roughhousing and being hard on his sons was the way to mold a man. To make a man grow. But to Kenzie, it was just their hero bullying them. She knew Jason wasn't getting stronger because of it—no, he was slowly folding into himself.

Turner always had this "good ol' boy" opinion of what a man was and what he should be: strong, fierce, aggressive. A leader at all costs. Fear and strength were the core of what Turner thought a leader conveyed. That the power of fear inherited respect and loyalty. That fear created toughness and virtues in a man.

And McKenzie, too, thought that was the way it was supposed to be. But like all the greatest leaders understand, fear is the opposite of what constitutes leadership. Fear does not cause one to learn or to grow. And the power to create fear is not the power of strength. True strength came in courage, in sacrifice, in facing fear. True strength came in service and in doing the right thing, like her Gram. But McKenzie was always just halfway there to that understanding. Because for her, there were no strong men in her life. There were no fathers or uncles or friends that helped her understand what a man was or what a man could do. What a man ought to do. Then, as time and adolescence told, she had experienced what it was like to be preyed upon and objectified by men because of the way she looked.

Then, Turner had gotten her pregnant.

As a single mother, she had learned what it was like to be a good-looking woman with two kids, trying to make ends meet all on her own. She had to be a woman and a man. A mother and a father.

Men were a judgmental obstruction, an antagonizing force, and that, in essence, was because there had never been a true man in her world.

The strongest person in her world was Gram.

And no one she'd ever met was as strong as her.

Gram showed strength through love, forgiveness, and truly listening. She was eternally passionate about kindness and wanted to help others. McKenzie had learned through Gram where real strength and leadership could be found: in the opposite direction of fear.

"I'll do it the way I should do it," Turner said, cutting into her, knowing he was speaking in his controlling, overbearing way. He was going to rough up Jason for his behavior and she knew it. Her knuckles tightened. If Turner were here in front of her, she would put her fist in his eye. Or her nails.

"Did you *hear* me? If you fucking touch him—"

"What?" he interrupted with a bite. "You'll sic your bitch on me?"

McKenzie took a long breath. She didn't want to win the argument. She wanted him to understand her, loud and clear. "If you wanna be a man and handle this like a man, then get off your high horse and work with me. But if you wanna bully me or our son, or pull that shit again like the other night, I'll walk your ass to county and make sure you got a fat fucking blemish on your pretty rodeo resume."

Turner went silent.

She had never once tried to get at him through his career. Through his dream. And he hated her for it.

"You know what, bitch? Forget Easter. Take the boys wherever the fuck you want."

"*Turner!*" she shouted just before he got out the last word. Her heart was pounding, and her blood was boiling. "If Jason shows up, you *call* me. Have a nice Easter. Hope your face is still busted, *bitch.*"

And she smashed the *End Call* button.

Her fists were shaking. She tried to breathe through it, but all she wanted to do was hit something. After a couple of deep breaths, she grabbed her next textbook and notes from her assembly line, then plopped down on the deck chair. As she did, an unmistakable piece of mail slid out from the pages. It was her mother's rehab bill. And it was due in two weeks. McKenzie shut her eyes and clenched them tight. She wanted to scream, yell, cry, punch the deck, when—

Rock and roll came booming up the block, rattling windows in the whole neighborhood. It was the Ford truck. Aiden and D.O.G. were sitting high on two mattresses covered in plastic in the truck bed.

"*Ow ow awhoooooooo!*" Aiden shouted as the large Ford bounced into the driveway. Nolan killed the engine, silencing the rumble and the wailing guitars of Led Zeppelin.

Aiden leaped out the back, then went around the back and popped open the truck bed for D.OG. The metal door slammed, and the dog hopped out. McKenzie just stood on the porch, not sure what to think of the commotion.

"We got beds!" Aiden yelled, grabbing some supplies off a plastic mattress in the back. Without even looking at his mother, he booked it for the front door. D.O.G. chased him the whole way, his tongue flailing as they burst into the house.

"What?" McKenzie finally asked, but Aiden was long gone and yelling back.

"I gotta clean my room!"

Nolan hopped out of the truck, still wearing her University of Arizona hat. He pulled a long and narrow box out of the truck as McKenzie stormed up, her blood still red hot.

"Why'd you do that?"

Nolan looked over. He slid the box out and leaned it against the truck. "I had a coupon."

"Yeah, real funny. Answer me." She softened, but was still angry. "You shouldn't have done that," she said. She didn't have a real reason to be mad, but she was.

Her independence and self-reliance were everything to her. And she never wanted nobody—and certainly no man—to help her, or think she would ever owe them something. She owed nothing to nobody and wanted it to always be like that. And now she was heated, staring at Nolan, her hip cocked and arms folded.

As he unloaded the other boxes holding the new bed frames, Nolan saw that she meant it. "Look," he said, stopping. "It wasn't hard to help. I wanted to." He stood there, firm, knowing that she would either get angrier, or let it go.

But she didn't know what to say or feel about it. Because it was different with Nolan. It was genuine. Whether he had the money or not, he did it because he wanted to. Because he could. Not because he had to.

Nolan lifted two long boxes and hooked one under each arm, expanding his shoulders and tightening his back muscles. His bruised biceps flexed, lifting what must have been forty-five pounds in each arm, bowing out with each four-foot-long box frame.

He stopped to look her in the eye. "You study, we'll build."

Then he headed up to the house. Kenzie just stood there, watching him go.

"You know he can't ride in the back without a seatbelt? It's illegal."

Nolan stopped, thought about it. "Shit," he said, then kept going.

She was agitated and felt like she had to protest—or at least get the last word in. Besides Gram, she thought of herself as the strongest person in her world—and right now she wasn't. She was flustered, and yet, she was happy at the same time.

"And you did tell him that's *your* dog, right!?"

Nolan was already pushing the front door open with the large frames. "Sorta," he said nonchalantly, then walked inside. Kenzie shook her head, standing alone in the driveway.

Then she smiled.

Jason's phone rang, but he still wasn't answering McKenzie's calls. She had to give it a rest now and put her focus back into her studying. As she returned to the last paragraph in the text, there was a calm that came over her. She could hear the boys tinkering away and building in the other room. Their constant talk and laughter were soothing. She had been studying for two hours now but had called Jason every twenty minutes.

The light was beginning to dip into shades of cool blue. She could see it happening through the kitchen windows, near where she had set up shop. It was the happiest and most efficient block of time she had had studying all weekend. And perhaps it was because she was at peace, knowing that she was doing the best she could, but also because her little boy was in the other room playing, learning, and laughing with Nolan.

There are few things sweeter to a woman than to hear a child truly happy. Especially for a mother.

The house was warm now, and McKenzie had changed into a low-cut black tank top, black skinny jeans, and her black boots. When she finally got up from her seat, she threw on her favorite red lumberjack flannel and headed to the bedrooms. D.O.G. immediately greeted her, as he had done over the past two hours, running in and out of each room, happy as hell to be in a new house full of scents and people.

Kenzie stood in the doorway. She found Aiden and Nolan working on the floor, nearly finished with the first new bed frame. Aiden sat on his new mattress to the side and lifted the power drill up when he saw his mom. "Almost done! See?" He pulled the trigger and the tip twirled.

"I see." She smiled approvingly. She could also see that Nolan was still wearing her hat. When he looked back at her, a smile came to his eyes.

He turned to the new bed frame and set a screw up for Aiden. He was determined to get both beds built tonight.

"All right, ready," Nolan said. Aiden excitedly leaned in with the drill and pulled the trigger, screwing one of the last bolts into his new bed.

McKenzie watched as she leaned in the doorway, petting D.O.G. "You boys wanna go to one of my favorite places?"

Aiden looked up. "Will there be food?"

"Maybe. After."

"Can D.O.G. come?" Aiden immediately asked.

"If Nolan does." She smiled.

Hearing his name, Nolan broke his focus. He looked up to see McKenzie in the doorway, smiling at him.

TO LOVE AND BE LOVED

T he white Ford roared through a long, densely forested road. The sun burst between tall trees and chased them through their open windows. Nolan looked over to find McKenzie, eyes shut, smiling into the warm light that caught her between the leaves. Nolan's right hand was atop the wide steering wheel and his left elbow leaned outside the window, protected by his denim jacket that blocked the cool air. The paved black road was long and winding, and it seemed as though they had been headed uphill for miles. In the truck bed were Aiden and D.O.G., slipping and sliding around and loving it.

Wind surged at them from every direction only to be broken by the kisses of sunlight. Nolan looked over again. Her hair flared wildly, and she smiled bright, lost in the light, pleasantly content, and in some ways, completely free. Nolan's eyes drifted between her and the road, making sure he drove as smoothly as possible. He watched her hair spill and fly with the wind. Then he realized that he was still wearing her hat. He wondered if he should give it to her.

Yet every time he looked over, it seemed as though she became even happier. Whether it was the forest or the sun or the endless flow of wind that rushed into the truck and scattered her hair, whatever the moment was—she loved it.

And Nolan couldn't help but look.

He didn't want to disturb her. However she felt, whatever she was thinking or feeling, he knew—something was perfect to her. Nolan's gut tightened and he looked away. He was trying to stop himself from pondering any further, wondering any further. He was already afraid of all that he might think…

Or what he might feel.

All that mattered now was that she was content. Nolan was just regaining his focus when she finally looked over to him. Her skin felt warm and rejuvenated and her smile was peaceful and true. Her cheeks dimpled and her lips pressed to one another until she finally spoke.

"Turn up there."

Nolan looked at her again. He could feel how happy she was. It was soaking into him, just looking at her. But before she turned with her smile, Nolan recomposed himself and looked to see what she meant. There was a trail road up ahead, just off the side of the road. He slowed the steel beast, its massive tires gripping and treading, then turned off onto a narrow dirt path that led to the mountainside.

The sun prepared to set over the western forest. The white Ford was parked high with its tail facing the panorama of an open valley, layered in miles of pine and hills and mountains. The expanse was wider than their eyes could perceive. The crystal clarity of the sky shared the descending sun, making the layers of mountains and hills feel completely endless. The truck was parked just before the cliff's ledge, separated by large rocks that clustered together like raw diamonds colored in browns, grays, and other shades of untouched earth. Nolan and McKenzie dangled their boots off the ledge of the truck bed while Aiden and D.O.G. ran behind them on the dirt road. Aiden was collecting and tossing thick pinecones for D.O.G. to fetch. His playfully high voice was having full dialogues with the dog, telling him every detail about his finds and the type of baseball throws he would ask him to catch.

McKenzie was smiling, but it was softer now, and when Nolan thought he could steal a look, he did, turning to his left.

Never did he imagine he would be there, looking at this amazing vista. Amidst the great many deserts and flatlands of Arizona, it was a place that he would have never known even existed. And to his left, this woman, who, in just a few days, had made their time spent together feel meaningful and effortless.

Like he had always known her.

And still...he couldn't help but think of moments in his past with *Her*. These two women were completely different, and yet there was something deeply shared between them, within them, something that smiled through their eyes and words and wounds and all of their movements.

He saw it. He felt it. Kenzie reminded him of *Her,* and yet, Kenzie was completely herself. And in so many ways different.

The silent mountain air was still and cool, but the gust of thoughts and feelings sent needles dancing up his spine. Not because he thought that McKenzie or *Her* were the same or different, but because he thought they were both incredible. Never did he imagine he would meet a person like McKenzie, especially after he had long lost someone who made him feel so much. McKenzie was someone who reminded him, like the greatest of people do, that we are always capable of feeling ourselves more, as well as those around us.

"When I was a girl..." she said, staring into the valley and interrupting Nolan's thoughts, "I'd come here to escape, or think. Or dream..."

The valley was everlasting. Stunning. But for Kenzie, it still carried the weight of her past. The last time she was here, she had been fifteen, and had run away from home. She was alone.

And she was pregnant.

Nolan's shoulder was slanted toward her and his chin turned just enough to see her without fully facing her. But he was listening, in every sense of it, trying to understand her.

"What would you dream about?"

She stifled a laugh. "It'll sound super heavy."

"Try me," he said confidently.

"Just *why*," she said. "Why anything. Why everything. Why *me*."

He wasn't sure what she meant, but he thought about his own life. They were words and feelings that had echoed throughout his own life. Throughout his entire mind. His entire heart. Especially after losing *Her*.

Especially now, here, looking at Kenzie.

"And?" he asked.

"And what?"

"And what do you think?" he insisted, wanting to understand.

She took her time. Her words were affirming and true to her. There was a faith and hope she had held onto, a faith and hope she'd had to keep since she was last here, fifteen and pregnant, with no one but her grandmother who wanted to help.

"I think everything happens for a reason," she said. "Even the things we don't want. I think we have to dig deep and make our own *why*. Things just make more sense that way. And I think, if anything, it shows us who we are, or who we can be."

He was hanging on her words. Her sense of depth, her sense of pain and hope and truth—they were things he saw. They were all things he felt. And to Nolan, it was as if she was speaking to him, for him, through him.

McKenzie finally turned to look at him. "What do you think?"

"I think you're pretty smart…for a country girl."

She pushed him. His elbows bowed out, but he kept his hands tightly in his pockets, accidentally brushing the Polaroid inside. He had forgotten it was there. His head lowered and he let go of his smile. He was at war with everything inside, and he knew it was more than what she knew, or perhaps could ever handle.

"Can I ask you something?" she said.

He looked to her, his stomach tightening.

"Why do you want to go to the Grand Canyon so bad?"

He turned to the wide valley in front of him. His fists clenched inside, and he was controlling everything within from moving or showing how uncomfortable he became. The sunset was almost under the brim of his hat and he kept his head low to hide from the light. He didn't want her to look into his eyes. He didn't want her to fully see him, judge him, or maybe…

Feel him.

"It was the last place *she* wanted to go," he finally said. "And I thought it was the last place I *needed* to go…"

She stared. Somehow, she knew exactly what he meant.

All this time, he hadn't been going to the Grand Canyon to visit. He had been going there to die.

And it made her furious. She exhaled, trying to hold back from letting him have it. "So, you were gonna just give up?"

He didn't answer. She shook her head at his silence. He kept his head low, blocking the light.

"Don't you believe in anything?" she accused. McKenzie huffed, then turned away.

He'd told her the truth, as best he could, but now he was left with his guilt. She was devastated he would ever consider such a thing. He was special to her. No—more than that. He was incredible. There were no other ways to describe what he was or what he meant to her now.

"Come on." She turned to face him. She wasn't going to give up on him. "Tell me what you believe in, Nolan."

She waited. "Use your words." she said.

His chin lifted. The setting sun found his eyes and filled his face with unobstructed shades of red, orange, and yellow. He felt the sunset, and he even dared to look into it for a moment before turning to the valley and fixating on something that wasn't even there.

"When I look at that," he said quietly, "I see God."

His eyes flicked up to the sunset, then submerged back into the valley.

"I see him, right in front of us. Everything he can do." He waited a moment, but it was no use—it was all he ever thought about.

"But how can I believe *anything* if he can control what happens? All the shit he lets happen? What he let happen to *Her*? How can I believe in him? How can I believe in *anything*?" He exhaled his last word as if he had held his breath the entire time, wanting to say everything.

McKenzie calmed. She understood him now. Now more than ever. She didn't think of his secret and why it made her angry. She thought about why it made him hurt.

"I don't know why things happen the way they do, but they *are* for a reason," she said quietly but firmly. "And I don't think God controls that. Or our happiness. I think what God is—what *that* is—is love." She was looking into all the colors now, bursting in the sky. "I think God is love."

Nolan lowered his head. The brim of the ball cap blocked it all.

"I think we just get so hurt by the things that happen, that we become too scared to face them, or learn from them. But how could we ever really live or grow if we don't learn from the things that hurt us?"

He was full of pain. Full of shame. And it all frustrated him, because deep down, she was right. Of all the things that made him strong, he still wasn't strong enough to face them himself, to face them like her. And now he was just angry with himself and with everything.

"So, what's your deal then?" he snapped. "You got it all figured out. What are you afraid of, Kenzie?"

She turned, thrown by the anger in his voice. He sounded like so many of the men who had hurt her in the past. And whether she had always known this about herself or had always felt this way about Nolan, she looked him right in his eyes, and her words immediately poured from her lips. "I'm afraid to trust. And I'm afraid to trust *you*."

They froze. Their eyes didn't waver for a second.

They were both charged, emotional, bewildered. He didn't know what she meant. And neither did she in this moment. But their anger dispersed quickly, like the song of the wind and fading light. It was dipping below the mountains now, and Kenzie, afraid to see his eyes any longer, looked to the sliver of light that lined the base of the mountains to the west. Nolan breathed in, discreetly as he could, masking his feelings again and turning to the remains of the light.

And although they were both turning inside, they both saw the very moment when the sun went down, together.

D.O.G. came flying toward them, just as Aiden jumped on the massive rear tire and grabbed the white Ford's metal bed, causing a loud *clink* sound, pulling the two away from the light. "We're hungry!"

McKenzie looked between Aiden and Nolan, who hopped off the back of the truck, his hands held tightly in his denim. Nolan stepped out to the rocky ledge alone. He didn't want the boy to see his face, knowing that he wouldn't be able to hide from both of them. He stood on the large rocks just above the mountain's edge and looked out to the remaining light.

McKenzie quickly changed the subject. "Well, guess who's down at El Charro hoping we'll come to dinner?" she asked, looking at her cell phone.

Aiden swung up and down, holding on to the side of the truck, squatting and popping back up. "Jackson, Tyler, Dylan, Tony, and Danielle?" he replied.

"Damn, kid," McKenzie said, surprised. "You nailed it."

"Are you coming, too, Nolan?"

He was standing on the ledge and gently rolling small rocks under his heavy boot. Nolan turned back halfway, his hands releasing their grip upon hearing his name come from Aiden. He thought about what to say…almost too long.

"Of course, he is," McKenzie jumped in.

Aiden smiled. She glanced at Nolan, then an idea came to her. "Hey, you know who else we could invite?"

"Who?" Aiden quickly asked.

"Let me see…" she said, and hopped off the bed of the truck, looking at her phone while walking to the front of the truck, toward the direction of town, hoping she'd get better reception.

Aiden jumped off the tire and dashed for Nolan. "*Hey*! Nolan!"

He ran so fast that Nolan's eyes snapped alert. Nolan idled just inches from the ledge, and Aiden was charging right at him. Nolan popped a knee forward and ripped his hands from his pockets, instantly striking out and stopping Aiden by the shoulders. "Easy, mate!"

"I know, I saw it!"

The dog stopped right between the two and they all stood there on the ledge.

"Oi, careful on these rocks, okay?" Nolan insisted.

"I know, I know," Aiden assured him.

Kenzie was standing just ahead of the truck's nose, frozen, her stomach knotted. If Aiden had made one mistake, one misstep, or simply tripped, he would have been gone. It was primal motherly instincts, feeling the danger in that instant, still rushing her entire body. Aiden had been running too fast, like he always did. And he could have gone over. But now, she watched them there on the ledge. She had one hand on her phone, ready to make a call, but she couldn't move.

Nolan looked down to Aiden, keeping his hands free. "You know what would happen if you fell down there?"

Without saying it, Aiden knew, peering over the cliff that plummeted a mile straight down into the valley.

Nolan smiled and poked Aiden's shoulder. "I'd have to climb all the way down and get ya."

Aiden looked up and grinned, thinking it was a clever thing to say, then he carefully went around a set of cliffside boulders. He was within eye shot of Nolan, but just out of sight from Kenzie. Aiden sat on a ledge with a small cliff below him, getting his own private view of the canyon. But Nolan and the dog leaned over their shoulders and watched Aiden, making sure he was safe and being smart.

And all this time, Kenzie was still staring. Nolan's right leg was elevated on a boulder higher than his left, and the dog was there on the ledge with him, between him and the valley, both looking at the little ledge that Aiden carefully sat on. The sky expressed streaks of orange, yellow, and blue, and the brightest part was a burst of sherbet light hovering over Nolan's shoulder.

Kenzie still hadn't moved. She thought about his words and what he'd told Aiden. She thought about what he said earlier and how deeply he felt. His hands were in his denim now, knowing that Aiden was safe, but he and the dog continued to watch him closely, his back to the light that streaked behind him like the rays of the state flag. Nolan was completely unaware, and it didn't matter to him—his eyes were on Aiden. Only Kenzie and Aiden could see the amazing light ahead of them, but nothing distracted her from looking at Nolan now.

He was bruised, he was strong, and he was kind. He looked like a ball player and could ride better than any cowboy she had ever known. He was mysterious, quiet, and yet, after only a few days, she felt like she had always known him. Especially through this boyish side she had now seen come to life around Aiden. He was just like her own two boys—owners of guarded, hopeful souls that would only come out when thoughtfully provoked with a playful joke, or with love. His pain was deep, much deeper than hers, and still, he selflessly cared about others. He cared so deeply for Aiden that she could see it. And she knew now what he meant to her. She had said in an instance of anger that she was afraid to trust him, but that wasn't it at all. She realized now that she was scared, because she completely *did* trust him. And in a great burst of final light and truth glowing over his shoulder, right before her, she knew now why any of this made her fearful, and why it had taken this very moment for her to understand.

She had fallen completely in love with him.

It was Sunday evening. They were downtown, parked in front of El Charro, a Mexican restaurant that had been in the old western building just south of Whiskey Row for over sixty-five years. McKenzie was introducing Nolan to a handful of friends. They were all in their thirties, some couples, some single men and women. Some carpenters, neighbors, and local bartenders. Nolan could tell they were all good people. A few of them had kids, who Aiden was quick to greet and run off with. McKenzie greeted and hugged them all with her way and her smile.

Nolan was quick to notice. It was a thing she possessed—this enveloping light that came about every time she saw someone she cared about. He was watching her, just being her. And they loved her. People *loved* her. Nolan couldn't help but smile, because he truly admired that about her. Then his smile unexpectedly grew wider, seeing someone he knew.

It was Goldie. He approached them from the street and hugged McKenzie, then he was quick to shake Nolan's hand. "How ya doing, young man?"

He realized then that Goldie was the person McKenzie had called from the forest lookout. Nolan's eyes said what his surprise couldn't—he was happy.

The interior of El Charro was covered in old brick, soft red mood lights and burning candles that made it warm and intimate. They sat at a long, family-sized table in the corner, facing the courtyard's window. Nolan could see his truck—he had planned it that way—and D.O.G., who was tied in the back, patiently sat and watched them through the restaurant's old glass window. They were all laughing and drinking margaritas. Nolan sat at the conjoined table across from Kenzie. She was facing the group and smiling.

She tucked a stand of hair behind her ear. Nolan noticed and watched as she spoke warmly with all of her friends surrounding them. He was content just to sit and watch her. She was easily the life of the party, along with Goldie, who was also thrilled to be amongst many good people, cracking his jokes and telling his old stories and proverbs.

Aiden ran up and down the restaurant dining room, then in and out of the building with his friends. They were excited to come back and play waiter, refilling everyone's drinks—especially the margaritas, which Aiden had somehow convinced the waiter he was equipped to do. It felt like friends and family all coming together to share a meal after a long week of hard work and sacrifice. A time of blood, sweat, and tears, met with a table full of people, just happy to be around each other. Just happy to celebrate. And Nolan was there, pleasantly observing, taking it all in.

This—Nolan thought to himself. Whatever *this* was, felt like family. Something he had only felt a handful of times in his life traveling across the world and living around Canada and North America. Being here was an inkling and memory of feelings that he recalled with the farmers and ranchers and fighters who had all raised him.

And *Her*.

He felt those feelings again. Here. Now. Looking at Kenzie and these people who loved her. They couldn't help but love her. And he loved that about her too.

Goldie dinged his margarita with his fork, getting the table's attention. He had to make his mandatory toast. He explained to them, just as he had to Nolan and Kenzie back on the ranch, "One must toast to the moment, whenever such a moment with friends and family should avail."

As he spoke, Nolan did not muse. All he did was look at her. The way she was smiling. It meant something to him now. *She* meant something to him, and more than what he was letting himself feel.

And then *she* caught him.

She saw the way he was looking at her. A wave inside rushed her. A movement in the depths of primal instincts and tender truths stored within the heart. And this time, amid the conversations and toasts and words and music and laughter, he did not turn away. When she looked over again this time, he was still looking.

She held eyes with him.

As if to challenge.

As if to understand that depth, surfacing in the other person. And truth came. The truth that only the resolute bonding of one's eyes could say. His fists were clenched and his fingers folded tightly into his hands, fighting to keep his composure as he looked right into her.

But she wouldn't look away either.

Then, under the table, her leg reached for his. She pressed her calf against his and leaned against him. And with a small shift in her eyes, she looked away, releasing her tension in a small, private smile. His fists released, his palms slowly opening.

He slid his leg, leaning into hers. Both of their throats tightened, then released. Something traveled up their stomachs and stopped at their hearts. He exhaled, his hands fully at rest.

And he knew.

He could no longer ignore it.

He was still looking at her because he couldn't look away.

He was in love with her.

OF FAMILY AND FRIENDS

M cKenzie chatted with a friend who had just begun his shift at El Charro's bar. For dinner, their table enjoyed several plates of hand-rolled tamales, chile rellenos, savory brown beans sprinkled with Mexican cheese, and a variety of salsa-drenched burritos. It was a true feast, and the kids all happily hopped around with their own bean and cheese burritos, each comparing the different-colored salsas they had scavenged from the waiters.

Nolan shared a couple chats with her friends. He was polite, but he was more interested in just sharing the space and observing these people. He knew he had to speak at some point, so he got to know Jeff, who was a mechanic across town. His kids had grown up with McKenzie's kids and they went to neighboring high schools. Despite how much McKenzie felt like she was on her own, Nolan came to see how many people cared about her. Maybe it was that she felt differently about herself or them. Maybe it was different because she only allowed herself to be vulnerable with very few. These were things that Nolan thought and could understand now. They were things he felt and wondered if he could one day ask her. Maybe talk to her about.

Nolan happily finished his second margarita, the same as Kenzie. He wanted to share the same level of intoxication with her. He had abused the drink before, whether as a scapegoat or as a crutch to his physical pain, but it had always been a crutch for his mental pain. Yet, while he battled his overthinking mind day in and day out, this feeling of celebration with these people felt good to him, albeit a lot of work, as he wasn't normally social.

When he saw that Jeff, Aiden, Goldie, and Kenzie were distracted, he slipped out the front door. Nolan took in the cool, quiet night with a deep inhale. El Charro's was loud, and it was good to feel the separation of sounds for a moment. He didn't want to overthink what he was feeling.

He went to D.O.G., who was elated to see him and quickly threw his paws on the side of the truck. D.O.G. shot his tongue out at Nolan, trying to lick him.

"All right, boy…all right." Nolan pet him, trying to sort out everything going on inside his head. He knew he had fallen in love with Kenzie.

On one hand, it was euphoric, like he could burst through his stitches and bruises, and on the other hand, it was absolutely terrifying.

All the while, he just looked at D.O.G., who stared, just happy to feel his attention. D.O.G.'s light brown eyes looked up and into the sharp eyes of Nolan, who asked aloud, "What would you do, if you were me?"

It was an honest question. He didn't know anymore. How could something like this happen—again?

How was it possible?

But the answer was interrupted.

A high-speed motor screeched from down the brick alleyway.

Nolan looked up, unable to see where it was.

Several motors screamed relentlessly. He could hear tires burning out, followed by a group of laughing teenagers.

Nolan knew it was the sound of dirt bikes.

He patted D.O.G. "Stay."

Then started walking.

The screaming engines and smell of burnt rubber became stronger. Nolan's boots clacked on the street, muted by the bikes. His hands tucked into his denim with his elbows bowing out, expanding his broad wingspan.

The alley of the building was unusually dark, and as he trekked, he could see broken beer bottles and rocks below shattered glass from the the streetlamps and building lights above. He cleared the alley into the dark parking lot, and found a group of teenagers circling recklessly on their dirt bikes.

And amongst them, was Jason, holding a beer. They were all drinking, and when they saw the largely built man in all denim, black jeans, and loud boots coming right at them, they knew they had to go. The five boys scattered, two jumping on their bikes, just as Nolan smacked a beer out of a kid's hand, splattering it on the ground. Jason's eyes widened, and he leaped onto his bike. The engine hummed, ready to take off, when Nolan swung his arm and clotheslined Jason clean off the seat. "Get off! Get the fuck off me!"

Nolan gripped him by the arm and neck, squeezing tightly so he couldn't run or resist. "You think you can run off and do this shit? Why didn't you go home?"

"I *did* go home!"

With all his strength, Jason twisted his body to face Nolan and swung a fist. Nolan stopped it instantly with an erect forearm, then tightened his grip on Jason's arm.

Jason wailed. But then, Nolan noticed something. He let go. Jason caught his breath and staggered back, turning his head away, but Nolan had already seen it.

Jason's ear was swollen purple.

Nolan could tell from the inflammation, he must have been struck more than once. Jason's earlobe was too swollen to be a mistake or from a bike accident. Jason knew Nolan had seen it. He quickly turned and ran for his bike. Nolan side-stepped in front of him, hit the kill-switch, and threw the key, just as Jason took another swing.

But it was blocked by a swipe of Nolan's palm.

"*Ahhh!* Fuck you!"

Jason threw another wild fist, but Nolan side-stepped him again, grabbed him by the neck and regained control of Jason just with his powerful fingers enclosed around his neck.

"Get away from me!" Jason cried out. Nolan clenched his entire arm to hold him at bay. Jason yelled in submission, giving up. Nolan pulled him in, trying to investigate his ear.

"Hey—look at me."

Jason did, breathing heavily between fury and fear.

"Who did that?" Nolan looked him dead in the eye while Jason held onto his wrist.

"The fuck you care!? You're not my fucking dad!"

Jason tried to yank away but Nolan, simply controlling him by the pressure points in his neck, walked him backwards into the alley. Jason nearly tripped over himself before being pinned against the brick wall.

"No, I'm not, you little shit."

Jason scrambled and winced from the pressure in his neck tendons. Nolan kept a thumb wedged in a pressure point behind his uninjured ear, surging Jason with nerve pain that shot throughout his entire skull.

"Who do you think cares about you, huh? Pulling this shit?" Nolan looked him square in the face. "Who do you think cares, your mum or your dad? She fucking loves you, mate. And she's scared shitless 'cause of you!"

Jason couldn't take it.

Any of it.

He finally gave in to the ideas destroying him. All the thwarted innocence and purity and confusion of a child in pain, came spewing. "Why don't they care about me!? Why don't they care!? They *bully* me, they *ignore* me, they *hate* me!" Jason burst out, crying through every bewildered word. It was everything he felt about his mother and father in a cloud of perplexed hurt. Their relationship, their separation, their love, their anger—all the lines were blurred. The idea of selling Gram's house, moving away, this foreign man showing up, nothing made sense to him.

But Nolan felt him now.

He released him.

Jason stood there, shaking. Nolan's hands drifted from his neck to his shoulders, and he held him there so the boy wouldn't fall. But Jason couldn't take anymore. He collapsed, sobbing into Nolan's chest. He wrapped his arms around Nolan and couldn't stop. The boy hadn't cried or been hugged in a very long time.

Nolan was shocked.

He didn't know what to do, until...

Nolan hugged him back. He held Jason, firm but gentle. Jason sobbed, trying to speak through his tears and Nolan's embrace.

"Everyone's got a normal family but me..."

Nolan took a long, deep breath and Jason's face rose and descended with his large chest.

"Mate," he said, his own voice softening. "There's no such thing as normal. I didn't even have a mum *or* a dad."

He wanted to tell him all the right words, but this time, he didn't even think about it. He just held him and told him what he knew. He told him what he felt. "They dropped me off on a farm and never came back. But your mum...she loves you. I know she does."

Tears streamed from Jason's red cheeks. He was so deeply confused and hurt. "But why doesn't Dad?"

"Look, I'm sure he does," Nolan replied, trying to help him understand his pain. "But not everyone knows how to show it. Not in the ways we want. But you can't hurt people you love just because you're hurting, and you can't let them hurt you like that either. You understand?"

They were words that didn't come from his own experiences or people. They were words that came from his heart.

They were things he believed in. Things he believed he could tell this boy, who was not far from his own age when his entire world had changed. Nolan pulled Jason from his chest and held him upright so he could see his face. He was gentle, keeping Jason on his own two feet and looking him calmly in the eyes.

"You gotta be stronger. You gotta protect *you*. So you can protect *them*."

Jason looked at him. He could hear how deeply Nolan was breathing, looking him square in the eye. Nolan, too, was vulnerable, and the tide of his tears rose, but he held them there and showed Jason through his voice and his eyes that he was not mad or displacing him. He was showing the boy what he needed to see now. He was showing him that he was calm. That he understood. That above all, he cared about him.

"You got a lot of family and friends in there having dinner together. They'd be really happy to see you."

"Mom will be mad," Jason said, his cheeks still damp and bright.

"For a second, yeah, because she loves you, mate. She wouldn't get mad if she didn't."

Jason considered it. He wasn't crying anymore. He was listening, trying to understand what he felt and what Nolan was doing for him.

"I...I don't want her to know about Dad."

218

Nolan nodded. He wanted to save the boy his embarrassment and ease the next challenge, but it was going to be difficult. "I'll talk to her, but you also gotta be strong enough to do the right thing, Jason. A man always does."

Jason wiped his face, hearing every word, but keeping his eyes low.

"Hey. You wanna learn how to fight?" Nolan asked then released Jason's shoulders. Jason finally looked up. "I can teach you how to protect yourself. From anyone."

"How?"

"I'm a fighter. Like you."

Jason thought about it. Nolan waited for his eyes and then he smiled. It was his true smile.

Across the alley, someone was watching. McKenzie had seen the entire thing. She was brittle with tears drenching her eyes, and she was about to fall on her knees with them. She quickly went around the corner of the alley and pressed her back against the brick wall.

Then she broke down in tears.

She saw everything that hurt Jason, and at the same time, everything that made Nolan strong. She saw the man she wanted and the father they'd never had. She couldn't intervene, she couldn't explain it, and she couldn't even understand it yet.

All she could do was cry.

Kenzie was cleaned up and talking with her friends at the table. Most of them were finishing their dinners or waiting on another pitcher of margaritas. She wasn't upset any longer, and no one could sense that anything was wrong.

No one except for Goldie, who could feel that something had changed in her energy when she slipped back in. He didn't think much of it, and when she sat back down, he just offered her his pleasant, reassuring smile. Nolan walked in from the back entrance with Jason by his side. They were both calm and walking casually, although Jason was hiding his nerves. McKenzie eyed them the moment they walked in. She watched them with strong but calm eyes, then she stood up and went to them.

Jason didn't say anything, expecting the worst. Instead, she took him in her arms and hugged him as tight as she could. She held him there as Nolan stepped around them and went to sit back down.

Goldie nodded to him, and after Nolan sat, he turned and watched them.

"Hey, you," she said to Jason. "What do you want to eat?"

It wasn't long before Aiden quickly ran up and tackled his brother from the side, almost tipping them both over, but Jason caught himself and hugged his little brother, who clung tightly. Kenzie brought Jason over to the table, and with a series of smiles, hugs, and handshakes, they all greeted him and pulled up a chair.

And that was it.

That was all it took for all of them to feel better. McKenzie returned to the table, but this time, she sat next to Nolan. He watched her as she entertained some questions from her friends about Jason's life and how high school was going. Jason was brief and non-telling, but they were kind to him and made him feel welcomed. He was the oldest of the kids there, and they had all seen him grow up, being McKenzie's first son.

And they loved him because they loved Kenzie.

But Nolan was becoming nervous. He had not met Kenzie's eyes since they'd come back into the restaurant. He knew he would help the boy as much as he could, and if she questioned him about why his ear was swollen, he would intervene to make any punishment or discussion softer for Jason. Nolan felt like he understood Jason because, like him, it had been a time and age of tumultuous confusion for Nolan. He had been fifteen when his parents left and never returned. He had been fifteen when he'd had to learn to fight, to survive, and to live.

The thought of that wrenched his stomach, not because of his past, but because he knew how truly hurt and confused Jason must be by his own father. He didn't care what Turner's justification was. To Nolan, no child should ever be abused. Not physically, not verbally, not emotionally.

And that included abandonment.

He thought about how, the next time he saw Turner, he would break his hand on sight.

McKenzie was resting her chin on her knuckles, listening to Jeff. She finally turned to Nolan. She was close. Close enough to see any movement, hesitation, or thought he had. They held their eyes there, intimately close, trying to read and understand the other person.

They each had a thousand questions and a thousand feelings, and they wanted to connect. But even with the briefest, simplest of eyes, they could deeply feel the other.

And in that moment, looking at each other, they both knew what it was.

McKenzie turned away. She didn't smile. Instead, her hand released from her chin and wandered under the table. Her fingers gently searched. They felt the rim of his denim jacket pocket—and he froze. Part of his hand was exposed, and with that, her fingers found their way into his denim and between his thumb and his index finger, she held him.

Nolan took a deep breath. He was vulnerable. His hand pulled from his denim to his side, and she held the top of it, tucking her fingers into his, interlocking with him. And without a single thought, he closed his fingers around hers, and that sudden rush of feeling overcame his fear and anxiety.

Because it was more than just feelings to them.

It was truth. It was an admission to themselves and to each other.

They were together.

And they were finally sharing it, here amongst family and friends.

THE TURN OF SPRING

They all rode home in the truck together. The boys were in the back with Jason's dirt bike strapped onto the chassis, and they shared the metal bed with D.O.G. Jason had been running his bike nearly empty since he'd left home. Nolan was happy to help. In the front, silent and looking out the window, was McKenzie.

They didn't speak the entire ride. Every once in a while, they gave each other glances here and there, but their eyes misconnected in between looks. Perhaps they were too nervous to see each other or to say something. Maybe it was an understanding.

Or the anticipation of what was yet to come.

They kept quiet, sharing the soft hum of the night and the laughter of the boys embracing the cold open air.

When they got to the house, McKenzie headed up for the door straight away, without saying a word. Nolan glanced a few times, but helped Jason unmount his bike and roll it to the side of the house. They chained it up then entered through the wooden patio's backdoor. When they got inside, Nolan noticed that her door was nearly closed. He paused, but then went straight back to setting up Jason's new bed. Aiden was already hopping around with D.O.G., explaining to Jason how he got to pick out the new beds, one for each of them.

And while Jason was reserved and quiet about it all, he was excited inside. "Next time, we'll get our own rooms," Jason joked.

Aiden squealed and jumped onto his new mattress. "Yeah!"

Next door, Nolan could hear Kenzie in her room, moving around. His ears were swollen from a lifetime of fighting, but his hearing was still sharp, always assessing where he was, and what was around him. It was possible that he could also hear better than most people because he listened more than most people. Nolan wondered what she was thinking.

Even more important to him now—what was she feeling?

Nolan finished the second bed's final screws as Aiden told Jason the story of his day and how he'd learned from Goldie that D.O.G. had fought an entire pack of coyotes by himself. While Jason mounted his new mattress onto his new bed, still listening to Aiden yammer, Nolan stepped out and creaked open the door to McKenzie's room.

She was sitting on her bed, thinking. Her eyes darted over, and she immediately went to him. She leaned in and reached behind him to partly close the door behind him.

She was close enough to kiss, looking up to him.

He stood there, motionless.

"I saw you. Outside El Charro."

Being this close, he wasn't sure what to say, let alone think. "You gonna kill Turner?"

Her eyes wandered a moment, actually considering it, but her voice stayed unexpectedly tranquil. "No. I'll do the right thing."

They were his own words. The same thing he had told Jason.

She reached up and put her hand through his beard. Then up the side of his face and into his thick hair, until she had to take his hat off. Her hat. He didn't move. His eyes fixated on hers. Her hand traveled his bruised face to his strong chin, then down to the taut symmetrical triangle in his neck. Her fingers pushed through the dark hairs on his chest, and traveled back to his hair, looking up, into his eyes. He stayed in hers. She came in...and kissed him.

And Nolan finally let go.

His large hands spread across the small of her back and he pulled her up into his kiss. She pressed back, pushing her entire body into him. She tucked her hands inside the warmth of his flannel and his body, and she leaned in even more. He towered over her as she fully pressed into him.

Close. Tasting each other's lips. Her breaths were heavy and becoming loud. His were hot, slow. His lips were powerful like his hands, and she felt it—all of it, matching her own strength, pressing her breasts and all of her body against his.

Their skin was hot under their clothes, and the sounds of their lips touching excited them. She couldn't help but push her hips toward his, holding down a moan, releasing and stepping back just enough to look up into his eyes again. He held her there. She caught her breath, almost holding it, desperate to taste him. They were barely past the doorway, against the wall, with their chests rising up and down against each other. Their eyes bright, vulnerable, and holding on to one another, wanting it all, until…

"I'm sorry…" She released him. "I…I don't know if I can."

But he knew what she meant. "Me too."

He felt the same way. His guard was gone. They had finally kissed. He wanted to. He wanted to do everything with her.

But not yet.

Nolan leaned toward her and her gut tightened. She wanted more and was hardly in control. But he was slow, careful, leaning forward and pressing his lips against her forehead. When he released, his eyes came down and found hers. He held her there a moment, both sharing the wonder and awe. Their bodies were heated, the tide of emotion was tasted, and their breathing finally relaxed until all that they had left was in their eyes. They stood there, looking at each other. And when it all subsided, what was felt was a releasing feeling of gratitude and respect for the other person.

"Is…your first test tomorrow?"

She nodded, her lips still wet.

"I want to see you after," he said.

She smiled. "I'll take that as a compliment."

Inside the boys' bedroom, Jason's legs were up on the windowsill extending from his new bed, and D.O.G. leaned against Aiden in his own new bed as he told them both a joke.

"Goodnight, boys," Nolan interrupted, stepping into the doorway with Kenzie.

"Goodnight," Jason said, hesitantly.

"Can D.O.G. stay with us, Nolan?" Aiden asked.

"No, he can't," McKenzie jumped in. "I already got enough animals to deal with."

Aiden shook his head. "First of all, we are not animals, Mom. Me and Nolan are wolfs. Are you coming back tomorrow, Nolan?"

With a soft laugh, Nolan blew air from his nostrils, then looked at Jason, who eyed him, wondering what his response might be. "Yeah," Nolan said. "I promised to do a couple things around here." Nolan shared a small look with Jason, then smiled at Aiden. "And you still gotta teach me how to fly fish."

"Okay!"

Nolan lifted his hand and made the wolf symbol using his fingers. Aiden returned it, his cheeks stretching with joy.

"D.O.G., come." And the dog knew. He leaped, happy to hear a command from his new owner. Nolan gave one last look to Jason, and with a small smile, he and McKenzie left for the front door.

The moon was soft and pale, shaped in a yellow crescent that hung low over town. Nolan and Kenzie stood under it by the truck at the front of the house. D.O.G. waited patiently inside the Ford, his head hanging out the window, staring between the two.

They were quiet and content. It had been a hell of a few days. Their smiles were subtle, but youthful. There was so much to say and so much to learn. Neither knew what to do or how to begin any of this. And yet, there was something unsaid between them that just felt natural and comforting.

"Hey," McKenzie finally spoke. "You wanna do Easter with us?"

"Here?"

"Goldie's."

"What?" He didn't understand.

"He offered to have it at his ranch. Said he'd like the kids and family around since he doesn't have any."

"He's a good man."

McKenzie stepped closer. He watched as her hand reached up and held his face. "So are you."

His mind wandered. He hadn't thought of himself like that in a long time. Perhaps he never had.

"Thank you," she said.

"For what?"

"For being *you*."

He didn't know what to say and she knew it.

So, she kissed him, long and hard, until they both needed to breathe. Then she turned and briskly walked back up to the house. Nolan watched her every step, then she snuck one last peek back at him, flashed a smile, and closed the door.

When Nolan turned, D.O.G. was staring with his tongue dripping in and out of his mouth. He had been observing quietly and happily the whole time.

"Yeah, yeah, what are you so happy about?"

And he hopped into the truck.

The sunrise over downtown stretched out to Williamson Valley and beyond to the greater state. The colors were new. As was all the new life. It was the turn of spring, and everything between the land and the valleys was growing. Lush green pastures left behind the memories of fall, and spring had sprung with blooming zest.

There is something to say about those who fall in love in their thirties. There is a degree of honor and maturity that is earned if one does. The way one thinks. The way one feels. The way things make sense about your past and past lovers. And yet, there is something so youthful and unforgettable that it leaps from your bones. To fall back in love in your thirties is to fall and to fly, the very same. It is something unforgettable, inexplicable, and magnificent.

For Nolan and McKenzie, it was as if they were teenagers again, absorbing the waves of what it was to feel something once more—the currents of first kisses, looks, and touches. They wanted to be subtle, but their eyes and their smiles could not. They were much older than the first time they had felt something like this, and they were very different people now. They had seen things, been through more, and experienced tribulations that had made their skin harder and their hearts softer. They had seen parts of the world through the heartbreak of others and the hurt done to them. They had seen the world through the hurt within themselves.

They had both been bruised, used, and left behind by the ones they loved. But, in every way, shape, and form, they were fighters. And with the turn of spring, they were young lovers once again.

Nolan spent two weeks working on Goldie's ranch. He hauled bales of hay from the valley to the barn and stacked them in a pyramid outside for the horses. He fed them every day and made a list with Goldie of things to repair on the ranch, like the old wooden fences around the premises. They shared freshly ground coffee in the morning, imported from Africa—something Goldie insisted on, despite his and his wife's love for all things French and Italian.

They took turns making breakfast together, which always happened within an hour of sunrise. They were both early risers, and one of them would always find the other sitting on one of the old deck chairs, overlooking the barn, the valley, and the rising sun every morning. It became almost habitual for them, sharing those moments together. Goldie loved to talk about Poem, and he noticed, with every new story and every new sunrise, Nolan was listening more and more.

He was opening up.

And while Goldie would never pry, he simply understood that there were things buried and not fully healed in the young man. He had known it from the very first moment he'd met him. But it gave Goldie comfort, because deep down, he thought he could help him in his own special way.

It was a blessing to have him work the ranch and do all the things Goldie could no longer do himself. Really, it was a blessing just to have Nolan around.

During the day, Goldie would tend to his practice in town and they would often share a late dinner or a night cap, if Nolan wasn't already doing so with Kenzie and the boys. After tending the horses and sharing breakfast during the sunrise, Nolan would go into town and work at the mechanic's. He and the shop owner were happy about this. He knew just as much about cars as the owner and the other mechanics did, thanks to his experiences ranching throughout Colorado, hitchhiking, and sharing homes with the country's countless talented laborers. A man had taken him in when a poor crop season had hit the land, and young Nolan had learned everything he could about trucks, cars, and motors.

Across the valley and under the tall pines, Kenzie would also wake before sunrise. But it was her time. It was the quietest period of the day for her, and was always the best time for her to get work or studying done. Yet what was most amazing was that she had done better on her finals than she'd thought she would. Some untapped energy had come with these new feelings, and it felt like she had more energy than ever before.

Even without a real plan after finishing Yavapai Community College, she believed that being successful at school was only going to build the next bridge for her to do well for her and her kids. She knew she had a shot here—she could enroll in an online degree or a trade school or maybe actually go to college somewhere. They were things no one in her family had ever done before. And she finally had a shot at a new road.

Whatever was to be, she was open.

Now more than ever.

During these two weeks, neither Nolan nor Kenzie called each other. Nolan had stopped carrying a cell phone long ago. But McKenzie knew that, every day, he would show up, either in the late afternoon before she went to work, or earlier on the days that he didn't work at the mechanic's.

Every day, without fail, he would come to her. They were the first thing each of them thought of when they woke up. And they were all that they thought about, every time they caught the sun rise or set.

And all of this was to say, that when they were apart or together, they were with each other. In each other's minds and hearts, like all lovers are, embedded within us since the beginning of time, just waiting to be found.

They saw each other every day in those two weeks. It was spring break for the boys. Nolan went on long walks with Aiden while he taught him how to fish "Aiden style," as he would proudly say. While Kenzie cooked dinner, Nolan would show Jason how to fight. But he always balanced it with lessons that were purely about self-defense and protection.

"Protecting yourself," Nolan told him one day on the porch, "is what a fighter really does."

All day, D.O.G. would run through the house and follow Aiden, and when McKenzie needed to research colleges, plan out finances, or simply be alone, she took her space and did it. They would all ride through the forest together to catch the sunset at the mountain lookout. Jason's dirt bike chased and zigzagged through the trails while Nolan roared up the road in his truck. Aiden would howl and Nolan would show him how much louder he could howl in return. They treated that break in spring like it was the very last day of summer or the very first. Every day was an adventure.

Nolan and McKenzie had little time alone, and they felt it longingly, every time they looked at each other. She would surprise him by cornering him in the laundry room, grabbing his hands, then kissing him. And every night that he left to take the long road back to the ranch, she kissed him like she would never see him again.

They were like teenagers, always flirting and anticipating what everything would be like for the first time.

They spent a whole day on the lake together, and Jason even showed up on his bike and dared them to jump in. Nolan didn't think twice before stripping down to his jeans and plunging in. They loved him for it. Kenzie, who lived to be challenged, stripped down to her black bra and jeans and jumped right in after. And after they froze during the twilight ride home, Nolan fixed the old, clogged fireplace, and they shared a gourmet soup that McKenzie scrounged together using packets of Top Ramen, shredded chicken breast, and every vegetable and grain she could scavenge in the kitchen.

During starlit nights, they would all lounge on the wooden porch and watch Nolan teach Jason how fight. He showed him nonthreatening defense stances, keeping his palms and fingers high and outward, with his chin low. Nolan showed him that the energy you put into your body and your eyes was just as important as what you did with your hands and your muscles.

He showed Jason how to use footwork to trick or evade an attacker, then he showed him how to use the entire force of the attacker's body and energy to counterstrike. Nolan showed him how to disarm a person who might grab his wrist, or put him in a chokehold, or simply swing a fist at him. Everyone was amazed by how quickly Nolan could move through these stances and techniques. He was like a different person—quick footed, sharp, and fast. He was naturally reserved and calm in his demeanor, but when demonstrating principles of fighting, his attitude and movements were alert, with eyes and ears perked like an animal.

Despite not being good in school, Jason loved to learn. He was starting to realize that maybe it wasn't always his fault. Nolan was showing him strikes, choreography, and takedowns, and he was understanding them and picking them up faster than he did sports, or math, or even when he'd started riding bikes. As many teachers had done for Nolan, it was always the power and the gift of a great teacher to unlock their student. And it was only with great passion that a student truly learned.

Their voices echoed through the old neighborhood with timeless laughter and sweet excitement. It was as if they were the only people there, joyous children playing into the night. When Nolan left for the evening, and they each returned to their rooms, separated by miles of immense valley and plains, Nolan and Kenzie sat on their beds alone, thinking of the other.

Every night from his cot on the ranch, he looked through the sliding glass door to the sky and thought of her. His hands folded behind his head, laying in his bed, daydreaming before falling asleep. She was always warm, he thought, and sometimes he could feel it from afar, just thinking of the times she'd grabbed him and pressed herself against him to kiss.

Kenzie, now with both of her kids sharing the same room, would listen to the soft ambiance of cool spring nights. She would sit up in bed, draped in warm quilts from her grandmother's history, enjoying the fresh air from her open window and wondering what could come with the next day.

The moon was always brightest in the valley where nothing but the Indian ruins, the tallest peak in the valley, would disrupt it. Sometimes Nolan would walk the perimeter of the ranch at night, and he could feel the glowing moon touch his skin.

From time to time, he would find the white stallion in the pasture, standing out on a small hill by itself. The horse would always be still, his gaze transfixed on the valley. Nolan thought that the stallion was a thinker, much like him. But on nights like these, when the stars were bright and the air was still and crisp, Nolan would watch him and know that the animal was at peace.

Every day became a new experience with Kenzie and the boys. Every day Nolan was exploring, hiking, playing, and kissing Kenzie—someone who, in many ways, he thought was so much stronger and confident than him. And every night after Nolan returned on the long journey back to his country bed, he found himself thinking more deeply through his heart. The things that had once pained him were now *different*. When he thought of *Her* in those faint moments before sleep, right when his eyes were heaviest, he no longer felt pain.

He felt gratitude.

He felt how he was so lucky to have met *Her*. To have loved *Her*. To have been loved by *Her*. And how now, be it through fate or destiny or life or miracles, he could still be loved by someone else.

Perhaps he would never know what was inside that made him worthy of this, or why his story had been written this way. Perhaps he would have never had the opportunity or chance to be here, if *She* hadn't come into his life. He could only shake his head in amazement and embrace the tears that welled within. He would have given his life if it could have saved *Hers*.

But in so many ways, she was the one who had saved his.

Because she had taught him how to love.

This was all because of *Her*.

He could love Kenzie, who said nothing that her eyes didn't already say. And he knew. He knew how she felt. It chilled his entire body, then warmed it like her kiss. Never would he have imagined that he would meet Kenzie. Not in this way, or in any way. Not in this life or another. She was the most emotional, intelligent, and strong person he had ever known, besides *Her*.

She was strong and kind to others. She loved to smile and play. But she wasn't afraid to defend herself or others.

It all baffled him. It all amazed him. While he did not yet know what was to come, he knew now what he wanted.

He wanted to be with Kenzie.

Because he loved her.

Those two weeks were the fastest days of their lives. McKenzie would take a final exam each day, and Nolan would pick her up, waiting out front in his truck. With his hands tucked into his jacket and leaning against the old steel, he would show up wearing her hat every time. She would see it and instantly smile, every single time.

They would either buy lunch together or joke up and down the aisles of the grocery store, contemplating pancakes or filets or huevos rancheros, then make lunch a surprise for the boys. They were never sure what it was going to be and yet they were just as excited.

One day, Nolan surprised Jason by how easily he could "shred" on his 300cc dirt bike. Nolan tore up and down their neighborhood road, screaming the engine, then he threw up the front handlebars, and his entire front wheel swung in the air while he propelled up the road. Jason and Aiden were amazed. Even D.O.G. watched with his ears standing up. Jason could wheelie on his bike, but not like Nolan. For the boys, Nolan always had surprises and secrets to share, and it was just another reason to spend time with him.

On Palm Sunday, Goldie invited them to ride the horses at the ranch. The white horse, the brindle mare, D.O.G., Aiden, Jason, McKenzie, Goldie, and Nolan all hiked up to see the sunset from the Indian ruins. It was the near end of spring break, and they all watched in silence. Although Goldie knew it, Nolan caught him looking out to some far-off part in the hills while the sun descended. The old man was quiet and kept his gaze in the opposite direction of the group. A tear navigated the wrinkles of his face and trickled down his cheek. He stared at a tall round hilltop just along the ridge of the Indian ruins. As the sun finally set, Aiden cheered, and the old man turned and found Nolan looking at him.

To his surprise, the old man smiled, and they turned back to the fading light together.

Nights were spent having dinner at Kenzie's or with Goldie, who loved to host just as much as she did. Time was fast and yet somehow also felt timeless and inevitable, like life had always been this way. Everything they did was simple and always started with a smile.

The boys spent hours at the lake fly fishing while McKenzie studied for her last exam in a hammock. Later in the day, they all picnicked and saw the sun dip and spread over the lake's horizon. Like many times before, Jason would fly up the mountain on his dirt bike to join them and get a new lesson in fighting.

They spent the last day of McKenzie's exams at the Dells, an endless collage of boulders that surrounded a crystal-clear lake. Nolan had seen many lakes in his time, but this one, like Goldwater, was one of a kind. It was as peaceful as the church, surrounded by textured, tan, round rocks, cold air, and colder water. It was a calming way to begin the closing of the boys' last days of spring break, as well as McKenzie's last exams. Although they were with each other every day during these two weeks, McKenzie and Nolan were never really alone with each other. They each felt a tugging desire that grew with the cool days and blossomed during candlelit nights.

By the end of those nights, they always found themselves kissing warmly against Nolan's chilled steel truck. They were afraid to do or to feel too much, even though deep down they felt it all. McKenzie constantly turned inside. Her body churned every time she saw him at the front of her school, waiting. When his shoulders bowed out as he walked to her, it made her stomach tighten. How he would always come to her with his hands in his denim, and how, by the end of the night, he would leave with his hands around her waist, pulling her in.

It was important to McKenzie that the boys knew she and Nolan respected them, and when they kissed, it was always in private or when saying goodbye. Each and every day, they felt more and more for each other, and still, they respected what the boys would or wouldn't see, even though Nolan and McKenzie always felt just moments away from having all of each other. But they both knew they wanted to trust each other. They wanted the boys to trust them. And it wasn't time yet. It was something unspoken, something understood in one another.

Trust, like love, was expressed in many colors.

To trust and to feel trusted was especially important to Nolan. In these boys, he saw parts of who he had been once, long ago. Aiden with his wide eyes, full of untouched youth. He was just like Nolan, before his parents disappeared. And Jason, he resembled everything Nolan had been after. He'd seen it in Jason that night on the porch, the destructive remorse in his eyes, running from home, riding into the night without a helmet, feverish and angry.

Fear and uncertainty always blur the truth and realities of life. When we live or operate in fear, our heart is pushed and pulled without any true resolution or understanding. But fear also tells us this: the reason we're afraid, is because, deep down, there is something hidden that we actually care about. The process of facing our fears is actually the process of unmasking our truth, and to unmask our truth is the foundation for us to express our love.

Little did they know, their fear was, in essence, showing them that they did care, that they each cared more deeply about each other than they could currently say. Because what they felt was beyond their ability to define with words. What they felt was real. And it was now.

In those two weeks together, everything was said with few or no words, but in the simple truths that only spending time with another person could express. When you spent copious amounts of time with someone, you learned to share the silence and the feelings of another. You learned the meaning of a single touch, a single smile. You learned how they thought, how they changed, and what made them move. All things were beginning between them, and it was more than just trust. Something was growing within each and every one of them. Nolan, without overthinking or understanding, succumbed to it. For the second, and most important, time in his life, he was embracing what he had lost, forgotten, and thought that he would never feel ever again.

He was embracing love.

And still, deep within, they all wondered in those small, hidden recesses of doubt and fear—what would come? They didn't discuss what Nolan was going to do, they only shared the day and what they *wanted* to do. Every day, Nolan would show up outside McKenzie's school, the church, or the bar. For two weeks he did this, sometimes without even knowing where she would be by the time he finished his work at the mechanic's or on the ranch.

Somehow, some way, without even talking to her, Nolan would just find her, and their day would begin. And every night when he said goodbye to her and to the boys, it became harder to leave. Perhaps that was why Kenzie kissed him the way she did. Kisses that felt tenderly forever. Kisses that wanted to hold on to him, and never wanted to forget the feeling. Every night, Nolan drove that single lonely road back through the valley and down the long winding dirt paths, back to North Star Ranch.

And every night, he wondered—did he have to leave?

234

THE POEM

It was Easter Sunday. Goldie beamed every time there was a knock at the door. The ranch's driveway was full of trucks and cars, from the barn doors to the front entrance of the house. There were kids and teenagers everywhere. Jason ripped up and down the dirt roads with his bike, and a few of his buddies zagged behind on their own.

Nolan was nervous, trying to manage interactions with the many good friends and family that had showed up on behalf of McKenzie or Goldie. But more than anything, Nolan was nervous to see McKenzie, who was coming later with Gram.

When they finally showed up, Nolan saw Kenzie in the doorway wearing low-cut brown cowboy boots, a yellow sun dress, and newly curled hair. He was stunned. She was like how spring sunlight complimented its flowers—natural, beautiful, and wild. He felt like a boy looking at her. Especially when her eyes found his and they smiled. Nolan approached and took her Gram by the hand. Kenzie watched, nervous too, as he kissed the back of it.

Gram, the wise and old woman with thick, white hair that stopped at her shoulders. She didn't think twice before smiling at him. "Well, there you are," Gram said, with her confident smile. It was just like Kenzie's.

Nolan smiled back, relieved. He was just happy to finally meet her.

McKenzie couldn't remember a single thing Nolan had said to Gram. She loved her so dearly, and was so nervous, that even she didn't speak. She was hoping that Gram would just talk to him and appreciate him for who he was. And she did.

When Kenzie went around to greet her friends and family, Nolan and Gram talked on the balcony together. They spoke of horses and Montana, a place she and her family had gone to many times in her childhood. The way Gram spoke about Montana, the movement of trees, and the tastes and sounds of rivers—it was exactly how Nolan remembered it. He asked her questions about her life and what made her most proud.

Gram smiled. "Many things. McKenzie, most of all."

The ranch was loud and full of life. Everyone important to Kenzie was there, and Goldie was happy to share his home with new guests. Goldie also took to Gram very well. There's something special about the wise and the kind. They greeted each other and shared space like old friends or family would. Goldie and Gram were very pleased to have another like-minded peer around.

They all dined at Goldie's long banquet table, filling it with people and dishes, while facing the wide second-story view of the ranch and valley. It had not shared more than two people for over ten years. The dinner was lush and full of every possible fixing, meat, and vegetable one could imagine for Easter. It was a pleasant day and becoming more joyful as everyone began serving and passing dishes to share the great meal.

McKenzie and Nolan didn't speak much—they were both incessantly surrounded by family, friends, and children. Gram was getting older and got tired easier these days, and McKenzie didn't want to leave her unattended. She only did when Goldie spent time with her, or Nolan. McKenzie spent the whole day smiling, but that little fear of anticipating her grandmother's feelings kept her wondering.

Yet, every time she went to get something for Gram, or left her alone momentarily, she found Nolan next to her again, asking her about her life, Montana, or Arizona. McKenzie caught glimpses of the unwavering attention and diligence Nolan kept up with her. He was listening closely and asking about her experiences and family history in Arizona. While Kenzie did not intrude, she could sense something in the way that her Gram was speaking to him, hearing some of her words and the feeling in her tone and body language—she was speaking to Nolan about life in all the special and fearless ways that she would. It was something about her that made her so beautiful to Kenzie. Gram was wise and calm about everything, especially her anecdotes on life. McKenzie could see that she and Nolan were sharing something on the balcony.

It was special to her.

Later, at the dinner table, Kenzie sat diagonally across from Nolan, who sat next to her Gram. She was wondering what they spoke about that seemed so personal, when Goldie stood up from the table with a glass high in his hand. Everyone stopped and looked to him, and the kids and teenagers sitting at the long side table slowly came around.

"Okay, y'all, bring it in now. Kids, you too."

Everyone rested their forks and held up their drinks. Goldie smiled, looking at each person there in his home, making eye contact. Goldie had always wanted to have family events like this.

He'd never gotten to.

"You know, Easter is about many things. For me, it has always been about new beginnings. It's always been about family. My family was small...and she's longer here," he reflected. Nolan's stomach tightened. "Looking around this room, I see mothers, fathers, friends, children...even strangers and dogs." He smiled at Aiden and D.O.G., who sat together with the rest of the youth at the long kids' table. Everyone listened carefully and with smiles. "But what I really see, is family." He looked at each and every one of them. "It's never too late to feel that. It's never too late to have that. Hell, I'm wise enough *and* old enough to know that. Cheers!"

Goldie smiled and lifted his glass even higher.

"Cheers to that, Goldie!" Kenzie called out.

As the many hands and glasses raised and toasted together, Nolan and Kenzie locked eyes in between it all. They had been thinking about each other the entire time.

The fireplace burned tall, and the twilight night was cloudless when most of the guests left. Some were still sharing dessert or preparing their goodbyes. Aiden ran through the house with D.O.G. and his friends, which all of the adults discouraged except for Goldie. They all shared drinks and wine around the large, plush, living room couches while Goldie stood by the fire, where he rested his drink and arm on the mantle. It was a warm and cozy home, and the night was perfect to Goldie. He had wanted to have nights like these with friends and family his entire life. Ever since he was a boy, he'd thought about family get-togethers like this, where the past and the future and the old and the young could all be together. Aunts, uncles, animals, grandmas, and children—they were things he'd yearned for. They were things he'd missed out on in life. To have met Kenzie and to share his large home with her many friends and family, was in every way a gift to him. It was something that he had dreamed about his whole life, and for many complicated reasons, he had almost never gotten to have.

Nolan leaned against the back wall near Goldie's piano. Kenzie sat comfortably on the couch under a quilt that Goldie had offered to her and Gram. Gram complimented the wonderful patchwork and hand-stitching, which pleased Goldie, seeing them throw it over their legs and knees. McKenzie's eyes jumped to Nolan. He was reserved, but she could tell he was content. Besides D.O.G. and his wild tongue, no one stood next to him or engaged him for a good thirty minutes. He wasn't one to talk anyway, she thought, and smiled, knowing that he had made solid efforts today. Kenzie had seen and was learning more and more about him each day that they shared. Actually, she thought to herself, in the past two weeks, this was the least amount of time they had shared in one space together without talking or touching.

But their feelings were palpable, even tense at times, as, throughout the whole night, they snuck looks at one another or asked how they were doing in between guests. Kenzie held her Gram's hand on the couch when Goldie flicked his glass filled with old '82. When he got their attention, everyone hushed and bound together. He was reflecting. The room became quiet, and Goldie kept his gaze down, thinking, the old Scotch making him sentimental.

"You know, this ranch was built twenty years ago. I built it...I built it for my wife." He thought through his words. It was deeper than that. "I built it *with* her."

Everyone became quiet, attentive. They could feel the shift in Goldie.

"The French, they have a way of saying 'I miss you.'" He smiled, but it was faint. "'Tu me manques,' which is actually to say, 'you are missing from me.'" He cleared his throat, then looked down. The faces around the room were still, hanging on to the old man's words. McKenzie was already emotional just thinking of her Gram throughout the day and how much she had been through, but now… she was thinking of her own life.

"It was just me and her," he said. "Forty-one years. Almost ten here. Many right here, in this room." Goldie took a deep breath. "So, I can tell you, what makes a family, what makes a home, what makes a life….are *people*. People we love."

He paused, then looked up. Nolan was standing alone, across the room. He was looking down, but listening, the melancholy of the past grabbing hold of him.

"I'm a bit of a writer—a little hobby of mine," Goldie continued. "If you could honor an old man, I'd like to share something special about this place. About *someone* special." He looked up and smiled. "And I'd like *you* to read it, young man."

They all turned. Nolan looked up.

"Me?"

Goldie extended a hand. "I would be so very honored."

McKenzie watched. She smiled sweetly, hoping it would nudge him. Nolan took his hands from his denim jacket and walked across the room. He took the letter and stood at the side of the fireplace next to Goldie. He scanned it, seeing what was written.

He took a deep, controlled breath before looking once more to Goldie's warm and happy eyes. Then he looked to Kenzie, who was both intrigued and nervous. She knew Nolan didn't like these situations, and now all the focus was on him. But, even more troubling, she knew he just didn't like to say much. And yet, something shifted as she gazed upon him. She saw something moving and working within his eyes as he scanned the text on the page. He finally spoke:

"With each step my foot sinks into the sacred soil.
Unspoiled and molded only by nature's touch.
From the stormy monsoons that wash over it,
To the small pine trees that stand humbled by the sun.
For miles only the land is visible, with no sight of man.
A gently sloping valley stretches to the next range of mountains.
With just a touch of imagination you can see the past…

The Great Yavapai roam the valley,
Hunting for the tribe's next meal.
Above on the ridge behind me,
They make their dwelling proud.
Preparing for the coming feast.
And the work never stops.
Children are happy and playing.
Using little more than their great imagination.
Remembering the stories from elders,
That have been passed on with pride.
A chill runs up my spine.
But the air is calm.
With that my spirit rises.
Knowing that I'm in a happy place.
Where honor could not be bought.
And money had no value.
Where love of one another was the rule.
And nature was respected for all its gifts.
As I stood there, my soul was at rest.
And my heart was at peace.
For a land with such a history,
Is a place to be cherished.
So I turned to see my future
As she stood silently transfixed
I knew she too felt all that I did
And I knew then
We were home."

Nolan stopped. The room didn't move. He scanned the paper one more time. He had spoken, reading aloud, and did not stop. He had spoken in a way that he thought he wouldn't—or perhaps in a way he thought he couldn't. But his voice was strong and clear to the very last word. And he felt everything he said.

He looked up.

The entire room was still looking. They were speechless. McKenzie was holding tears while Gram held her eyes on Nolan, a gentle smile on her lips as she looked effortlessly at his soul.

Goldie's head was low and looking into the fireplace. He felt his own words in a way that he never had before. He had not shared this poem with anyone, until now. He had written it the day they came here—to Arizona. He had not heard the words aloud for twenty years. Until now.

Goldie inhaled long and deep, then he released, smiling to the room. "Thank you. Happy Easter."

And they all smiled and relaxed, releasing from the moment.

But then Aiden started clapping in the other room. "Go, Nolan!"

Kenzie shook her head and a few guests laughed until Goldie rallied the whole room, laughing happily and clapping the loudest.

Later that night, only McKenzie's closest family—Jason, Aiden, Gram, and a few others were at the ranch. The boys and their cousins were preparing a slumber party in the living room with a makeshift fort and sleeping bags, while Gram told stories of how Jason used to do the same. They all talked in the background while Nolan stood alone on the balcony facing the valley.

He was looking at the moon. When he turned back, he saw McKenzie and Jason sitting together by the piano, getting along. Of all nights, the moon was full, and it illuminated the darkness of the valley that was peppered with bushes, hills, and the barn under its pale blue cast.

Something was stirring within. Why had those words startled him? He felt some medley of emotions, traversing between his past and present. Some kind of thread strung between memories and thoughts and feelings. A thread that held all truths between two people he now loved.

He thought of Goldie. How strong he must be to continue without his wife for so long. The notion stung in his chest. Then, something came anew. That pain was soon met with warmth and gratitude for where he was now. For what he was experiencing at this exact moment of his life. And while he felt so much gratitude, a new fear came with it. It was more than the fear or pain of remembering his past. In the storm of emotions that fostered and shared this new love, he was becoming afraid of what pain might come with a new future. He knew it—he was open now. All of him.

With all of his bruises and his eyes and his heart.

He was open, and he was in love with Kenzie. He was in love with all of them. And that both thrilled him and terrified him to his soul.

"Thank you for that," Goldie said, walking up.

Nolan knew he was overthinking again. He nodded to the old man, then looked back to the moon. Goldie stood there, holding his old '82, sharing the stillness and the space with him. Nolan didn't understand why the old man had done that—why he'd asked him to read his words, but, suddenly, Goldie began coughing harshly.

Nolan turned. Goldie's throat scraped, hacking hard up his esophagus, trying to catch up to his lungs. The old man fought it off and got ahold of himself.

"What's wrong with you?" Nolan asked directly. He knew Goldie had been hiding it for weeks now.

Goldie considered what to tell him, settling back in. "Poem and I," he said, looking at the moon, "we learned everything from each other. We shared everything. Thick and thin. But you know what gift she gave me, that keeps on giving?"

Nolan turned and waited for the old man, who simply stared at the moon. He turned to face Nolan.

"She reminded me to live."

And with one last look, Goldie went into the living room with the others. Nolan watched him go. It was the simplest of words and it felt as if the old man knew everything—everything he was afraid of, everything he'd lost, and everything that he now stood to lose. But how could he? Nolan had told him little to nothing about his life.

Nothing about *Her*.

Yet, he felt that the old man somehow knew…and when he looked across the room at all the many happy faces and children and neighbors, his eyes crossed Kenzie's. She was happy. But with one glance at Nolan's face, she knew something was wrong.

To Live

Nolan had snuck off while everyone played or lounged in the living room. He was down in the den, laying on his cot and peering up at the ceiling. He needed time to breathe freely and to work through his thoughts from the night. There was much to unpack and to understand between him, Kenzie, the boys, and everything Goldie had told him. And the only way he was going to do that was alone.

Jason had taken Gram home in Kenzie's Jeep as most of them had been drinking, even McKenzie, who had had a little bit of Goldie's Scotch. Aiden, his cousins, their friends, and a few of McKenzie's own friends had opted to stay on the ranch. But what amazed her was that, even though it was thirty miles round trip, instead of going home to the house or staying at Gram's, which would have been more convenient, Jason came right back the very same night. He did it just so he could be around his family and cousins some more. It was special, McKenzie thought, seeing him get along with his cousins and the younger kids. He was a natural leader.

It was almost midnight now, and Kenzie was dressed for bed, wearing a yellow and purple flannel, a low tank top, silky night shorts, and her moccasin slippers. Aiden was hollering to her from a massive living room fort, saying that it was a holiday, and they should be able to stay up as late as they want.

"Well then, you need to keep it down. You aren't the only ones sleeping here."

"Okay, Mom. Nighty night," Aiden complied.

"Night, Mom," Jason followed, slumped on the leather couch, his feet on the coffee table.

The others said goodnight too.

"Goodnight, my little wolves."

"*Awhooooo*!" Aiden called out.

Kenzie hushed him through a small smile, then walked out of the room, putting the wolf symbol up high in her hand. The boys called back, keeping their howls low. McKenzie walked through the large ranch dining room, then into the hallway where bedrooms divided between the upstairs rooms and the downstairs den. The door to Goldie's room was closed and her room for the night was beside his. Down in the lower den, she saw that Nolan's door was still closed. A rush came over her. She wondered if he was still awake and how he was doing. He'd left the party early and without saying goodnight. She took one more look at his door, then went to her room.

Through soft and thin linen curtains, she saw a full, pink, glowing moon. She pulled the curtains open to see its grand, robust shape. A rush of coolness emitted from the cold glass and danced chills up her spine. Her skin prickled.

Downstairs in the guest room, Nolan was looking at the very same moon. He had been thinking for hours.

About *Her*.

About Kenzie.

About everything he had been through. It was a moon full of thoughts and feelings and words. But now he was finally alone, and he was thinking about something Kenzie had told him not long ago, atop the Indians ruins: it wasn't that he "didn't feel," it was he was *afraid* to feel.

He thought about every moment and every day that had passed before he came to this town. How, for over a year, he had felt little to nothing outside of his pain. As if he had been incapable of feeling anything outside of guilt, or remorse. No bruises, no knuckles, no cuts hurt enough to make him feel that deeply into his soul.

The only thing he had felt was empty.

Until he met Kenzie.

This inspired him and terrified him all the same. There was a sense of wonder and fear with these feelings. And he was here now, fixated on the moon, his soul drifting through these thoughts and ideas that all led him to one thing: whatever he had survived in his story, in his history, in his life—everything led him to here. To now. And he was grateful.

While Nolan didn't say the words aloud, in his heart, he knew he thanked God for his life. He thanked God for giving him this moment, whatever it was, and whatever was left of it. Even though he had cursed the powers that be so many times before, even though he was perpetually discouraged by the world, he was here now and embracing his gratitude. He was embracing what the universe and what God had gifted him. He had never been a religious man, but, in this moment, Nolan embraced this moon and these feelings as if God had intended for him to have them. He embraced it all as if he knew—this was the end of a long, long repentance.

And the door creaked open.

It was her.

Kenzie stood in the moon-kissed doorway with bare feet and soft eyes that missed him. His chest thumped, and he pulled himself up to sit in bed. He gazed at her, not sure if it was really Kenzie or some thought or vision of her. She tiptoed across the cold wooden floors and came to his bedside. She put her hand to his beard and looked down and into his eyes.

It was Kenzie.

And they both knew then all the reasons she came.

She straddled him atop his dark jeans. He leaned up and into her, kissing her first. She pulled her lips from his, then combed her hair from his brightening blue eyes. She wanted to see them. Tender and slow, she pressed her lips against the bruises just above his eyes. They were calm again.

His large hands traveled her, unbuttoned her flannel to the sides. It dripped from her shoulders, then he watched it slide down her skin, showing herself to him for the first time. She looked into his eyes without turning, and a strand of dark chestnut hair fell down her face.

Calm, content. He tucked her soft hair behind her ear. She pressed her chest against his, then peeled his shirt slowly from his lower back. He pushed himself up higher on the cot and she rode up with him. His lips pressed deeper, and their eyes closed together. Their lips enveloped completely, then pulled away, wanting to see each other and taste each other, but too excited to decide. His hands covered her lower back and slid up her waist, then under her arms and stopped, the space between his index and thumbs cupped under her breasts, holding her firmly. She lifted her knees and pushed into him to taste more. And they loved each other, having all of each other, all through the night. Moments inside each other's eyes and touches. In softness and folded hands. In lips and wetness. He was strong in ways that heated her body, and she was soft in ways that gave him chills.

And it made them hungry for more.

For everything.

For all of each other.

They didn't speak a word until an hour before sunrise. They tasted, they trusted, and they gave each other everything. When the sun came up and poured light into the valley, McKenzie was only in her skin, lying atop Nolan's wide chest and nestled into his dark hairs. They watched the light rise together.

"Was your Gram okay?" he asked softly.

"She had a good time."

They were quiet again. Exhausted from everything they had given.

"Are you?" She was wondering if he was okay with the night, with dinner, and with everything that had happened.

"Yeah. You?" He was thinking the same.

She nodded, strands of her soft hair spilling down his body and to the top of her chest. She was thinking of the night and about things she had always wondered about him.

Especially now.

"Do you..." She was careful to ask. "Do you think of *Her?*"

She knew the answer, but some small itching worry made her ask anyway.

Nolan inhaled slow and calm. Her head rose with his chest. She tilted her chin to see him.

"Yeah." He said it gentle and true.

She wasn't sure what else to ask, but it just came forth. "A lot?"

Nolan knew nothing he could say would express what he had been through with *Her.* Or what he was going through now with Kenzie. It was pain, it was peace, but, in all essences, it was hope. It was hope for him and for everything he felt now. For everything he once had and everything he had dreamed of having again.

He didn't know what to give her or to tell her.

Instead, he told her the only thing he thought mattered now.

"I'll always love *Her*, but…" He pulled his chin down and looked her in her eyes. He was looking at her in the same way that he knew, the very first time. In the way he knew now. "I love *you*."

It hit her soul. It elevated her, it frightened her, and it filled her. And at the same time all her wonders and worries came with it.

"Why?" she asked.

Nolan didn't turn away. "Because you're *you*."

Her eyes focused on him, full of tears, until she couldn't hold them any longer. It would never be the same now. Not for either of them. His words were sweet and true just like his eyes, and they held no barrier to her. She scooted up to him and he turned to her so they could see each other, equally again.

They were there together.

He meant it and she knew it.

And for the first time in years, Kenzie let herself go again. She leaned in and kissed him. She kissed him in all the ways that she loved him.

When the sun finally peeked over the ruins, Kenzie was already up and cooking for everyone. She had bacon, crisped hash browns, buttermilk biscuits, and some of Goldie's African coffee brewing. Jason and Aiden's cousins were still at the ranch with them, and Goldie was thrilled to join in and help her prepare a big breakfast for everyone. Nolan tended to the horses as he always did just after sunrise. The two recognized him now, as he had become their caretaker during this time. It was something the beasts knew as well. Just as they did his feelings of truth that had been hiding inside. It was all aglow now. His love for Kenzie came through his entire being. And sometimes with animals, all it took was one look, and their own pure, unconditional love would reflect back the same. The horses were happy, and Nolan was, too, smiling, feeding them with open palms. What a thought, his mind wandered—he had smiled more in this time in Prescott than he had in a long, long time. It was no longer the past that held his mind. It was his future. It was Kenzie.

The kitchen was full of animals and laughter and Aiden howling for more hash browns, extra thin and always crispy, with his bacon. Goldie made fresh orange juice in a steel juicer, and Jason was told to cook some sausages on the balcony's porch grill. Nolan came in wearing a used, but clean, mechanic's jumpsuit.

"Will you look who it is," Goldie poked. "Lookin' good, young man."

"It'll do for now." Nolan smiled.

Aiden yelled, "Nolan, are we gonna see you later?"

"Of course."

He went to McKenzie, and without hesitation, she kissed him with loud smacking lips and said nothing else. It was louder than the bacon crackling in the pan. Aiden gawked with his nose scrunched. Even Jason heard it and stared in from the porch.

"Ewwww!" Aiden finally erupted, causing Jason to shake his head.

Nolan and McKenzie shot them looks.

"See ya later," Nolan said, patting D.O.G., then walked to the back door. Aiden gushed with kissing faces to his two younger cousins, but Jason, still turning sausages on the patio, turned and smiled to himself. His Mom was happy, he thought. She deserved it.

And that made him happy.

Nolan was working under a bright red, vintage Ford pickup truck. It was a 1948 F1, in mint condition with newly set tires. Nolan felt like a kid in a candy store, tinkering with the old nuts and bolts inside the classic vehicle. He felt a kick at the bottom of his boot. He slid from under and found the mechanic hovering above him with a big smile.

"You gonna get that thing done or just tickle her all day, mate?"

"Hey, nobody knows how to touch this beauty but me."

The mechanic laughed, as did the other guys working in the garage. "Yeah, yeah, only you can service her, we get it. Don't enjoy yourself too much."

He kicked Nolan's boot playfully and walked off with a grin. Nolan slid back under the truck, amused. They were good men, he thought, and he was grateful they offered him cash work.

"Payout's Friday." The mechanic said then disappeared into his office as Nolan continued his day's work. He had nothing in his pocket and nothing to his name. He had nothing to lose, but for the first time in a long time, he felt like he had everything to gain. He was building a new life. Lying under the truck, his true smile came to him.

It's funny, he thought, how quickly and how greatly things could change. Later in the afternoon, he wondered what McKenzie was doing and if they should all go to dinner or stay at the ranch another night. It was really nice, he thought, sharing the ranch with everyone. Though he hadn't been used to being around so many people, not since his days ranching or day-working, he was starting to remember the good feelings that had come with it. It felt like family, or at least, what he thought family was. It was hard to describe, and the closest thing before this was the people who had come in and out of his life after his parents—and then there had been *Her*. Although it was hard for him to open up or make small talk or chit-chat, Nolan was looking forward to the next time he could be a part of that. There were many things he had to look forward to, he thought. Especially Kenzie.

A set of loud snakeskin cowboy boots came clacking across the cement of the shop's garage. Nolan was still on his back under the body of the truck when he felt his foot kicked again and a voice that came with it. "How she looking?"

"Good. Doing a final polish—" And as he pulled his head out, he finally saw who it was.

Turner.

Nolan's hands were black with oil, but his knuckles tightened so hard they turned white.

Turner smiled, chewing a wad of cherry-red gum, the same color as his truck. He shook his head in almost pleased disbelief. "Oh, man. Didn't know Mike had you working here, *mate*."

Nolan's eyes locked with Turner's. He stood up to face him, but Turner winked and walked straight into the mechanic's office.

Turner had been in the office with the door closed for twenty minutes.

Nolan wasn't sure what he was doing, but he knew he had to try and stay calm. If he had caught Turner anywhere else in town, he wouldn't be walking or talking. Nolan sealed up a valve, washed his hands spotless, and leaned against the truck. After a couple of lofty and loud goodbyes, Turner threw the office door open with a grand smile. Nolan caught the mechanic shaking his head as Turner walked toward him, then he saw Nolan, his face full of shame as the door closed him inside. Turner dawdled up, his boots clacking loudly, and his thumbs tucked under his shiny rodeo belt buckle. He stopped in front of Nolan and smirked, chewing a fresh wad of gum. "How you doin', partner?"

"How's your son doing?" Nolan fired back.

Turner eyed him but his confident grin didn't fade. "Why don't you tell me?" Turner knew damn well how much time he was spending with his boys.

It was a stare down, each man standing in front of the beautiful and bright, fire-red truck that was Turner's and Nolan had unknowingly tuned up.

"You think I won't muck my hands," Nolan whispered, "and put your head all over this paint?" He was fearless.

But so was Turner. "You oughta talk to your boss first." He sniffed, then went around the bed to get into the truck. Nolan considered what he meant by it.

Turner fired up the engine. The taste of revenge was sweeter than the gum, and just looking at Nolan, who was filthy and confused, made it all the more sweet to him. "Let me tell you something…" Turner said, leaning through the window. "Those boys—they're mine. I ain't going nowhere. But you are."

He revved the engine and pulled the truck out. Nolan immediately turned and headed to the boss's office. The other mechanics in the garage were watching silently the entire time. Nolan flung open the office door and found the mechanic in his desk chair.

"He your buddy?"

The mechanic shook his head, trying to make sense of the situation. "Nolan, you know I asked you to work here. You know I think you're solid hands." He paused, eyeing Nolan. He was being truthful and straightforward. "Tell me you got papers."

Nolan knew Turner must have provoked this. And now it was his past again, coming back to haunt him. "No," Nolan said, quiet and firm.

The mechanic sighed. "Look, it's hard enough running a shop in a small town. I can't be having an illegal here. He'll report the both of us."

Nolan almost laughed, shaking his head.

"You think I want him running me up and out of town for this? Or you?" the mechanic asked, staring. "I told 'im I'd let you go."

Nolan waited a moment, then nodded. He knew there was nothing he could do now. He unzipped the jumpsuit showing his dirty white undershirt, then walked out the door.

No matter how clean his hands were, to some people they were always dirty. Something was going to change.

TO SAY GOODBYE

The sun was setting over Goldwater Lake. Nolan's left hand was clenched in his denim pocket, and his right hand tightly held the Polaroid of *Her*. It was a bad dream. The same dream, happening over and over again. He was reconsidering it all—over and over again. But this time, he couldn't escape, run, or hide. He was stuck and empty and isolated, all at the same time. He'd been engaged to *Her*.

He had spent his whole life drifting or running or hiding—and then she had arrived. He had known he'd be with her forever. But when he buried her, he'd left her the ring. It didn't matter that they hadn't been able to get married in time. At the time, all that had mattered was her survival. But no matter what he'd done or how much he'd loved her, she was going to die. This sickness had her. The choice had been made. It had been written. And now he was here, the past repeating itself again.

He had come so far from so much pain. And now, he had come so far back, and so far from that sense of peace. Life was a perpetual cycle of pain and peace and pleasure. And in between was the fear. The fear of it all. The fear of loss. Nothing made sense again. There was no reasoning to explain this. He was lost again. Abandoned again. And he didn't even want to ask why. Because it all hurt too much. And what made him hurt the most, was the fact that he cared. He cared deeply about McKenzie and the boys. And he knew they cared sincerely about him. He knew he had to make a choice. His last choice. And everything inside twisted and turned and agonized over what he was about to do.

McKenzie walked through the house, maneuvering around D.O.G. and Aiden, who pulled pillows and chairs to build a fort in their room. They were all waiting for Nolan, and she wondered what was taking him so long. Over the past two weeks, he had always shown up much earlier than sunset. On most days this spring, they had ended the day watching sunset together, then deciding on dinner. She was sitting on her porch chair, wearing tight, light-colored jeans, brown boots that gave her an extra heel, and a form-fitting long-sleeved top. She thought they could all go out for pizza and beer. Or maybe just a walk through town until their noses caught something delicious.

Either way, she wanted to celebrate. Her final grades at Yavapai College had now rolled in. She had done great on all her exams. In fact, she had done better on those tests than she'd ever done on any test before. She knew it was partly the intense work she had put in—and partly because she was more open and motivated than ever before. Things were happening, things were changing, and like a breath of deep, fresh, nurturing new air, she was ready to celebrate and change with it.

It was twilight when Nolan's truck thundered down the hill. He came down from Goldwater Lake, through the backwoods and the mountains. The white Ford's engine shook the neighborhood as his tires tore down the road and roared into the driveway. McKenzie came out just as she heard the sound of his metal door close.

His eyes were heavy, and his hands were already in his pockets. He leaned against the truck, waiting. Nolan had made her smile everyday just the same way, by parking and waiting for it, then finally looking up to see her. But when he looked up, her glowing smile faded. His was not there.

"What happened?"

Nolan shifted in his boots, leaning against the truck. He didn't know what to tell her. She stepped closer, then reached up and gently held up his face. She held the same part of his temple that once had been bruised. Nolan couldn't handle it. He had to say it. "I gotta go."

She went still. "What do you mean?"

"I mean...I can't be here anymore."

Her breath was short, and that fire inside was forced to the surface like so many times before in her life. "Why are you running?" she demanded.

"I'm not."

"Then what are you doing?" Her eyes were fierce.

Nolan looked at her. He couldn't say.

"You wanted to fuck me first? Was it worth it?"

He was shocked and she was wrong. "What? That's not it at all…"

"Then what is it?" she bit.

Nolan shook his head.

She stepped in close, as if to hug him, but instead she peered directly up and into his eyes. "Nolan! Use your words!"

He couldn't take his own painful silence any longer. "I don't want those kids to wake up one day and be told I'm not here! That I'm gone, forever. I don't wish that on any of you!"

He was undoubtedly tormented by this, and yet she didn't fully understand. "What are you talking about?"

But Nolan only shook his head.

"Hello?" she barked.

"I'm talking about everyone in my life! *Everyone.*"

She was baffled. A wave of fear and anger flooded her while Nolan began to cool. He was grieving. All he kept thinking was that his parents had left him around the same age as Jason—they had left and never come back, and now he was gonna do the same. But he wouldn't tell her that. He could only try to make sense of what he had chosen to do.

"I can't promise you anything…" he said, looking for the right words.

"You think I want promises? You think the boys do?" She shook her head. "I want *you*, Nolan."

"*Why*?" he snapped back.

"Because I love *you!* Loving you isn't gonna solve any of my problems! Not my bills, not school—"

"Then what's it gonna *do*?"

"It's gonna make me *happy*. It's gonna make *you* happy."

She was hurt, but clear. She knew what she wanted. Neither of them wanted to yell or be like this. But she no longer knew what to ask or say. They stood there, quiet now.

Nolan took a deep breath, his fingers locked and sweating in his denim pockets. "I think you need something different—you need someone *right*," he said.

She stared him dead in the eyes and shook her head. "And I think you're full of shit. And scared. For every reason you just told me."

They both held there, looking into each other's eyes. They were both fighting, but for different things.

Aiden and D.O.G. came running out. "Nolan! We made a fort between the beds. Hurry up!" And he bolted back in with D.O.G.

She looked at Nolan.

"I gotta go," he said.

"You mean you gotta run."

Every second of this was killing him. And her. He pushed off the side of the truck, then went around the bed and got in.

When Nolan got in his seat and put his hand on the key, they knew it was over. He looked at her through the window. She hadn't moved. He was trying to be as honest as he could, knowing that he couldn't tell her everything, that she just wouldn't understand.

And she didn't. She didn't know about Turner or his threat. She didn't know why he was running instead of choosing to fight. She didn't know any of it.

"Kenzie…" His voice was folding in. "You deserve everything. And I don't know how to give that to you."

"If you think that's what I want, then you don't know what I deserve." Her tears came, but she didn't weep. "I trusted you."

She turned with her last words and went straight up to the house.

She didn't look back and Nolan couldn't look a second more.

This loss—this time—would cripple him more than anything before. He was *done*. And he knew it.

Jason walked out just as McKenzie rushed past, trying to hold her tears in.

"Mom?"

But she went right into the house. Jason just stood on the porch—the same place that he first met Nolan. But now he was on the high ground, looking down at Nolan, whose hands were on the steering wheel, looking forward, idling senselessly.

He caught Jason's eyes. His face…it was a punishing hit to the gut. Nolan turned away and put the truck in reverse. Jason watched, not understanding what was happening as the Ford pulled away from the house. But he could feel it—Nolan wasn't going to say goodbye.

And he wasn't coming back.

SEASONS AWAY

W*hat does one feel when going away? When we finally move on from our past, or choose to move on from our present? Or even the idea of turning away from a future, when we refuse something new and foreign? How do we feel when we give up, when we give in, or choose to move on?*

To go forward and to move on are melancholic things unto themselves. You always leave something or someone behind. We embrace the tides of change and the winds that whisper what was, and we find ourselves ruminating on what had been, or even, what could still yet be. But sometimes, we do not move on— we run away. But this running always leads us right back to where we left. Ignoring and returning to the very problem we first fled. We run right back into the person we avoid to face—ourselves. Often our choices speak from our fears, trying to protect us. A fight or flight emergence from our hearts. Yet no matter the merit in our instincts to protect ourselves, where there is fear, there is never clarity on what should be done, and what right choices there could be. Only love tells us that. And I hope—I truly truly hope, that you will listen to that love, McKenzie. That you will listen to it, above all, and forgive. Whether it be your mother, yourself, or anyone. To forgive and to love. That is what truly sets you free.

Goldie set down his pen…finishing the last sentence. He took a long breath. They were truths that both hurt and soothed. And there was much more to be said. To everyone.

Nolan rode through town and the valley. He felt everything he thought he had overcome. Anger. Regret. A debilitating soreness that shadowed his heart and clouded his head. Across town, McKenzie was sitting in her room. She didn't move. She didn't know what to think or feel. All she knew was that she was trying to keep herself strong, when all she wanted to do was cry.

Nolan's truck flew up the dirt road coming up to the ranch. Twilight was ending and the darkest skies were rising, but Nolan didn't care. This time around, he didn't want to waste one more second. He had made a choice, and he was going to drive all night to the Grand Canyon if he had to. He had done it before. He had done worse. And now, it was time to go. He was going to the Grand Canyon to finish what he had started. And he didn't need the gun to do it.

Nolan rummaged angrily in his den and packed as fast as he could. The Polaroid was with him again, and he shoved his past back in his denim and filled his duffle with all that he came into this town with. When he came up the stairs, he saw that Goldie's door was open. It was nearing sunset, but there was a light emitting from inside his room. Nolan was sweating with frustration and anger, and more than Goldie could understand. But despite everything that tortured him, he didn't want to hurt the old man. Nolan walked up the stairs and saw from the doorway that Goldie was in his bed.

Nolan knew, as he had always known, but had not confronted it, the old man was sick.

"Sounded like quite the ruckus down there," Goldie said, laying on his back and looking toward the ceiling.

Nolan was no longer going to ignore his roundabout ways: "What's wrong with you, old man!? Out with it!" He was furious and had no time to waste.

But Goldie, calm, tired, and worn, took a deep breath. "I think you know."

Nolan inhaled. Then again, and again. Deeper and deeper. Adrenaline rushed him, triggering him like he was preparing for a fight. Blood, memories, and pain flooded him as he stood there in the doorway.

But Goldie remained calm and kindhearted. "Sit with me."

Nolan exhaled powerfully and dropped his duffle to the ground. He went briskly to the old man's side and sat. His fists were locked tight, his way of curbing the pressure that built everywhere else in his body.

"Now I have something to ask of you," Goldie said, looking into his eyes. "Stick around until I go."

Nolan shook his head, gritting his teeth—he didn't want to fight, and he didn't want to explode.

"You don't understand what I've been through," Nolan said through a squeezed jaw.

But Goldie kept his eyes on his. "I do."

"No, you *don't!*" Nolan lashed out. "You *all* do this. All of you! My entire *life.*" His eyes were swelling with tears, filling Nolan's face with feelings that he had packed down for so long.

"I do," the old man repeated.

Nolan finally began to cry. Tears rushed from his eyes and trickled down his bruises, his cheeks, and his tired, bearded face.

"You think Poem never hurt me?" Goldie asked.

"Don't give me your life lesson bullshit, Goldie! You *had* a life with her. Mine got ripped away." Tears erupted through erratic breaths. He was trying to bury it all down, and the more he tried, the more it all spewed.

"You're right, son. You're right," Goldie said, quietly. "And if you keep yourself closed up, you ain't gonna have any life either."

Nolan lost it.

He was trying to regulate his breathing, the same way he did through any fight or injury to mask the pain. But he couldn't. Everything flooded. Everything flowed.

And the old man waited. "I'm not trying to change you," he said, slowly extending his hand and holding Nolan's strong forearm. Nolan's hands were locked, pushing hard into his pockets. "I'm trying to be here for you. And I'm asking you to be here for me." Goldie's hand was gentle, grasping Nolan's arm. "Until I go."

Nolan yanked his sweaty palms from his pockets and covered his face. He couldn't stop the flow of tears. He pressed his palms to his eyes harder and harder.

Goldie reached up and grasped his hand again, the shock of touch taking away Nolan's strength. Gently and slowly, Goldie pulled Nolan's hand from his face. His eyes and his cheeks were red with tears and regret and all that he wanted to hide. But he couldn't any longer.

"Don't you know?" Goldie asked, smiling sweetly. "You're a fighter."

Nolan looked at the old man, who had showed him in every moment that he loved him like a son. His respiration slowed and became rhythmic again. He relaxed his sore, tightened hands while Goldie waited, still holding on to him.

Nolan exhaled with the last of his tears. He became calm.

"Someone once told me not to judge a book by its cover," Nolan said.

Goldie smiled. "Can you imagine all the adventures we'd miss if we did?"

The sun rose over Prescott. In an instant, it reached over the valleys and the plains and the ranch and the road, then pierced onto McKenzie's home. She was on the porch, watching that first break of light. By her side, with his chin on the deck, was D.O.G. She looked back to the sunrise. Had she been wrong about Nolan?

In her mind, she had overcome years of broken trust, letdowns, and bad people. But Nolan wasn't like that. He wasn't a bad man—he was the total opposite. But there was something about him that she did know. He had not healed. He was still living in some fear. Still living in that past.

And it pained her. Because to live in fear was not truly living. She knew there was nothing she could do. Whatever his decision was—to leave and never return, or even worse—she had to accept it. Like the sun rising above the pines in front of her, it was something she had to embrace.

But the greatest, most painful irony to her was this: sometimes letting go was the only way to embrace someone. Sometimes letting go was the only way we truly had someone, because what was truly left of them when they were gone, was what they left in our hearts.

D.O.G. looked up to her. His large, light brown eyes held her the way they held onto Nolan.

She reached down and stroked his fine brown and auburn hair. All she could do now was just be grateful for what she had been given in life.

Like her Gram had always said: "Everything happens for a reason."

Across the land, past the town, and beyond Thumb Butte which overlooked it all, then through the cold stems of grass and fields was the still morning valley. All was quiet.

And just like the sunrise that came and went, so did the sunset.

Then days.

Weeks.

Seven months.

And all this time, Nolan was there, on the ranch.

On one cold morning, he was chopping wood, sweat rolling down his long, shirtless back. It trickled between muscles and scars, then what little skin was left untouched by tattoos. The sweat rolled down the face of the permanently inscribed wolf that sprawled across his shoulders, then puddled at the muscles in his lower back.

He was trying to be active. He was trying to kill time. All he could do now was keep his word to the old man, then go forth. Every day, he chopped wood for the night's fire. The wood split easy, like slicing stems of aged spring flowers. He swung up and rolled his wide shoulders over and around, then brought the cold steel down, splintering log after log. And when he had enough wood, he chopped some more. Some days, he wouldn't stop until the day's end came with the sunset or his muscles were shot from overuse. But on this day, it was different. Over the Indian ruins, the moon was tall and suspended in the sky. It was odd, he thought, the moon and the sun were almost parallel in height. Each was present, beaming within plain sight of the other. One was ahead of him, the other behind.

He wiped his forehead with a navy bandana wrapped around his swollen hand. Perspiration streamed down the trails of thick veins in his forearm and slicked his tanned skin. But before he moved on from the distinct sight, something in the wind caught his ear.

Somewhere afar, sharing the plains lands and the valley, a series of cries became pronounced and clear: the call of wolves. It was a small pack, somewhere, howling between the moon and the sun. Then he heard the huff of the beast. Over his shoulder, the white stallion was looking into the valley. He stood on a mound of land outside the barn, still, calm, looking into the unknown. Nolan wiped his head, then rested on a log, listening with the stallion.

His eyes lowered.

More weeks passed.

Somewhere up the valley road, Jason was racing his dirt bike with his buddies. They zig-zagged and laughed down the two-way stretch, swerving their bikes between both lanes and screeching across the farmlands. But Jason, hidden in his helmet, wasn't laughing at all. He was gunning it as hard and as fast as he could. The bike's motor screamed, speeding down the paved road. He accelerated faster than the others, his T-shirt whipping through the air against his body. The winds were cold and cutting, but he didn't care. He blasted ahead, right down the center of the road. His buddies couldn't keep up, Jason nearly maxing his engine. He knew what was coming—he soon saw the turn off to North Star Road.

And so he sped even faster, dusting his friends behind, who watched him recklessly blaze ahead, pushing the motor, ignoring his anger, and the spiking gauges. He didn't care what would happen next. Nothing mattered or made sense anymore. No one made sense either. Especially his family. Especially Nolan.

Night after night, McKenzie worked the bar. She was there all night, every night, and yet, she never felt awake. This time without him felt empty, routine. She couldn't explain it. Her boys were quieter, her mornings were louder, and every new day felt longer and like nothing had ever really happened. He was a ghost now, though those memories and feelings were real. They *had* happened. When people asked her what was going on, she put the blame on her mother's rehab bills. Or the fact that her mother didn't want to see her again, despite all she had done. It was an easy escape from questions she didn't want to answer. They were questions she wouldn't even know *how* to answer. It was hard enough trying to explain to Aiden that Nolan wasn't coming back. She didn't even try with Jason. His face told her everything already. It was too deep and he was too hurt. They both were.

More than anything, she didn't want anyone to know how low she had gotten. How weak she felt. Night and day, she thought about schools and where she should go. She thought about how leaving town might have been the reason for this. How maybe this had all happened because she was meant to experience absurd pain so that she could finally experience incredible growth. Whether it was her faith or her Gram's conscience, or that leaping fire that blazed and burned and rose inside her, that she had barely kept within, she wasn't going to stay like this, or here, much longer.

McKenzie had studied the best she could, but this all ruminated in her mind during the week of her tests. No matter how she felt about them now, or how much she struggled, they were done. And no matter what was to happen next, she had done something for herself that no one had ever helped her with or even understood. She had given years to finishing her high school and community college education, and she did it by herself. If anything, maybe these past few months were to show her who she was and what she was capable of. Whatever it was and whatever it was to be, McKenzie knew, she had to keep her faith. That was more important than any pain or fire she had ever walked through.

The change of seasons was slow, but like the sun drifting between the mountains and the sand, they came again. And when the first powdery snow sprinkled into town, all became quieter and slower than ever.

It was the winter of thoughts and words. Nolan made Goldie soup and sandwiches every day, and Goldie, day in and day out, would tell him about his life and all he had done with Poem. How he'd met her on his birthday in Paris. How he hadn't come home for nearly two years. How he'd found himself living with Poem in Rome the entire time. Throughout his life, Goldie had taken a leap of faith over and over again. He told Nolan stories about their travels and moments around the globe. How it had always felt like it was them against the world, even though, to them, the world was such a beautiful place.

And he told Nolan about their life here on the ranch. The old man was optimistic and positive about everything, even the terrible things he had been through. During these days, Nolan just wanted to listen. It helped the old man, too, because he had no one to share his stories with. Although he rarely said much or even asked a question, Nolan was amazed.

By all of it.

The only thing Nolan ever did really say, was that the old man should leave the bed. But each day, Goldie shook his head, even though he constantly talked about the sunset and how, every evening, his balcony had been his favorite place with Poem. But one night, when Nolan got Goldie drunk enough off of his old '82, he lifted him up and carried him to the balcony. He had made a steak and sautéed spinach dinner for Goldie and had some more of his '82 ready for him, all laid out on the balcony table, facing the entire ranch.

When Nolan put him in his chair and the pink and orange light of the setting sun touched their faces, the old man cried softly through his smile. Nolan smiled with him. Goldie told him that, for someone who didn't say much, "you really are romantic."

Nolan laughed, but disregarded the comment, as he did with anything that reminded him of his past. But he felt something of himself through Goldie's stories, just as he did when he smiled or shed tears. It was the way he talked about Poem, the way he thought about her. The way he completely, utterly, adored her. It was unforgettable. Nolan saw himself in that. He saw Kenzie. He saw his life and every color of the seasons and sunrises and sunsets. But that's just what it was—Nolan always understood things better through other people. His life and his feelings always made more sense and were expressed better through the people that he loved.

On the days or nights Goldie skipped meals or slept, Nolan would ride through town. He knew he might see her again one day, so he always bought their groceries outside of town. But on certain nights, when the Row was its coldest and most quiet, he wanted to ride in to see it. During the winter, everything in Prescott was painted in Christmas lights, decorations, and snow. He remembered once, in the spring, when McKenzie had described it. "It's one of the most beautiful times and places in the world. I think that's one reason why people love it so much here."

She was right. The air was thick and cold with a soft, white mist, and the snow shared the reflections of beautiful lights that covered the courthouse, the gazebo, and all of Whiskey Row.

But on this night, if Nolan had stopped at that corner—that very same corner they had once crossed together, months back, when they'd first talked, and he'd walked her to work—he would have seen her. Tucked into a long, black overcoat, a knitted scarf, and long black boots, she was there. She had left work a little earlier that night, just to be alone. She wanted the peace and comfort of silence. She needed it, because inside, she felt contorted, like she was starting over and moving on at the same time. But, if Nolan had made one more lap around the courthouse, or had spared one more minute at the grocery store or the gas station, or perhaps, if just one more moment in time had been just a little bit different, he would have seen her.

Or she would have seen the white Ford.

Instead, they were miles apart, heading on different roads.

Nolan's beard grew long and his hair even longer. He hadn't touched it since the spring. It was wild and curling, and it helped block the winter air. But none of that mattered to him. His entire body was sore from the winter, as was his mind. He had returned to that place that he once was, buried in the desert. That place of isolation. Of silence and thoughts. The place before Prescott. His own abyss.

Every day, he felt that pain. But all he wanted to do now was keep his promise to the old man. So, he chopped wood through the winter too. And when his hands bled from the day's frost, he chopped even more.

Yet on some days, like this very last, there was something invisible and pulling, something that called out to him from the valley. On this day, he rode the stallion through the still, frosty air. His navy bandana tied around his neck, stuffed into a large wool and suede winter coat with a high collar. His unruly beard fought freckles of drifting snow as he rode throughout the plains. It was times like these, with the white horse, that he couldn't help but wonder:

What was McKenzie doing? What did she feel?

Had she forgiven him?

Would she?

As they rode through the empty valley, Nolan's mind roamed with it.

What would *She* think now?

Was this it?

Was this all there was to be?

Eight months had now come and gone.

He counted every day, as Goldie became thinner and thinner. Goldie was in pain, but hid it well. Some nights, Nolan would go out to the barn and vomit in the snow. Watching the old man die a bit more each day made everything but his stomach feel numb. Seeing him like this brought him back to those days with *Her*. How he had stayed with her as she suffered, till the very end. And it was happening again. But he couldn't get mad at the old man. It was what we asked—what he wanted. It was only days like today, on the back of the white horse, galloping through the open valley, that Nolan felt his strongest. Within the serenity of the snowy valley and the silence of winter, he felt the changes. The snow had come earlier than ever before, Goldie told him. And as Nolan rode and roamed and wondered, the silent bond shared between him and the powerful beast that propelled him forward through the plains and the snow—made him feel again. Deep within, something had to change.

He had to do the right thing.

YOU

The night was warm in Goldie's room. Nolan always made sure he was comfortable and never cold. Every hour, he checked on the old man and his bedside fire, just to make sure it kept ablaze and that he was at ease under his quilts. Each day was getting harder for both of them. No matter how kind Nolan could be or what he could do, Goldie was bedridden, and his smile was fading fast. It was a night like this, where the old man struggled to breathe, that Nolan felt his chest fold inward. He knew loss and death better than he had ever known love.

Or so he thought.

But tonight, Goldie was truly happy. The two were having an early dinner. Goldie loved the warmth of food during the twilight hours, before the darkest parts of night would freeze the land. The ranch was quiet, and Nolan had just finished preparing a soup, while Goldie warmed up first, sitting upright in his bed sipping the end of his old '82. Nolan knew the old man's body had taken a turn for the worse, because on nights like these, Goldie didn't talk much. Not about Poem, not about anything. Nolan poured a splash of '82, but made sure the rest was left for the old man. When he looked up, he saw that Goldie was fixated on something—an old handmade wooden clock above the windows that faced the valley and the barn. The minute and hour hands were resting precisely on "11:11."

Goldie's nose flared. He wanted to laugh. But the muscles in his face were too weak and his breath was short, so he smiled instead.

"What?" Nolan softly asked.

"Funny," Goldie said, looking at the clock. "We're all afraid of time tickin', when all we should fear is time wastin'."

Nolan's eyes lowered. He thought about his ride that day.

He thought about Kenzie.

He was wasting time and he knew it.

Then it dawned on him, something he had told himself so many times before. Goldie watched him think through what was stirring in his head. He knew Nolan had something to ask.

Nolan looked up. "Do you believe in second chances?"

Goldie's smile blossomed in that bright, ageless way. The way it had before this sickness had anchored him to the bed. "All of life is a second chance," he said. The old man held his smile, and his eyes closed. "Look at me, living to see another season." He opened his eyes again. "But there's a secret," he continued. Nolan watched. He was truly listening now. "Il n'est rien de réel que le rêve et l'amour."

"And what's that?" Nolan asked.

The old man smiled. "I'd tell ya, but you're too old to believe me."

Nolan finally smiled. Goldie smiled back. The old man would never change, Nolan thought.

And he never wanted him to.

Goldie took his last sip of old '82, then nestled softly and sank himself into his bed, the way a child would, slowly drifting asleep.

Nolan watched, and his true smile came.

"Goodnight, *young man*," he said.

Goldie smiled back. "Goodnight, *old man*."

The white stallion squealed with a powerfully pitched whinny.

Nolan's eyes shot awake. He put on his navy flannel and boots, then threw his denim jacket on. He always woke before sunrise, but today it was much earlier in the morning. Every once and a while, the stallion would speak to the sun like this, but his room was dark, and Nolan knew that the morning light had not yet arrived. He went up to Goldie's room to ask if he wanted coffee or tea first before breakfast. Often, he said that the coffee was becoming too strong, so he would choose an Irish Breakfast tea from time to time. But when Nolan got to his room, Goldie wasn't there.

Nolan walked through the chilled ranch house. Winter had arrived much earlier and even though it was defiantly crisp, the end seemed closer than before. Nolan walked through the hall from the family room, into the living room, and saw that the porch was open, letting in cold, fresh air. He slowed in his steps. He could see from across the room that Goldie was bundled up in his chair on the balcony patio. Nolan smiled and went to join him.

The white stallion neighed again. Nolan approached the patio. It was the break of dawn and the sky shared the fading blues of the moon and the radiant light of sunrise's birth. He looked down at the old man, and his smile faded. Goldie was there, resting peacefully. His eyes were open, but they did not move. He was watching the sunrise from beyond.

Nolan took a slow, deep breath. The horses were on the prairie, facing them. And now they were silent. Nolan's eyes began to swell.

Goldie was gone.

He meant more to him than he could possibly know.

And he wished now that he had told him.

He wished the old man knew.

But all was quiet.

The colors of the sun crested over the ruins, then the ranch. And still, the horses just stood, watching Nolan and Goldie, witnessing the colors of pain and sadness in Nolan's heart.

But it was more than sadness. It was something beyond.

Something that told Nolan how much he cared.

How much he loved the old man.

He hadn't even tried—and he'd been a father to Nolan.

On the table next to his body was his empty glass of old '82 and an unsealed envelope. On the top of the envelope was Goldie's handwriting:

MICHAEL J. GOLDSMITH
LAST WILL AND TESTAMENT

Nolan inhaled and his tears came. He was no longer ashamed to cry. Not over Goldie, or anything. He felt honored the old man would trust him like this. And when he picked it up, he found another letter, perfectly folded and placed under it. And on the front, it read:

THE INCREDIBLE EXISTENCE OF YOU

With both hands freeing from his pockets, Nolan took it. He clutched both sides of the letter, holding it, not knowing what it was or what might be written inside. He only knew one thing—whatever it was, it was because the old man loved him.

Later that afternoon, Nolan stood atop a tall, rolling hill that overlooked the entire valley. It was just south of the Indian ruins. A place he had not yet seen. Nolan was looking down at an old wooden cross, and now, a newly planted one. The old, weathered cross had the following written on it:

POEM ELLA GOLDSMITH
1944 - 2012
"Il n'est rien de réel que le rêve et l'amour."

Beside it, was a newly dug plot. Goldie's. Under his cross and name was a handmade plaque made of ponderosa wood that Nolan had cut and carved from the land himself. And under it read:

"All that matters are dreams and love."

Nolan was there, looking across the valley. In his heart, he knew how much he loved Goldie. He had grown to believe now that the old man must have known too. There was so much unsaid that made sense now.

The pain of not saying what we actually feel to our loved ones, in so many ways, often becomes our life's greatest pain. What words we feel deep in our soul, but we withdraw and refrain from saying. We always feel so much, yet say too little. And we always seem to feel that it's always too little, too late. And that is why it is our truest responsibility to always search, to always dig, to always find our truest feelings, and express them.

Now more than ever, Nolan knew. Even though, somehow, deep down, it was a truth he had always known. But as with the cycle of life, death, and growth, it sometimes took the magnitude of loss to awaken our truth. The wind whispered through his long hair, his denim's wool collar, and whipped his navy bandana around his neck. His eyes squinted, calmness and poise came to the valley. He looked out to where *she* would be.

Nolan had more to say. He needed a second chance.

He needed Kenzie.

Back at the ranch, Nolan scurried, throwing a backpack full of clothes and supplies into the bed of the truck. He hopped in, and without another hesitation, he roared off, leaving North Star Ranch in the wake of his dust. As the large tires spewed melted snow and dirt, he saw through the open barn doors that the white stallion was standing there. He was watching him leave.

Nolan rode the long dirt and snow-dusted path out of the valley farmlands until he hit the main road. It was the only road on this side of the valley, and he was at the head of only two directions he could go: toward downtown, or toward the Grand Canyon.

He thought about it one last time. His hand swung the large truck wheel to the left and he blasted down the road for town.

When he got to McKenzie's house, his eyes bulged.

A real estate sign was planted on the lawn: *SOLD*. He couldn't believe it. His stomach twisted and every muscle in his body tightened. He was bracing for the impact of what it meant.

Was he actually too late? It couldn't be like this. It couldn't end like this. Not after all he'd learned and all that he'd had been through. Nolan's mind raced. He swung the truck wheel one more time and gunned it for downtown.

Nolan raced down the sidewalk and burst into McKenzie's bar. She wasn't there. No one had seen her for a week. He barked and demanded they tell him anything and everything about where she was, but no one knew.

Nolan flew out of the bar and looked around, thinking and walking as fast as he could. He had to find out. He had to find her. The town was busy—the season was changing and new tourists were coming with it. In a split second, he had a moment of inspiration.

Nolan ditched his truck and hauled on foot up the street to the church. With his hands stuffed into his pockets and his boots slamming the concrete, he prayed. He hadn't prayed in years, but he was praying now. She was going to be there again, like she had been before. Like how she'd found him. That was it, it made sense. Because he hadn't found her, Kenzie had found *him*. She had opened him. She had done it on her own. She was meant to, because she had been his second chance all along, looking right at him, smiling and being kind, in her loving way that was hers and hers alone. So, he was praying. And he was hoping that, this time, he would find her and finally say all the things he had not said before.

He knew now, it wasn't that he *couldn't* tell her how he felt, it was that he *hadn't*. And that was no longer a guilt he could live with. He needed to tell her. He needed to see her. He needed McKenzie.

Because he loved her.

Nolan detoured up the street to the church and moved through the neighborhood to see if her Jeep was where she'd normally park to keep it hidden. But it wasn't there. He exhaled deeply, the fear of losing her torturing his body. It was fight or flight now. Nolan hauled ass to the church entrance. The stained-glass windows were aglow, and with every brisk step in his boots, it wasn't fast enough. The large holy doors were just ahead, and he was already trying to regulate his breathing with every step. He gripped the large metal handles and threw them open. The doors flung to the sides, and he stood in the aisle, facing an empty church and the man hanging on the cross, looking down on him.

She wasn't there.

His heart stopped. Everything inside him was throbbing, punching, pulling. He'd waited too long. He had lost his chance. It was clear. It didn't matter what Goldie had done for him. It didn't matter what Nolan knew or how he felt now.

She was gone.

His fists clenched in his denim as if he could destroy the first thing or person he saw, and as his fingers tightened and his knuckles protruded with cracking winter skin, he felt the crumbling texture of a piece of paper that he had in his pocket. Nolan burst from the church and hurried for the busy street. Whatever this suffering of loss and guilt was before, it had become a sickness to his soul.

But he wasn't giving up.

He was determined to go to the courthouse and then to every bar on the Row if he needed to. He'd talk to someone, ask everyone, beg anyone, whatever must be done to get some information. He told himself he'd go to the antique shop, or the grocer, or the mechanic, or even to Turner if he needed to. He wasn't going to give up.

Not this time.

He would stop and ask every single person in this town if that was what it was going to take. And as he trudged across the street, fists clenched, Nolan made a promise to himself: he was going to find her and tell her everything.

His hands were tight in his jacket and his head low, rushing down the boulevard just as a wave of people came out of the old Elks Theatre. The well-dressed citizens poured out, fresh from a show. Then Nolan heard a voice.

"Nolan!"

It was Aiden. Nolan dashed across the street toward him. With no hesitation in his bones, Aiden ran up and wrapped himself around Nolan's waist. He hugged deeply, his eyes closed, and he squeezed tightly. Nolan's heart skipped. "Where you been!?" Aiden blurted out, but he wasn't upset, he was simply aglow at the sight of Nolan. "There were so many javelinas this morning, dude! Me and D.O.G. chased like twenty!"

Nolan was speechless.

He couldn't stop his smile. Of all the things Aiden could have felt or said, it was if nothing had changed. As if Nolan had never left.

And then another voice came. "Aiden!"

It was her.

Kenzie stood at the entrance of the theater wearing a long, navy dress. The seamless fabric dripped down her shoulders and waist, then cascaded over her curves and fell down to her tall black heels. It was all elegant and fit her beautifully. Nolan had never seen her dressed up. Everything around him stopped, stunned by the sight of her. Then he realized there was a man next to her.

Kyle, her longtime family friend. He was dressed up, too, wearing a simple suit and tie, with a thin but grown beard which made him more handsome than before. Kyle stood, staring with firm eyes, observing the out-of-towner he had heard so much about.

Aiden was looking back at Kenzie, who fumbled with her thoughts. She finally looked to Aiden. "Go with Kyle."

Kyle put out his hand. "C'mon, bud. Let's get ice cream."

Whatever pieces were left of Nolan's heart—they shattered.

All he could do was stare. She moved through the crowd, her whole body tightening as she came closer to him. She was shocked. He was here, of all times and all places. And she knew how he must feel, seeing her with Kyle. She wasn't even sure he knew that Kyle was the agent who had sold her home, or if he had been by the house since it had sold. They had moved in with Gram, preparing for the next journey, whatever that was to be. Kenzie stood at a distance from Nolan, her arms folded while people filled the sidewalks, celebrating and discussing the show they had just seen.

"What are you doing?" she said.

But Nolan couldn't speak. He was brittle, he was hurt, and Kenzie could feel it. It took two seconds in his bright blue eyes to feel everything again. Her hands were shaking, trying to hold her elbows, and she was ready to burst into tears at any moment, just by looking at him.

"Just tell me you're happy," he finally spoke.

"What?"

"Tell me you're happy so I can go."

She shook her head, holding everything back. "Why are you saying this?"

"Kenzie. Are you happy?"

She gawked, but she couldn't respond.

"Are you *happy*? Just tell me and I'll go!"

"I…" she hesitated. "Why are you saying this?"

Nolan exhaled, fuming like the stallion. "Shit, I don't even care. Just lie to me!"

Jason came out of the theater. He stopped dead in his boots, seeing Nolan.

"You ran away!" she yelled.

"I did!" he yelled back.

"Why, Nolan?"

In one of those few, sacred times in his life, Nolan's heart poured without restraint, without thinking. "Because I'm *scared*. Because I don't have *papers*. Because everyone I love, I *lose*. And because I love *you*. I love *all* of you. And that scares me too."

She was unable to move. Jason either.

He was speaking to all of them. He loved *all* of them. And Jason knew it too.

"But if you're happy," Nolan finally breathed, "if you're happy, Kenzie," he shook his head, "I'll do the right thing and I'll go."

It was silent for only a moment.

"But if you're not..." His hands left his pockets and reached out toward her. "I'll never leave you again. I'll never leave any of you."

McKenzie's knees couldn't hold any longer. She fought herself, she fought her anger, and now she was fighting her tears.

Jason stared in awe. He had never seen any man or person act this way.

"You disappeared for eight months. I didn't even know if you were alive. Why? Why now?"

"Goldie said he wrote you..."

"Yeah, and why didn't you!?" She hit back.

Nolan took a breath. He felt everything. But he wasn't going to shed tears. Not now.

This was his second chance.

He needed to say everything. He needed to be strong. And for him, that meant using every word he could to say what he truly meant. But more importantly to him and to her, he needed to say what he truly felt.

"I told myself I gave *Her* everything. I told myself I was nothing left." Nolan shook his head, finally looking away from her. "I'm the only one who didn't know I was wrong."

She watched his every move.

His palms opened and he looked into her eyes. "Everything does happen for a reason. Goldie's gone, Kenzie. And everything he said about me, everything you said, *it's true*. I stopped fighting for what I need. I'm fighting now. I need *you*, Kenzie."

She couldn't look at him any longer. It was too hard.

"Why…"

"Because I love *you*." He took another breath. "You make me feel. You make me feel everything."

It was everything she wanted and everything she had prayed for. But in this moment in time, it didn't make sense to her anymore. It had been so long. So much had changed.

"Nolan…" she said his name softly, keeping her eyes down. "I can't." And she began to walk away.

"You can't? Or you *won't*?" Nolan quickly called out.

They were Goldie's words.

But she took one last look, and he knew that she meant it.

McKenzie walked away. Jason was still there, speechless. And when he saw that his mother would not turn back, he turned to go with her. But he looked back at Nolan, baffled. Nolan was still standing there, in utter disbelief.

Nolan's right here in front of us! Jason thought.

He didn't want him to leave again. He knew how Nolan felt, because he felt it himself. And he didn't want to leave Nolan. He shouldn't have to pick sides or turn his back on either of them, he thought.

But that was it—he knew that his mother always meant everything she ever said, and she was walking away now, even though he could feel how fragile she was. Jason kept following. If anything, he had to be there for his mother now.

They walked up the street while Nolan stood there, watching. He could fight no longer. No fight amounted to this. No victory or defeat could parallel this feeling. It was beyond anything he had experienced inside the ring, or out of it. He stood there, senseless, his hands wide open, empty, watching Kenzie walk away forever.

Jason turned back once more. For whatever reason, he wanted to give Nolan one last look. Something happened when he did. His heart had grown enough now to understand what it felt in that moment.

It was loss. True loss. And it sunk him as he trudged up the street behind his mother.

Inside the ice cream parlor, Kyle sat, looking back and forth between a local real estate magazine and Aiden, who kept his head low, purposely ignoring him. Kyle had tried to get him to lighten up, but now he just had to respect that the child wasn't going to. While Aiden was devastated, Kyle was still happy about the huge sale he shared with Kenzie through her grandmother's house. And he wondered what he could sell or do next with her. McKenzie stepped through the entrance with Jason following just behind her. She immediately sat at the table with them, then forced her smile—something Kenzie never did.

Kyle scanned her up and down, trying to decipher her feelings about what had just happened.

"Hey, is everything—"

"It's fine."

But it was clear to everyone it was not. She was hurting, and since she had walked through the door, Aiden hadn't look up once. Jason was slumped in his own seat at their table.

Kenzie took a breath, her eyes moved from Jason to Aiden, then watched him closely. Through her many gifts, she knew Aiden was devastated that Nolan was here, but not coming back. Something she had had to tell him several times over, for months, and it had killed her every time. She had had to tell Aiden that she and Nolan were no longer "together," that he also couldn't be Aiden's friend any longer. They had been some of the most difficult and complex words she had ever said. And now, what was left was her heartbroken son, who wouldn't look at her, and instead stared at the end of the table.

"Aiden, what'd you get?" She was referring to the ice cream, though there was none there. Kyle was finishing his vanilla cone and holding another real estate magazine.

"Nothing..." Aiden said in a low voice. The same voice he used when his back used to hurt. Or when his father had let him down.

Jason looked at McKenzie, then Kyle. There were only a few people inside, but more coming in from the theater. Inside Jason's chest, he felt the weight of things he could not explain. It all felt like a hollowing hit to his chest, the kind that Nolan had showed him could knock the wind out of any man. He remembered that Nolan had taught him not only how to do the strike, but how to protect himself from it, and how to keep it from knocking him breathless.

Jason sat upright in his chair and his shoulders raised and lowered with rhythmic breaths. They were angry and deep, but were soon becoming melodic. He was breathing the way Nolan had taught him.

"You guys wanna go play ball at my house? I'm sure Dog would," Kyle asked, finishing his cone.

"It's *Dee-Oh-Gee*! Not *dog*! I told you!'" Aiden blurted.

Kenzie was shocked. She wasn't going to sit in this atmosphere for much longer. She couldn't have herself or her boys go through this all over again.

As she was considering what to do or say, Jason finally spoke. "I don't get it. Why don't you love him?"

Aiden's eyes darted up to his brother, then to his mother. He wondered too. McKenzie felt a train hit her chest. She was on the spot, in front of all of them. Aiden stared, holding attentive eyes between tears and hope. McKenzie saw them, and now her chest ached. She could see how much he cared. Then she looked to Jason. He didn't understand their situation or choices, and he didn't care now. He asked his question with conviction, and he deeply cared about the answer. Jason knew what he felt about Nolan, and he wanted to understand what his mother felt and why.

Kyle began to sweat uncomfortably. He and McKenzie were unofficially dating, and he knew all about Nolan from friends and relatives, and the little that McKenzie had shared. But he knew she was still grieving him. Kyle did care about her, and that was part of the reason why he had waited so long then persisted for another chance to date her.

McKenzie repeated Jason's words in her head. *"Why don't you love him?"*

She asked herself over and over again, while they all watched her. Her eyes searched, repeating the question inside her head and her heart until out of nowhere she blurted, "Shit."

Everyone gawked, not knowing what to make it of it, until...

"Kyle, can you leave? Please?"

Now they were all really confused. Kyle slowly put down the magazine. "What?"

And then her confident, clear tone came. "Thank you for taking us. I'll call you tomorrow."

"Really?" he asked rhetorically.

She stared. He stared. Everyone stared.

"So, what, you trust that guy over me?"

"I don't know." She shook her head. "But I trust my boys."

They were all shocked and confused now. It was a long, awkward pause before Kyle made a choice. He stood up and walked out. Jason watched his mother trying to figure it out in her head. She was calmer, digging deeply. Jason wouldn't tell her for years to come, but he knew in his heart that all of his real strength—everything that made him strong and compelled him to do the right thing—came from her. Especially from this moment.

Aiden's mind raced, still trying to understand what was happening here. "What's wrong with Nolan, Mom? You don't love him?"

Kenzie couldn't help but cry now, and her soft words came with it. "I do."

Aiden immediately became anxious. It was the first time he'd seen his mother cry. Jason was still breathing rhythmically. Breathing in the way that Nolan had explained would help center him. He had to be strong, like Nolan had once said. And he wanted to be strong for her.

"Do you know why I do?" Jason asked.

When she looked up at her very first child and saw the clarity and strength in his eyes, her own eyes were ready to flood.

"Because he loves *you*," Jason said. "And he loves *us*."

They were words that meant the entire world to her. She had been frail and on the brink of letting it all go, but now she pulled herself together. She sucked up her tears and even smiled. The boys stared. Then, McKenzie nearly laughed, and she said it again: "Shit!"

The white Ford tumbled up to the ranch. Nolan had taken the long way home. A detour through the mountains and the lake, and then the long way to the back valley through the very first farmlands in the county. His thoughts were scattered, replaying every moment in his head. All of them. Like he had been hiding them and blocking them all out to protect himself from the insurmountable pain and regret he had for letting them all go.

McKenzie was his second chance.

It wasn't anyone else's fault for losing her.

It wasn't God or fate or destiny.

It was his fault.

When he got to the top of the ranch, he killed the engine, jumped out, slammed the steel door, and stood there in the dirt driveway. It was silent all around him. It was only him now. His head was low, and his hands were raw from chopping wood and from what constantly tightening his knuckles had finally done to him. Nolan walked into the ranch house and was met with more silence. There was no wind, there was no rustling in the bushes, or even bugs. Standing in the doorway to this empty house, he didn't know what to do. The white linen curtains to the balcony floated, but they, too, were silent. There was no gust or chirping birds or horses. Everything was silent, gray. He was stuck, in every sense. And it was worse than death. It was emptiness again.

Nothing made sense now and nothing would.

Nothing existed.

Until right then.

He heard the tumbling of tires flying up the dirt road. Nolan looked to the patio and through the flowing curtain. It was Kenzie's Jeep, and it was hauling ass down the road, spewing dust everywhere.

Nolan's eyes jumped, and he bolted out the door. His hands flew, running with him, and then his boots slammed in the driveway, planting himself right in front as she pulled up. She was still wearing her navy dress when she hopped out, but she hiked it up her legs and her black heels dug into the dirt. She stormed up the driveway, looking him straight in the eyes.

"We can stay here and fight, we can go west, we can go east—I don't care!" She stopped just a few feet away, angry, clear, and ready. "I wanna be with you. My kids wanna be with you."

He was speechless.

"Nolan, I do love you, and I don't want to lose you."

She was about to cry again, telling him, opening herself up again. Her voice softened with sincerity that only a strong woman could possess. "We gotta make this work."

His jaw was locked. His eyes were slow moving and overwhelmed, trying to understand this moment. He had to think—he had to make sense of it and all that he felt.

He was stuck in his head and Kenzie could see it—she could always see it.

And now she cried, truly afraid that Nolan couldn't handle this any longer. Her voice reached through desperate tears. "Nolan, *please.* Use your words."

His chest filled, taking the deepest breath he could, and his hands, as they would always do, buried into his pockets. She watched, tears running, ready to burst. He was going to close up again. He was going to run away again.

In his right pocket, Nolan felt the texture of old paper. He clutched it and slowly took it out.

He opened it.

With one last look in her eyes, the eyes he loved, he began to read:

"How I see you in me.
How you see me in *you*.
Fire, brimstone, sunset, rain.
All my dreams, all my history
All my life, all my pain.
You unlock
everything
As you say I do for you.
It inspires me
It terrifies me
and it
opens me.
To everything.
Everything I should be.
Everything that is me.
Everything that is *you*.
The Incredible Existence in Me
is found
in *The Incredible Existence of You.*"

Her breath stuttered in her throat, with eyes full of tears that poured down her face. Nolan stayed in her eyes, holding them, waiting, and he wasn't going to let her go. Not now, not ever. He stayed calm, but let his own tears flow.

"You wrote that?" she asked.

"Goldie. But he always could say what I feel." He paused. "Just like *you*."

Nolan looked at her in that way that she remembered, seasons ago. In the way that she felt him. The way that she saw him. The real him. He looked at her in the way that he loved her.

And she didn't wait another second.

"I'll take that as a compliment."

Kenzie walked up, grabbed his entire face, and kissed him with everything.

Nolan dropped the letter and surrounded her with his arms, pulling her in, pressing their lips together completely, feeling all of their pain and their love and their souls.

Everything. In one single kiss.

All of existence.

In one single moment.

EXISTENCE

The hills were endless in the northern state land. The mountains afar could be seen from anywhere. Old roads, new roads, and roads not yet paved—it all existed under the clouds and the sky. And below, heading north, was the old white Ford.

In the truck's bed was Aiden, Jason, and D.O.G, their feet and paws up on one of their old bed mattresses with D.O.G. on top, and Aiden, sitting in a custom-built chair and seatbelt, in which he happily stayed kaput. In the front, with windows open and air flowing through her hair and her white summer dress, was Kenzie. She was there again, in her free, special place. And Nolan kept looking, glowing, wearing her new college's old hat.

They passed through the plains and mountains and forests until they reached a place of tall pines and wide, clean, paved roads. It was a crossroads, a place people from all over the world had come to see. Cars from all fifty states shared the road as they all adventured high and low to come to this place. After a couple hours' journey north from Prescott, Nolan's truck finally pulled up and parked. Jason had his feet up on the metal side of the truck, lounging across Aiden's old bed mattress. He took a peek over the bed to see if they had arrived.

McKenzie turned to Nolan. "Ready?"

He was nervous, but he was ready. "Yeah."

Aiden popped his head in from the back window. "Are we here!?"

McKenzie beamed. "Yeah!"

"*Well, let's go!*"

They all walked together. Kenzie had her arm around Nolan's, whose hands were in his jacket, but they were free, relaxed, holding on to nothing inside. Aiden and D.O.G. raced ahead, and Jason followed behind, looking around, not knowing what to expect. When they finally saw it, they all slowed until their feet planted and they could no longer move. They were utterly amazed.

"Whoa," McKenzie whispered.

"*Whoa*!" Aiden glowed.

Then Jason arrived. "Wow."

But Nolan just stared. It was farther and wider than his eyes or mind could see.

The Grand Canyon.

Open. Endless.

Aiden grabbed D.O.G.'s new blue collar and held him, looking around, amazed.

Tears started to fall from Nolan's eyes. *Goldie was right.* Everything about this place—the shades of tan and red and rock, the layers of earth and sky and limitless horizon—it was all poetry.

When Kenzie saw Nolan's tears, her eyes immediately did the same. She turned, stood on the toes of her brown cowboy boots, and kissed his cheek. Then she pulled a hand from his pockets and held it. Nolan didn't resist. He held hers back and kept looking forward, scanning the great expanse just ahead. When their silence finally made Jason look over, he could see that they were both crying. Aiden saw it, too, and he became anxious again.

Jason understood more about Nolan and his mother now. There was a maturity within him that had arrived. During this time in his life, he saw and experienced many complications and complexities about life, family, and love. He had tried to make sense of his anger, his parents, and their resentment toward one another, just as he had tried to make sense of his own. But what he saw and learned was that all of life was a second chance, everything did happen for a reason, and that it was never too late to become all that you were meant to be—whether you were an old man, a young man, a woman, child, or dog.

Watching Nolan and his mother now, he felt them in a way that reached deep and held him within. And he knew that, even though tears were streaming down their faces, they were tears of love. But then he saw Aiden, who was startled, watching his heroes stunned and crying together. It was hard for all of them, Jason thought. He could see it, looking at his family. And he wanted to be strong for them. There was something he had to do.

"*Ahwoooooooooo!*"

They all turned. Jason's hands were cupped around his mouth. His howl shook them awake and the echo soared throughout the canyon.

Aiden glowed. "*Ow ow awhooooo!*" he returned, and D.O.G immediately barked, sharing the excitement.

McKenzie put her hands up to her mouth, and through tears and laughter, she howled back "*Ow ow awhoooooooo!*"

And finally, with a smile—Nolan's real smile—he raised both of his hands to his mouth and cried louder and longer than all of them. "*Awhoooooooooooooooooooooooooo!*"

They all howl together now, facing the openness and the endlessness of what lies before them. Howling, from what lies within them.

Made in the USA
Las Vegas, NV
05 December 2021